It might be...
passion...
guarante...

Celebration

Three brilliant, intense, emotional
stories, perfect Christmas reading,
by much-loved author Carol Marinelli

Passion
Lynne Graham
June 2011

Pleasure
Sandra Marton
July 2011

Seduction
Miranda Lee
August 2011

Fascination
Carole Mortimer
September 2011

Satisfaction
Sharon Kendrick
October 2011

Celebration
Carol Marinelli
November 2011

Carol Marinelli
Celebration

MILLS & BOON

DID YOU PURCHASE THIS BOOK WITHOUT A COVER?
If you did, you should be aware it is **stolen property** as it was
reported *unsold and destroyed* by a retailer. Neither the author nor the
publisher has received any payment for this book.

All the characters in this book have no existence outside the imagination of the author, and have no relation whatsoever to anyone bearing the same name or names. They are not even distantly inspired by any individual known or unknown to the author, and all the incidents are pure invention.

All Rights Reserved including the right of reproduction in whole or in part in any form. This edition is published by arrangement with Harlequin Enterprises II B.V./S.à.r.l. The text of this publication or any part thereof may not be reproduced or transmitted in any form or by any means, electronic or mechanical, including photocopying, recording, storage in an information retrieval system, or otherwise, without the written permission of the publisher.

This book is sold subject to the condition that it shall not, by way of trade or otherwise, be lent, resold, hired out or otherwise circulated without the prior consent of the publisher in any form of binding or cover other than that in which it is published and without a similar condition including this condition being imposed on the subsequent purchaser.

® and ™ are trademarks owned and used by the trademark owner and/ or its licensee. Trademarks marked with ® are registered with the United Kingdom Patent Office and/or the Office for Harmonisation in the Internal Market and in other countries.

Mills & Boon, an imprint of Harlequin (UK) Limited, Eton House, 18-24 Paradise Road, Richmond, Surrey TW9 1SR

CELEBRATION © Harlequin Enterprises II B.V./S.à.r.l. 2011

Italian Boss, Ruthless Revenge © Carol Marinelli 2008
One Magical Christmas © Carol Marinelli 2008
Hired: The Italian's Convenient Mistress © Carole Marinelli 2008

ISBN: 978 0 263 88988 8

009-1111

Harlequin (UK) policy is to use papers that are natural, renewable and recyclable products and made from wood grown in sustainable forests. The logging and manufacturing processes conform to the legal environmental regulations of the country of origin.

Printed and bound in Spain
by Blackprint CPI, Barcelona

Carol Marinelli recently filled in a form where she was asked for her job title and was thrilled, after all these years, to be able to put down her answer as writer. Then it asked what Carol did for relaxation and after chewing her pen for a moment Carol put down the truth—writing.

The third question asked—what are your hobbies? Well, not wanting to look obsessed or, worse still, boring, she crossed the fingers on her free hand and answered swimming and tennis, but, given that the chlorine in the pool does terrible things to her highlights and the closest she's got to a tennis racket in the last couple of years is watching the Australian Open—I'm sure you can guess the real answer!

Look out for Carol Marinelli's latest exciting novels, *Heart of the Desert* and *Cort Mason—Dr Delectable*, available in July and September from Mills & Boon® Modern™ and Medical™ romance respectively.

Italian Boss, Ruthless Revenge

CAROL MARINELLI

PROLOGUE

'RANALDI'S here!'

A shiver of anticipation went around the lavish hotel reception—starting with a nod from the doorman to warn the concierge, who in turn signalled to the receptionists—and Caitlyn noticed everyone's backs seemed to straighten just a touch more, hands all moving to flatten ties or hair, as a sleek limousine pulled up outside.

'The question is—' Glynn, the manager, blinked nervously as he flicked his fringe back off his face '—which one?'

The answer was, for Caitlyn, more relevant than Glen could possibly realise.

Here on work experience, shadowing the staff and completely supernumerary, it shouldn't have mattered a jot to Caitlyn *which* one of the dashing Ranaldi twins was pulling up outside—after all, both were legends.

Lazzaro and Luca Ranaldi both headed up the sumptuous Ranaldi chain of luxurious international hotels—and, along with their sister, were heirs to the vast wealth their father had created and subsequently, following his death last year, left behind.

Impressive? Yes.

Newsworthy? No.

Unless, of course, that vast wealth happened to have landed in the laps of stunning identical twins. Not one but two immaculate prototypes, who regularly hit the headlines courtesy of their jet-setting, depraved existence. Since their father's death, and their sister marrying and settling there, the stunning pair had loosely based themselves in Melbourne—two irrepressible playboys, who made no apologies and certainly offered no excuses! Only last week Luca had been in the papers for a fight at the casino, and there had been a few drink-driving scandals recently that Caitlyn could recall.

A dark-suited man stepped out of the limousine, and Caitlyn found herself holding her breath…

'Which one is it?' Caitlyn whispered.

'I'm not sure yet…' Glynn mused. 'They're both identical, both divine…'

Caitlyn hoped it was Lazzaro.

Not because he was considered the most powerful, the true leader of the two, but for a reason Glynn would have trouble believing.

Watching as two strappy sandals hit the ground beneath the car door, Caitlyn chewed on her lip, wondering what on earth she'd do if Roxanne came into view—wondering how the other hotel staff would react to her if they knew the strange truth…

Luca Ranaldi was dating her cousin.

'It's Lazzaro,' Glynn confirmed as, without waiting for his date, the dark-suited male walked through the gold revolving doors.

'How do you know?' Caitlyn frowned. 'I thought you said they were identical…'

'Lazzaro doesn't wait for anyone...' Glynn hissed out of the side of his mouth before stepping forward to greet his boss. 'Not even a beautiful woman!'

Oh, she'd seen him before—had seen him in the papers, his photo being on the cover of a business magazine she was reading for her course—but nothing, *nothing* had prepared Caitlyn for the impact of seeing him up close and in the flesh. Well over six feet, as he walked in it was clear to all that he owned the place—and not just literally. Confidence and arrogance just oozed from him, and as he walked over to the desk Caitlyn realised he wasn't just stunning—he was absolutely beautiful. His jet hair was longer than it was in the photos, with a raven fringe flopping over his forehead, and as for those eyes... Caitlyn actually gave a little sigh. Thickly lashed, they were black as the night and just as dangerous. As his gaze met hers, it was bored, utterly uninterested and he soon looked away. But, for Caitlyn, it was as if his image had been branded on her brain, freeze-framed so she could examine it at her leisure—see again that straight Roman nose, see close up his smooth olive skin and that sulky, full, incredibly kissable mouth.

Realising she was staring—gaping, even—Caitlyn tore her gaze away and looked at the woman who had walked in behind him. She was now sitting on one of the plush lobby sofas as she awaited her master—and Caitlyn couldn't help the tiny ironic smile that pursed her lips.

Though it wasn't Roxanne, it might just as well have been.

The raven beauty who accompanied Lazzaro certainly hadn't been striving to achieve *au naturelle* when she'd applied her make-up. Dark glossy hair tumbled, albeit strategically, over shoulders that were so evenly tanned it could only have come from some serious hours on a sunbed combined with a regular spray tan.

'Welcome, sir.' Glynn's outstretched hand went ignored.

'How are things?' Lazzaro didn't return the greeting, his eyes narrowing as they scanned the reception area. 'Any problems?'

'None at all,' his manager assured him.

'Has Luca been in?'

'Not as yet,' Glynn said, discreetly omitting to mention the drunken call he'd taken earlier, demanding that the best room in the hotel be somehow vacated and prepared for his arrival.

'How's the wedding?'

'Excellent,' Glynn enthused. But as Lazzaro's burning gaze fell on him, he coloured up just a touch. 'Well, there's one teeny problem, but we're taking care of it now.'

Lazzaro raised one perfectly arched black brow, and, though he didn't say a word, the tiny gesture clearly indicated that he wanted more information.

'The bride's father, Mr Danton—'

'Gus Danton is a close personal friend of mine,' Lazzaro interrupted, and though his English was excellent, his deep, heavily accented voice held just a tinge of warning.

Caitlyn's eyebrows shot up just a fraction—after all, if he was such a good friend, how come Lazzaro hadn't been at the wedding? She didn't say it, of course, but Lazzaro was either a skilled mind-reader or had felt the breeze from her eyebrows raising, because, as if answering her very thoughts he deigned to give her a brief look.

'There are not enough Saturday nights in a year to attend

every wedding to which I am invited but—given Mr Danton has chosen my hotel, and given Mr Danton is a friend—naturally I will come in for a drink. Of course, I hoped to hear there have been no problems…'

'Quite.' Glynn swallowed.

'So?'

'Well, he's asked that the bar remain open for another hour. Of course we're more than happy to oblige—it's just that his credit card has been declined. I was actually on my way to have a discreet word with him now.'

'Bring up his details.' He snapped his fingers in Caitlyn's vague direction, and even though she'd been bringing up guests' details for most of the night, this *almost* mastered skill had never been tested under such stressful conditions.

'Er, Caitlyn's only here on work experience, sir,' Glynn said, rushing over to the computer. One black look from Lazzaro halted him. 'She's studying hospitality, and—'

'Since when has a work experience student stayed till midnight on a Saturday?' Lazzaro cut in, staring at her name badge, lowering his eyes to her suede stilettos, and then lazily working them upwards—taking in the rather cheap navy skirt and white blouse that comprised her uniform. In absolutely no hurry, as Glynn chatted nervously on, he scrutinised her face, staring into her blue eyes and doing the strangest things to her stomach.

'Caitlyn was very keen to witness a busy Saturday night…'

God, she wished she'd had warning—wished she'd had time to dash to the loo and redo her heavy blonde hair. She could feel her attempt at a French roll uncoiling before his eyes. And she wished the mouth he was staring at had just a little bit of lipstick on.

'And she has been dealing with guests?'

'Yes,' Glynn croaked. 'Well, she's been closely supervised, of course.'

'She has been bringing up details for paying guests?'

'Er, yes…' Glynn nodded. 'But, as I said, only with supervision.' Which wasn't strictly true—Glynn had been out for more smoke breaks than Caitlyn could count. Still, she was hardly going to tell Lazzaro that.

'If she is good enough for my guests,' Lazzaro responded, with the martyrdom only the truly pompous could muster, 'then she is good enough for me.'

If he called her *she* again, Caitlyn decided, then *she'd* jolly well give him a piece of her mind.

As his black eyes fell on her, Caitlyn recanted.

Well, maybe she wouldn't actually *say* anything. Still, she could *think* it—divine he might be to look at, but he was a loathsome, arrogant, chauvinist brute. Blushing with a mixture of annoyance and embarrassment, she furiously backspaced as she spectacularly mistyped. After an exceedingly long moment, Gus Danton's details finally flashed on to the screen.

Momentarily!

'His account,' Lazzaro snapped, clearly expecting that with a few rapid clicks Caitlyn should bring up the necessary page. But his impatience only unsettled her more.

The cursor wobbled on screen as suddenly he was behind her, standing over her, his hand hovering to take the computer mouse—effectively dismissing her efforts. She should have stepped back—only he was behind her. She should have moved her hand to let him take over—only his was above hers.

Perhaps it was the prospect of physical contact with him, perhaps it was nerves, or an impossible combination of both, but at *that* second precisely her hope for a glowing reference from the Ranaldi Hotel for her work experience melted away as rapidly as Caitlyn clicked the mouse—not once, not twice, but as if her finger had suddenly developed a nervous twitch. She repeatedly tapped away—panic rising as she deleted Lazzaro Ranaldi's number-one guest's entire financial history before his very eyes. He should step in, Caitlyn thought, frantically hitting the back arrow, sweat trickling between her breasts as his hand still hovered. His breath was on the back of her burning neck as an unfamiliar system command popped on screen, to taunt her.

Put Susan to Bed.

What?

Oh—she should have pressed cancel. As soon as she tapped okay, Caitlyn recalled the meaning of the strange prompt—that she really *didn't* want the computer system to shut down on the day, that she really, *really* didn't want to do the *one single thing* Glynn had told her she must never, ever do. But as the screen went black, Caitlyn knew that Susan wasn't just in bed, she was snoring her head off and completely unrousable as somewhere in the system she tallied and recorded the day's figures and guests' comings and goings.

Caitlyn never swore—well, never in front of her boss—but her curse was out before she could stop it. Glynn's alarmed expression told her that her frantic whisper had reached his ears.

'Everything okay?' Glynn checked nervously, from the other side of the desk, and Caitlyn looked up to face the lesser of two evils but Glynn's visible terror at her horrified expression held nothing that could console her. 'Everything is okay, isn't it?' he hissed.

'There seems to be a problem with the system.' Caitlyn attempted a calm voice, only her mouth seemed to belong to someone who had just stepped out of the dentist's after having a root canal procedure. Her lips struggled to form the words, her finger was still tapping away, but her whole body was absolutely rigid. She was wishing that she'd gone home when she could have—when she *should* have.

'What the hell do you mean?' Glynn snapped, moving to race his way around the counter. 'A problem with the system? What on earth have you done, Caitlyn?'

Ended her career before it had even started, probably, Caitlyn thought with dread. Lazzaro Ranaldi's temper was legendary amongst the staff—and something she'd never wanted to witness, particularly aimed at herself. Bracing herself for his caustic tongue, for a few choice expletives to fill the lavish reception area as he told her exactly what he thought of her computer skills, of her woeful inadequacy to work for such an exclusive hotel, bravely—*stupidly*, perhaps—Caitlyn lifted her head and craned her neck to face him.

Her terrified expression turned to one of bemusement as she saw that the eyes that met hers weren't hostile at all. In fact, if she wasn't mistaken, there was just the hint of a smile playing on the edge of his mouth.

'It's fine, Glynn.' With one perfectly manicured hand he halted his manager's progress. 'You have guests to attend to.' Lazzaro's eyes fell on a rather affectionate couple at the desk, who really should get a room as quickly as possible. 'As Caitlyn said, there is a small problem with the system—nothing I can't sort.'

Was there really a problem with the system? Caitlyn wondered hopefully as Glynn went to sort out the couple, her eyes darting back to the now flickering screen of the computer.

'Nothing that can't be fixed...' He was leaning right over her now, as she stood frozen to the spot—and not just her feet. Caitlyn's hand was still clutching the mouse like a frozen claw. Her throat tightened as his warm hand closed around hers, guiding it up to the little red arrow at the top and closing the programme—something Caitlyn was sure, positive in fact, that you shouldn't do. Her heart was thumping in her chest as he removed his hand—she should really step aside. Only she didn't. In fact, still she stood there, as his hands came around either side of her waist and moved to the keyboard. Her heart leapt up into her mouth as, without a single mistake, he calmly logged in and with impressive speed typed in the necessary details to retrieve Gus Dalton's information.

'Luckily everything is backed up.' His voice was low in her ear, and she waited for relief to flood her—waited for grateful breath to escape her lips as the crisis was averted. Only it never came. Her body was resisting the call to relax, and her mind was telling her in no uncertain terms that now certainly wasn't the time for complacency. Every nerve was on high alert, every cell, every shred of DNA was quivering with tension. Only it had nothing to do with her career, nothing to do with her boss catching her making a stupendous mistake, but everything to do with the man who was leaning over her, the heavy scent of him, the absolute undeniable maleness of him, was having the most dizzying effect.

'How…?' Caitlyn blinked. 'Glynn said that once Susan was put to bed…'

'All the day's data is sent to me for checking,' Lazzaro explained then elaborated, still tapping away. 'Nothing that happens on this computer is deleted till I am satisfied it is okay…'

'Thank goodness for that.'

'So long as you're not attempting a dash of embezzlement…?' He'd stopped typing now, put the delicious prison of his arms down as he stepped back, and Caitlyn thankfully exhaled before she turned to face him.

'Of course not!' Caitlyn giggled.

'Or having a few friends paying mate's rates while staying in the Presidential Suite?'

'Please!' Caitlyn laughed.

'Or mooning behind the desk checking e-mails and doing a spot of internet banking on my time?'

'Er, no.' Caitlyn wasn't laughing now. In fact she was having trouble forcing a smile.

'Or checking your horoscope…?'

Caitlyn didn't even attempt a denial. Her face was burning an unattractive shade of scarlet, but if she'd had the nerve to look up she'd have seen that he was smiling.

'Everything in order?' Glynn was positively dripping with nerves as he came over.

'Of course.' Lazzaro shrugged. 'I see that Gus paid in advance forty-eight hours before the reception…'

'Still…' Glynn cleared his throat. 'I thought I ought to warn him…'

'Lazzaro!' Smiling, loud, and as red in the face as Caitlyn, Gus Danton crossed the foyer. 'Come in and have a drink!'

'I was just about to.' Lazzaro nodded. 'I trust everything has gone smoothly tonight?'

'It's been perfect!' Gus enthused. 'Everything's gone off without a hitch. Actually…' Gus turned to address Glynn. 'Did you sort out the bar, like I asked?'

'All done,' Lazzaro answered for his manager. 'You'll be posted an itemised bill next week.'

'Details, details…' Gus waved them away. 'Join us, Lazzaro.'

'I'll be there in just a moment.'

As Gus headed back to the ballroom, Lazzaro gave a nod to his waiting beauty. And though he didn't whistle, though he didn't wave a lead, as she jumped up eagerly, the only thing Caitlyn could liken her to was an over-eager dog, finding out it was about to be walked.

Every staff member stood rigid, every polished smile was perfectly in place as he stalked towards the ballroom, yet, like a leaky balloon, one could almost feel the tension seeping out as the ballroom doors were opened and Lazzaro and his date entered. But just as shoulders drooped, just as everyone prepared to exhale *en masse,* as if having second thoughts, he turned around—striding back to the reception desk and fixing a stunned Caitlyn with his stern glare.

'Why did I do that?' he demanded. 'Come on—you are here to learn. Why, when this is a business, when I know he may not have the funds, would I choose, for now, to ignore it?'

'Er…' Caitlyn's eyes darted to Glynn's in a brief plea for help, but when none was forthcoming she forced herself to look back at Lazzaro. 'Because he's a friend?' Caitlyn attempted. Seeing his frown deepen, she had another stab. 'Because he's a guest and, rather than embarrass him tonight…' The frown was still deepening as she frantically racked her brain. 'Because he's already paid so much…'

She was clearly completely off track. Her mind raced to come up with an answer, only she had none left. Bracing herself for the cracking whip of his putdown, she gave in. And he did the strangest, most unexpected thing.

'All good reasons. But…' That inscrutable, scathing expression slipped like a mask and broke into another smile of which Caitlyn was the sole beneficiary, and it was like stepping out into the sun unprotected— dazzling, warming, blinding her with its intensity, knocking her completely off guard, a smile that magnified everything. 'He has three more daughters and all of them are single—so if tonight goes well, that is three more weddings…'

He didn't finish. Bored now, he turned again and headed back to his date, and towards the ballroom.

And this time, for Caitlyn at least, the tension had only just started—and there wasn't a trace of breath left in her lungs to be let out.

There were several clocks in the reception area, each giving the different times around the world—ten minutes to midnight in Melbourne, ten minutes to two in the afternoon in London, and ten minutes to nine in the morning in New York—and Caitlyn glanced up at them, freeze-framing them in her mind. Because suddenly it was relevant; for the first time in her life Caitlyn actually understood the saying that time stood still...

Because it did.

At ten minutes to midnight Caitlyn's eyes were dragged back to Lazzaro's departing back, watching as he walked into the ballroom and out of her view, taking with him just a little piece of her very young, very tender heart.

'You might as well go home,' Glynn said a little while later. 'There's not much to do.'

'There will be, though.' Caitlyn coloured up a touch, her work ethic for once having nothing to do with her wanting to hang around. 'Once the wedding reception finishes.'

'It's all under control.'

'What are you going to do about Luca?' Caitlyn asked. 'All the best rooms are booked out for the wedding.'

'He'll be so wasted he won't notice if I put him in the broom cupboard.' Glynn rolled his eyes, then smiled. 'Have you thought about what I said? About working here while you study? A lot of our chambermaids are students.'

Caitlyn nodded. 'I'm going to put in my résumé on Monday.'

'Well, you can put me down as a reference,' Glynn said. 'You've done really well—here.' He handed her a cab voucher.

'What's this for? You don't have to do that!'

'Don't worry—I haven't gone soft. Lazzaro insists the hotel pays for a taxi if staff work after eleven—and given that you're practically staff, he wouldn't hear otherwise!'

'So he can be nice, then?' Caitlyn fished. 'Despite what everyone says?'

'Unfortunately, yes.' Glynn sighed. 'Which means one always ends up forgiving him when he's being bloody! Night, Caitlyn.'

Chatting idly to the doorman, Caitlyn shivered—not with cold but with tiredness as she waited for ever for her taxi. But her weariness was quickly forgotten when Lazzaro's rather ravishing date came out alone and boot-faced, and was gobbled up by his limousine.

'Lovers' tiff.' Geoff winked, once she was safely off into the night. 'You'd think he'd have had the sense to wait till morning to get rid of her!'

'Have they been together long?' Caitlyn attempted to be casual but her face was burning.

'Never seen her till tonight,' Geoff said cheerfully. 'I'll give your taxi another reminder—mind you, the tennis is on. Why don't you wait inside and I'll call you when it comes?'

And she would have—only Lazzaro Ranaldi himself was coming through the revolving glass doors. Lazzaro Ranaldi himself was smiling at her as he walked past.

'You're either very late leaving, or arriving incredibly early.'

'I'm waiting for a taxi,' Caitlyn mumbled.

'You'll be waiting a while—the night match at the tennis just wrapped up.'

'I heard.'

'Would you like a lift?'

Just like that he said it—just like any *normal* person would say it. Only he wasn't just a normal person, and Caitlyn had difficulty coming up with a normal answer. She just stood there mute for a moment as a few hundred thousand dollars' worth of sleek silver sports car pulled up and the valet handed him the keys.

'I was expecting the limousine!' She put on a plummy voice and raised her nose in distaste at his stunning car—then panicked that he wouldn't get her rather offbeat humour.

'Sorry about that… You'll just have to slum it in this…' He didn't just get it, he topped it! As Geoff opened the passenger door for her, Lazzaro peered inside at the immaculate leather upholstery. 'I can look in the boot for a newspaper or something for you to sit on, so you don't mess up your skirt.'

'I'll be fine.' Caitlyn gave a martyred sigh and climbed into the seat, wriggling down in the baby-bottom-soft leather and returning his smile as he joined her, watching as he punched her address into the sat nav. And just like that she forgot to be nervous—just like that they purred off into the night, chatting about anything and everything—including her age.

'How old are you, then?' Lazzaro asked as she rattled on about her studies.

'Twenty,' Caitlyn lied. Then, realising he could look it up, she recanted. 'Well, I will be on Thursday.'

He made a mental note to tell his PA to send flowers and book a table—Thursday suddenly seemed an impossibly long way off.

'Turn left at the next roundabout and your destination is on the right,' came the very calm voice of the sat nav.

'The trouble with these things,' Lazzaro said, smiling as he turned off the engine and faced her, 'is that you can't pretend you're lost and prolong your journey.'

'I know where I live,' Caitlyn pointed out, but her heart was soaring at his blatant flirt.

'Nice place.' It was—a massive old weatherboard in a very nice street, just a stone's throw from the beach. Either there were a thousand students crammed in or, Lazzaro realised, she still lived at home. 'Someone's still up.'

'My mum!' Caitlyn frowned at the twitching curtain, wishing she'd just gone to bed, embarrassed all of a sudden and feeling about twelve years old. 'Or my grandad.'

Only it didn't bother him a bit—in fact, there was a certain novelty to it all. Lazzaro was used—too used—to sophisticates seductively inviting him up, having already gone down!

'Then you'd better go in.'

He watched her face fall an inch, and, though he wanted nothing more than to reach over and kiss her, Lazzaro knew exactly how to keep a woman wanting more.

God, she was gorgeous, though, Lazzaro thought as she walked up her drive.

The front door was opening before she even got there.

Funny too, Lazzaro mused, smiling as he drove off into the night. He'd put her out of her misery and ring her on Monday—put himself out of his misery too, Lazzaro thought, shifting uncomfortably in his seat.

Once he'd dealt with Luca he'd ring her.

Luca.

His face hardened when he thought of his twin brother—he was not relishing a bit the task that lay ahead.

Monday suddenly seemed impossibly close.

CHAPTER ONE

'You bit him!' Black eyes fixed her with a stern glare as she stood at his desk. *This* was the very last thing Lazzaro needed to be dealing with today, and a petty row among the domestic staff was something he didn't usually have to.

'I didn't bite him,' Caitlyn snapped, and Lazzaro actually blinked. Her denial was not what he had been expecting—especially given the evidence. But her irritation, her indignation, even, told him that this five-minute problem that had landed on his desk at five p.m. on a hellish Friday was actually a rather more serious one. Jenna, his PA, had tearfully resigned on Wednesday, and *her* assistant was off with the flu that had swept through half his admin staff, which meant that today Lazzaro was dealing with what was usually expertly delegated. Only maybe it was just as well he was dealing with this particular scenario. It would seem that Caitlyn—he glanced down at the file on his desk—Caitlyn Bell, had a side to her story that he needed to hear.

Even if he really didn't want to.

'It was just a little nip.' China-blue eyes held his—eyes

that were familiar somehow…eyes that were just as blue as Roxanne's.

Where the hell had *that* thought come from?

This woman was nothing like Roxanne.

Caitlyn was as blonde as Roxanne was dark, and the woman who stood before him was petite whereas Roxanne was curvaceous, but those eyes… A tiny swallow was the only evidence of his inner turmoil—he was angry with himself that even after all this time the memories, the pain, could still wash over him at the most unexpected of times.

'It's not as if I sank my teeth in.'

Lazzaro dragged his mind back to the conversation, grateful to escape his own thoughts, and it was quite hard not to smile at her description, quite hard *not* to compare it to Malvolio's—who had roared and ranted so loudly, his hand wrapped in a handkerchief, as if it was about to fall off. He hadn't known what to expect when he'd called her to his office. He was the last person who would normally deal with one of the hotel's maids, and when he did they were usually cowering in the chair. But not this one.

She'd declined his offer to sit, and was instead standing at his desk—jangling with nerves, perhaps, but curiously strong. Long blonde hair that was presumably usually neatly tied back was tumbling out of its hair-tie after the *incident,* her arms were folded across her chest, and the blue eyes were glassy from her trying not to cry. She kept sniffing in the effort not to, and somehow, even if she was tiny, even if she was clearly shaken, somehow she was incredibly together too—her rosebud mouth pursed and defiant as she refused to relent.

'I need more information.'

'I really don't see what all the fuss is about.'

'One of my staff members has been bitten by another—'

'Not just any one of your staff members…'

This time he deliberately didn't blink. He held his expression in absolute check as she interrupted, and, though few usually dared, he let the fact go as Caitlyn Bell got straight to the rather awkward point.

'Malvolio is, I believe, your brother-in-law.'

He gave a terse nod—a nod that was actually respectful, acknowledging what she had to say even while quickly disregarding it. 'The fact Malvolio is my brother-in-law has no bearing in this matter—none whatsoever. Now, I want to hear exactly what happened.'

'As Malvolio said, we were discussing a promotion—he tripped and, like a reflex action, he put out his hands to save himself—'

'Caitlyn—' Rather more usually, it was Lazzaro interrupting now, but unusually someone overrode him—someone's voice got a touch louder and more insistent as Caitlyn spoke over him.

'And—like a reflex action—I bit him.' She gave a tight smile. 'Or rather, I gave him a little nip.'

'I want the truth.'

'You just got it.'

'Caitlyn, you are one of my staff…'

'Not any more.' She shook her head. 'I just resigned.'

'No.' He wasn't having it—he saw just a flash of tears in those stunning blue eyes, and loathed Malvolio for causing them. 'You do not have to lose your job over this…'

'I was already leaving. That's why I was having a discussion with Malvolio in the first place. I've got an interview next week—a second interview, actually—for a PR position with the Mancini chain of hotels.'

'A PR position?' Lazzaro frowned. Alberto Mancini was both his friend and his rival. Both had hotels all over the world, both had formidable reputations, and both were choosy with their staff—and a chambermaid, no matter how well presented, wouldn't cut it in PR. 'You are a chambermaid. How can you have an interview for a PR—?'

'I've been working as a maid while studying.'

'Studying?'

'Hospitality and tourism…'

He was only half listening—that jolt of recognition he had experienced when he saw her was explained now. That was where he knew her from. She'd been on the desk—funny that he could remember, but he did—and there had been a wedding… The Danton wedding…that was it…

'You did work experience here while you were studying?' Lazzaro checked. 'A couple of years ago?'

'That's right…' Caitlyn blinked, stunned that he remembered, wondering *what* he remembered. 'Just for a few days. I filled in an application form at the time, and I've been working as a maid while I've been studying ever since.'

He ran a hand over his forehead and trailed it down over his cheek, fingering for just a second the livid scar that ran the length of it. And for the second time in as many moments, Lazzaro came up with another logical explanation as to why this particular woman's face remained in his memory.

Before.

The weekend before it had happened.

The weekend before, when life had been so much easier.

When laughing had come so much more readily.

He'd kissed thousands of women he couldn't recall. Funny that he remembered one that he hadn't.

'Why haven't you applied for a position here—given your history with the place?'

It was a perfectly reasonable question, one that her family and colleagues regularly asked, but one she simply couldn't answer—and especially not to Lazzaro.

How could she tell him that for more than two years he'd been on her mind, that the king-size crush that had hit her that night—despite her busy life, despite dancing and fun and boyfriends—still hadn't faded?

That she really needed to get a life.

One away from Lazzaro Ranaldi and the stupid torch she carried for him.

Maybe if his brother hadn't died...maybe if she hadn't started work as a chambermaid...maybe if he hadn't been linked with Roxanne and it hadn't been on every news bulletin and in every paper or magazine Caitlyn had opened...then, after that initial meeting, she'd have moved quickly on, forgotten the feel of his eyes on hers, forgotten the thrill in her stomach as that dark, ruthless face had been softened by a rare smile. Only in the days after that meeting she'd seen the pain in those closed features screaming from the newspapers, had winced at the scurrilous gossip that had ensued, the blistering row between brothers that had preceded Luca Ranaldi's sudden and tragic death. But still working in the hotel—instead of moving on—she had caught her breath whenever she'd gleaned an occasional glimpse of him striding through the hotel, blushing in her maid's uniform as—naturally—he didn't deign to give her a glance. Though Caitlyn did. That perfect face, marred since that tragic day by a livid scar along his cheek, with lines now fanning his dark eyes and his mouth permanently set on grim. She could see the tension he carried in his shoulders, and wanted somehow for him to smile again.

Just the way he once had.

She hadn't spoken to him since that night—not even once. And thank goodness for that, Caitlyn realised, because despite more than two years between drinks, so to speak, still he absolutely moved her. Despite the angry scar on his cheek, despite the closed, much more guarded expression he wore now, despite the pain in his eyes—still he was absolutely beautiful.

'I need a bit more variety...' Caitlyn answered truthfully—because she did. She needed to sample a world that didn't have his name on every sheet of paper, needed to check her bank balance and not see 'Ranaldi', needed to just get over him—for good.

'You'll find nowhere better than right here.'

'You're probably right...' Caitlyn's face twisted slightly at the unwitting irony of his statement. 'But I really think it's time for a change—so you see today really doesn't matter. I was leaving soon anyway.'

'But it *does* matter, Caitlyn. You have worked for this hotel for two years and one month.' He gave a small swallow as her eyes narrowed, and he glanced again at her file, as if he'd gleaned the information from there. Only he hadn't—the date was indelibly etched on his mind, but she didn't need to know why...

It had nothing to do with her.

'If anything untoward has happened, you have the same

rights as any other staff member. Just because Malvolio is family...'

'I hear your sister's having a baby...' She pulled a crumpled tissue out of her pocket and gave her nose a rather loud blow.

'What does that have to do with this?' Lazzaro's voice was completely even, his face impassive, but he had to stop himself from drumming his fingers on the desk—actually had to remind himself to keep looking her in the eye as she voiced his very thoughts. How the hell would Antonia cope? She had just started to get her life back on track after Luca's death, the new baby was due in just a few days, there was his niece, Marianna, just four years old—what the hell had Malvolio been *thinking?*

'It has everything to do with this!' Caitlyn gulped. 'Look, I'm fine—I really am—and I don't want any fuss. I just want to get my things and leave.'

And, though it must surely be the last thing she wanted after the day's events, all *he* wanted to do was to walk around the desk and put his arms around her, this little spitfire who had marched into his office on his command and was about to walk out against it. And, yes, technically it would be so much easier to let her go. But it would be wrong, so very wrong, if he did.

'Caitlyn—let's just talk about this. It can be dealt with—you really do not have to leave.'

'Oh, but I think I do,' she countered. 'As I said, I've got the Mancini interview...I can muddle through till then. Though...' Her voice faded, her head shaking at the impossibility of explaining her problems to him.

'What?'

'It's complicated.'

'Probably not to me.'

She managed a wan smile, realising she had no choice but to tell him. 'I've been doing a lot of overtime for the last two months. A *lot* of overtime,' Caitlyn reiterated.

'I will ensure that you're paid.'

'It's just that...' Caitlyn took a deep breath. 'I'm applying for a mortgage, and I need three months of payslips to show my earnings.' She scuffed the carpet with her foot. 'I told the bank it was my regular wage.'

'Without overtime?' Lazzaro checked. 'But wouldn't that show up on your payslip?'

'Quite!' Caitlyn blushed.

'So you lied to the bank?'

'Not lied exactly.' Caitlyn gulped. 'Malvolio said it...' She watched his eyes narrow, realised he must be thinking there was something more to their working relationship. There truly wasn't. She had asked and he had agreed—it was as simple as that. 'Oh, it doesn't matter.' Caitlyn shrugged. 'I need three payslips anyway.'

'Then stay.'

'I don't want to.' She stood firm. 'I'd rather not put Malvolio down as a reference. I know he deals with the domestic staff, and I know he usually would be the one, but I...'

'You can put me—I can assure you I have more influence with Mancini than Malvolio does, and I will ensure it is extremely favourable.'

'How?' Caitlyn frowned. 'How can you write my reference when you don't know anything about me?'

'Oh, but I think I do.' Her words, only spoken through

his lips now. He stared over at her—little, but strong and, unlike his brother-in-law, unlike the father of the baby, this stranger actually gave a damn about the woman who was carrying his child.

'I will get the forms and have your pay made up. I will do it on Monday—that way, if you change your mind over the weekend—'

'Could you get the forms now, please?' She wasn't looking at him now, instead staring out of his vast windows somewhere over his shoulder at the Melbourne city skyline. 'I won't be changing my mind.'

'Just think about it.'

'I'd like the forms now.'

This time she didn't add please.

This time Lazzaro knew there was no persuading her otherwise.

'Where's Malvolio?'

Storming through the Admin corridors, Lazzaro caught everyone by surprise. Admin staff with bags over their shoulders, hoping to slope off a little early, suddenly sat back down and started tapping at blank screens; the raucous laughter coming from the boardroom that signalled end-of-week drinks that Lazzaro supplied for his team, which should start at five but in fact seemed to start around lunchtime, snapped off as if the power had been pulled as he stormed into rather unfamiliar territory. His suite was on the top floor, and he had a private lift that absolutely bypassed the usually well-oiled engines of Admin.

But come five p.m. on Friday, the wheels fell off somewhat!

'He's gone!' Audrey Miller, Malvolio's assistant, gave an anxious smile. 'He had to dash off—Antonia rang and said she was having some cramps…'

'Antonia's in labour?'

'I'm not sure.' Audrey gulped. 'But the staff got a bit excited, as you can see…'

There wasn't a hope in hell of getting the termination forms—let alone a final cheque cut.

He'd deal with the lot of them on Monday.

Right now, his sister could be in labour.

His brother-in-law by her side.

The same brother-in-law who had forced Caitlyn Bell's resignation for all the wrong reasons.

CHAPTER TWO

DAMN!

Pacing the floor of the huge office, Caitlyn paused for a moment to blow her nose again, and rummaged in her bag for her compact, powdering her reddened face and telling herself to hold it together for just a little while longer.

She'd surely get another job—but she also needed those three blasted payslips just in case the court ruling went against her mother.

It wouldn't, Caitlyn consoled herself. Their lawyer had assured them that everything was under control. A moan of horror escaped her lips at the thought of that same lawyer's bill, sitting on the dining room table—a bill that had to be paid before he'd proceed further.

What the hell was she going to do?

She'd lied to Lazzaro about a second interview with the Mancini chain—she hadn't even had the first interview yet. Her application was still sitting half-typed on her computer! Actually, she'd lied to Lazzaro about everything. There had been no discussion about a promotion; Malvolio had just been his usual sleazy self. She'd been sitting on her afternoon break, minding her own business, when he'd come into the coffee room and again suggested they catch up for a drink after work.

Again she'd declined.

'You've got something in your hair.'

He'd come over, had stood behind her where she sat, and, as if being touched by a lizard, she'd flinched as his hand had made contact with her hair. She had screwed her eyes closed as he'd brushed something that surely wasn't there away, wishing the horrible moment over, only the horror hadn't even begun. The lizard had been on the move.

'Come on, Caitlyn...stop teasing me...'

His filthy hands had crept down; she'd been able to hear his breath coming short and hard behind her.

'I'm not teasing you...' Her head had been spinning. The confrontation she'd dreaded—dreaded but convinced herself would never happen, that she was surely imagining things—was actually here. *'Malvolio, you're married...'*

'Antonia....' His hand had moved down. *'She is so wrapped up in herself and the baby. You and I could be so good together....'*

Paralysed, she'd sat, watched his fingers sneaking at the top of her dress, her brain literally frozen. It had been like being stuck in a nightmare, where you couldn't scream. She'd known that by doing nothing she was implying consent...and if she couldn't speak, if she couldn't scream, then there were two other choices that had sprung to her panicked mind: vomit or bite.

Caitlyn had chosen the latter!

She could still hear his screams of rage—hear again the vile torrent of words he'd spat at her as he'd jumped back—and, like a child, she put her hands over her ears, blocked out what he had said to her. She just didn't want to go there right now.

How, Caitlyn begged herself as she resumed her pacing, could he think she'd teased him? She'd gone out of her way to avoid him, though she had felt his unwelcome eyes on her for months now, had done everything possible to avoid… Her eyes shuttered in wretched horror. The consequences of her resignation were starting to hit home. The prospect of going home and telling her mother that she no longer had work… Oh, a chambermaid's wage wasn't going to change the world, but for now at least it meant holding onto her mother's.

A single mother, Helen Bell had done *everything* to provide not just for her daughter, but for her own father. When Caitlyn's grandmother had died, two years after Caitlyn was born, concerned about her father's declining health and mounting financial problems, Helen had moved back to the family home, working several jobs to pay the mortgage and bills and had gradually cleared his debts. It hadn't all been a struggle, though—the home had been a happy one, with Caitlyn's grandfather more than happy to mind his grandchild while Helen worked hard. And in later years, as his health had declined, both Helen and Caitlyn had in turn been more than happy to care for him—nursing him at home right till the end.

Caitlyn's aunt Cheryl had rarely put in an appearance—until after the funeral. Of course the family home Helen had worked so hard to keep and pay for had been left to her. But Cheryl had had it valued—the beachside suburb close to the city was prime real estate now—and Cheryl wanted not only the generous cash sum that her father had bequeathed to her in his will, but half the value of the family home. Egged on by Roxanne and a greedy lawyer, she was moving heaven and earth to ensure that she got it.

'Bloody Roxanne and Aunty Cheryl...' Caitlyn hissed. Why couldn't they just leave them alone?

The ringing of the phone halted her pacing for less than a second. Her mind was so consumed with her own problems that at first she didn't even give it a glance.

She needed work so badly, but here it would be impossible. Lazzaro was hardly going to fire his own brother-in-law. It would be her word against his. And what about Malvolio's poor wife? How—?

The phone resumed its shrill, and irritated now, unable to ignore it, Caitlyn picked it up.

'Lazzaro Ranaldi's phone. This is Caitlyn Bell speaking.'

She didn't notice Lazzaro come in at first, just listened as a rather exasperated female voice demanded that she be put through.

'I'm sorry, Mr Ranaldi isn't in his office right now. But if you'd like to leave your name, as soon as he returns I'll let him know that you called...'

Half turning, she saw him, and was just about to hand the phone over when instinct kicked in somehow. The dash of bitters in the woman's voice was telling Caitlyn that perhaps this was one call Lazzaro might be glad to miss, so instead of handing him the receiver, she grabbed a pen and scribbled down the woman's name. *Lucy*.

She even managed a little smile when he grimaced and shook his head while Lucy vented her spleen down the phone.

'Of course,' Caitlyn said sweetly. 'I'll be sure to let him know.' Replacing the receiver, she turned to her very soon to be ex-boss. 'You're a bastard!'

'Thank you for passing it on.'

'And she knows you're there and just refusing to talk to her.'

'Anything else?'

'Er, that was pretty much it,' Caitlyn lied. Well, she was hardly going to tell him that 'just because he's fabulous in bed, it doesn't make up for the way he's treated me'. Though she did give him a rather edited version of the teary conclusion to the call. 'She'd like you to call her—any time,' Caitlyn emphasised. 'Any time at all! So…' Noticing his empty hands, she raised her eyebrows. 'Where are the forms?'

'In a filing cabinet.' He gave an apologetic grimace. 'Only I'm not sure which one…but I will write you a cheque now…'

'A cheque's not much good to me at this time on a Friday.' She didn't want to stay another second. Another second and she'd start crying; another second and she'd crumple. The brave façade she was wearing so well was seriously falling apart—the hem unravelling along with the seams—so she hitched her bag on her shoulder and headed for the door. 'Just have it all posted to me on Monday.'

'Caitlyn.' His strong voice summoned her back, but she kept on walking. 'Just listen to me for a moment. What if I were to offer you a job as my personal assistant?'

Now, that was enough to stop her in her tracks—only not enough to make her turn around.

'Me?'

Her hand paused as it reached for the handle and Lazzaro spoke on. 'Clearly I need someone, and you have no idea of some of the poor efforts the agency has sent. You handled that call well, you are qualified, and you are clearly...' he gave a slightly uncomfortable cough '...discreet...'

'I can't.'

The words shot out on instinct—her dream job, everything that she'd wished for coming true, and the money, oh, God, the money would make *such* a difference. Only she couldn't do it—just couldn't do it. And bitter, so bitter, was her regret.

'I can't face seeing Malvolio again.' Her voice was shrill, and still she didn't turn around. Her hand was on the door now, but not to open it, more for support. The horrors of the day were finally catching up, the feelings she had denied, had willed herself not to examine until she was safely alone, were making searing contact with her brain now. 'I don't think I could stand to be...'

Silence filled the room. Only it wasn't peaceful. It was that horrible silence of a strangled sob, the thud of reality, that moment when it all catches up and there's nothing that can be done to push it back down—when you can't keep smiling as if you're stupid, when you can't pretend that you don't care and that it didn't really matter that filthy hands had dirtied your life. Yes—in a while she'd no doubt be able to shrug it off; in a while she'd probably put it all into perspective and apportion the correct blame. In a while it wouldn't matter as much as it mattered now.

But right now it mattered.

And it mattered to Lazzaro too.

Seeing her convulse—seeing this proud, strong woman wilt for a second—he found it mattered enough to propel him from his desk, to literally peel her trembling body from the door, to turn her around to face him and hold her. Like some mountain rescuer he reached her on the cliff-edge and tried to imbue her with his warmth.

'I hate him...' She wasn't talking to Lazzaro; he knew that. 'I *hate* him.'

'I know.'

'I'll be okay soon.' She gulped, knowing she would, just confirming it to herself. She was embarrassed now at letting him see her cry, but he held her closer as she started to pull away, and after just a second of protest she let him—let him comfort her, let him hold her as the horror slowly receded, her breathing slowing at just listening to the soothing thud of his heart in his chest.

For Lazzaro there was one inevitable end to holding a woman in his arms. The luxury of having a penthouse suite as your office meant there was a bed just a door away, and as he stared down at lips swollen from nibbling teeth and salty tears, instinct told him to kiss her—to soothe her in the way he soothed women best. Only a deeper instinct prevailed.

Morality—which was usually void—crept in. His kiss was surely not what she needed now.

Only it was.

It felt like for ever that she'd dreamt of being in his arms, but now it had happened Caitlyn found out dreams didn't actually compare. Being held by him was so blissfully consuming, the circle of his arms so strong and safe, that nothing else could invade. She felt the shift in him, felt the shift from comfort to more, and she actually *wanted* him to kiss her, wanted his hands on her to erase the grubby stains Malvolio's had left.

But he didn't. Instead he held her for just a little bit

more, held her close as she assimilated all that had taken place and put it into some sort of order, and when finally he let her go, when finally she could stand alone again, the world was certainly a nicer place than the one she'd left just moments ago.

'Malvolio manages the housekeeping staff. He's rarely in the office and I'm rarely here. The job would involve a lot of travel…' His voice was low, his gaze direct as he told her he hadn't changed his mind.

'But even so…' Caitlyn protested. 'I'd still have to see him sometimes…' Again she shook her head, but she wasn't so certain now. Lazzaro believed her. Lazzaro knew. And he would, she was sure, sort it.

That thought was confirmed when Lazzaro spoke next. 'He will not trouble you at all—I will go and see him and make very sure of it. You do not have to leave.'

'I haven't got any experience…' She was being offered her dream job, a fast-track to what would normally take years to achieve, and even if it was foolhardy to show how woefully inadequate she was for such an esteemed position, really she had no choice.

'You haven't picked up any bad habits, then.' For the first time today she saw him smile, then he gestured to the desk. 'Sit down.'

Formality was welcome.

Formality she could actually deal with.

So she listened as he took her through her new role, blinking at the description of international flights and luxury hotels that would now pepper her existence, at a salary that made her eyes widen, and at the prospect of a life, as Lazzaro strongly pointed out, that would be basically put on hold to accommodate his.

'My time is valuable,' Lazzaro said, and she nodded. 'Take today—I should not be going to Admin to get forms, and nor will you be able to. That is why you too will have an assistant. My former PA has a list of names somewhere, of people who can be put through to me without question, people who first you check and people who, like Lucy, you will have to deal with.' He gave a tight smile. 'At times your work will be menial, and at times it will be downright boring—such as sitting in a car waiting for me. At other times the stress and demands will be intense. Each morning we will go through my day—each week we will plan my schedule. For example, in a couple of weeks we will fly to Rome—'

'I don't speak Italian…'

'Lucky for you then, that nearly all my staff in Rome speak excellent English… Still, if you do decide to remain in this position, that is something you might be wise to address.'

If she decided to remain! Who would be mad enough to leave such a fabulous job?

Lazzaro must have caught the slightly incongruous dart of her eyes.

'I have never had a PA stay for more than a year—that is how long you will be contracted for. Towards the end of your term we will discuss your future. This is an exceptionally demanding role—and, yes, I am an exceptionally demanding boss. I have high standards, a formidable workload, and at some point you will no doubt decide that no amount of money or perks can make up for it.'

'Is that why Jenna left?' Caitlyn asked, because she'd heard that you should find out the reasons any position was vacant. Though when Lazzaro answered she rather wished that she hadn't.

'Jenna had certain demands that I wasn't prepared to meet.'

Like monogamy? Caitlyn was tempted to say, but thankfully she didn't—their private affair had not been so private, given it was she who had changed the sheets!

'At some point,' Lazzaro continued, 'you will want to resume your own life—I accept that. However, a period of working for me will open many doors for you.'

'I just don't get why me, when it's clearly such a demanding role...' Caitlyn's mouth was suddenly dry—she was acutely aware that she was sitting in a chambermaid's dress, suddenly being interviewed for a plum position. 'And though naturally I'd love the opportunity, I just don't understand why you'd just hand it to me. If it's because of what happened with Malvolio—'

'After several unsuccessful interviews, I wasted yet another hour this afternoon attempting to explain to a very boutique recruitment agency my needs,' Lazzaro interrupted. 'Outlining what it was I was looking for in an assistant. Next week I will be paraded with a number of what they consider suitable applicants. I do not necessarily want someone who speaks fluent Italian. I do not want someone who on paper has "excellent interpersonal skills" but in reality cannot read a situation. I want someone who, without being told, writes down the name of a caller they assume might be difficult.' His eyes narrowed thoughtfully as he looked over at her. 'I guess you just know sometimes that you've found the person you're looking for.'

'Quite!' Caitlyn croaked, then coloured up, biting on her

bottom lip, wishing she were hearing that from him somewhere other than in an interview.

'And,' Lazzaro continued, 'I want someone who has the guts to be honest.'

'I *am* honest…' Caitlyn flared.

'Just not with your bank.' He grinned. 'Look, I am not asking you to sign away the rest of your life. I understand that the role is too consuming, too demanding to expect longevity. But most people I interview are using this as a stepping stone—are prepared to work hard for a few months because of the doors it will open. I want someone who is prepared to work hard, full-stop. So when you are thinking of leaving—which you will—I want you to tell me.'

'Okay…' Caitlyn nodded, only she didn't sound very convinced—wasn't convinced at all, in fact, that she would ever leave. Still, maybe this was the way to get over him, she decided, looking at the multitude of positives. Maybe witnessing his legendary bloody nature first hand might just get her to put out the light on the stupid torch she'd been carrying for him.

'Are you in a relationship?'

'Excuse me?' Caitlyn's response was suitably appalled. 'I hardly think that's relevant.'

'But it is,' Lazzaro countered. 'He is going to have to be one very patient man to accept that he's hardly going to see you—that if this goes ahead, as of Monday, I come first!'

'Well, I'm not in a relationship.' Caitlyn sniffed. 'We just broke up.'

'Excellent.' Lazzaro smiled. 'How long were you together?'

'Why? Are you worried I'm going to be crying into my tissues instead of concentrating on you?'

'I'm just curious.' Lazzaro shrugged. 'Given that we're going to be working so closely together, we're going to get to know these things about each other.'

Hardly! Caitlyn choked back the word—she couldn't imagine asking Lazzaro to pass the tissues as she cracked a bar of chocolate and told him that the reason she and Dominic had broken up was because—because... She closed her eyes and cringed. Because of the things she *didn't* do. Because, at the ripe old age of twenty-two, she was still a virgin!

'Purple!' Caitlyn said instead, giving a tight smile at Lazzaro's bemused frown. 'I'm wearing purple knickers, before you ask, and we were together six months. He ended it, but I was actually about to. Is that enough information for you?'

'For now...' He gave her a very lazy smile, and stared at her for the longest time without even attempting to speak. For Caitlyn it was excruciating as she awaited what she knew was about to be a summing up. 'You're very...' he paused before he delivered his verdict '...different.'

'I am.'

'Very interesting...' Lazzaro mused.

'I'm hard bloody work, actually!'

'I like hard work.' Lazzaro grinned, and she nearly shot out of her chair at the look he was giving her. 'Well, I look forward to working with you. That will be all.'

'Not quite.' Caitlyn saw his frown of surprise and she took a deep breath before speaking. 'Generally at the end of an interview the interviewee is asked if she has any questions or anything she'd like to add.'

'Do you?'

'Actually, yes...' Caitlyn hesitated for a second—could absolutely hear the horrified shriek of the little devil that sat on her shoulder as she decided to be upfront. But there was no point in taking this job, no point at all, if one thing wasn't made perfectly clear from the start. She'd heard Lazzaro was a tough and demanding boss, that he had no qualms at all about speaking his mind—loudly on occasion. That she could accept, so long as Lazzaro could accept her. 'I admire the fact that you speak your mind. However...' her blue eyes locked with his '...so do I.'

'I'd already worked that one out,' Lazzaro countered. 'Though stand-up rows with my personal assistant I can do without.'

'Oh, there'll be no stand-up rows.' Caitlyn smiled. 'I'm more professional than that. But, before you formally offer me the position, you should know that I do have a tongue, and one that I'll use if I think I'm being spoken to inappropriately—no matter how good the salary, manners cost nothing.'

Lazzaro, though his face never moved a muscle, was actually smothering a smile; listening to Caitlyn was as unique as it was refreshing—almost as if *he* were the one being interviewed for the job.

'So I am to watch what I say?'

'No,' Caitlyn corrected. 'Just don't expect me to hide behind a pot plant till your mood passes.'

'I don't have any pot plants.'

He stared at her thoughtfully for a moment, and for Caitlyn it lasted for ever. She was wondering if she'd blown it, if she was about to kiss her dream job goodbye, but suddenly he smiled—not a wide, generous smile, more a brief upturn of his lips, but for Caitlyn it was wonderful.

'I will see you on Monday at seven-thirty. You will need a suitable wardrobe, of course. I will arrange an account for you—'

'I *have* a suitable wardrobe,' Caitlyn interrupted. 'I don't generally walk around dressed like this.'

'As you wish.' Lazzaro shrugged. 'But I expect smart.'

'You'll get it.'

'I mean *really* smart,' Lazzaro countered—and winced as the phone rang.

'Allow me.' Caitlyn grinned, rolling her eyes as an expensive voice purred out her new nearly boss's name.

'*Bonita,*' Caitlyn mouthed, expecting him to shake his head, and more than a little miffed when he didn't.

His manicured hand reached for the phone, his voice surprisingly gentle and familiar as he greeted his caller and then asked if she minded holding for a moment.

'You represent me…' Lazzaro continued, but he was distracted now, clearly wanting this meeting over so he could get back to his call. 'My hotels are the best in the world. A high street suit and cheap luggage is not going to—' He saw her colour up, a little pink tinge come to her cheeks, and he reached in his drawer and scribbled down the name of several stores where he held accounts. 'This is not a favour; this is part of your role if you want the job.'

'Tha—' She stopped herself from thanking him. 'Of course.'

But he wasn't listening. His focus was already elsewhere as he waved her away, and even before she'd closed the door behind her she could hear him talking into the phone.

Only, as much as Lazzaro was listening to Bonita, for a moment his mind was still on Caitlyn.

Watching her walk out of his office, Lazzaro knew he had made the right choice—she was smart, capable, and she had enough guts to stand up to him—and she was damned attractive too… His mouth split in a thin smile. He had absolutely no qualms about mixing business with pleasure…and Caitlyn Bell was going to be just that; he knew it.

An absolute pleasure.

CHAPTER THREE

OPPORTUNITY always knocked when one was least expecting it.

But not only was Caitlyn not expecting it—she actually didn't have time for such a once-in-a-lifetime opportunity to come knocking this weekend. She had a wedding to go to tomorrow, which meant she already had a hairdresser's appointment booked, and then the wedding post mortem on Sunday—in fact, she still hadn't even bought a present.

Which left her about two free hours this evening to buy a fabulous executive wardrobe that would see her through not only her new job in Melbourne, but also a quick dash to Rome.

Stepping out onto the street, Caitlyn walked through the crowded city, her head spinning—not just from Lazzaro's job offer, not just because in a matter of an hour or so her whole life had been turned around... She should be walking on air, but instead her legs felt like lead. It felt as if she was walking through mud and, giving in, she leant against a wall for a moment, watching but somehow not watching a tram clattering through the busy street, the spill of suits leaving their offices, eagerly awaiting their weekends. And though it was the last thing she wanted to think about, though there were a million other things she would rather dwell on, it was Malvolio she couldn't rid from her mind.

A nauseous feeling rose in her throat as she relived the horrible scene. Saw again the hate in his eyes when she'd bitten him, heard again the vile spit of words as he'd stormed out of the door.

'You're a cheap slut, Caitlyn—just like Roxanne.'

Roxanne...

Caitlyn closed her eyes, willed her heart to settle into a more normal rhythm. The name he'd hurled meant that he knew who she was—a revelation she hadn't been prepared for.

After ascending the elevator in a city department store, as usual she got off on the fourth floor. It took about ten minutes of blind panic for her to realise that no half-price suit in a sale was going to do for Lazzaro.

He wasn't doing her a favour.

She said Lazzaro's words over and over to herself as she stepped back on the elevator and ascended to the hallowed sixth floor, swallowing at the price tags on the exclusive designer labels, and even accepting the help of a very pushy assistant, whose rather snooty stance noticeably softened when Caitlyn stammered out her predicament.

'You're Lazzaro Ranaldi's new personal assistant... So Gemma has left?'

'Jenna.'

'That's right! Jenna shopped here regularly. I know all about how she just *had* to look the part.'

'Really?'

'Your new boss has very exacting standards where his staff are concerned. Absolutely I'll help you.'

Standing in the changing room, Caitlyn stared at her reflection—the safe black suit she'd initially chosen had been tut-tutted away by the assistant and replaced with a slate-grey one, which was gorgeous, a cream linen one, which Caitlyn wasn't sure about, and an olive one which was fab too—although the skirt was just a touch too short for her liking. Now she was wearing a chocolate-brown suit that, as the assistant had promised, did work well with her colouring. It calmed her complexion and brought out the blue of her eyes, and with her hair done, with make-up on and the right shoes... Standing on tiptoe, Caitlyn assumed a snooty pose and decided that she actually might just pass as Lazzaro Ranaldi's assistant—and she could afford to help her mother now, could pay the lawyer and, if the ruling didn't go their way, would be able to pay off Aunty Cheryl and Roxanne.

Roxanne...

Sitting on the bench in the changing room, Caitlyn buried her head in her hands and dragged in the stuffy air. The knot that was so familiar in her stomach these days tightened another notch, as if Roxanne and Cheryl were on either side, pulling, tugging so hard it would be easier sometimes to just let it snap. Their vile conversation was still playing on her mind as clearly as if it had taken place yesterday instead of two years ago. And not for the first time, maybe for the millionth, Caitlyn wondered if there was anything she could have done—anything she could have said—that might have changed the appalling outcome.

They'd gone to Roxanne's on the Sunday—Helen to

plead with Cheryl to please come and visit now and then. Caitlyn and Roxanne had left them to it, taken a bottle of champagne upstairs and attempted a girls' night in.

Attempted—as they had since they'd been little girls—to pretend they were friends.

'What's this?' Roxanne's eyes had lit up as Caitlyn's bag had tipped off the bed, the photo of Lazzaro she'd torn out of a magazine falling on the floor. 'You've got a crush on him, haven't you?'

'No!' Caitlyn had snatched back the picture, her face burning. But an excuse to talk about Lazzaro had been just too impossible to pass up. 'But you should see how he runs the place—he's pretty amazing.'

'He's hot…' Roxanne had grinned. 'I'll give you that.'

Brave or foolish, Caitlyn hadn't been able to help but show off a little bit to her cousin. 'He gave me a lift home last night.'

'You?' Roxanne scoffed. 'He's ferrying the staff home now, is he? Things must be getting tight!' Roxanne stared down at her newly painted toenails. 'I'm sick of the Ranaldis. I thought I was on to a good thing with Luca, and it turns out the guy's a complete loser.'

'Hardly a loser,' Caitlyn countered. 'And if he's anything like his twin then he must be stunning.'

'He's broke,' Roxanne groaned. 'Luca Ranaldi's a drunk, and he's broke.'

'Broke?' Caitlyn frowned. The words 'broke' and 'Ranaldi' didn't exactly belong in the same sentence, but Roxanne just giggled, opening her wardrobe and pulling out dress after dress, then pulling out a box and smiling at Caitlyn's shocked expression over the glittering array of jewels. 'He's bought you all *this?* But I thought you just said he was broke.'

'What salesperson would even think to check *his* credit rating? He's living off his reputation—though not for much longer,' Roxanne said darkly. 'Lazzaro's covering all his rapidly bouncing cheques.'

'So what the hell are you doing, accepting these things?' Caitlyn said hotly. 'Roxanne, if the guy's going under…'

'Then he might as well go under in style. Anyway, a few piddly dresses and some jewels are a drop in the ocean compared to his problems. I was actually going to dump him today, but he said that he'd take me car-shopping on Monday.' She tossed over a few brochures. 'I'm thinking I might go for red.'

'Roxanne!'

'Oh, get a life,' Roxanne snapped. 'Once I've got rid of Luca I intend to.'

'How are you doing? I've got some luggage for you to—' The shop assistant whipped back the curtain, her painted smile wavering as Caitlyn looked up. 'Are you feeling all right?'

'I'm fine.' Caitlyn ran a tongue over dry lips and stood up. 'Just fine.'

They were so in love.

The words taunted her as she stared in the mirror. Aunty Cheryl had said them over and over, her mother too—it had even been in the newspapers, with a photo of Roxanne having to be held up as she walked behind Luca's coffin.

But Caitlyn knew the truth—and it would seem that Malvolio did too.

* * *

'What's happening?' Lazzaro frowned as, not only was the phone picked up at his sister's home, but Antonia herself answered.

'Nothing. Why?'

'I thought you had pains? That you were—'

'Hardly...' Antonia sighed. 'I don't think this baby's ever going to come out. What are you doing?'

'Driving... Is Malvolio there?'

'He's just outside. I'll get him—'

'Don't worry.' Lazzaro interrupted his sister. 'I'll call over—I'm just a few minutes away.'

'Well, stay for dinner. I could—' Antonia started cheerfully, then stopped mid-sentence as the phone cut out—not that she gave it much thought. Her brother Lazzaro wasn't exactly known for his small talk.

Putting down her book and trying to heave herself off the couch, Antonia smiled as the housekeeper opened the front door and her brother strode into the lounge. 'I was just asking if you wanted to stay for dinner before you hung up on me.'

'No...' Lazzaro shook his head.

'Stay,' Antonia insisted, but still he shook his head.

'Zio!' Marianna's squeal was delighted as she padded into the living room, dressed in pink pyjamas and a dressing gown, her dark curls bobbing as she ran delightedly towards him. Normally he scooped her up, rained her fat baby face with kisses—only he couldn't today. He felt sick with indecision as he looked from his sister to his niece, not wanting to be the one to burst their bubble.

'Hey...' Lazzaro ruffled Marianna's hair, tried not to notice the disappointment in the little girl's eyes at his cool greeting. 'It's good to see you, Marianna.' He turned his attention back to his sister. 'I just wanted to have a word with Malvolio—about work...' he added, completely unable to look at her now.

But Antonia wasn't having it, and called to the housekeeper, asking her to take Marianna for a play, before talking to her brother.

'Is everything okay, Lazzaro?' Antonia checked. She hadn't seen Lazzaro as bad as this for ages. Tense, distracted, he was like a coiled spring. 'You seem...'

'I'm just tired,' Lazzaro answered, forcing a smile of his own. 'It's been a busy week. You heard about Jenna leaving?'

'Poor you. Let's hope you get someone soon.'

'I already have.'

'Already? That's quick. Normally it takes you for ever to find someone suitable.'

'Not this time.'

'So stay for dinner,' Antonia pleaded. 'Marianna would be delighted, and so would I—it would help me take my mind off this little one.' She ran a hand over her swollen stomach. 'I'm getting more nervous by the minute.'

'You're going to be fine,' Lazzaro said, and even tried to smile as he did so. 'You're both going to be fine. What are you reading?'

'A baby name book—I'm down to about thirty names for a girl, but if it's a boy...' She paused for a second, watching as Lazzaro swallowed, pain flickering across his usually impassive features. 'I want to call him Luca.'

'That's good.' Lazzaro nodded. 'That's how it should be—it is the right thing to do.'

'You're sure? I mean, I know...' She didn't finish her sentence, waited for Lazzaro to fill in the impossible gap.

Only he didn't, instead running a hand over his forehead, then squeezing the bridge of his nose between his thumb and forefinger for a second.

'Talk to me, Lazzaro.'

'There's nothing to say. I just...' He couldn't even think it, let alone say it, and Antonia tried to help him.

'You think you'll never be able to say that name again without remembering...?'

'I'll always remember,' Lazzaro countered, because he always did. His late brother was a constant and was always on his mind.

'Without feeling pain, then?' Antonia suggested, but still she didn't get it—the pain too was always there.

'Without regret,' Luca said finally. 'I don't think I will ever be able to think about Luca without feeling regret.'

'Please don't say that...' Antonia's eyes filled with tears—not for her dead brother, but for the agony that remained with the living one. The agony that could never, *had* never been fully discussed. And from the shuttering of his eyes, from the shake of his head, Antonia knew that this was as far as Lazzaro was prepared to go. Only it didn't stop her from trying. 'Lazzaro, if Luca's safe, if he's still with us somehow, then he understands why you had to say what you did—and something *had* to be said, Lazzaro. He was out of control.'

'I know that.' Lazzaro nodded, only they both knew it wasn't the point.

Bravely, Antonia continued. 'And I'm sure he's forgiven you for what you did...' She walked over to him, her voice thick with tears as she pleaded for him to listen. 'If it's any help at all, I forgave you too—a long time ago…' She put up her hand to his cheek, to touch the scar there, but he couldn't let her, pushed her hand away. His sister's forgiveness was not what he needed. 'Lazzaro, you have to let it go…'

'I *have* let it go.'

'Oh, but you haven't, Lazzaro. You're hardly here, and you've hardly been in the same room with our mother since it happened.' Her voice was rising, as if she was anticipating him talking over her, anticipating him terminating the conversation, as he always did. 'We have to talk about it.' There was an almost begging note to Antonia's tone. 'This is killing you—I can see that.'

'There is no point going over and over—'

'We haven't been over it *once!*' Antonia sobbed, her every feature, every movement exhausted—not just from her pregnancy, but from the strain of the past two years. 'Since that day at the hospital it has never been discussed, and we need to do that, Lazzaro—with Mamma too. We need to talk. I need to hear—'

'No, Antonia, you don't!' Lazzaro snapped the words out, watched her recoil at his harshness and hated himself for it. But he consoled himself with the truth: Antonia didn't need to know more of what had happened that day, just as she didn't need to know what had happened this day. If somehow he could carry it alone, somehow he could deal with it, keep it from her, then surely it was the right thing to do? But his voice was a touch softer when he spoke next. 'Is talking going to bring him back?'

'You know it's not.'

'Is talking going to change what happened that day?

Change what Luca saw?' He watched her shake her head in regret. 'Then how the hell can it help?'

'Lazzaro, please...' Antonia begged, but she knew it was useless—knew there was no getting through to him tonight—knew that she had no choice other than to let it go.

'Where's Malvolio?'

'He took his drink outside...' Antonia's voice was flat with weary resignation as she wiped her cheek with the back of her hand and tried to resume normality— whatever the hell that was in this family. 'I'll tell him you're here.'

'I'll go and talk to him out there. You rest up.' He waited till she'd lowered herself back onto the sofa, tried to keep his voice normal, to not betray the bile that was churning in his stomach, the fury that was straining to break free, to look, to sound, to act as if he'd just popped over to see his family.

Family!

In a couple of weeks Malvolio and Antonia would have another baby—a brother or sister for Marianna... What was that bastard doing to his sister, to his niece, to the baby that wasn't even born yet?

As he strode out through the French windows, his mind involuntarily went one step further. What had that bastard done to Caitlyn?

Lazzaro didn't plan things—that was what he paid his staff to do. His busy life was a well-oiled machine that left him free to walk into to any meeting, any boardroom, and instinctively take over—no preparation required for his brilliant mind to assess any situation. But he wished he had prepared for now.

He saw his brother-in-law, his colleague, and to this

point his *friend* standing leaning against the stone wall, a sticking plaster on the hand that was holding his glass. Malvolio's eyes were completely unable to meet his, and for a second Lazzaro truly didn't know what to say.

The truth was so damning, so utterly reprehensible, so loaded with consequence, he wanted to dispute it.

Wanted Caitlyn to be wrong—almost *wanted* her to be *lying*.

Only—sick to the stomach—he was sure that she wasn't.

'What did she say?' Malvolio's face was as white as chalk, a muscle pulsing in his cheek. 'What did that little bitch have to say—?'

He never got to finish. He was yanked forward by his jacket a generous few inches, then slammed back hard against the wall.

'Shut it,' Lazzaro snarled, his face inches away from Malvolio's. 'You make me sick.'

'You believe her?' Malvolio gave a nervous but mocking laugh. 'You believe her against your own family?'

'You are married to my sister,' Lazzaro snarled. 'You are not my blood. What the hell are you doing, messing around?'

'I wasn't. She's the one who was coming on to *me*. She's the one who set me up.'

'Rubbish,' Lazzaro snarled. 'Don't try and lie your way out of this. You go near her again and I will not be responsible for my actions.' Lazzaro's hands were still pushing him up against the wall, his voice low and menacing. 'You stay well away from her.'

'You mean you haven't got rid of her?' Malvolio's voice was aghast.

'Why would I get rid of her when it was *your* mistake?

She is my personal assistant now—and one wrong move from you and don't think I won't tell my sister.'

'She set me up.' Malvolio had rallied. 'She's set you up too.'

'What are you talking about? You were the one trying to lure her with talk of a promotion, watching her all the time—and that's not from Caitlyn; that's from another staff member.'

'Lure her!' Malvolio let out an incredulous snort. 'She was the one coming on to *me,* Lazzaro. Now she's got her fancy qualifications she thinks she's entitled to the top job—she wanted to know if, with Jenna gone, I could find an opening for her. She's always after favours—wanting her payslips fiddled. You should have seen her…'

Malvolio raked a hand through his hair, his breathless voice growing stronger with every word as Lazzaro stepped back, shaking his head, refuting it and yet hearing it—hearing and starting to if not believe it, then… His already loosened tie seemed to be choking him, and Lazzaro pulled at his collar, the open-and-shut case that had assured his tirade wavering at the final summing up as Malvolio continued.

'She was all over me. I didn't know what to do—I told her you were interviewing, that I couldn't do her any favours, and the next thing she bit me, screaming that I'd come on to her—'

'You're lying.' Lazzaro snarled the words out. 'Lying to save yourself—because without my family, without your job, without us, you are nothing. Without me propping you up you would be the nothing you were before you met my sister.' He hissed out a curse. 'Why am I protecting you? She would be better off without you…better off knowing the truth…'

'No!' Malvolio shouted the word. 'I love Antonia—as if I'd jeopardise things with a tart like that. As if I'd mess up the kids' lives like that,' Malvolio went on. 'She was so upset by me that she had to leave, was she?' He gave an incredulous laugh. 'Only she wasn't so upset when you upped her salary. It would seem she can stomach staying if the price is right. She can't be *that* distressed by me…'

Lazzaro could hear the blood pounding in his temples, a drench of relief flooding him. Because if Malvolio was telling the truth then his sister was okay, the kids were okay. And as for Caitlyn… The shot of relief was temporary. He knew the pain in her eyes had been real. He was sure. He'd felt her heart fluttering in her chest when he'd held her. Lazzaro knew women—knew when he was being lied to—she couldn't have played him that well.

'You know who she is, don't you?'

Malvolio's voice seemed to be coming from a long way off, but he didn't get to finish. The French doors were opening and Antonia was stepping out. Thankfully though, Lazzaro was saved from faking casual in front of his sister—as his mobile trilled he left it to Malvolio to make the small talk and tell her they'd be in soon. It took a moment to tune his brain into the conversation, as the clipped voice introduced herself as a saleswoman from a downtown department store.

'Just to confirm some spending on a new signatory. I need to run through the purchases, if I may?' And he listened—listened as designer suits, coats, shoes and boots were reeled off, listened as he heard how the woman who had insisted she could manage smart, had actually in less than an hour managed to pretty much top Jenna's annual clothing budget. 'And a full set of Oroton luggage. You're aware of all these purchases?'

'I am.' Lazzaro nodded, more to himself than to the woman on the other end of the line. Jenna had cost a fortune to kit out initially, he recalled. Of course Caitlyn would need coats and boots for Italy. He'd never questioned a bill like that in his life, and he wasn't about to start because of Malvolio.

Turning off the phone, he smiled to his sister as Malvolio assured her they'd be inside in just a moment.

'Everything's okay, isn't it?' Antonia checked nervously.

'Of course.' Lazzaro smiled, but it faded the second his sister was back inside, and the conversation resumed exactly where it had left off, the whole sordid mess of this afternoon taking a darker, sicker twist.

'She's Roxanne's cousin.' Malvolio sneered the words and Lazzaro's face visibly paled.

Caitlyn Bell was Roxanne's cousin.

Roxanne Martin was the person he hated most in the world.

The woman who had pitched brother against brother.

The woman who had so much blood on her hands she might as well have killed Luca with her own bare ones.

'You're the one talking about family,' Malvolio carried on savagely. 'You're the one talking about blood relations. Well, your new personal assistant comes from the same gene pool as Roxanne Martin.'

No!

Lazzaro's brain tightened in denial, the word on the tip

of his taut lips. The woman he had spoken to this evening, the woman he had held in his arms for a short while, was nothing, *nothing* like Roxanne.

But just as he was about to refute it, sense took over. Denial was dangerous.

Denial—the impossible dance that had led Luca to his early grave.

Only he was stronger than Luca.

The eyes that had held his were swimming into his vision—only with dangerous undertones. And though he was initially tempted to ring the store, to cut her credit, to retract his job offer, instead a bitter smile twisted his lips... So what if he'd hired a manipulative, lying, little bitch? It could be worse—he might not have known it!

'You'd better be telling the truth—because if you ever hurt my sister...' Lazzaro pinned his brother-in-law with his eyes, watched as he shrank against the wall. 'If I let you live, it will only be to ensure that you regret it!'

'And Caitlyn?' Malvolio's eyes darted as he voiced the unpalatable question. 'You'll get rid of her? I mean, given what I've told you...'

'Get rid of her? Why would I do that when things are just starting to get interesting?' Lazzaro's dark laugh was mirthless. 'If Caitlyn Bell thinks she can play me then she hasn't done her homework properly. I'm actually looking forward to it.'

CHAPTER FOUR

'IT SAYS here Roberta called.'

His voice held the warning ring that was becoming increasingly familiar. Her first week working for Lazzaro and already she was looking at the clock, willing the next few hours to just please hurry up and go, so that she could wave goodbye to him till Monday.

'She did.' Caitlyn gulped, not looking up, staring instead at the note he had put on her desk—focussing not on the message she'd written but on his tense fingers that were drumming over it. 'Half an hour ago. But you were on another call…'

'And what did you say to her?'

'Just that,' Caitlyn offered. 'I said that you were on another call and I'd let you know…' A rather shaky finger hovered near his and pointed to her note. 'Which I did.'

'She told you it was urgent, I presume?'

'She did.' Caitlyn cleared her throat. 'But nearly everyone—'

'You do realise that I've been trying to get hold of her for two days?' His voice was pure ice.

'She sounded anxious,' Caitlyn attempted. 'She sounded like—'

'She probably *was* anxious, given that I told her that if she didn't get back to me by five p.m. Friday I would be commencing legal proceedings—which I was just in the process of till I saw your little note. Why the hell didn't you think to check? Of all the bloody incompetent—'

'Now, hold on a minute!' Standing up, even in killer heels, she was no match for his height—or his wrath—but she gave it her best shot. He'd been bloody all week—nothing like the man who'd interviewed her—and Caitlyn was seriously wondering if she'd see out the first week, let alone last a year! 'Her name wasn't on Jenna's precious list, and if I put through every anxious, depressed, teary or tipsy woman who calls for you, you might as well get rid of your desk and sit at one of those old-fashioned switchboards! "Mr Ranaldi..."' she mimicked—who, she didn't know, but she was boiling angry now. '"Just connecting you now!"'

'Next time someone you don't know calls for me,' Lazzaro said tartly, but his mouth was actually twitching as he tried not to smile, 'you are to check with me.'

As if on cue her phone rang and, still bristling, Caitlyn picked it up, introducing herself calmly. Just a teeny glint came to her eye. 'One moment, please. I'll just check.'

'Tanya.' She smiled sweetly, but her eyes were mutinous. 'Should I put her through?'

'No!' Lazzaro snapped.

'Only she says it's urgent—she sounds quite anxious, actually!'

'Tell her I've left for the weekend.' He raked a hand through his hair. 'But now you've bloody put her on hold she's going to *know* I'm here!'

'I'm so sorry to keep you waiting.' Taking Tanya off hold, Caitlyn was as sweet as she was convincing. 'I thought I might be able to catch him at Reception for you, but he's already left for the weekend—I'll be sure to let him know that you called, though.'

Replacing the receiver, she waited—would wait till Monday if she had to.

'Okay…' He gave the tiniest shrug. 'Next time just…' His voice trailed off.

'Just what?' Caitlyn pushed. 'Do you want me to put them through, check with you, or use my initiative? Which, given I don't possess psychic powers, isn't always going to be spot-on!'

'Okay! *Okay!*' He threw his hands up in exasperation before storming off. 'I accept that.'

'So do I,' she said to his departing back. 'Your apology, that is.'

And for the first time in the whole week—at five past five on Friday—he smiled. Actually turned to her and smiled.

'You're pushing your luck now! I still have to ring Roberta—*and* call off my lawyer.' But he was still smiling! 'Look, why don't you go home?'

Which was better than an apology, given that every other night she'd been here till well into the double digits. 'Well, if you're sure…' Caitlyn sniffed, still refusing to completely forgive him.

'Of course. You've worked hard this week.' It was the first compliment he'd paid her since she'd started, and all her anger just evaporated. Finally returning his smile, she reached for her bag. 'I'll see you at seven a.m.'

'Seven a.m.?' Caitlyn blinked. 'But it's Saturday tomorrow.'

'Which is exactly why I want to check out the peninsular resort. I'm considering buying it to offer my overseas clients a break from the city at weekends—so naturally I want to spend a weekend there.'

'But it isn't booked,' Caitlyn said hopefully, visions of collapsing in the bath, shaving her legs and putting on a face mask, or just doing nothing, fading as the reality of this job caught up.

'We'll ring on the way.' Lazzaro shrugged. 'I'd like to see what they come up with at short notice, and we'll use an alias—I don't want them to even have a hint that it's me who's arriving.' He registered her frown. 'I'm always one step ahead of everyone, Caitlyn, that's why I'm so successful. You'd do well to remember that.'

And even though he was still smiling, somehow it didn't reach his eyes—somehow, as Caitlyn headed for the door, she felt as if he was warning her.

It wasn't so much a question of juggling her life around her career, Caitlyn thought at seven the next morning, as Jeremy pressed the remote control and the heavy gates opened to Lazzaro's impressive home—working closely with the great Ranaldi there could *be* no life. The role of Lazzaro's PA, as she'd found out in her first week, was an all-consuming one. They either met at the hotel or at his home—whatever his schedule dictated—and, boy, did his schedule dictate. In the week she'd been working for him, Caitlyn had racked up more air miles than she'd had in her entire life up to now. Lazzaro used helicopters the way other people used taxis, and Interstate trips for a two-hour meeting barely merited comment. Waking before sunrise, showering and dressing before Lazzaro's driver collected her, and the draining day began—then she'd crawl into bed, often not before midnight, only to sit bolt-upright as her alarm trilled and the whole exhausting circus started again....

Taking a final gulp of her take-away coffee, and hoping the caffeine would get to work soon, Caitlyn wearily climbed out of the car and, fixing a smile in place, knocked on his heavy front door, wondering what sort of mood she was going to find behind it.

'Good morning!' Used to not getting an answer, Caitlyn pushed it open, her high heels echoing on the floorboards, then silencing whenever she hit one of the thick luxurious rugs. Her new shoes were already starting to hurt as she called out into the empty hallway—this was only the third time she'd been to his home in the morning, and on both other occasions Lazzaro had greeted her from the kitchen with the briefest of good mornings and a rapid rundown of their schedule.

But not this morning.

Feeling like an intruder, she walked along the darkened hallway—the luxurious surrounds were not quite familiar enough yet to fail to impress. His Toorak mansion home had been meticulously decorated, with no expense spared—exquisite antique furniture clashed marvellously with the latest in everything modern—but it was definitely a male home. Feminine touches were markedly absent—no flowers brightening corners, no splashes of colour to take away the rather austere lines, no photos on the heavy wooden furniture to draw the eye.

Glancing into the lounge as she walked past, she saw the usually immaculate room was dishevelled—given the ungodly hour, it hadn't been attended to by the housekeeper—but it was the cushions that were tossed on the floor that had Caitlyn pausing. Like a cat sniffing the air, sensing an intruder, she caught an unwelcome whiff of a heavy, exotic perfume, saw the impressive stereo system flashing like a beacon in the darkness. Presumably he hadn't had time to turn it off before he'd headed to bed. Knowing it shouldn't irk her, but accepting that it did, Caitlyn gave her head a little shake and her mind a little talking-to as she headed into the kitchen.

Get used to it, Caitlyn. Living in Lazzaro's pocket, she was going to have to get used to stumbling on his loose change—oh, and there was plenty: Lucy, Tabitha, Mandy, Tanya... Each name twisted the knife in her stomach a notch as it purred down the phone—and each time Lazzaro refused to take the call it loosened a little. Maybe it was Bonita, Caitlyn thought drily—the woman whose calls he took without question; a woman whose thick, throaty voice could haul Lazzaro out of any meeting.

Caitlyn gave an uncomfortable swallow, wondering if it was Bonita she was about to meet and telling herself she could deal with it—reminding herself that she was his employee, his assistant.

It mustn't matter a jot how she felt about him.

Still, no amount of reminding herself of her place in his life was going to stop it hurting, and as she entered the kitchen Caitlyn tried and simultaneously failed not to notice the empty champagne bottle on the stone bench...tried and failed not to notice the two glasses beside it.

Tried and failed not to notice the lipstick marks on one of the glasses.

For an appalling moment she wondered if she was disturbing something—braced herself as she heard footsteps on the stairwell for the sight of some ravishing, exotic beauty.

But it was only Lazzaro!

Bloody hell! Caitlyn thought, ducking from under the light and hoping the shadows would hide her blush as she busied herself with her briefcase. Couldn't he at least put some clothes on?

Dressed *only* in trousers, the button not even done up, damp from the shower, patting his freshly shaven jaw with a towel, the usually immaculate Lazzaro was unusually untogether—and, though not the one she'd dreaded facing, he was certainly a ravishing, exotic beauty. The swarthy olive skin that so far Caitlyn had only witnessed from the collar up or the cuffs down was blissfully exposed now...

'I'm running late...' Damp jet hair flopped over his forehead, and the musky tang of freshly applied aftershave mingling with damp skin almost asphyxiated her as he brushed past—only it wasn't the scent that was causing her throat to tighten, trapping her breath in her lungs, it was the man wearing it. 'Coffee?'

A simple question—a needless one, almost, as caffeine was the one thing that had got her through the previous week. But though Caitlyn had shared more coffees with him than she could count it seemed different somehow— here in his home—with Lazzaro making it.

'Coffee?' He frowned at her muteness, at her hesitant

blushing nod, then turned his back—which didn't help matters much. She could feel her nails digging into her palms as he stretched up and opened the cupboard above him, the simple movement allowing a teasing glimpse of muscle definition. She *really* wished he'd put some damn clothes on—wished normal services could be resumed. Because with Lazzaro semi-naked in the kitchen, her thought processes scattered like leaves in the wind, and she could only hope he didn't pull out three cups—that Lazzaro's *visitor* wasn't going to be joining them or, worse, that Lazzaro wasn't going to take *her* a drink.

Lucky the woman who woke to him…

The leaves caught in a gust, her thoughts fluttered skywards. She was picturing the heaven of that usually inscrutable face smiling down at her with tenderness upon waking, then feeling that surly mouth awakening her with a lazy kiss.

'Here…' Unlike hers, his hand was completely steady as he handed her a coffee, as he served her a front-row, best seat view of his chest, and she actually couldn't take it from him—just couldn't. She just sat on a kitchen stool and swallowed as he leant over her just a little bit and placed it on the bench behind her, treating her to a generous glimpse of his underarm hair as he stretched. She'd read somewhere that women shouldn't shave there, that underarm hair was just loaded with lusty fragrances that would dizzy your lover if only you dared. Whoever had written it must have been right because, whether Lazzaro was fresh out of the shower or not, something animal was happening—her head was spinning as the air between them seemed to still. His nipple was in her face, and she wanted to lick it. Torrid, unfamiliar thoughts were pinging in—intimate thoughts. This was their morning. She glimpsed her dreams and elaborated them a touch. This was what it could be like each and every morning...

God, but she was gorgeous. A bag of nerves, perhaps, but utterly, utterly gorgeous.

The last week had been difficult in the extreme—with Lazzaro waiting for her to make a mistake, waiting for her to slip up, to show her true colours. Only to date all she had been was a breath of fresh air...clipping in and out of his office with her wide smile, charming his colleagues and the boss to boot! There was no question she was capable of the role—would, in fact, be *extremely* capable once she'd mastered a few more of the basics.

Sometimes he actually forgot for a moment just who she was...

At moments like this one he actually forgot that she was Roxanne's cousin. Lazzaro could see her hands in her lap, her knees bobbing up and down, and he wanted to still them—wanted to trap her legs with his thighs, wanted to take that mouth with his and taste it. Why couldn't he have felt like that last night? Listening to Mandy—or was it Mindy?—droning on and on. As beautiful as she was, he hadn't even been bothered enough to shut her up with a kiss, hadn't even felt a stirring—which for Lazzaro had proved extremely worrying. Rising to *any* occasion had never, ever been an issue—only it would have been last night. Which was why he'd had his driver take Mandy home—why, after a quick drink, he'd pleaded exhaustion.

Lazzaro wasn't tired now, though—in fact he was very, very awake. The air was thick with arousal, and the heat that was burning from her mouth warmed him. Their breathing matched. He could see the curve of her bosom as it rapidly rose and fell, and it actually felt as if they *were* kissing. He could see her tongue bobbing out, rolling over her bottom lip. Both were silent, both just staring, both feeling it—an *it* that was impossible to deny—this bit of ice that reared between them now and then. Ice that really needed to be broken…

'Should we just go upstairs? Get it over with…?' His voice was low and gruff, his eyes smiling down at hers.

If anyone else, under any other circumstance, had said that, she'd have died. But she actually laughed, grateful that he'd acknowledged it, made a sort of joke about it, so that she could too.

'Only I don't think I can walk about like this all day—it would be extremely uncomfortable!'

'Well, you'd better get used to it,' Caitlyn retorted. 'Because I've seen your schedule and we certainly haven't got time for any of that nonsense—anyway, I've just done my make-up.'

He laughed, and amazingly she wasn't blushing any more. In fact, Caitlyn realised, she was flirting—she, Caitlyn Bell, the last virgin on earth, the most unskilled flirter alive, was actually teasing the sexiest man of them all. And she was doing it rather well, she realised, as he actually pushed just a little bit harder, and she actually glimpsed a note of regret when he smiled and winked.

'Pity!'

Now she *could* pick up her cup, and she took a drink.

'Pity,' he said again. 'It would have been marvellous, you know!'

Skimming the newspaper as they left the city behind, still he managed to dish out his orders.

'Book a massage for you—all the best treatments—and book golf for me. Tell them I need to hire everything,' Lazzaro prompted as she pulled out her phone.

'Women do play golf too,' Caitlyn responded tartly as she dialled the number. 'Some rather well…'

'Fine.' Lazzaro bared his teeth in a smile. 'You play golf, if you prefer—I could use a massage, actually!'

Given the only thing Caitlyn knew about golf was that it sounded boring, she made reservations for 'Mr Holland' and his assistant Miss Bell, blushing as she did so. Definitely *not* refusing to give in, she ordered a few rather luxurious-sounding treatments for herself.

'Not much of an alias,' Lazzaro drawled as she clicked the phone off.

'I'm not the one with anything to hide,' Caitlyn teased back. But he mustn't have got her sense of humour, or something must have been lost in translation, because instead of smirking back at her, as she'd expected, his face hardened, his eyes narrowing for a moment, staring at her as he had all last week.

Looking at her as if he didn't even like her.

The mobile ringing in his pocket went unanswered, Lazzaro instead flicking his eyes away and staring moodily out of the window. The sun was rising on an already warm day, hitting the high-rise towers of the city, and despite the air-conditioned car, Caitlyn felt drained. Even after the strong shot of coffee, Caitlyn suddenly felt weary—the teasing fun they'd had this morning but a distant memory now. It was clearly going to be another very long day.

'Caitlyn Bell.' When her own mobile rang she answered without checking—glad for the diversion, actually, with Lazzaro suddenly in this black mood. 'Oh, Antonia,' she said, and Lazzaro looked over sharply. 'How are you?'

'Today's the day…' Caitlyn could hear the excitement laced with fear in his sister's voice. 'We're on our way to the hospital now. I've tried to get hold of Lazzaro at home, and on his mobile—he's not with you, is he?'

Caitlyn was saved from having to answer by Lazzaro giving a rather irritated sigh and snapping his fingers for her to hand over the phone. But when he spoke to his sister his voice was light and easy—though Caitlyn couldn't help but notice every bit of his body language said otherwise.

'How are you?' Lazzaro greeted his sister. 'That's fantastic!' He paused and laughed. 'Well, don't be—you know they say the second labour's always much easier.'

Since when was Lazzaro such an expert on childbirth? Caitlyn thought, irritated. But clearly Antonia, in her present state, had no trouble voicing it!

'You should know by now that I'm an expert on *everything*!' Lazzaro responded. 'I thought you weren't due for another week.' His fingers were tapping on his thigh as Antonia answered. 'It's just bad timing at this end—I can't cancel this weekend. It's been booked for ages.'

And Caitlyn watched—watched as he lied through his very white teeth, and didn't even blush as he proceeded to lie a whole lot more.

'I wish I could, Antonia, but there's nothing I can do about it. You are to let me know the second there's news. Good luck!'

Clicking off the phone, he handed it back to Caitlyn without a word—then turned again to the window as Caitlyn's mind whirred like a merry-go-round. Oh, she'd heard Lazzaro lie to women—had lied to them on his behalf on more than a couple of occasions—but what she couldn't fathom, what she was having trouble comprehending, was that he'd lie to his own sister. A sister who, over the past week or so, Caitlyn had spoken to. A sister he seemed genuinely fond of—*his* sister, who was clearly in labour.

He didn't have to cancel this trip—they hadn't even been expecting him!

Lazzaro could sense her disapproval, and for once it unnerved him—though his assistant's approval was usually the last thing he required as he got on with the business of being a Ranaldi. Yet he was tempted to tap Jeremy on the shoulder and tell him to stop the car and let him out. He wanted out of the car and away from the bloody lot of them.

Tapping his fingers impatiently, Lazzaro dismissed the odd impulse. He didn't really want to be alone with his thoughts today of all days. It wasn't Caitlyn's disapproval that was gnawing at him—it was his own dread and loathing.

He was trying to centre himself. It was as if he was surrounded by a million scattered compasses, and the needles which had hovered without direction for so long were suddenly settling, all homing in as the universe moved the world along, as everything aligned to bring things to an unwelcome head. A new life was coming into the world—a new life that meant his shattered family would have to meet, might talk…

That he might have to face the dead.

CHAPTER FIVE

THE entire day was to be exhausting.

Oh, the resort was fabulous—as they swept up the pebbled drive the lush green of the golf course was a rare sight after the long drought-filled summer. Water was spraying into the sun, and on appearance alone the temperature seemed surely to have dropped a few welcome degrees.

Before his sister's telephone call, when Lazzaro had been capable of talking in more than single syllables, he'd explained that a lot of his overseas clients tired of the city and hotel life—no matter how luxurious—and often went away for the weekends. Lazzaro had shrugged. Why not ensure that their spending money went straight into *his* account?

The building was cool and welcoming as they entered—understated, yet utterly luxurious—and from the second they set foot into the cool, pale lobby, and were then shown to their luxury suites, Caitlyn could see why he wanted it!

Glancing at the vast white bed, it was all Caitlyn could do not to peel off her shoes and just collapse on top. She felt as if she'd worked a full day and it wasn't even nine o'clock! Still, there was no time to feel sorry for herself.

Brimming with energy, Lazzaro tapped on her door about eight and a half seconds later and set her to work.

If Caitlyn thought she'd seen him in action before, today he was absolutely formidable—interviewing key staff as Caitlyn took copious notes, scanning the books as the accountant coughed and fiddled under Lazzaro's very direct line of questioning. Even lunch wasn't relaxing. They'd barely been seated when Lazzaro took an impromptu tour of the kitchen, and then proceeded to order the one thing on the menu that wasn't available.

'You look pleased with yourself.'

'I am…' Lazzaro responded, swirling an asparagus head in butter, then popping it in his mouth. 'Because, despite appearances, this place needs a lot of work.'

'But it's divine,' Caitlyn countered.

'It will be,' Lazzaro affirmed. 'But I've managed to knock at least a couple of zeros off the asking price—they need to sell, and fast.'

'How do you know?'

'Because it's my job to know. Today has been extremely worthwhile.'

'Good.' Caitlyn concentrated on her food as she spoke. 'So, does that mean we'll finish up soon?'

'Why? Do you have plans tonight?'

'No, but you might.' Forcing herself, she looked up at him. 'We've got a lot of work done today. If we push on, maybe we can head back to Melbourne, and you could—'

'Have you any idea how much this place is worth?' Lazzaro interrupted, and though the figure he gave was impressive, Caitlyn remained tight-lipped. 'I am hardly likely to make such a decision before I have seen more of the resort's workings myself. Anyway—' he tried to lighten the tone '—you have a massage booked, and I really should wander over to the golf course.'

'I can't really picture you as a golfer.'

'I'm not.' Lazzaro gave a small unworried shrug.

'You can't just bluff your way through a game of golf.'

'Bluff?' Lazzaro frowned.

'Pretend you're good...' Caitlyn attempted.

'Ahh, but I'm *very* good,' Lazzaro said, standing up. 'I just hate the bloody game—it's not my fault I'm excellent at it.'

There certainly were perks to being Lazzaro Ranaldi's assistant, Caitlyn thought as she lay down on the massage table. Having been exfoliated practically to the bone, and peeled, tweezed and waxed till there wasn't a superfluous hair or skin cell left on her body, it was time for the skilled hands of the masseur to massage away all her tension. Closing her eyes, she tried to relax, tried to close her mind to the jumble of thoughts—and it did help. But only for a little while. Because just as she was almost relaxed, just as she was about to sink into mindless oblivion, it was as if two hands dived in and pulled her up, forcing her to the surface, back to the constant whirl of her thoughts.

When finally she was wrapped in a fluffy robe, sipping a ginger, camomile and lemon tea in her room, Caitlyn honestly wondered if she had the strength to face Lazzaro at dinner tonight. The man whose company she had craved for two years was just too exhausting, too bewildering for her today.

Maybe she could ring in sick?

No such luck. Her phone trilled and, glancing at the caller ID, Caitlyn knew she was going to have to face him.

'Hi, Antonia!' Caitlyn said warmly. 'How are you?'

'Great...though I really wanted to talk with Lazzaro. I'm having no luck getting him on his mobile, and his room phone just keeps ringing out.'

'He's playing golf,' Caitlyn said helpfully. 'He probably didn't take his phone...' Hearing the sigh on the other end of the line, imagining how *she'd* feel if she had such a massive piece of news to share, Caitlyn relented. 'I'll go and knock on his door, and if he's not there I'll pop a note under.'

As she opened her door to do just that, Caitlyn jumped with nerves. The man himself was striding past, frowning as she called out to him— 'It's Antonia...' Slinking back into her room, embarrassed and awkward, Caitlyn sat down and sipped at her disgusting tea as Lazzaro took the call— the call he'd clearly been dreading.

'Fantastic...' For once Lazzaro's usually clipped voice was effusive. 'You've already told her? She must be thrilled!'

If Caitlyn closed her eyes, if she just listened to his words, she'd believe him—could almost envision him pumping a fist into the air at the joyous news. Only Caitlyn's eyes weren't closed, and she could see Lazzaro—leaning against the wall, his shoulders hunched, his forehead resting in the palm of his hand, his profile rigid, a muscle flickering in his cheek as he took in the 'happy' news.

'I'm sorry, Antonia—it's just one thing after another. We're stuck here tonight and most of tomorrow. You should be with Malvolio anyway... Well, I am *buying* this golf course—it seems prudent that I at least give it a go. But I'll be there as soon as I can, and I'll let...'

Caitlyn watched as his free hand bunched into a fist, saw

the little bit of colour that was left in him literally drain away. His Adam's apple bobbed a couple of times before he managed to carry on. 'How was Mum?' He closed his eyes on the excited chatter, raked his hand through his hair and dragged in vital oxygen.

'Of course I hope to see them. It just depends on when we go to Rome... I'm glad you're calling him that—no, really. I'm fine with it now...'

Just for a second his voice broke, and so evident was his pain, so abject his misery, Caitlyn had to force herself not to go over—had to literally stop herself from walking over and taking the phone from his hand, telling Antonia he would call back later.

But Lazzaro recovered quickly, nodding blindly and forcing himself to go on, his cheery voice absolutely belying his hopeless stance. 'Luca would be very proud.'

'A boy?' He didn't look over, just clicked off the phone and stared out of the window into the darkening night. She rued answering the phone—rued that he had taken the call in front of her. She knew, just knew, that this was a side to Lazzaro that he had never wanted her to see.

'They've called him Luca.'

Normally congratulations would be in order. Everything told her they weren't here.

'After my brother...my twin...' He turned just enough to look at her, his eyes holding hers, accusing, almost, and suddenly Caitlyn was nervous. 'Did you ever meet him?'

'How would I have met Luca?' Caitlyn croaked, with no idea why she was blushing guiltily when she hadn't done anything wrong, why he was staring at her as if she had.

'When you were doing work experience, of course.'

Lazzaro's eyes narrowed. 'When did you think I was referring to?'

Did he know Roxanne was her cousin? Caitlyn could feel the sweat beading on her forehead, and despite the massage that had practically rendered her unconscious, and despite a scalp soaked with lavender oil, every muscle in her body was taut with tension.

'I don't know…' She attempted a shrug. 'But, no, I never ran into him. Look, do you want me to book transport?' She was attempting normal, attempting professional, trying to do what a good personal assistant would in these circumstances. 'If we get the helicopter—'

'Tomorrow.' Luca shook his head. 'There is too much to do here.'

He didn't elaborate—because, Caitlyn realised, he couldn't. The lies he'd told Antonia didn't match with the truth—and now she knew for sure that today wasn't about sampling the delicacies that would be on offer to his elite patrons. Today served one purpose and one purpose only.

Escape.

And that was reinforced when Lazzaro snapped back into business mode, demanding that she pull out her planner and, despite her rather inappropriate attire, proceeded to go through his schedule.

'We are supposed to be flying to Rome next week. Rearrange things—tomorrow would be better.'

'But what about your sister?' Caitlyn asked. 'Don't you want to arrange some time so that you can see—'

'I do not need you to organise my private life—that I can take care of myself,' Lazzaro interrupted. 'Could you arrange a gift for the baby—and of course flowers…'

'You want *me* to buy your nephew's gift?' Caitlyn tried to keep the slightly ironic note from her voice. *This* from a man who almost in the same breath had told her he could handle his own private life? 'Do you have any idea what you'd like to get him?'

'None,' Lazzaro snapped. 'That will be all.'

As he stood to go, she halted him. 'Lazzaro, can I—?'

'Make a suggestion?' he sneered. 'Are you going to suggest that perhaps I should shop for my own nephew? Or that I should delay going to Rome so that I can spend some time with my family? You know, I really do *not* need to hear your advice, Caitlyn.'

'I wasn't about to give it,' Caitlyn said evenly. 'I was just going to ask if I could have my phone.'

Every question that had flashed into her mind, every question she would never have considered voicing, Lazzaro had just answered—and seeing this proud, strong man look awkward, even for a moment, seeing embarrassment actually taint his features as he offered her her phone, Caitlyn wished she knew him well enough to ask them—wished somehow she could help him.

'I know it must seem...' His voice trailed off, his voluntary attempt at explanation fading before it began. 'You just don't understand.'

'I know I don't.' They were both holding the phone, both holding onto this inanimate object, both staring at it, both looking at it—neither letting go. Behind the strength of his voice she could hear the pain. Behind the terseness she could hear fear. 'I wish I could say the right thing.'

'You can't.' Letting go of the phone, he dragged his fingers through his hair. She half expected him to walk out without another word—could feel the tension in him, the indecision, and nodded when he asked if he could use her bathroom.

He felt sick as he went over and over the conversation with Antonia. He hoped to God he'd sounded happy enough about the news. His mother would soon be on her way—with her latest boyfriend on her arm, no doubt. Running the tap, he splashed water on his face, then did it again, taking in the lipsticks and perfumes that adorned the surfaces. It was easier to focus on nothing than what was in his head. Contraceptive pills, toothpaste—ordinary things, just so out of place in this strange, strange moment.

Baby Luca was here, bearing the name that drenched him in sweat each night, filled his nightmares. The name that he choked on was one he'd have to say daily now… He could see the beads of sweat on his grey complexion—could feel the bile rising within him, no matter how many times he washed his face. God, should he cancel dinner? For the first time he truly didn't know if he could manage normal for an evening—yet at the same time he didn't want to be alone.

'I wish I could help.' She was standing at the open bathroom door, walking in behind him, staring at his reflection in the mirror. And he stared back at her—infinitely better than staring at his own face—so much easier to focus on her beauty than deal with his own demons.

For a moment she'd seemed bold—but as he turned around to her, suddenly she was shy. Lazzaro lifted her chin with his fingers—staring down at her when, as if opening the lid on a velvet box, her eyelashes lifted to show two brilliant sapphires…entrancing, dazzling… bewitching.

The same eyes as Roxanne's. The shade of blue identical. Hell, sometimes he forgot, actually *forgot* that she was using him—actually *forgot* his conversation with Malvolio, actually *forgot* that she'd lied and schemed her way into his life. She was probably lying and scheming right now— right now, at this very minute—trying to worm her way into his heart, trying to get inside his head. Right now, when it was so hard, so very hard to be alone.

When Luca had died he'd sworn never to let a woman get close—never to let a woman under his skin in the way his brother had. But, staring at Caitlyn, blinded by her beauty, it was scarily easy to renegotiate with himself, so very tempting to take the comfort he needed now, to lose himself in the urges he had been resisting since the moment she'd stepped back into his life.

They *were* the same shade of blue—only he could see a swirl of black around each iris that intrigued him. He'd never stared into Roxanne's eyes like this—had never been lulled into the dizzy whirlpool of attraction with Roxanne, never wanted to lower his head to hers the way he did now, towards Caitlyn's...

Only he'd sworn that he wouldn't.

Supremely focussed, incredibly driven, self-control was something he had never had to knowingly exert. He worked hard and, when time allowed, he had the funds and the stamina to play equally hard. His dark good-looks ensured an endless *smorgasbord* of suitable playmates, and his conscience was rarely if ever pricked.

He never promised anything of himself.

So why the dilemma? Why, when never had he craved oblivion more, was he hesitating?

She did something to him—altered his usually direct

thought processes until they were scattered to the wind. Her image darted into his mind's eye over and over throughout the day, and her scent reached him even when she wasn't present—overwhelming him, just as Roxanne had Luca.

This was a woman who *could* get under his skin.

His lips were so close that if she moved a mere inch they would be touching. Only still he hesitated. Still he wrestled with something deep inside. And if life was a series of choices, in that split second Lazzaro's was made: he *would* lose himself in her, *would* drown in the balmy oblivion of lovemaking, *would* bathe in the warmth of her body—only on his terms. He knew he was strong enough to hold back, to take only what he needed tonight and nothing more.

'I don't bite.'

Foolish words, perhaps, but they actually made things easier for him, reminded him of the woman he was dealing with. No matter how sweet her exterior, inside she was as hard as nails—would use him as a means to an end.

Just as he would now use her.

'Oh, but you do!' A smudge of a smile relaxed his lips, but it didn't soften his eyes.

His mouth moved that last delicious fraction, and it was Caitlyn's eyes closing. The bliss of flesh on flesh, of his lips finally on hers—the moment she had dreamed of for so, so long was actually eventuating... His hands were on her shoulders, his mouth moving with hers, and if ever there was a textbook kiss then this was one. His lips were tender, measured, skilled, his tongue sliding around hers... Only as perfect as it might be, even if there wasn't one single thing she could fault, the best Caitlyn could come up with as his mouth moved over hers was that it wasn't *her* perfect.

Dreams were dangerous. Dreams let you inhabit a world that didn't exist—let you savour and taste what you'd never had, what didn't or couldn't exist. Because, as adept and as proficient as his kiss was, no matter how she tried to go with it, no matter how she closed her eyes and attempted to relish this moment, the reality of it didn't match up to her dreams.

'Lazzaro…' She pulled back, shook her head, knowing perhaps she would appear a tease—might in that contrary moment be giving credence to Malvolio's vile accusations—only she couldn't pretend. Couldn't just go along with something that wasn't okay. 'This isn't…'

He felt her detachment before she pulled back. Knew he had lost her before she had gone. But just the taste of her, the smell of her, the feel of her, had him hungry—hungry for all of her. A fierce need was coursing through him, every nerve in his body shrilling demands that their master must not deny them now. And he could do it, Lazzaro said to himself, as he pulled her back in and lowered his head again. He *was* strong enough, Lazzaro told himself—he *could* give just a little bit more of himself and *then* detach.

One hand snaked around her waist, finding the small of her back and wrenching her in as the other knotted into her thick blonde hair, holding her head till there was nowhere else she could go. Kissing her, kissing her as she should be kissed, as he'd wanted to kiss her from the second he'd laid eyes on her, his tongue devoured her, tasted her, drank from her.

His chin was hard on hers, scratching at her skin, his body not just warm but hot through her bathrobe. She could feel herself sink into him, melt into him. His kiss, *this* kiss, was all she had ever imagined—all it should be.

He smothered her—smothered her with rough, urgent, hot kisses that burnt somewhere deep inside, that offered only temporary satisfaction. Every taste made her hungry for more. His hands were on her bottom, wedging her groin into his in an almost needless gesture because she was pressing herself against him too. She closed her eyes as his mouth kissed her hairline, her eyelids, almost bleating with pleasure, with fear, as his tongue explored the hollows of her neck. This time when she pulled back it was for a very different reason—stupidity and inexperience were two different things entirely, and Caitlyn knew exactly where this was going. Knew because her body was telling her—knew that for the first time it felt absolutely right—that this was what to date her lovers' kisses had been missing. And she knew he needed to know.

'I haven't done this before…'

His mouth was still on her neck, kissing her deeply and making her head roll.

'Done what?'

She could feel the warmth of his words on her neck, and the warmth of her blush spread down to greet them as she told him her truth.

'This.'

'What?'

He wasn't kissing her now. Standing to his full height, he was staring down at her, taking in the blonde dishevelled hair. The oil from the massage made it look wet—as if she'd just stepped out of the shower. Her face was flushed, as if the water had been too warm, and her gown had parted just enough to reveal one soft bosom that he wanted so badly to taste.

'I've never made love before.'

Did she think he was *that* stupid?

China-blue eyes stared up at him. That full mouth was quivering with nerves, waiting to be kissed some more, and he was tempted to silence her with just that. What the hell was she playing at? He'd seen her pills in the bathroom, for God's sake, and she'd told him that she'd just broken up with her boyfriend of six months—now she was telling him she was a virgin?

Please!

A very scathing remark was on the tip of his tongue— whatever game she was playing with him was about to be abruptly concluded. The muscles in his arms tensed as he prepared to push her away—only he didn't.

If she wanted to play virgin, if she wanted to pretend that he was her first, then who was he to stop her? In fact, somehow it made it easier to just block out the whys and hows—easier to lower his mouth to hers, to play whatever game it was that she was playing and lose himself.

Pulling her back towards him, Lazzaro kissed the shell of her ear as he spoke. 'Then we'd better take things slowly!'

So slowly. The weight of his mouth on hers was less urgent now, more a slow, languorous kiss, as intimate as it was passionate, exciting her even while simultaneously calming her, telling Caitlyn there was no hurry, no rush on this journey. So she took the time he allowed to explore him—inhaling him, inhaling the undertones of his cologne that couldn't mask the masculine smell of want, feeling the scratch of his face against her skin, coarse, bruising, delicious, and then, because she knew where it was going, because there was nothing to stop her now, allowing herself to concentrate on the blissful feel of his tongue against hers. It toyed with hers, stroking not just where flesh met flesh, but somewhere deeper inside, stirring her slowly, and the weighty band of arousal around her groin danced to the puppet strings he pulled with his mouth.

Lazzaro's hands slipped inside her gown, emitting a groan in their entwined mouths as he encountered the silken smooth, heavily oiled weight of her breasts. He held them in the palms of his hands like ripe fruit, then rolled her nipples between his fingers. Her robe fell in a puddle as he lowered her on the bed, his mouth working its way steadily downwards, and Caitlyn felt her heart still in her throat with nervousness, then trip back into life as she momentarily relaxed, remembering that she had her panties on.

Lazzaro was in no hurry to remove them, but he was kissing her stomach as thoroughly as he'd kissed her mouth, and as his tongue slid down his fingers toyed with her panties, then stopped. She almost sobbed at what was to come. The tease of his tongue through the fabric, the scratch of his jaw high between her legs, the nibble of teeth on lace had Caitlyn squirming with want in his skilful hands as his tongue worked on. But she couldn't relax, couldn't let go and enjoy, because if he didn't stop soon… She could feel her breath catching in her throat, panic building inside. Because if he didn't relent, didn't give her just a second to gather herself…

Her hands were pushing his shoulders, only Lazzaro wasn't letting her go. His shoulders were immovable against the pressure of her hands. *His* hands were stronger as he cupped her bottom and pressed her engorged flesh harder against his mouth. His tongue was inside her panties now, his lips pressed against her, tasting her, drinking her, frenzying her—and her own imagination had been a woeful substitute for reality. The glimpses of satisfaction she had soothed herself with were nothing, *nothing* compared to this. On and ever on he pushed her, and her throat was constricting, stifling her pleas, a sob was catching in her throat.

'Don't…' He whispered the command, and for a second he paused, for a second he looked up…

Fleetingly she asked the question in her jumbled mind—don't what?—but as he dived back down, as his mouth pushed aside her soaking knickers, as his tongue hit her delicious tender spot, she gave herself up to the pleasure of her flesh, her thighs tightening, her bottom arching to his hungry mouth. Her hands were not on his shoulders now, but knotting into his hair. Her intimate lips were kissing him back with a hungry beat that he savoured, in an orgasm that went on for ever, made her almost want to beg for it to stop, and when it was over—when all she wanted to do was curl up her legs and recover—he leant back, smiling down at her as she slowly came to.

'Right…' His voice and his breathing were completely even, his expression utterly deadpan, but there was a glint in his eyes that was almost dangerous as he took in her dishevelled state. 'Let's get started, then…'

Bloody hell! It was the only thing that came to mind as his low voice directed her to the front of the queue for a rollercoaster ride. She'd just had the most amazing orgasm of her life, and Lazzaro hadn't even taken off his top!

God, she was gorgeous… A considerate lover, Lazzaro took pleasure in pleasuring—not out of any sense of duty, more because he loved women, loved feeling them come alive, giving in under his hands, his lips. Only with Caitlyn there *was* a measure of selfishness in his seemingly generous actions—the sweet scent of her skin, the taste of her on his tongue, the moans of pleasure from her throat, had Lazzaro precariously close to ruining his rather formidable reputation.

Lowering himself on the bed beside her, his mouth on hers, feeling her tentative hands running over his chest as they kissed, exploring him, moving with feather-light strokes downwards, Lazzaro knew he wouldn't last a second once inside her. And he so badly wanted to be inside her. His tongue was on her neck now, his lips sucking the tender flesh as his hand moved down to where his mouth had been. His palm held her warm mound as he slipped his finger into her wet, warm space. Biting into her neck, he felt her pleasure as his, felt her moisten beneath him. His erection was dragging on her thigh, nudging its way homeward, hovering there, teasing her, massaging her, tempting her, till it was Caitlyn who had no restraint.

Caitlyn guided that first delicious stab, and then it was Lazzaro, sliding a little way in, then pulling back, staring into her eyes as he did so, monitoring her reaction, tempting her with just a little bit more till her body begged. With each motion her body accommodated this new sensation; with each measured, controlled thrust he held back just enough to make her want more—until she wanted him all: the weight of him on top of her, the feel of him deep inside her, giddying her. Every nerve in her body was fighting the pleasure—because some pleasures were just too great. The control she had lived by, had *had* to live by this past week, was very close to abandonment now.

'Don't.'

He said it again as she fought with herself—said what he had before, the word short and stilted. She could see his shoulders above her, looked down to where he was sliding within, and it was the most erotic thing she had ever seen, the shadowed length of him moving inside her. Only this time he finished what he was saying as a scream curled from her.

'Don't—hold—back.'

'Like you do?' Caitlyn gasped, staring into those black pools and holding them. Because he couldn't ask for all of her without giving all of himself too—and she could feel his restraint, even though it was bliss.

Their eyes locked as they came together, each contraction, each pulse spasmed, and her body squeezed out a scream, her nails digging into his taut shoulders, her mouth sucking on his salty chest as she felt him bucking inside her, felt Lazzaro shuddering his release, their bodies damp, sliding against each other...

'What do you do to me...?' He was still coming, and so was she, and it almost hurt to give so much. She almost hated him for the response he so easily elicited, hated him for making her want him so, for being the one man she wasn't able to resist.

'I told you...'

They were lying in bed. Lazzaro was playing with her hair and Caitlyn was wondering if he was about to get up and leave when his rich voice reached her.

'I told you this morning it would be marvellous.'

Was it? She wanted to check. *Or are you just saying that?* Oh, it had been marvellous for her, but the thought of the beauties he had bedded before was doing nothing for her confidence right now.

She did her best to manage a sophisticated smile as she answered him. 'You did too!' Only she couldn't keep up the charade for long. 'So, what happens now?' Frantic eyes turned to him. 'I mean, it's not very professional…'

'Says who?'

'Says everyone.'

'You only listen to me. I'm the boss; I make the rules.' He realised his words had done nothing to soothe her. 'We'll just be discreet. Obviously we can't make it public—you are my PA, and it would make things awkward on so many levels if people knew that we were…'

He didn't finish. She wished that he would. Were *what?* Caitlyn wanted to ask, only she didn't have the courage.

'Just be discreet.' He kissed the tip of her nose. 'Now, go to sleep…'

He was holding her, still holding her, and she waited, turned her face away from him, waited for him to pull back the rumpled sheets and get dressed and go.

She couldn't bear it for a second longer. 'Are you staying?'

'Why—do you have other plans?'

'It's just that…' She blinked up at the ceiling, her thoughts tumbling out as he smiled and watched. 'Well, actually I'm starving. And I've promised myself that I'll fall asleep every night with my headphones on… I'm doing this crash course in Italian…'

He halted her by leaning over and picking up the phone. And though he cursed at the state of the after-hours menu, never had a club sandwich and icy champagne in bed tasted so good…

Later, Caitlyn reflected. Who needed headphones when she had her very own personal tutor? Her very own Latin lover, whispering in her ear throughout the night and teaching her words that she was sure wouldn't go down too well at any meeting….

CHAPTER SIX

HE WAS very nice to wake up to.

Not that they'd done much sleeping... Caitlyn's inexperience was a distant memory by morning, as Lazzaro had delightedly given her a crash course in lovemaking. A very intensive course in lovemaking, in fact—and she was a very willing pupil, utterly devouring her new-found knowledge and incredibly keen to utilise it!

But lying there, watching him sleeping—watching that normally severe face, that tense body, for once relaxed beside her—she thought that never had he looked more beautiful. His scar just added mystery, though it confused her in some ways. He was hardly vain—Lazzaro took about two minutes to shower and get ready—but for a man who had the best of everything, surely he could have had it seen to...? Caitlyn stared closely at the jagged edges. She could see where the sutures had been placed, and she was so tempted to reach out and touch it, to touch his pain and somehow kiss it better.

As his phone rang, black eyes opened on blue smiling ones.

'Morning...' She reached over to kiss him, unabashed

after last night's intimacies—although if her lack of experience in lovemaking had been taken care of, she was a complete novice in other areas. She had trusted him last night and assumed she could trust him this morning—she had given him her heart and, having fallen asleep in his arms, had never considered it would be handed back in the light of morning.

'Let me see who it is...'

Caitlyn could already see—*Bonita* was flashing up on his caller ID. Her only solace was that he chose not to answer.

'We should get going.' He didn't kiss her back—didn't even try to pretend for a second. Just peeled back the sheets and climbed out of the warm bed. 'I'll meet you downstairs for breakfast.'

'Lazzaro?' She watched his shoulders stiffen at the question in her voice—and knew, because it was indisputable now, that the intimacies they had shared last night didn't extend into the day. Learning fast, and hating the game she found herself playing, Caitlyn checked the slightly needy note in her voice. 'I'll be down in twenty minutes.'

He was far bolder than she could ever be. He didn't even attempt to pull on yesterday's grubby clothes, just wrapped a towel round his waist and picked up his things before heading off to his own room to get showered and dressed, leaving Caitlyn blowing her fringe skywards as she lay on the bed, trying not to cry—determined not to give him the satisfaction of her tears.

Sciocco! Sciocco!

The word pounded in Lazzaro's head as he showered

and dressed, beating in his temples like a pulse as he headed down to breakfast.

Fool! Fool for forgetting who she was—and he *had* forgotten.

Holding her, making love to her, kissing her, tasting her, he'd lost himself, lost his mind… For a few blissful hours he had forgotten about everything—Luca, Antonia, the baby, Malvolio…

Lazzaro's face hardened.

She'd lied to him—she still hadn't told him that Roxanne was her cousin, and as for being a virgin!

Lazzaro snapped his fingers at a waitress, jabbed at his cup for her to refill it.

Well, she might have won this round, but the game wasn't over—a fool he'd be no more.

'Good morning!' His deadpan face didn't even change as she staggered into the dining room—utterly business as usual, he was looking through his schedule and tapping away on his laptop as a very untogether Caitlyn rather shakily poured coffee and picked at a croissant.

'Jeremy will drive you back to Melbourne. I have a few things I want to finalise here and I will get the helicopter back—I also need to see to a few things back at the office…'

'I've rearranged our flights.' Somehow she managed to sound efficient. 'Our plane to Rome now leaves at ten. So we need to be at the airport by eight. Do you want me to meet you at the office?'

Lazzaro shook his head. 'Buy a gift for my sister—then you'll need the rest of the day for yourself, to pack, pay bills, whatever…'

So he *did* acknowledge that she actually had a life? Small comfort, though, when she knew she was being got rid of.

'Jeremy and I will pick you up around six-thirty—we can stop at the hospital on our way to the airport.'

'Fine...'

He watched her fumble with her pastry. He could see the bewilderment in her eyes and it angered him—what the hell did she expect? Breakfast in bed?

'Lazzaro!'

Antonia's vibrant greeting caught them both unawares. Caitlyn was just about to sit herself down in the rather opulent waiting room of the private maternity hospital to catch up on some notes while Luca visited his sister before they headed to the airport. In fact, the only reason Caitlyn hadn't stayed in the car with Lazzaro's chauffeur was the fact that she knew Malvolio was still safely at the hotel, and there would be no chance of banging into him. But—looking radiant, pushing a crib along the carpeted corridor from the nursery towards her room—it turned out Antonia was the one who greeted them.

'It is so good to see you—meet your nephew!'

'Shouldn't you be in bed?' Lazzaro frowned, barely giving the infant a glance.

'I was just fetching Luca from the nursery.'

'Don't the nurses do that?' Lazzaro asked, but Antonia just laughed.

'So, what do you think of your new nephew?'

If it had been anyone, *anyone* else, Caitlyn wouldn't have been able to resist peeking into the crib and staring at the newborn. Only her eyes were on Lazzaro, watching every flicker of his reaction as he stared down—and she could see the grief stamped on his face even though he smiled, could see the bob of his Adam's apple as he swallowed while staring at the baby.

'He's beautiful...' His voice was soft, but raw, his hands bunched into fists as if he was fighting with an instinct to touch him.

He looked so lost and wretched that Caitlyn was fighting with instincts of her own, tempted to wrap her fingers around his closed ones, to support him somehow in this difficult time—only that wasn't in Lazzaro's strange rule book, Caitlyn reminded herself. Discretion was the key— and communication outside the sheets taboo.

'Mum says he's the image of you and Luca when you were born.' Antonia was looking at Lazzaro too, her kind, weary face etched with worry, and Caitlyn's heart went out to her. She was sure this was just as impossible for her too.

'Where's Marianna?' Lazzaro dragged his eyes away from the infant. 'Malvolio said she was at the hospital with you.'

'She is—she's with Mum...come on.'

'She's already here?' Lazzaro didn't even attempt to keep the appalled note out of his voice. 'But how?'

'She flew out as soon as she found out I was in labour. If you'd answered your phone, Lazzaro, you'd have known a few hours sooner too! Marco's with her...'

'Marco?' Lazzaro frowned.

'Her boyfriend.'

'Hardly a boy...' Lazzaro sneered, but Antonia wasn't listening.

'Come and say hi—you too,' she offered Caitlyn. 'There's no need to sit in the waiting room. The more the merrier.'

Caitlyn was about to politely decline, positive her presence would be the last thing Lazzaro would want at this intimate family gathering, but just as she was about to shake her head, before the words could even form on her lips, Lazzaro gave a nod.

'Come!' he clipped, in his usual Spartan way, and then he did the strangest thing.

His hand took her elbow and guided her alongside Antonia. And though it was Lazzaro holding her, somehow Caitlyn was sure it was otherwise—sure for a moment that she was the one holding him up—and though common sense argued loudly, told her he was merely being polite, somehow she knew better.

Lazzaro didn't *do* polite.

Entering Antonia's room, he headed over to his mother, kissing her and ignoring Marco, and talking in rapid Italian as Caitlyn hovered uncomfortably.

'Thank you for the flowers.' Antonia smiled at Caitlyn as she opened the gift. 'And thank you for these…' She grinned at Caitlyn's slightly non-plussed look. 'Lazzaro would never say such thoughtful things…or choose something so heavenly.' She held up the tiny outfits Caitlyn had so carefully chosen earlier that afternoon, and the silver rattle that she had hoped was expensive enough to be suitable!

'I *did* put a lot of thought into them!' Lazzaro countered with a half-smile. 'I choose my staff very carefully.'

Although Antonia made an effort to include Caitlyn, Lazzaro's mother ignored her, clearly more than used to having staff around. They spoke in Italian, with Marco bouncing little Marianna on his knee as the *nona* scooped up a sleeping Luca, and though her last week had been spent falling asleep with *Speak Italian in Seven Days* playing in her ears, Caitlyn still really didn't understand a word of the colourful language.

No command of Italian was necessary, though, to comprehend what Lazzaro's mother was saying when she held out the tiny infant and offered him to her son. *'Desiderate tenere il bambino?'*

'Non posso.' Lazzaro shook his head. 'I can't. We have to be at the airport…'

'Surely you can give him a quick cuddle?' Antonia pushed, and though she was smiling, Caitlyn could see tears brimming in her eyes as Lazzaro remained adamant.

'We have to go—there is fog in Europe, and the planes are all off schedule. We really ought to make a move.'

'Do you like my baby brother?' Marianna's eyes, as black as Lazzaro's but a lot more trusting, caught Caitlyn's.

'He's beautiful.' Caitlyn smiled. 'Like his big sister!'

'He's named after my dead uncle.'

And no icy European winter could match the sudden drop in temperature on the hot maternity ward.

'Come.' It was Lazzaro who broke the appalling silence, but his single word unleashed the dam. His mother sped after him, talking in rapid Italian, and as the baby started crying to be fed, unsettled by her new brother, and her uncle who was leaving, so too did Marianna.

So too did Antonia. And her throaty pleas for her brother to just give his mother what she wanted—five minutes of his time—were the ones that finally stalled Lazzaro. A terse nod and a surly shrug implied that there really wasn't an issue, that of course he had no problem spending time with them. Then another brief nod as his mother spoke again.

'We will go for a coffee.' Lazzaro gave his sister a smile 'You feed the baby, we'll take Marianna, then I'll come back and say goodbye.' He glanced over to Caitlyn. 'Meet me in the car in half an hour.'

Which was normal—in the little while she'd been working for him, waiting in reception areas or in the car, chatting to his driver, was a rather regular occurrence, while Lazzaro wined and dined his way through business lunches. Her peripheral presence was necessary in case he wanted her to pluck some figure from her laptop, or—and she still couldn't quite get her head around it—to buy him some mints!

What wasn't normal, though, was being left alone with his sister. What was horribly awkward was pretending nothing untoward had taken place and offering her a smile and rather forced congratulations as she turned to leave. But Antonia's strangled sob as Caitlyn reached the door was utterly heartbreaking, and whether she was Lazzaro's PA or not, whether she was nothing more than a convenience, she was still a woman, and few women could have ignored another in such obvious distress.

'I'm sorry…' Antonia sobbed as Caitlyn came over, her tears spilling onto the screaming baby, his mother's distress making him wail all the louder. 'I'm upsetting Luca…'

'Here…!'

Peeling tissues out of the box on the bedside table, she handed them to the upset woman. When it was clear more than paper was required, Caitlyn relieved Antonia of the screaming baby, rocking him in her arms, trying to hush him as Antonia sobbed on.

'It's all just falling apart…' Antonia was inconsolable.

'I thought with a new baby, if we were all together, then maybe we could move on...' The tears were stilling now, but her distress was just as raw. 'It's never going to get better, is it?'

'Of course it will,' Caitlyn offered helplessly. 'These things take time.'

'It's been more than two years!' Antonia choked. 'Two years of grieving for one brother and watching the other disappear. There was a row, a terrible row, before Luca died. Lazzaro confronted him. Luca was in debt to the eyeballs, spending money like water, completely out of control...'

'I know...' Caitlyn nodded—because she did know, and not just from Roxanne. Like everyone else, she had read the newspapers at the time, watched the journalists deliver the court's findings on the evening news. 'But Lazzaro couldn't have known what was to come...' And he couldn't have, Caitlyn reasoned. He couldn't have known Luca would walk out of the argument and into a bar—would get behind the wheel so loaded that the second he turned the key in the ignition the outcome was inevitable.

'It was Lazzaro's fault.' Antonia's sobbed the words out. '*Why*? *Why* would he do that?' Antonia stopped as quickly as she had started, pleading eyes looking to Caitlyn's.

'You said yourself, he *had* to...' Caitlyn attempted. But as Antonia placed her shaking hand over her mouth, closed her eyes in horror, she knew Antonia had said more than she had intended—knew that what she had just heard was something she shouldn't have. 'What happened, Antonia?'

'I can't say...'

She was a pitiful sight. A woman who seemingly had everything—money, looks, a doting husband, beautiful children—only Caitlyn's heart went out to her. Whether Antonia knew it or not, her world really was falling apart. 'I am scared for my brother—scared he is heading down the same path as Luca.'

'Lazzaro doesn't gamble,' Caitlyn soothed, 'and he hardly drinks. Lazzaro—'

'Is in hell…' Antonia finished. 'Just look out for him… You are working with him, closer to him at the moment than his own family.' Antonia's eyes met hers as Caitlyn handed her back little Luca. 'I'm just asking that you look out for him.'

'I somehow don't think Lazzaro would appreciate it.' Caitlyn gave a wobbly smile. The lines were suddenly blurring. He was her boss, nothing else. It was something she had to remind herself of constantly—to remain professional and aloof at all times, and even when he kissed her to somehow remember a kiss was all it was—that even if he had held her last night he had dismissed her in the morning.

Could she do it? Caitlyn wondered as she farewelled Antonia and walked along the hospital corridor. Could she really put her life on hold for him? Fall more and more in love with him? Only to walk away at the end? Because somehow, even when he was loathsome, the more she saw of him, the more she wanted him, and the more he allowed her to have the more she gratefully received—but then what?

What happened when she upped her demands? Would she be dismissed, like Jenna? It was Caitlyn now suddenly near to tears.

When he'd decided he'd had enough, when she'd served her purpose or dared to make a demand, it would be over—

not just a fantasy figure to get over, but her first love to recover from.

'What are *you* doing here?'

Malvolio's voice made her jump, and her eyes darted along the corridor, her heart thudding in her chest as for the first time since he'd tried to kiss her she faced him.

'Lazzaro came to see his sister.'

'I'm not asking about Lazzaro...' Malvolio hissed. 'Stay the hell away from my family—got it?'

Head down, she nodded, walked quickly away. But Malvolio hadn't yet finished.

'Oh, and, Caitlyn—you might think you're on to a good thing, in your fancy new clothes and with your fancy new title, but let me tell you one thing about my brother in-law.' She kept walking, refusing to look back, but his black voice caught up with her before she'd turned the corner. 'He doesn't give a damn about anyone—not even his own family. When he's finished with you—when you've served your purpose—he'll spit you out along with the pips.'

Lazzaro's face was as grim as Caitlyn's when he finally joined her in the car. Climbing in, he didn't even bother to say hello—just told Jeremy to step on it.

'Everything okay?' Finally he deigned to look at her.

'Great!' Caitlyn's eyes met his in the darkness, glittering with tears and holding his for an impossibly long time. 'How about you?'

'Great!' Lazzaro snapped. 'Things couldn't be better.'

CHAPTER SEVEN

THEY breezed through check-in and Customs and took off on time. The journey was in fact perfect—except for the two coiled springs sharing the first-class cabin.

As they hurtled across time zones, Caitlyn played a game with the night sky—convincing herself that the day that had started so perfectly was being extended so it could end on a better note, that somehow he'd look over and smile, as if pleased the universe was giving him these extra hours. Only Lazzaro didn't use them wisely. Barely a word passed between them even as they landed and renegotiated Customs—and stepped out into the freezing morning.

Freezing!

Melbourne winters weren't exactly warm, but they were positively tropical compared to this. Her breath was blowing out white clouds, her teeth chattering as they headed to the waiting car, jumping like a puppy left behind into the heated warmth as the driver loaded their cases.

But nothing—not Lazzaro's black mood nor her earlier confrontation with Malvolio—could dim the beauty of Rome, as the sleek black Mercedes drove them at breakneck speed through the ancient city. She longed to ask the driver to slow down—had to stifle a squeal as the Colosseum came into view.

'It really is in Rome…' She rolled her eyes at Lazzaro's old-fashioned look. 'Right in the middle.' Pressing her nose against the window, at that moment Caitlyn didn't care about his bloody mood, or *her* bloody mood, or what was happening, or where things were going. She was in Rome—*in Rome*—and it was beautiful. The people were beautiful. Stunning groomed women, trailing scarves clipping through the cobbled streets. Elegant men, in long coats… Not caring what Lazzaro thought, she opened the window, closed her eyes for a second against the icy blast of air that hit her, then opened them on a carnival of noise. Mopeds weaving through the heavy traffic, drivers shouting and cursing—she'd never seen so many people. Rush hour in Melbourne was like a Sunday stroll in the park compared to this.

'Close the window,' Lazzaro snapped. 'It's cold.'

'It is!' Pushing the button, blocking out the noise, just for a second, one very defiant second, she looked at him and gave him a little piece of her mind. 'In fact it's probably warmer outside!'

There were five-star hotels, Caitlyn realised as the car door was opened and she stepped out, and then there were *five-star hotels*. Heavy gold revolving doors spun her into a stunning foyer, and Caitlyn didn't know whether to look up or down. Marble pillars stretched to a magnificent high-domed ceiling, and a chandelier surely the size of Caitlyn's back garden, and thick exquisite rugs dotted the black and white tiled floor. And the beauty of her surroundings was only surpassed by the stunning guests.

Ranaldi's Roma was clearly the jewel in the Ranaldi crown.

Lazzaro's bloody mood wasn't aimed solely at her though. After the briefest shower and change in history, with barely a second to take in her stunning suite, there was a sharp rap at her door and work began. Lazzaro met with his staff throughout the day and picked fault with everything—from the food and the selection in the private wine cellar to some unfortunate bellboy whose shirt wasn't tucked in properly. He waltzed through the place, knowing he owned it, and everyone quailed—and Caitlyn trailed. In fact, by the time the old-fashioned lift creaked her up towards her room that evening, not for the first time since taking the position of Lazzaro's assistant, all she felt was exhausted...and not just physically.

His rejection, his cruel dismissal, had cut her to the very core of her being—yet there had been no chance to examine it, no time to process it, to retreat and lick her wounds.

Till now—only now she was too damned tired.

There were no fancy swipe cards here. Instead she opened her door with a key that was as old as time, and thankfully closed the door on the longest day of her life. Her tired eyes took in her suite: the vibrant clash of golds and reds that worked so brilliantly, the intricate flower arrangements, the white shutters at the endless thin windows. Even the vast carved walnut bed couldn't dominate the massive bedroom, but it was the only thing that held her interest. Not even bothering to take off her make-up, Caitlyn dropped her clothes to the floor and brushed her teeth, then sank into bed, trying to summon the energy to book a wake-up call.

She sighed at the soft knocking at her door, choosing to ignore it. She was just closing her eyes as the maid let herself in—no doubt to turn down the bed she was already in…

'Caitlyn…' Though softly spoken, Lazzaro's word made her jump.

'What the hell are you doing in here?' Sitting bolt-upright, she pulled the sheet tightly around her, scarcely able to believe his audacity. 'Don't tell me—you've got a master key to the place.'

'You didn't lock your door,' Lazzaro pointed out, sitting down in the darkness on the bed beside her. 'Look—'

'No!' Without waiting to hear what he wanted, she shook her head. 'I know it's only seven o'clock, I know you warned me that we'd be busy, and you've probably got a million things you want to do this evening and a million people you want to see—'

'Just one.'

'Please,' Caitlyn said, not even attempting to keep the note of weariness out of her voice, 'can't you manage it without me—just this once?'

'Probably,' Lazzaro said, his fingers moving to sheet, his breath warm on her cheek. Caitlyn realised he wasn't here about work. 'Only it wouldn't be anywhere near as nice!'

His depraved response eked out of her the tiniest shocked laugh, and Lazzaro pounced, his mouth claiming hers. But Caitlyn pulled back.

'Don't!' she sobbed. 'You've been vile all day…'

'That was work…' He was raining kisses on her face, his hands pulling her rigid arms to her sides, and, brimming with loathing and longing, she fought to resist as he clouded her mind.

'Not just at work...' He was kissing her quiet, his mouth dulling her words, but again she pulled back. 'You ignored me...'

'I'm not ignoring you now...' Lazzaro husked, then groaned into her neck. 'Caitlyn, please. This endless day has been hell...'

Naked beneath the sheet, her body begged for no more questions. He was here, he'd come to her, somehow he needed her tonight, and it must be enough to hush her worried mind. His hands were cupping her face as he kissed away her doubts, and her sob of anger was aimed at herself as she pulled at his suit, as her fingers tore at his clothes.

Could she do it? Caitlyn begged of herself as he entered her.

Could she be the woman he came to at night if he gave nothing of himself in the morning?

'Yes!' Caitlyn sobbed her answer out loud, then sobbed it again. 'Yes...' she whimpered, her nails digging into the taut muscles of his back as he moved deep within her, tears spilling out of her eyes as he took her to the edge, then toppled her over.

Staring down at her as she slept, her face as pale as the pillow in the moonlight, her hair spread on the sheet, her lips swollen from his attention, her shoulders bruised from his kisses, he knew he was as weak as he was hard.

He had sworn he wouldn't go back—yet here he was.

Sciocco.

No! Lazzaro's jaw tightened—he was still in control, was wise to her games, was one step ahead. He would trip her up on her lies some time soon...but for now... Pulling her, soft and warm, into his body, he felt her hair tickling his chest as his arm wrapped around her. He stared at the ceiling as the word taunted him again.

Sciocco.

Perhaps a little, Lazzaro conceded, but he could handle it—wouldn't let himself forget for a moment that he was living in a fool's paradise.

'To be the best...' Lazzaro gave her a black smile as they sat in his room on Saturday and for the second time he sent back his food with complaints to the chef '...you have to give the best—every time.'

'Well, my lunch is perfect,' Caitlyn said defiantly—because it was!

She'd been taking notes since eight a.m., a pounding headache her companion as Lazzaro bombarded her with his findings, snapping his fingers as he had the night they'd first met as—not quickly enough for his impatient liking—she retrieved reams and reams of figures from her laptop. She had been grateful, so grateful, when lunch had appeared—and, unlike at the peninsular resort, in-room dining at Ranaldi's Roma was a slice of heaven. A trolley as vast as her dinner table at home had been wheeled in, groaning under the weight of a sumptuous spread of cold meats and pastries, syruped fruits and cannolis, and coffee as thick as treacle had cleared her thumping head—yet still he found something to complain about.

Taking a bite of her cannoli, tasting the sugared creamed cheese, ignoring the inevitable icing sugar moustache, Caitlyn was insistent. 'It's heavenly, in fact.'

'Because *you* know no better!'

God, he was poisonous at times. The man she shared her bed with, shared herself with at night, was unrecognisable against the man she barely tolerated by day.

'Tonight we check out the competition.'

'I thought it was Signor Mancini's party tonight.'

'It is—he is still the competition, and I am his. I can guarantee everything will be perfect—as it should be here. You need to get ready for tonight—your hair is...' He gave her a curious look that inflamed her.

'I didn't wash it this morning,' Caitlyn hissed, 'because I'm having it put up for the party! You-don't-wash-your-hair-the-day-you-get-it-put-up-or-it-comes-down!'

'Thank you for telling me.' He gave her a very on-off smile. 'I was just going to say that you will stand out tonight—there are not many natural blondes in Rome.'

'Oh!' She was jolly well sure he *hadn't* been about to say that, but, given she'd so spectacularly jumped the gun, she'd never know. 'I've chosen one from the dresses you had sent over—don't worry, I won't let you down. So, what are we doing for the rest of the day?'

'I've told you—you are getting your hair and make-up done.'

'It's one p.m.,' Caitlyn pointed out. 'I don't take six hours to get ready!'

He frowned over at her. 'Your eyebrows need doing too...'

'Excuse me?' Caitlyn blushed in anger at yet another rude observation. 'How rude!'

'Tonight you are going to be mingling with Rome's most rich, most beautiful. So I suggest you go and start to prepare. I am just letting you know—'

'Well, don't!' Caitlyn snapped. Her heavenly lunch was

sitting like lead in her stomach, and not for the first time she wondered if she was up to this—wondered if her mother's mortgage was really worth the humiliation. She consoled herself that at least the rose-coloured glasses she'd worn over the years were well and truly starting to clear. 'And if we're being personal…' She stared over at him, wishing he wasn't so damn perfect, trying to find a fault to pick. When there wasn't, annoyed at herself for being so childish, she made one up. 'You've got something on your teeth!'

'I have not.'

'You have,' Caitlyn insisted. 'A great big green bit—right there.' She tapped at her own teeth. 'I just don't want you to embarrass yourself when you abuse your staff!'

He laughed—actually threw his head back and laughed—and, most annoyingly of all, he didn't make a single move to check. Which was probably just as well, Caitlyn thought. Because there was nothing there. Despite herself, she started to laugh too.

'Gone?' He smiled that lazy smile that did something to her deep inside—that made her relent when she'd sworn she wouldn't.

'Gone!' Caitlyn conceded, because for the moment at least it had. Not the imaginary thing on his teeth—they both knew that—but the black cloud that had engulfed them since he'd stepped out of her bed. She was dazzled momentarily by the rainbow of his smile.

'Go!' He said it nicely—rather too nicely, in fact…sort of undressing her with his eyes as he did so…sort of warning her to get out while the going was good. 'Enjoy your afternoon…'

If only she'd picked up her bag then and headed to her suite. But when Lazzaro was being nice there was no one nicer...when Lazzaro was looking at her like that there was every reason to stay.

'Lazzaro...'

The deep, throaty, *familiar* voice made her start. Utterly unprepared, all she could do was sit as he stood, as he took the stunning woman in his arms and kissed her as only Italians did—only there was a tenderness there, a protectiveness there that she'd never witnessed before—and certainly not for herself. There was a gentleness in Lazzaro as he greeted this woman that made Caitlyn's heart bleed.

'Bonita, this is my new personal assistant, Caitlyn Bell—Caitlyn this is Bonita Mancini...' He gave Caitlyn a sudden smile. 'Of course—stupid me. You two will have already met.'

'Met?' Caitlyn frowned, and so too did Bonita.

'We've spoken on the *telefono,* yes?'

'That's right.' Caitlyn nodded, then turned to Lazzaro. 'We've never actually met.'

'But surely at your interview for the PR position...?' Lazzaro was still smiling, but there was a dangerous glint in his eyes. 'Oh—sorry, Caitlyn. I didn't introduce you properly—you see, not only is Bonita Alberto Mancini's wife, she's head of PR. That's how they met, in fact!'

'Still he keeps me working!' Bonita laughed, but her laughter faded as her eyes—not her Botoxed forehead—crinkled in concentration. 'You say you had an interview...?' she attempted, her voice fading as she attempted to place Caitlyn.

'It must have been with another hotel chain.' It was

Lazzaro who broke the appalling silence. 'My mistake.' He might have broken the silence, but nothing could take away the awkwardness—everyone present knew he never made mistakes—at least not when it came to work!

'I'd better get on!' Caitlyn forced a smile and excused herself, reeling from the news that Bonita was Bonita *Mancini,* and looking back just once, in time to see his arm slide around her shoulders and pull her in—in time to see her rest her head on his chest as if she'd missed him for ever.

CHAPTER EIGHT

SHE looked... Caitlyn stared back at her reflection and actually said the word out loud. *'Fabulous!'*

And it had nothing to do with the flattering mirror!

There was no place for self-deprecation tonight—it was about self-preservation. And, oh, the gods had been kind tonight, because if ever she'd needed to pull out all the stops to face Lazzaro, if ever she'd needed to know not just that she was okay, but to *know* she was fabulous—it was tonight.

The hairdressers had practically fallen over themselves to do her hair—and though she'd planned to wear her hair up, in her usual safe French roll, after a glass of champagne and a large boost to her ego Caitlyn had, for the first time in her life, actually listened to what the hairdresser had to say. Instead of staying safe, why not play up her natural asset? Why not wear a head full of blonde curls?

So now she stood, curls snaking around her face and onto her shoulders—her eyes unrecognisable after the skilled attention of the makeup artist.

'Uno o l'altro,' the beautician had explained as she'd scrutinised her face, and Caitlyn had understood—she could play up either her eyes or her mouth, but not both.

The eyes had it!

Slate-grey eyeshadow and lashings of eyeliner and mascara brought out every last glimmer of blue in her eyes, soft blush accentuated her cheekbones, and her lips were full but teasingly neutral. As for the dress—black had never been less safe. A million hand-sewn black glass beads covered every inch of fabric, and the deep empress line showed off her bosom—and from the second she'd slipped it on, feeling guilty for being greedy, Caitlyn had been wanting to ask if it was hers or on loan.

Well, for tonight at least it was hers.

And for tonight at least she had enough confidence to deal with Lazzaro—was enough of a woman to walk away from the man of her dreams.

She'd always thought that he'd come back.

That the bitter man, so twisted by grief, would one day return to the man she had first met. She had been sure in her heart that the man she had fallen in love with was in there somewhere.

Only he wasn't.

Tears glittered in her eyes as the door to her heart closed to him—closed to a man who could do such a thing to his friend. It was all she'd thought about all day, as she was primped and preened to within an inch of her life, to make her fit to grace the arm of Lazzaro Ranaldi when he attended his good friend's birthday party. The friend whose wife he was having an affair with.

'Are you ready?'

It was hardly an effusive greeting, but Caitlyn was relieved not to have to make small talk as she tried to squeeze lipstick, face powder and her key into the tiniest of bags—relieved because in all her efforts to look the part she'd forgotten to prepare herself for the sight of him. Always effortlessly stunning, tonight, when he *had* made an effort, he quite simply took her breath away. Black hair was smoothed back from his face, and his tuxedo was so superbly cut it accentuated his already broad shoulders. The white of his shirt and immaculate trousers highlighted the smooth planes of his stomach and the thick muscular legs that seemed to go on for ever.

'Is that all you're taking?' Lazzaro frowned. 'You know we'll be staying there?'

'Where?'

'At the Mancini hotel—of course.'

She hadn't known, *of course*—though now she thought about it, it seemed obvious. Someone with the wealth and resources of Alberto Mancini would ensure his guests were extremely well looked after.

'It would be rude to decline…' Lazzaro gave a pompous shrug as Caitlyn turned to race to pack an overnight bag. 'Even if my hotel is better.'

'How was your afternoon?' Caitlyn asked as the elevator doors clanged behind them.

'Long,' came the single-word reply as he stared fixedly ahead.

Lazzaro was holding his breath—trying to block out her heady scent—trying not to look at her. Oh, he'd always known she was stunning—that with the right clothes, the right make-up, she could rival any of the A-list beauties who would be paraded tonight—but knowing what he knew, what he'd found out today, seeing her so sleek, so polished, instead of melting him it did the opposite. Tonight she turned him to stone.

He strode out of the lift and across the foyer and into the waiting car. Caitlyn struggled to keep up, tossing her bag to his driver and not offering a single word as the car sped through the wet Rome streets.

A blonde Medusa—bewitching, beguiling. Well, not tonight. Tonight he was impervious to her charms. Tonight he would hold onto the truth—the truth that was becoming clear, no matter how she, how *he*, tried to gloss over it. So many times he'd been tempted to trust her, to ignore the red flags—to just deny what he knew—see only the good... She bewitched him, just as Roxanne had Luca—one look at those eyes and he was gone.

Well, no more!

Tonight he would confront her.

'Lazzaro!'

Alberto Mancini was, of course, the guest of honour at his own party, but Lazzaro clearly came a close second. Their host quickly excused himself from the gathered crowd and made his way over, talking in rapid Italian as he greeted his friend, but politely switching to English as soon as Caitlyn was introduced.

'So, you are Lazzaro's new personal assistant—congratulations! No doubt we will be seeing quite a bit of each other.'

'It's a pleasure to meet you,' Caitlyn dutifully answered.

'May I say you look stunning? Every head turned when you walked in.'

In Lazzaro's direction, Caitlyn wanted to point out. But instead she murmured her thanks.

'This is my wife, Bonita...' Alberto said cheerfully, sliding an arm around his wife's tiny waist as she came over. 'Looking stunning too—though so you should, darling,' he teased good-naturedly, 'with the amount of time you spent at the parlour today! Bonita, this is Caitlyn—Lazzaro's new personal assistant!' And from the tiny nervous dart in Bonita's eye, from her polite response and the kiss on Caitlyn's cheek, if any confirmation had been needed that Alberto knew nothing of his wife's whereabouts that afternoon, then she had it.

As Alberto excused himself and wandered off to mingle with his guests, all pretence at politeness was dropped. Bonita reverted to Italian, taking Lazzaro by the arm and guiding him away, leaving Caitlyn awkward and alone and trying not to show it. She sipped on her drink and made occasional small talk, standing on heels that hurt with a smile that ached—and a heart that was literally breaking.

In a room of beautiful people, somehow Lazzaro topped them all.

He stood just that bit taller, that bit straighter than the rest—with beautiful women floating around him like humming birds, like butterflies...like angry bees, Caitlyn thought sometimes, watching through narrowed eyes as he danced with many—or merely stood as they fought for the beam of his smile, for a second dance with the master, for the chance of a night with him. Alberto Mancini joined him, chatting and laughing and utterly, utterly oblivious—and it made Caitlyn feel sick.

'He's an attractive man...' Bonita was beside her as the painful night was thankfully drawing to a close, sipping on champagne and watching the proceedings. 'Your boss.'

'So is your husband,' Caitlyn answered tightly, her back straightening as if it had a rod in it, her hand so tight on her glass she half expected the stem to snap.

'He is...'

The affection in Bonita's voice confused Caitlyn.

'A lot of people, my family included, think it can only be about money...why would I look at him otherwise? They do not know how he makes me feel.'

'How *does* he make you feel?'

'Safe,' Bonita answered. 'When I am with Alberto, my world is safe.'

Then what the hell are you doing? Caitlyn wanted to scream at her. Only she didn't—just stiffened more, if that were possible, as Lazzaro caught her eye. Her whole body was torn between want and loathing as he excused himself from the masses and made his way over.

'We were just talking about you, Lazzaro.' Bonita smiled.

'All good, I hope?' he drawled, but his face was grim. 'I think Alberto has had enough.'

'I agree.' Bonita gave a tight smile. 'Will you...?'

'I have told him.' Lazzaro nodded. 'He is just saying his farewells—I will help him to his room.' His eyes were thoughtful as he looked over at Caitlyn. 'I'm sorry if I have left you to your own devices...'

'I'm not your date, Lazzaro,' Caitlyn answered tightly. 'This is work.'

'Then, when I return, it's time I asked my assistant to dance.'

A heart that should be utterly unmoved by him somehow leapt when finally they danced.

Even as he held her, even as they danced, it was at arm's length—the boss and his assistant—the duty dance. But even if his hands barely touched her dress, even if her body wasn't against his, the energy was undeniable—the space between them thick with loathing and bitter attraction. Her hair occasionally tickled his cheek, her scent filled his nostrils, and the awkwardness between them was arousing somehow. He wanted to bury his face in her hair, to pull her soft, warm body to his hard one, but instead he spoke.

'Thank you...' His voice was low in her ear. 'For not saying anything to Alberto about this afternoon.'

'Don't thank me.' His hands were loosely around her waist, their bodies somehow close enough to look as if they were comfortable with each other even while barely touching—oh, but she ached, longed to move that dangerous couple of inches, to rest herself against him, to close her eyes and feel him, have him hold her. But Caitlyn knew if she did she'd be lost. 'Don't make me a part of it.'

'I'm not with you—a part of it?' Now and then he did that—his English was seemingly not quite so perfect, needing her to translate—but Caitlyn knew better. Knew he was, in fact, just buying a little more time.

'Don't...' She looked up to him. 'Don't ever put me in that position again. I'll lie to your girlfriends, Lazzaro—but not to their partners.'

'I never asked you to lie...'

'Should I have told him Bonita and I had already met?' Her words hissed into his ears. 'When she came to your suite. Should I have told him that the reason his young gold-digging wife's looking so fabulous—with that flush on her face and her sparkling eyes—has nothing to do with hours at the salon, but everything to do with your—?' Her voice stopped abruptly as his hand caught her wrist.

His words were caustic as they reached her. 'How dare you judge me by your own standards?'

'At least I *have* some standards!'

They weren't even pretending to dance now, just standing in the middle of the dance floor, bristling, bursting with unsaid words. But thankfully the music paused then, the room rippling with applause, and Lazzaro's hand tightened around hers, practically dragging her across the dance floor to a secluded table.

Only there was no such thing as total seclusion when you were Lazzaro Ranaldi. A waiter appeared—offering drinks, pouring water—when all they wanted was to be left alone.

'What standards?' Lazzaro sneered, picking up the conversation exactly where they had left it. '*You're* the liar…'

'Me?'

'It was confirmed today—you never did have a second interview lined up with Mancini.' He watched as she coloured up, watched her hands tighten around her drink, and couldn't help but smile in triumph. It was Caitlyn playing for time now. 'You never even had a *first!*'

'No,' Caitlyn finally answered, glad for the water that had been poured—glad that there was actually something she could do with her hands as she fiddled with her glass.

'You never even sent them your résumé, did you?'

'Why bother asking when clearly you've been checking up?'

'Of course,' Lazzaro answered evenly. 'What? Did you think that I wouldn't? Did you expect me to just trust you? Did you think that I really thought I had the hotel name wrong?'

'I'm surprised you had time to even think of me when you were with Bonita,' Caitlyn spat. 'I'm surprised I even entered you head.'

'I don't have to explain myself to you.' In a curiously insolent gesture Lazzaro raised one shoulder, then dropped it. 'But clearly, after your little display, it has slipped your mind that I am in fact your boss, and you *do* have to explain yourself to *me!* So, why did you lie?'

But suddenly he changed his mind—the question he had just voiced temporarily forgotten as angrily he leant over the table.

'Alberto Mancini is my friend—how dare you insult me—*how dare you insult Bonita too*—when you know nothing of what has gone on? Nothing!'

'Then tell me,' Caitlyn begged. 'What the hell am I supposed to think, Lazzaro? She's on the phone every five minutes, and coming up to your room, and clearly Alberto doesn't have a clue...'

'Why would I tell you? I don't trust you,' Lazzaro sneered. 'So come on—why did you lie?'

'I just did.' Caitlyn shrugged tightly.

'Surely in an interview you must—'

'When I *lied*,' Caitlyn interrupted, 'I wasn't even aware I was *being* interviewed. In fact, if I remember correctly, when I *lied* to you, Lazzaro, I was trying to *leave* my job, not wangle another one.'

'You said you had another job practically lined up,' Lazzaro pointed out. 'You specifically said—'

Caitlyn put down her drink and stood up—she didn't

need this sort of inquisition now, didn't want to go over that awful day again. And she was also angry—angry at the accusing way he always looked at her, the accusing way he so *often* looked at her.

'Oh, I lied,' Caitlyn flared, 'and you were bloody grateful at the time, if I remember rightly. Grateful that you didn't have to explain to your precious sister the type of man she was married to—grateful that you could put another Band-Aid over a raw subject rather than deal with it!'

'I never asked for you to lie! I told you I wanted the truth.'

'Perhaps!' People were looking at them now, heads turning in their direction—the Italians were not exactly known for their discretion—but Caitlyn couldn't have cared less. 'But please don't sit there and try to tell me you weren't just a little bit relieved when you didn't have to face up to it, didn't have to actually deal with it—just like you don't want to deal with your br—' Her mouth snapped closed, her voice abruptly halting as if a plug had suddenly been pulled.

'Go on.' His voice was like ice. 'Finish what you were going to say.'

'I—I don't want to…' Caitlyn stammered, horrified at what she had just said, horrified at where this argument had led. But Lazzaro wasn't letting her leave it there.

'What is it I don't want to deal with?'

'Lazzaro, don't.'

'Clearly you have an opinion on me,' Lazzaro continued, utterly ignoring her words. 'And I'd like to hear it!'

There was no chance of even pretending this evening was going to conclude politely—no chance of making small talk when the big talk was hanging in the air. 'I should go…'

She stood up. Hand shaking, Caitlyn reached for her bag—but Lazzaro caught her wrist. 'Why would you leave when the conversation is just starting to get interesting?'

'I'm going to bed.' She pulled back her hand, and he let her go, but even as she turned, even as her shaking legs tried to walk her out of the ballroom, she knew that he was behind her.

Momentarily she lost direction—the Mancini lobby was unfamiliar—but, locating the lifts, she clipped towards them, knowing it wasn't over. Without looking over her shoulder, Caitlyn closed her eyes as he stepped in the lift beside her, but her eyelids couldn't dim the burn of his eyes on her. Her body was drenched in his anger—her mind trapped in the maze of a row that hadn't yet happened but, thanks to her careless words, it would seem now had to.

He walked her to her door uninvited, leant against the wall without a word as it took her three goes to get the blasted swipe card to work, and even as she stepped in, even as she went to close the door, she knew she hadn't seen the last of him.

'What?' His face twisted into a smile that was completely false as his foot jammed the door. 'Aren't you even going to ask me in for coffee?'

And she nodded—because it wasn't him she feared, but what she had unleashed in the terrible, public moment she'd so poorly chosen to discuss his private agony. Or maybe it had been the right moment, Caitlyn reflected as she stepped back enough to let him in. Because he hadn't silenced her, or halted her...hadn't run from the issue—in fact, he'd followed her here to face it.

The room had been prepared—the bed turned back, chocolates placed on her pillows—and she stood there trembling.

'You were saying?'

'Your brother.' Finally she concluded what she had to say—the plug back in, the power back on. And the light was a relief after the darkness they had plunged into. It had been a necessary darkness, though, Caitlyn realised—the panic, the fumbling, the searching, all needed to bring them to this point, where finally she could look at him as she said the word that no one was really allowed to. 'Luca.'

'I deal with Luca's death every day.' Lazzaro attempted a dismissal.

'Every minute of every hour of every day,' Caitlyn countered, watching as he closed his eyes. 'I know you must feel awful...'

'You know, do you?'

'My grandfather died six months ago—'

'You compare the death of a young man—'

'No!' Caitlyn interrupted with a shout of her own. 'No, but I know how it feels to miss someone, and I know how it feels to love and mourn someone. But I also know peace, Lazzaro, something that seems to elude *you* even two years on!' Her voice was softer now. 'I know you rowed before he died—I read it in the papers, and Antonia said it was awful. But by all accounts Luca was out of control, something had to be said—and I don't get it. You'd have been prepared for his anger. How did you let him hit you? How—?'

'Drop it!' His voice had a stern warning ring—angry, even. Only it wasn't aimed at her, instead it was turned onto himself. The past few days had been hell—the past few weeks, in fact. Knowing his family would soon all be together, that Luca's name would be said again. Like living in a sewer—the filth and grime seeping through the floorboards no matter how much he tried to gloss it over. And now here she stood—understanding in her voice, eyes that seemed to reach inside him—and it would be so, so easy to push aside doubt, to convince himself that she actually was different, that here was someone he could tell.

And how he wanted to tell. Only Malvolio's warning was ringing in his ears like the doomsday bell, and eyes as blue as Roxanne's eyes were staring back at him, just as they had that fateful day.

'It shouldn't be like that, Lazzaro…'

'How should it be, then?' Lazzaro fixed her with his glare, tried to warn her off—to get her the hell back—tried to ward her off, tried to keep his head, before she melted his heart again.

'I don't know…'

'That's right, you *don't* know—you don't know,' he repeated. 'So don't tell me I'm not dealing with things properly when you have no idea what happened that day.'

'Tell me, then,' Caitlyn begged.

'Why?' he asked.

'Because I want to know.'

'Why?'

'Because…' Like pulling the cork on a champagne bottle, she could feel the trepidation, feel the pressure building inside, and she didn't want to do it, didn't want to release what was inside. Only she couldn't hold it back, and just closed her eyes as she let it out—as the cork hit the wall and words spilled and bubbled and overflowed. 'Because I care about you, Lazzaro—and I'm sorry if that's not what you want to hear, or if it troubles you. I'm sorry if I'm not supposed to have feelings for you and I'm only supposed to be around when my services are required, but I happen to care about you—'

'What?' He was practically sneering. 'You want me to open up to *you?*' He mocked her with a black laugh. 'So you can use it on me later?'

'Why would I use it on you later?'

'You contradict yourself,' Lazzaro jeered, because it was easier—easier to keep her at arm's length than let her drag him in. 'One minute I am the lowest form of life—a man you say would sleep with his friend's wife—yet in the next breath you tell me you care. How?' he roared. 'How could you care about someone like that?'

'I don't know,' Caitlyn whispered. 'I just know that I do.'

There was the longest silence—his eyes were scales that weighed her up, his mind was begging him to see reason. Only he didn't want to.

Really didn't want to.

He wanted her to care—because so did he.

'Caitlyn, I have not slept with Bonita—I would never do that—I'm asking you to believe me.'

'Bonita's not the problem...' Thick black tears were rolling down her cheeks. She knew that because she saw the streaks on her hand when she wiped them away, pathetically grateful when he peeled off a wad of tissues and handed it to her. 'I'm just not up to this, Lazzaro. Hot one minute, cold the next...I don't understand why sometimes you choose to hate me...'

'Look, can we just start again?' His usually steady voice was rapid, interrupting her. 'Can we forget all that has been and start again?'

'Can we?' She truly didn't know.

'I can.' Lazzaro nodded.

'And you won't hate me again in the morning?'

'I never hated you…' Lazzaro said slowly. 'How can I hate you when all I do is want you?'

But it wasn't enough. She knew that, *knew* that, but she couldn't question him, didn't want to question him further, because his mouth was on hers, and it was surely sweeter than the truth.

His mouth was ravaging hers—his want matching hers—and the earth shifted as he moved closer into her space. She could hear the zipper of her dress as he pulled it down, the chill of air on the small of her back, and she braced herself for his hand on her bottom. At that moment she would have forgiven him for heading down instead of up—only he didn't. Each rib, each space was fingered with such lingering expertise that her panties were a damp mass when finally he found her bra, unhooked it. But instead of removing her top, instead of undressing her, he lowered his head and kissed her through her dress and the lace of her bra, his teeth nibbling round each areola, her dry-clean-only dress neither dry nor clean as still he worked on. His greedy hands pulled her dress down at the straps, and a thousand glass beads cascaded to the floor, crushed beneath their feet in the race to get out of their clothes. But there was no time. Caitlyn was whimpering with need to have her hungry nipple in his mouth, and if he hadn't taken it then she'd have begged.

It hurt.

Oh, but it was a delicious hurt as his mouth stretched her nipple to its greedy length. His lips paused, then he smiled up at her and suckled till it was indecent, till Caitlyn was moaning, her hand fumbling with his trousers, with his belt. One need was satisfied and she was greedy for more now, as still he suckled, trying to get rid of things that didn't matter to reach the things that did.

She was naked from the waist up and flaming from the waist down, but still he paid her breasts lavish attention as he slid her panties down her thighs. And the bed was just a little bit too far, so the dressing table sufficed, the mirror cold against her back, the surface hard against her bottom. But absolutely the pain was worth the gain, and the angled mirrors gave her never-ending views of him as she laid her head on his shoulder. She gazed at their reflection, saw his arms tighten around hers as he slid inside her, could see her thighs wrapped around his waist as she pulled him in closer, see the dint in his buttocks as her hands went there.

'Lazzaro...' she pleaded, and she wasn't looking any more, but sucking, biting on his salty shoulder, dragging her lips as she tried to hold it in.

But thankfully he wasn't taking his time tonight. He was swelling deeper inside her as she coiled into him, and she wasn't sure if it was people in the next room knocking or the thud of the mirror against the wall, didn't even care *where* they were as he arched his body and leant back, as somehow he climbed deeper inside her...as somehow he took just a little bit more than she knew she should give.

And after, when they were in bed, when maybe she should have just left it, bravely she didn't. Boldly, yet terribly tentatively, her fingers traced the length of his jagged raised scar. She watched as he closed his eyes—not gently, but sort of squeezing them together, as if anticipating the hurt her touch would cause, as if the wound was still raw—and Caitlyn knew then that it was.

'What happened here?'

His fingers caught hers, closed around them. Caitlyn was sure he was about to pull her hand away, and mentally kicked herself for asking too much too soon, but instead of pushing her away his fingers straightened her hand out, till it was the cool of her palm pressing against his cheek. And though they'd just made love, though never in her life had she felt so close to another human being, for that atom of time they weren't just close, they were together—his pain hers, her comfort his to have.

The tension permanently etched in his features faded away as she leant forward, soft lips on his wound, trying to kiss away the agony. Her salty tears bathed his scar, but only for a little while. Not roughly, but gently, he pushed her away, turned his face away from hers as she voiced the question again.

'What happened that day, Lazzaro?'

But even though she'd asked, even though she was sure she could deal with it, his voice told her that maybe she couldn't. The hollows of his pain and raw grief were so evident it made her wince, made her close her eyes as, albeit gently, and albeit tenderly, this time he pushed her away with three little words.

'Ask your cousin.'

'Going anywhere?' Brave, but scared, she smiled down at him the next morning.

Two strikes and he was out for good was her unwritten rule—but Lazzaro's eyes weren't avoiding hers this morning. In fact, utterly relaxed, he even managed to make her laugh.

'Just to my room…' His hand was under the sheet, exploring her shamelessly. 'I'll meet you at breakfast and tell you what our plans are until our flight this evening.'

'Go, then…' Caitlyn grinned. She loved him all of the time, but liked him more when he was like this.

'You *know* the only place I'm going,' Lazzaro drawled, making her gasp as he did something indecent, 'is here.'

'How was your night?' Alberto Mancini beamed over them.

The mood was rather more relaxed as his intimate, though very well-bred friends gathered for a lavish breakfast.

'I trust you were comfortable?'

'The bed was a bit lumpy,' Lazzaro teased goodnaturedly. 'But for a second-rate hotel—not bad!'

'Come,' said Alberto. 'I am going to speak with the minister and his lovely wife—and before I make my speech, can I borrow your boss?'

'Of course.' Caitlyn smiled, swallowing hard when Bonita slipped into Lazzaro's vacant seat.

'Thank you,' she said, 'for your discretion yesterday. I am so glad last night is over. If it wasn't for Lazzaro, I don't know how we'd have got through.' She gave a tired smile. 'I know that Lazzaro tells his PA everything.'

'Not this one…' Caitlyn started, but her voice faded as Alberto took the floor, greeting his guests, thanking them for coming. That much Caitlyn understood, but after a moment he handed the microphone to Lazzaro, and she watched as he spoke on his friend's behalf. Whatever he said made everyone laugh—only not Bonita. Her hand was dry as it reached for Caitlyn's.

'Thank God for Lazzaro...' Bonita said in a strangled whisper. 'Alberto is forgetting names, slurring his words sometimes—I did not want him to look a fool, or for people to think he was drunk, so I asked Lazzaro to stick by him...to cover for his memory lapses...' She dabbed at her cheek with a handkerchief, then saw Caitlyn's shocked expression, and for a second it was Bonita consoling Caitlyn.

'You really didn't know? Lazzaro never told you?'

'I thought...' Caitlyn winced in misery, but Bonita actually laughed.

'What *must* you have thought? Oh, but you are new—you would not know what a wonderful man he is just yet.'

Oh, but she was starting to.

'Alberto is sick,' Bonita explained, her voice brave, but her hand slipping into Caitlyn's again, and clinging onto it as she spoke. 'He is to start treatment as soon as possible, but we want to wait—his daughter gets married soon. Just two more weeks is all we are asking,' Bonita rasped. 'If we can just hold it together for two weeks, till his daughter gets married—*then* we can tell everyone.'

Just for a second Caitlyn met Lazzaro's gaze—guilt and regret were washing over her for her harsh assumptions—for thinking the very worst of him. And she was proud too—proud that even last night, with his back to the wall, he hadn't betrayed his friend's trust.

Hadn't told her the truth when it would surely have been so much easier for him.

CHAPTER NINE

'I WISH you'd told me,' Caitlyn said, wondering how the sky could be so blue and the sun could be out, yet it was so cold as they emerged from the hotel. Finally she was to be treated to a real glimpse of the Eternal City…

'It wasn't my place to tell.'

'So you let me think the worst?'

'You chose to think the worst,' Lazzaro pointed out.

'So do you…' It was the hardest thing she'd ever said, offering a fact that was only based on her feeling. 'Lazzaro, surely it's something we should talk about—?'

'Not today.' He silenced her with a kiss. 'Let's just enjoy today.'

There were only a few hours till they headed back to Australia—and though she'd braced herself for coldness, for distance between them, it was anything but. And once breakfast was over, he'd suggested they spend the day wandering Rome.

They stopped in tiny cafés, where Caitlyn practised her appalling Italian and Lazzaro winced in apology at the waiters. She took her camera out at every turn. She ate chestnuts out of the bag, and, even though they were possibly the most disgusting thing she had ever tasted, somehow she finished the lot.

'You should get a memento...' Lazzaro was steering her towards shops with names that were more likely to be represented by fakes in her wardrobe. But even though she'd probably rue it later, even though her friends would never understand, and even though they were the most glamorous she'd ever seen, the boutiques around Piazza di Spagna held little interest for Caitlyn—even when Lazzaro prompted her to choose a bag, 'or shoes, or whatever it is that women like.'

'I like walking.'

So they did—moving away from the shops to the Spanish Steps themselves, where Caitlyn, just a little bit shy, pulled out her camera again and asked Lazzaro to take her photo. Blushing, she shook her head when a cheerful tourist offered to take the camera and take a photo of the two of them.

'Thank you, but no...'

'Why not?' Lazzaro laughed at her blush as they walked on. 'Don't you want to remember us together today?'

She would *always* remember today—with or without a photo—would always remember walking around the most stunning of cities with the most stunning of men. Would always remember the thrill of the feel of his hand slipping into hers. For a little while they were just another couple—another pair of lovers wandering the streets talking about nothing and everything, watching the world go by—and for today at least it was a nicer world with the other there.

She didn't need her tourist guide to know they were at the Trevi Fountain—didn't need to ask what Lazzaro was doing when he rummaged in his pocket and offered her a coin.

'You know the saying…' His hand was absolutely steady as he offered her the coin. 'If you throw in a coin, it is guaranteed you will be back—take it.'

Only she didn't know if she wanted to.

No matter how beautiful the city was, it could never be as beautiful as it was today—and Caitlyn truly didn't know if she wanted to come back if it wasn't with him. She wanted to remember it just as it was.

Oh, today they were fine, between the sheets they were fine—when it was just them, just the two of them and nothing else came close, then there was nothing better— only somehow she knew it couldn't last. Their world was a fragile bubble that somehow couldn't survive the elements.

'Take it.'

And finally she did—watched as it sank to the bottom and joined a million other wishes—closed her eyes as he put his arm around her—leant on him for just a little while longer—tried to convince herself they were really okay— that the little bit they had was enough to sustain them in the real world….

CHAPTER TEN

THEY *did* have enough to sustain them.

As long as they were careful—as they long as they weren't greedy and lived solely in the moment—didn't look at the past or glimpse the future. As long as he made love to her at night and kissed her in the morning—as long as they didn't address the issues—*then* they were okay.

'Hi, Mum!' Sitting at her desk a week after they returned, Caitlyn couldn't keep the happiness from her voice. But she checked it a touch as the thought of her mother's problems brought her rapidly back down to earth. 'How are things?'

'Great!' Her unusually effusive responsive had Caitlyn frowning.

'Great?' Caitlyn checked.

'The lawyer just called—we've won!' Her voice broke then, laughter turning to tears. 'We can keep the house.'

And even though their lawyer had said over and over that Cheryl had no case, that her grandfather's wishes had been clear, that her mother's contribution to the home had been documented, to have it confirmed, to know that it was finally over brought such a sweet flood of release that only then did Caitlyn actually realise the strain she had been under.

'Thank you…' Helen cried into the phone. 'I know what I've put you through. I know it wasn't fair to ask you to take on such a huge mortgage…'

'I didn't have to, though!' Caitlyn smiled.

'But you would have,' her mother pointed out.

'And you did,' Caitlyn said softly. 'You did it for your dad, remember?'

'Why wouldn't they have a bridal registry?' Lazzaro was utterly perplexed as, smiling, she walked into his office. 'Of all the stupid things… What are *you* looking so happy about?'

'I just am.'

She'd never told him about her problems. The sum of money that was so huge to her was a drop in the ocean to Lazzaro, and worse for Caitlyn than him not understanding would have been the prospect of him sorting it out—the idea of somehow being beholden to him. As she took Alberto Mancini's daughter's wedding invitation from him, her smile widened. 'I actually think it's nice that they don't have a registry! It means that people like you can't just click their mouse and have their gift dispatched—it means pompous, arrogant people like you actually have to stop and think about what their friends might want for a wedding gift.'

'They are not my friends.' Lazzaro flicked his hands skywards in exasperation. 'She is the *daughter* of a *friend* of mine—a daughter I have not seen for five years, and I have never even *met* her fiancé. How could I possibly know what they want?'

'Well, you'd better think fast,' Caitlyn said cheekily. 'You fly out on Thursday.'

'Come with me.'

'I can't.' Caitlyn groaned. 'I know you're used to it, Lazzaro, and I know we'll be travelling first-class and I can sleep all the way there—I know all that—but honestly…'

'Okay—I get it…' he relented. 'You need your weekend off.'

'I do.'

And, oh, she did. Just needed a weekend to catch up with friends, to sleep in, to see her mum, to read… Lazzaro had said the job would be demanding, and it was, but add to the most demanding of jobs the most demanding of lovers, and Caitlyn was actually looking forward to a weekend of…nothing.

'So you're definitely not coming.' He gave a regretful smile, then shot her a look that had her in flames. 'Which means I won't be either.'

'You'll survive!' Caitlyn gave a saucy wink.

'I guess I'll have to—but for your sins *you* can choose the gift.' He waved away her protest. 'That is why us pompous, arrogant people have assistants—off you go.'

What did you get someone who had everything? Someone you'd never met, someone who… Racking her brains, Caitlyn trailed the shops, wishing she knew enough to come back with something fabulous and meaningful… Why the hell *didn't* they have a bridal registry? Caitlyn thought as she trudged back a couple of hours later to the hotel—defeated and empty-handed, but still smiling. She'd splurged on a bottle of champagne—she would bung it in the fridge at work and open it the second she got home tonight…

'Ms Bell?' Caught unawares, Caitlyn started at the sound of her name, swinging around and frowning at the woman who promptly thrust a microphone under her nose. 'What do you have to say about the rumours that Lazzaro Ranaldi is dating his rival's wife?'

'Pardon…?' Like a rabbit in headlights, Caitlyn froze as she saw the television camera zooming in on her.

'We have it from a reliable source that Mr Ranaldi has been seeing rather a lot of Bonita Mancini—we have photos of them at lunch, and we have heard that he spent the afternoon of Mr Mancini's sixtieth birthday with her. And that night he put him to bed drunk and then consoled his wife—'

'No!' Caitlyn's denial was immediate, her mind whirring. It was just a week to the wedding—all Bonita had wanted was for her stepdaughter to marry before hearing the news that her father was terminally ill—and now somehow the press had twisted what few facts they had into something sordid.

'But Mrs Mancini *did* spend the afternoon in Mr Ranaldi's suite…?'

Caitlyn didn't answer. Two spots of colour were burning on her cheeks, and she wished she was better prepared for this. She knew, as Lazzaro's assistant, that she should have just walked away at the outset, should have said nothing, should neither have confirmed or denied.

'And she did spend the night with Mr Ranaldi?'

'No.' Caitlyn was adamant now. 'She didn't.'

'How can you be sure? My sources state that—'

'I'm quite sure Mr Ranaldi didn't spend the night with Mrs Mancini.' She knew even as she said it that she would regret it, but knew she had no choice. She had to quash the rumours now.

'And you're sure because...?'

And even if it was a rushed decision it wasn't blind—Caitlyn could still feel Bonita's hand in hers, feel the love that everyone denied she had for her husband, and she knew that even if it wasn't what was wanted, it was something she had to do.

'I'm sure he wasn't with Mrs Mancini, because Lazzaro Ranaldi spent the night with me.'

Turning, she walked away—away from the hotel—disappearing into the crowds, wondering how she would face him, wondering what Lazzaro's reaction would be when he heard what she'd done...

Never for a second did she imagine the truth.

The frown on his face as he watched after his sister rang him on his mobile and told him to turn on the news, the black anger as he heard the reporter's allegations.

His hand jerked to his desk phone, to ring Bonita and warn her, but his grim face broke into a smile as he heard her blurt out her admission—as Caitlyn Bell dragged them out to face the world.

'She's lovely...' a forgotten Antonia said down his mobile.

'Not exactly discreet, though!' Lazzaro pointed out, but he was still smiling.

'So what are you going to do about it, brother?'

He didn't answer straight away, just stared out of his vast window down to the city streets below, knowing she was down there—imagining her embarrassment, her horror at what she had done, and wanting to soothe it.

To tell her it was okay.

To tell her that *they* were okay.

For the first time in the longest time he breathed

without pain. For just a moment or two Lazzaro felt peace creep somewhere into his soul—glimpsed a future that was bearable.

'Lazzaro?' Antonia pushed excitedly, smiling herself when her brother spoke again, then hung up the phone.

'*We'll* let you know.'

But numbing a toothache didn't make the rot go away. Even if the pain was deadened for a while, still the damage went on inside—weakening the roots, prolonging the inevitable, till it erupted in an agony that couldn't be escaped. And then extraction was preferable to treatment.

As Lazzaro clicked off the phone, as he wondered if he should just ring her now and tell her to stop hiding, the door opened and his smile faded—as the one woman on God's earth he'd hoped never to see again walked into his office and plunged him out of his momentary oasis and straight back into hell.

CHAPTER ELEVEN

'WHAT the hell do *you* want?' Lazzaro sneered out the words, contempt blazing in his eyes as he stared at the person he hated most in the world. 'Who let you in?'

'Audrey let me up—she still remembers me.' Roxanne flicked back her dark curls, strode across his office as if she owned it. ' I thought we should clear the air…'

'Clear the air?' Lazzaro spat. 'The air stinks when you're here. The stench of you makes me—'

'Better out than in!' Roxanne's red lips smiled sweetly at him. 'I saw Caitlyn on the news—she's good, I have to admit that. When she sets her mind on something she always gives it her best.'

'What?' Lazzaro snapped, then shook his head—because he didn't want to hear it, didn't need to hear, didn't want to be in the same room as Roxanne for even a second. 'Get out, Roxanne—you make me sick.'

'Did you fund her lawyers, Lazzaro?'

'Lawyers?' Narrowed eyes watched his smudge of a frown appear. 'I don't know what you're talking about.'

'You mean she didn't tell you? Did sweet little Caitlyn forget to mention when she had her legs wrapped around you that, even though her mother had freeloaded off my grandfather for years, not satisfied with living there, because Helen Bell couldn't afford to raise her bastard child herself, even after he died they refused to move out, that they're refusing to give my mother her fair share?'

'You're full of it,' Lazzaro sneered. 'You couldn't tell the truth on your deathbed.' A thud of papers on his desk held his gaze for a second. Legal letters. He pointedly pushed them away, but he was rattled now—and she knew it.

'Why would I lie?' Roxanne stared at him, those blue eyes the same as Caitlyn's, but utterly, utterly steady—not even a hint of a flicker as they pinned him—and at that moment Lazzaro truly didn't know what was real and what wasn't. Whether it was Roxanne looking him in the eye and lying, or Caitlyn who couldn't.

'Knowing Caitlyn, you were probably her plan B.'

'What do you want, Roxanne?' He gave a mirthless laugh. 'As if I didn't already know.'

'I want what my mother's entitled to.'

'If she's so entitled the courts would have seen it that way.'

'Unlike Caitlyn, I don't have access to limitless funds to pay lawyers—unlike my cousin, I'm not screwing a Ranaldi!' Her face twisted with bitterness. 'You really think she's all sweetness and light, don't you? You're so bloody quick to make out I'm the bitch here.'

'That goes without saying.'

'You know, she always said she'd get you in the end…' Roxanne watched his jaw tighten, but he shook his head.

'You're a liar, Roxanne,' Lazzaro hissed. 'You're just rotten to the core.'

'I can still see her the day before Luca died, with that

stupid photo of you she carried around, rattling on about how you'd given her a lift home and how she was already a shoe-in.' Watching his face pale, watching as a muscle pounded in his cheek, Roxanne was sure that she had him. 'Anyway I'm tired of playing with lawyers. Journalists are far more fun—they actually pay to listen—and I'm sure they'd be delighted to hear the full story about Luca!'

'How much do you want?' Pulling out his chequebook, somehow Lazzaro's hands were steady—but his face was as white and as cold as marble.

'My mother's share.' Roxanne spat out the figure, her blue eyes boring into his as he wrote not the sum she quoted, but two *very* choice little words. He watched her greedy hand snatch the cheque from his, watched her mouth twist in rage as she read his none too polite request for her to leave.

'Talk to your journalist,' Lazzaro jeered as she screwed it up and hurled it at him. 'But, as you pointed out, I have limitless funds—and if you do talk I will spend whatever it takes to ensure you never see a single cent. I tell you now that I will devote the rest of my life to making yours hell. Never threaten me again, Roxanne, and never try to bribe me. I don't deal with dirt!'

'Oh, but you do, Lazzaro—and, just like your brother, you're too foolish to realise!' She turned at the door, excising her jealousy, her venom, her hatred, with every spiteful word. 'The only difference between Caitlyn and me is that she chose more wisely. My cousin happened to hitch her star to the *right* wagon!'

Her smell lingered long after she'd left—a sickly-sweet perfume that seeped into his pores, the same sickly scent she'd had on that day…here, right here. Sinking into his seat, he closed his eyes, waited for the nausea to recede—only it didn't.

'Luca…' He closed his eyes. He could see his brother's face. The face that had always been the same as his was different, and it wasn't just the years of agony, regret and bitterness that had wreaked changes… Lazzaro's fingers ran along the jagged line on his cheekbone—the numb knot of flesh, the scar that Luca had inflicted on his last day on earth.

Still numb.

Memories he'd spent more than two years quashing were bobbing to the surface now, and no matter how quickly he pushed one down, another popped up. He was locked in a shooting range—each image a target, each picture shot down, only to reappear stronger and more relentless than before.

Two years on the pain was still just too big to deal with—but, like an anaesthetic wearing off, sensation was starting to creep in, raw wounds that weren't ready to be exposed yet were starting to make themselves known.

Only he didn't want to feel—didn't want to face it.

But that was exactly what Caitlyn did—she made him face the impossible.

As soon as she walked into his office, Caitlyn realised he couldn't have heard her knock. Knew, somehow, that she was glimpsing a side to Lazzaro Ranaldi that he would prefer no one, not even his lover, to see.

His head was in his hands, his shoulders slumped, his complexion grey beneath his fingers. She should turn, Caitlyn thought, walk out and knock again, save them both the embarrassment of explanations. But in that frozen second he looked up.

'I'm sorry...' She spilled the words out. 'What I said to the press—I know it was indiscreet, I know I should have called you straight after. I was just so embarrassed...'

His expression gave her nothing, no clue at all, and even though he was looking at her it was as if he was looking straight through her—as if he wasn't even hearing her.

'I was just put on the spot. I knew how important it was that it didn't come out about Alberto, what it would do to him if there was even a hint of an affair...'

The clap of his hands was like the crack of a whip, making her jump, making her eyes widen in confusion as it continued—as Lazzaro leant back in his chair and gave a slow hand-clap, on and on, as she stood there mute.

'Bravo, Caitlyn.' He'd stopped clapping now, but still it echoed in her head, stinging her ears as he stared at her now—stared at her as if he hated her. 'You're wasted as a PA. You should try your hand on the stage after I fire you.'

'Because of what I said to the press—?' she started, but her words were cut off by his.

'Don't play a player, Caitlyn. Especially not one as good as me.'

'A player? I don't know what you mean.'

'She's still playing...' Lazzaro jeered to an absent crowd. 'Hey, why the champagne, Caitlyn? Come on—get out the glasses...'

'I don't know what you mean...'

Tears were pricking her eyes, her head spinning, but he pulled two from the shelf and grabbed the bottle, popping the cork against the wall as a sob escaped her lips.

'What are we celebrating?' Lazzaro smiled, but his eyes were black with hatred. 'Your little announcement about us to the press? Or the fact you've screwed your cousin out of her inheritance?'

'How do you know about that?' Caitlyn's teeth were chattering now.

'I make it my business to know. Come on, Caitlyn.' He pressed a glass into her hand. 'At least you won't need to use plan B.'

'Plan B?'

'Your *cousin*—' he spat the word out '—the one you omitted to mention, the one who just happened to be dating my brother when he died, just paid me a little visit…'

'Please, you don't know what she's like…' Caitlyn begged. 'You don't know what she's capable of…'

'Oh, but I do!' he roared. 'How many chances have I given you? How many times have I tried to ignore your lies?' His voice was ominously calm now. 'So innocent…' He chinked his glass against hers. 'My innocent little virgin, who just happened to be on the pill.'

'They're for my spots…'

She shuddered. She didn't have to justify herself to him—didn't have to tell him anything. Her shaking hand placed her glass on the table, spilling champagne. She was trying to leave, only her legs wouldn't move.

'You lie to the bank, lie on your résumé. It comes so naturally I'm sure you don't even know when you're doing it. Hey, Caitlyn—when you told Roxanne you'd get me, did you really believe it? When you cut out my photo from a magazine…?'

Her cheeks were burning, humiliation seeping into her

bone marrow. It was like being stuck in a nightmare, her mouth opening to speak but the words not coming out.

'When you set your little cap at the big prize, did you honestly think you'd win? Did you honestly think I wouldn't see through you? Did you really think that by announcing things to the press you could push me into marrying you? Didn't you realise that I'd only ever marry a woman I love—and that was never, could never, be you.'

'I'm going.' Her voice was a mere croak, her legs like jelly, but at least they were moving.

'Good!' Lazzaro snarled, and he was already ahead of her, brushing past her as he stormed out. 'Get your things and then get the hell out. You've got five minutes—I don't want a single thing of yours left behind. You make me sick.'

'I hate you!' she screamed out at him. Her voice was back now, and there was agony, truth, in every word. 'And I wish to God I'd never fallen in love with you!'

She watched his shoulders stiffen, could see his knuckles white on the handle of the door for just a second—and then he slammed it closed behind him.

There would be time for tears later—but right now, after her outburst, she was numb, frozen, mute. She shook as she stood in the office, trembling at the task in hand, then moved, heart pounding, on a strange kind of autopilot—picking up her things, her books, her pens, her overnight bag that was permanently packed in case they jetted off at a second's notice... There were things to leave too. She pulled out her purse, put down the credit card, wondered what to do with the phone. But it was too much to think about, too hard to stand and delete messages. Somebody else would have to deal with those.

'You've served your purpose, then?' Malvolio stood in the doorway, and she was too numb to be shocked at the sight of him. 'The great Ranaldi's tossing you out?'

'Your brother-in-law's a bastard!' Caitlyn retorted. Her mind was just not there. Her brain was hypothermic, frozen by Lazzaro's brutal words, all her responses slower, her thought processes functioning at basic survival level.

'I could have told you that and saved you the trouble.' Malvolio came over, smiled down at her sympathetically. 'The Ranaldis are all bastards—or bitches,' he added. 'We're not good enough for any of them...'

Her defences were utterly down. She wasn't seeing the red flags that were waving, wasn't hearing the frantic urgent alert as her brain struggled to hit her warning bell. And then she did. Like a fog horn screaming in the darkness, suddenly she heard it, and panic, fear, was gripping her. Only it was just a little bit too late. She could taste the whisky on the mouth that crushed hers, the putridness of his breath, the blood on her lips. There was hate and anger in him as he wedged his body against her—and she knew, *knew* what was going to happen. Knew that even though she was kicking and screaming, his hate was stronger. And as he slammed her to the ground all she could hope was that it would be quick.

That this hell would soon be over.

CHAPTER TWELVE

WHAT the hell had he done?

Lazzaro paced the lobby, his hand clamped over his mouth, his breath hyperventilating into his hand, as his staff watched on bemused. Glynn the only one with the nerve to approach him.

'Is everything okay, sir?'

He didn't answer—didn't even hear him. His mind was with Caitlyn, hating what he'd done to her. He could see her in his mind's eye, standing frozen as he'd shamed her, humiliated her—and for what?

Because once she'd wanted him?

Because all this time she'd loved him?

It was like an axe splitting his skull open—and he hated himself more as he remembered *that* night they'd first met. Hell, if he'd had a photo of *her,* if *she'd* been in a magazine...

Roxanne was poison—she twisted things, blurred the truth—and she wasn't Caitlyn.

Just as he wasn't Luca, so Roxanne wasn't Caitlyn.

Sweet, trusting Caitlyn—which she was.

She *was!*

He trusted her. For the first time in the longest time he

trusted someone—actually believed in someone—and it truly terrified him.

'Sir?' Glynn's face blurred out of focus. 'Is there anything I can get you?' He could see the worry on his manager's face. 'Malvolio was just looking for you—I said you were in your office. Maybe I could call him for you…?'

'Malvolio!'

He was running now, pounding the button for the lift with his hand. Caitlyn *had* been telling the truth. All along she had been telling the truth—and that meant right now *he'd* left her alone with him.

Never had a lift taken so long. Every second as it sped him upwards felt like an hour. Vainly he parted the sliding doors with his hands in frustration in his haste to get to her, racing through the gap and into the hell he'd created—just in time to see her pushed to the floor.

Ripping him off her, slamming him across the room, he knew someone was looking after him—someone up there was looking after him. Because with every fibre of his being he wanted to slam into Malvolio, to hit him, to rip him a new face. But if he did, he knew he'd kill him.

He'd kill him.

His fingers were somehow pressing the security alert button, and that tiny pause was long enough to regroup, to see her sitting on the floor, hugging her knees, to acknowledge that he'd got there in time. And then he faced the bastard—only Lazzaro wasn't the only one filled with hate. Malvolio had his share too.

Screaming like a demented woman, his eyes bulged in fury. 'You think you're so good. Your whole family thinks it's better—you're users—'

'Shut it.' Lazzaro was in his face, but Malvolio wasn't to be contained.

'You swan around like God on the day of reckoning—judging us, shaming us, humiliating us. No wonder Luca hated you!'

Security was there then, already alerted by Glynn. And Lazzaro's office was a ball of chaos for a while—but only a little while. Lazzaro cleared them all out quickly, for which Caitlyn was grateful—because she didn't want to see Malvolio ever again. She would make statements and all that later. Just not right now.

Sitting on the edge of the plump sofa, holding a tissue to her lip, Caitlyn watched as he closed the door, stared at him as he came over to comfort her—stopped him with her eyes as she delivered her words.

'He's right.'

'Caitlyn—'

'Everything Malvolio said is right.'

'Don't—'

'All I ever did wrong was fall in love with you, and you took something nice, something pure, then turned around and shamed me with it.'

'Don't talk about that now.' His usually strong voice was a croak. 'I need to know that you're okay. Did he hurt you anywhere else, apart from your lip?'

'*He* didn't hurt me!' Caitlyn shouted. 'At least nowhere near as much as you did. You made me feel cheaper and dirtier and more ashamed than Malvolio just did…'

'I'm sorry…' He tried to take her hand but she pulled it away. 'I was coming back to say I was sorry.'

'Well, you were already too late.' On surprisingly steady

legs she stood up. 'I've forgiven you so many times, Lazzaro—and I swear I never will again. I swear that I'll hate you for ever.'

Friends were golden.

Real friends. Because, even if he'd started as a colleague, Glynn *was* actually a friend. He came without question when she buzzed him, put his arm around her and led her out as Lazzaro stood there. He drove her home and poured her some wine and called in the troops—an army of friends who swarmed like butterflies, who held her hand every step of the horrible way and told her over and over, till she almost believed it, that none of this was her fault—that she was absolutely better off without him.

CHAPTER THIRTEEN

Ask your cousin.

During the grim post-mortem that came at the end of any romance—where you bargained with yourself and beat yourself up over the *mistakes* that actually weren't mistakes, were just you—in the sleepless nights when you rang your voicemail just to hear his voice, replaying every conversation in a futile search for the clue that's going to unlock the mystery of what went wrong, Caitlyn actually found one. She heard for the first time not just the agony but the loathing in his voice as he'd said it—felt again his hand pushing hers away as she touched his pain and he shut her out.

'Ask your cousin.'

So she did.

She reacquainted herself with her wardrobe and her make-up bag, and stepped out like a foal on wobbly legs, into a world that seemed just a little too bright and loud, and bravely asked the question she had to.

She'd sworn she'd never go back to him.

Would never set foot in the hotel again, would never be

in the same room with Lazzaro Ranaldi as long as there was a breath left in her.

She'd sat and drunk and cried with friends, had read the self-help books and grudgingly accepted that he just 'wasn't that into her'—she had done all the things a girl had to do when she'd had her heart ripped out and stomped on: rung friends instead of him, deleted his mobile number so she wasn't tempted to text him in the middle of the night, removed him from her inbox. And she'd waited.

Waited to feel better.

To believe that time healed.

That one guy didn't fit all.

That of course there were others.

Millions and millions of others, walking the globe at this very minute...

But there was only one *him*.

Only one man who could literally stop her heart as she walked into the hotel bar and saw him sitting there. Only one man she'd actually have done this for—whether it made her brave or stupid that when he'd called her and asked that they might meet she'd agreed.

For closure.

Closure for him as much as for her.

'Thank you.' It was impossible to look him in the eye when he greeted her—impossible, because if she did she'd start crying. 'Thank you for coming.'

'It's fine.' She'd insisted they meet in the bar, unable to face his office. 'I'm sorry it's so public. I just couldn't face the...'

She couldn't even say it—couldn't stand to go back to the office where it had all happened.

Lazzaro understood. 'I know how you feel.'

'I know you do.' She gave a tight smile, because he must—because she didn't actually know how *he* did it, how he sat in the same office not just where Malvolio had been so vile, but where he'd fought so bitterly with Luca.

Why he put himself through it.

Even if Caitlyn couldn't look him in the eye, still she could see the pain etched on his face. The scar that was gouged on his cheek was red and livid today—as if the hell, the cesspit of demons inside, were all clamouring surfacewards now. She wasn't conceited enough to consider it had anything to do with her—she knew his rivers of pain went far deeper than that.

'How's Antonia?' That wasn't why she was here, they both knew that, but she wanted to know. She cared for the other woman whose life had been upended.

'She's doing very well.' Lazzaro managed a small smile at Caitlyn's surprised expression at his upbeat response. 'She really is. The marriage wasn't good—well, we knew that. But it turned out she knew it too. Not about the affairs, of course…'

'Affairs?'

Lazzaro nodded. 'It would seem that when you stumble on the truth you find a lot of untruths.'

'Who said that?' Caitlyn frowned as she tried to recall.

'I did.' Lazzaro gave a tight smile. 'Very Zen of me.'

God, why did he—*how* could he—still make her laugh? How, on this, the blackest of days, in the midst of an impossible conversation, when nothing about this was easy or right, could he, even if for just a second, manage to eke out a laugh?

'She really is okay,' Lazzaro continued. 'It turns out that

she had wanted to end it for a long time—only she didn't know how, didn't feel she had enough reason to walk out on her marriage.'

'Now she has.'

'She is sorry for what happened, and concerned for you too.'

'She doesn't blame me?' Tears that had been held firmly in check couldn't be contained now. A big fat one was rolling down her cheek, and she quickly wiped it away—but it was a pointless exercise, because when he answered her, when this usually distant, emotionally absent man spoke, the softness, the tenderness in his voice, was so unexpected, so laced with the right words, it lacerated her.

Not just what he said, but the fact that it was him saying it.

'You have nothing to feel guilty for. You did nothing wrong, Caitlyn. Antonia knows that, and so must you.'

'I do know that.' She nodded, because now—hearing him say it, knowing Antonia had said it—finally she did.

'I should have taken your first complaint more seriously…'

'No!' She shook her head, because that really was pointless. 'It's done now. I'm just glad that Antonia's okay.'

'She is. She said…' His voice trailed off and Caitlyn frowned.

'Said what?'

'It doesn't matter.' Oh, but it did to Caitlyn. But he shook his head, that part of the conversation clearly over. Which brought them to the next, and Lazzaro swallowed hard before he spoke again. 'I owe you an explanation.'

'You do?'

A muscle was pounding in his cheek, his face was moist with perspiration and his tongue moved to moisten dry lips. When that didn't work, Caitlyn watched as he drained his drink in one gulp. She could almost feel his fight or flight response, knew that he might just stand up and walk out. Because she was feeling it too—was sitting there with her neck so rigid, her nerves so taut, that at any moment she could walk out too—just not go ahead with this appalling conversation.

Only Lazzaro didn't get up and walk out. He sat there and faced it, and so too must Caitlyn.

'After I offered you the job I found out you were Roxanne's cousin. From that moment on…'

'You were waiting for me to reveal my true colours?'

Bitter with regret, he nodded. 'I didn't want to like you, knew that I must never trust you…only more and more I did. When Roxanne came that day, told me about your legal battle when you hadn't even mentioned it…'

'What would you have done, Lazzaro?'

'I would have helped.'

'No.' Caitlyn shook her head. 'That would have proved to you that I was using you. My mother grew up in that house. Apart from a couple of years when she had me, she's lived there all her life. She's renovated it, decorated it, furnished it…'

'You don't have to explain…'

'You've made it so that I do,' Caitlyn pointed out. 'It wasn't about money—and it wasn't even about the house. It was about her home. My mum offered to Cheryl to leave it in her will equally to both Roxanne and I…'

'I misjudged you.'

'You did.'

'I have misjudged many things—you see, Roxanne and I...'

His hand tightened on the glass he was holding, and she wanted, *how* she wanted, to reach out and hold it, to comfort him, console him somehow as he served up his wretched past. Only it wasn't her place any more.

Never had been her place, Caitlyn realised, because Lazzaro had seen to that.

Lazzaro had refused to let anyone in.

'There was an incident,' Lazzaro bravely started. 'One that didn't reach the newspapers. When he came to my office, I told Luca that I had arranged rehab for him, that I would stand by him so long as he made some attempt to sort himself out—only he wouldn't go.' His voice was surprisingly calm—resigned, even. 'He just wouldn't accept there was a problem—but everyone could see it. His drinking, the gambling—he had debts everywhere. I was running around cleaning up the messes he was leaving behind him, and I just couldn't do it for ever...'

'Of course you couldn't.' Caitlyn's voice was strong. 'He had to acknowledge it before he could get help...' But that wasn't the issue today, and they both knew it.

'Roxanne turned up as he was leaving. He sort of pushed past her and knocked her over. She was upset—we were both upset. I helped her up and she started crying, so I comforted her...' It was as if he were giving a police statement, his voice unnervingly even as he reeled off the appalling train of events, delivered brutal words in an impassive tone. 'I told her I was sorry for all Luca was putting her through...'

It was Caitlyn whose throat was dry now, and she was

grateful when he picked up her bottle of water and topped up her glass. She took a sip, but just about missed her mouth because her hands were trembling so much.

'I started kissing her, telling her I would treat her so much better than Luca... Things were getting a bit out of hand, and then...'

'Luca came back?' Caitlyn finished for him.

'Luca caught us.'

'That's when he hit you?'

'He went crazy...said that I had always been the better one, the older one, the smarter one, that I had screwed up his life, that I had taken everything good from him and now I was taking the woman he loved, that I'd humiliated him over and over...' He pinched the bridge of his nose, screwed his eyes closed as he relieved that hell. 'He said quite a lot more than just that.'

'I'm sure he did.'

'Then he stormed off. And I went to the hospital to get stitched.'

Caitlyn watched, tears streaming down her face, as he gagged out an expletive and this strongest of men almost fell apart.

And for the first time he faced it.

As if a fist had gone into his stomach, he let out a shudder of breath, almost doubled up in agony—and he told her. Or did he? Because he truly didn't know if he was talking it or living it again. At that point he wasn't sitting with Caitlyn, he was back pacing in that hospital cubicle, a wad of gauze pressed to his cheek, so incredibly angry he was climbing the walls. He just wanted the hell out of there, wanted to get stitched so he could go and find Luca, to make things right, to fix his brother. Then everything had just faded into oblivion. Aghast, he'd watched as a stretcher whizzed past his cubicle. It was as if he was looking at himself in a mirror, and he'd seen the horror on his own face mistaken by a nurse, who'd pulled his curtain tightly closed. Only Lazzaro had opened it, striding into the resuscitation area despite the protests of the staff. Their angry shouts had been dim in his ears, theirs the shocked expressions as they'd looked down at the body they were working on and seen it was the mirror image of this intruder who had marched in. And he had seen the wretchedness in the doctors' eyes as they'd realised he was his twin.

'I'm so sorry.'

Paltry words that had been delivered by a doctor even before Antonia had arrived.

He hadn't even needed a local anaesthetic when they'd sutured him—his whole body had been numb with pain as he'd lain on the hospital trolley and the needle had slid in and out of his flesh.

'I'm so sorry.'

Paltry words that had been delivered hours later, as he'd held his brother's cold blue hand, had stared at a face that might as well have been his—had felt as if it *was* his.

'I knew he was dead the moment I saw him...' The tirade that had spewed from his mouth abated a touch, and still Caitlyn listened. 'I knew he was dead, and that nothing they were going to do would bring him back. It was over by the time Antonia arrived, and then my mother...'

'Roxanne too?' Caitlyn checked, and he nodded.

'Antonia called her. She didn't know at that point what had happened.'

'But you told her?'

'Roxanne did.' Lazzaro let out a long breath. 'She was hysterical. She said that we'd as good as killed him, that if I hadn't come on to her, that if he hadn't caught us...' His skin was grey, the lines around his eyes so dark they looked as if they might have been pencilled in. 'He came back, Caitlyn. God, he came back—and maybe he was going to get help. Maybe if we hadn't been—'

'Maybe he'd forgotten his car keys,' Caitlyn snapped back, surprising even herself with her bitterness. But she was cross—cross with Luca, the Saint Luca Ranaldi he had somehow become, the man who in death had been excused his mistakes, exempted by his brother, by his family, for his appalling leading role in all of this—who'd had so much and been so careless, not just with himself, but with the happiness of those who'd loved him. 'Maybe he'd come back to borrow some more money, or to tell you where to get off.'

'Get off?' Lazzaro frowned. Even if his English was excellent, sometimes he missed a point—but not this time, because Caitlyn wouldn't let him.

'I could put it far less politely—but I think you know what I mean. So, what did your family say?'

'A lot. My mother was hysterical—she hit me...' His voice was void of emotion now—detached, even. 'She actually tore some of the stitches I had just had... Antonia vomited, told me she would hate me for ever, would hate Roxanne too—I told them it wasn't her fault...' He gave a mirthless laugh. 'There are a lot of people who will hate me for ever...hell isn't going to be lonely.'

'I don't hate you, Lazzaro.' She looked at him for just an atom of time, saw the dart in his eyes, the tiny flicker of relief on his tired face. 'Maybe I did at the time, or maybe I just said it to hurt you, but I don't actually hate you now.'

'Thank you.'

Which led to another tear—but only one. What she had to say, what she had to hear, was just too important to lose to emotion. 'That's why you and Roxanne didn't carry on seeing each other afterwards?' Caitlyn continued, watching him, watching every flicker of his reaction. 'Just too much guilt?'

'Of course.'

'Of course,' Caitlyn repeated in a clipped voice, watching again as he frowned at her response. 'I don't believe you, Lazzaro.'

'What are you talking about?'

And for the first time since she'd sat down she *did* manage to look him in the eye and hold it—was able to stare into those dark liquid pools. Because, unlike Lazzaro, she had nothing more to hide now—nothing she couldn't or wouldn't reveal. Hell, she'd already told him she loved him, and had accepted his rejection. Funny, though, that through it all, dignity prevailed—that she, Caitlyn Bell, was actually incredibly strong.

'You're lying.'

'Lying!' His mouth opened incredulously. 'I've been more honest with you than I've ever been. I've told you, *told* you what happened, and you have the gall to sit there and tell me—'

'That you're lying!' Caitlyn finished for him, shouting the words almost, not caring who was watching, who was listening.

'I spoke to Roxanne.' She hurled the words at him. 'I went to the woman I hate more than anyone in the world and I asked *her* what happened *that* day.'

'What did she tell you?'

'The same as you.'

She watched his frown, saw the confusion in his tired eyes.

'Roxanne's a liar—we both know that,' Caitlyn spat, furious not with him, but *for* him. No, she conceded, her mind racing at a million miles an hour, furious *with* him too—for the agony, for the self-infliction of such pain, such guilt. 'And you're a bloody liar, Lazzaro, and you're still making excuses for Luca, still cleaning up the mess he made.'

She stood up, hardly able to believe what she was doing—that she was walking out, walking out when perhaps he needed her the most, that she was furious when perhaps he needed calm. But she couldn't help it—couldn't contain what she was feeling within the parameters that might better fit.

'After everything that's happened, after all I've been through—*with* you, *for* you—you can sit there and look me in the eye and bloody well lie to me. If, after all that, you can still hold back the most essential piece of yourself, then—you know what? I don't actually want the rest.'

'Caitlyn!'

His voice barked at her to come back, ordered her to turn around and not walk out. But she *did* walk out, and she did what you're not supposed to—Caitlyn looked back, just once, and she was actually glad that she had. She saw him sitting there, set in stone, frozen, immutable, and by choice completely alone, by choice refusing to get angry, refusing to see his brother for what he was, refusing to grab at life and move on. It was all the impetus she needed to walk faster—to shake her head in contempt and get the hell out of there. She was walking so fast she was almost running.

She could hear the frantic clipping of her shoes on the polished marble as she dashed through the foyer crying, not in pain but in anger, and she heard him run behind her, tempted, so tempted, to slap him as he grabbed her wrist and spun her around.

'How?' His eyes were livid, his question a howl. 'How do you know?'

'Because I know *you*.' She jabbed the fingers on her free hand into his chest. 'I know you're a callous bastard, and I know that you've got a few scruples missing, but I know, *I know,* that you'd never, ever have stooped that low.'

'How?' He said it again, not livid now, more bewildered. 'How could you know that?'

'You already know that I love you...' Tears were coursing down her face. 'What you've consistently failed to see, though, is that I'm actually a nice person—and I happen to have very good taste...' She even managed a smile as she said it—could smile because *he* actually smiled a bit. 'And I have my standards, and I trust myself, and I just don't think I'd have fallen so hard for someone I couldn't trust. Someone who wouldn't do it to a friend leads me to believe that he would never, *ever* have done it to his own brother.'

'Not here...' His voice was urgent as he glanced around at the lobby—the lobby where they'd started this journey and should probably end it.

Only she couldn't. She conceded one final demand and nodded as he gestured to the lift, joined him as they headed towards the office—and it actually didn't bother her as much as she'd thought it would. Lazzaro's issues were somehow overriding hers.

'Roxanne did come on to me—and I was pushing her off.' He spoke even as the lift took them skywards. They were standing at either side, staring at the door rather than looking at each other. 'I told her to get off—and I am using your polite expression here.' She did look over to him then, and even if it wasn't a big one, there was a small smile as somehow they slipped into their own world, their own language, the bit that was just about them. 'She was all over me—saying she'd always wanted me—she dated Malvolio too, you know…'

The lift door sliding open went unnoticed. Caitlyn was stunned at this revelation, yet as they walked into his office she knew it somehow made sense.

'That was how she met Luca?' Caitlyn asked.

'Malvolio was her ticket to Luca.'

'Unlike me.' She gave a tight shrug. 'I just went straight to the top.'

'Never,' Lazzaro said seriously. 'Never again will I compare you to her.'

'She was even a horrible little girl…' Caitlyn rolled her eyes and let out an angry breath. 'Always messing up my things, breaking my toys—anything I had she wanted. You know, I'm not excusing Malvolio…' Caitlyn was thinking more than talking, thinking out loud. 'But you can see now why he'd hate you so—hate me too…'

'I don't want to think of him at all,' Lazzaro interrupted. 'I don't even want to try and understand his twisted mind.'

And she didn't want to think about him either. She wanted to think about Lazzaro, wanted to try and finally understand.

'Why didn't you tell your family what really happened?'

'So I could humiliate Luca all over again?' Lazzaro shook his head. 'How, with his body still warm, could I tell my family that he had nothing? That the one good thing he thought he had in his life—?'

'So you took the blame for him?' Caitlyn said. 'You let them think that it was you coming on to Roxanne instead of the other way around?'

'Luca said that I took everything from him—maybe I did. I just couldn't take that last piece.'

'Luca blamed you because that's what he did best— blamed you for his mess because it was easier than blaming himself, easier than admitting he had a problem, easier than facing up that his *life* was a mess. Luca knew what had happened as much as *I* know what happened,' Caitlyn responded firmly, nodding her head as he shook his. 'Hell, yes, he was jealous, and he probably wanted to think it was you, but he knew—he knew exactly what happened that day. He just didn't want to face it—the same way he didn't want to face anything…'

'You really think he knew?'

'Absolutely.' And she watched as her words sank in, watched him blink as he opened his eyes to the truth, and it was like watching the clock go back, as if a great, filthy weight was being lifted.

'Oh, Caitlyn…'

He was holding her, holding her so tight, kissing her face, kissing her tears, his hands everywhere—and even if he didn't love her, would never love her, even if she should just push him off, she couldn't. She would rather end it like this than the way it had ended before—would give him this because she needed it too, needed to feel him one more time.

Urgent, frantic sex *was* a great balm. His hands were pushing up her skirt even as hers grappled with his buckle. His mouth was hot on her neck, biting, bruising, thrilling. Lowering her to the floor, he was pushing her, but somehow supporting her, tearing at her stockings, her panties, and Caitlyn's want was as prevalent as his. Pushing down his trousers, feeling his taut buttocks, she was holding him, holding the bit of him that she needed, wanted, adored—and it was beautiful—and it belonged inside her.

With each delicious thrust he called out her name, and somehow he was kissing her too, kissing her, licking her. His shoulders were over her and she was watching him, watching him and trying to capture him, to remember this for ever—and he *had* held back before, because even if the sex had been wonderful, this was *it*—this wasn't him and her, it was *them*, one person almost. And maybe she *had* held back too, Caitlyn realised. He was so deep inside her, his hips grinding into hers, his body filled with a delicious tension that begged release. Perhaps she had held back, but there was no need to now. He knew she loved him; there were no secrets any more.

'Oh, God, Caitlyn.'

He was calling out her name, and she was calling his, until she couldn't, her throat closing on his name before she screamed it out, every muscle in her body tensing, her legs wrapped around him, her thighs dragging him in as he groaned his gift into her, as she accepted it, breathless, dizzy, but amazingly calm.

Afterwards they lay there—holding each other, staring at the ceiling, waiting for the world to come back.

'Every time I look at this room now, instead of thinking about…' He gave a laugh. But it wasn't funny, and it wasn't sad, it was just better.

'You'll remember me, then?'

'Remember you?' He propped himself up on his elbow, stared down at her. And she wasn't crying, she was able to stare right back, to look at him and love him simply because she did. 'I don't have to remember you—I see you every day.'

'You won't be seeing me every day, Lazzaro. It can't work…'

'What was that, then?'

'Sex.' Caitlyn stared bravely back at him. 'Fabulous, wonderful, and much-needed sex.'

'That wasn't *sex;* that was making love.'

'For me it was.' She gave a tight smile. 'But we all know that *you* don't need to love a woman to—'

'I need to love a woman to make love to her like that…' He frowned down at her. 'You were really going to walk away—after that?' He shook his head in wonder. 'You know, you're a strange girl, Caitlyn…' He kissed the tip of her nose. 'A very good girl who is actually a very bad girl too.'

'But in a good way?' Caitlyn sniffed. She wasn't actually thinking about that now. Her mind was trying to concentrate, to focus on what he'd just said, and her heart that had just slowed down was tripping into tachycardia again as she wrestled with the impossible. 'What you said about loving…?'

'I meant it.'

'Meant what?' Caitlyn asked gingerly, nibbling on her bottom lip, scared to check, scared to ask, in case she didn't like the answer, scared to even hope.

'That I love you.'
'Oh.'
'I love you,' he said again.
'Me?'
'Yes, you.'
'Say it again.'
'I love you.'
'So, what does that mean?'

He smiled down at her, massaging her raw and bruised ego with his eyes and words, and she let him. She needed to hear it. 'That I don't want to be without you—ever.'

'And?'

'That I want to wake up to you in the morning. I want you to annoy the hell out of me. I want you to confuse me—I don't ever want to know you—'

'That doesn't make sense,' Caitlyn interrupted. 'What you meant to say was that you *want* to know me...'

'I know exactly what I am saying. I want to spend the rest of my life trying to work you out. I love that you confuse me.'

'Oh.' Caitlyn smiled, closing her eyes—because she could now, because she knew that when she opened them he'd still be there.

'In fact I fell in love with you a long time ago.'

'When?' Her eyes were still closed, and she was smiling, his words like the warm sun on her face. 'At the hotel? Or was it in Rome...?'

'Shut up and let me talk.'

So she did just that. And she was so, so glad that she did, or she might never have heard his amazing answer.

'On the stroke of midnight the night we first met.'

'It wasn't midnight.' She opened her eyes and her heart to him. She couldn't be quiet, just couldn't contain it. Because it was just so wonderful, so amazing, that he'd felt it too—that love, *their* love, had always been real, that the torch she'd carried for him had had heavy-duty batteries for a very good reason. 'It was ten to twelve. Because I specifically remember looking at the clock. It was at ten minutes to twelve that we fell in love.'

'Just because you move fast, it doesn't mean that I have to… I like to take my time and think about these things.' He kissed her, kissed her between sentences—like a gorgeous long meal, like a wonderful smorgasbord, where you didn't have to rush, could just pick and choose the good bits and go back for more whenever you wanted. You could start and finish with dessert if you wanted, or just get full on a thousand prawns. 'I went into the ballroom and everyone was talking. I had friends around me, a good malt whisky in my hand and a beautiful woman on my arm, and I looked at my watch, and I looked at the closed door, and I wanted to be on the other side of it. I had everything a man could want—only it didn't feel right because you weren't there.'

'I'm here now,' Caitlyn said softly.

'So am I…' He rained her face with butterfly kisses, and she rained them back, kissing away all the hurt and the grief, chasing away all the horrible, scary shadows till there was only light left. 'I'm here, where I belong.'

EPILOGUE

'Do you want me to say something?' Caitlyn offered as Lazzaro called for the bill.

'The food was fantastic,' Lazzaro said. 'Let's not make a fuss.'

'But every time we come here they get it wrong! I specifically ordered the mushroom risotto, and we got vegetarian arranchini.'

Lazzaro peeled off another note and added it to his already generous tip. They were sitting in one of the smartest cafés in Rome, and the waiter had in fact done an amazing job—deciphering somehow, from Caitlyn's truly appalling Italian, that they wanted rice and vegetables.

It *was* bad.

Even after a year of flying between two amazing cities—even after having a son who had been born here in Rome—Caitlyn's mastery of the language was poor, to say the least. But her Italian was delivered with such flair, such passion and enthusiasm, and such a warm, generous smile, that no one—not the doctors, nor the midwives, nor the hotel staff or even a waiter—had the heart to tell her.

'*Che era meraviglioso—grazie.*' Caitlyn beamed at the

bemused waiter as she clipped little Dante into his pram and wheeled him out of the restaurant.

'That was wonderful—thank you...' Lazzaro loosely translated, rolling his eyes and mouthing another thank-you to the waiter, then joining his wife and new son on the street outside.

'You'd think they'd never seen a blond baby.' Caitlyn smiled as everyone who passed cooed into the stroller. 'Mind you—he *is* gorgeous.'

And the image of Caitlyn.

Blond, already lifting his head and taking in the world, smiling and cooing at six weeks and refusing to sleep, he was a carbon copy of his mother—and Lazzaro, just as he was with his wife, was completely smitten.

'Right—time to look for a gift. I still don't get why some people don't have a bridal registry,' Lazzaro said as they wandered the streets.

'We didn't...' Caitlyn pointed out.

'Because you refused to—and just look at the pile of rubbish we ended up with.' Lazzaro stared moodily into a gallery. 'She's been married already—she got everything she wanted the first time around...'

'And she got everything she wanted in the divorce.' Caitlyn giggled. 'How about that?' she asked, pointing to a painting in the window of the modern art gallery.

'It could have been done by a five-year-old—in fact, give Dante a brush and he could do better.'

'It's divine,' Caitlyn breathed.

'It's three circles within a circle.'

'Antonia, Marianna and baby Luca, and circling them, looking out for them, is Dario.'

'I still think the wedding should be at Ranaldi's.' Lazzaro was still staring at the picture and trying to see what she saw—trying to work out Caitlyn's impossible, crazy take on the world, trying to take in that Antonia was marrying his friend Alberto's son. 'I would have done it better.'

'Probably.' Caitlyn shrugged. 'But I'd never have seen you—you'd have spent the night marching around the kitchen insisting everything was "the best". This way, you get to enjoy yourself...' She was suddenly serious. 'Anyway, Alberto is enjoying organising it—it's good to see him happy after the year he's had.'

'I know,' Lazzaro conceded.

'And talking of weddings...' A mischievous smile was on her lips, but two circles of red were burning on her cheeks as she broached a terribly taboo subject. 'Can you believe Roxanne and Malvolio sent us an invitation to theirs? Can you believe they actually invited us?'

They were inside the gallery now. Lazzaro was ignoring the owner's effusive attempts to discuss the delightful piece they were buying—instead handing over his credit card and giving the details as to where it should be sent.

'They deserve each other!' Lazzaro hissed as they stepped outside.

'Well, they've got each other.' Caitlyn laughed. 'Thanks in small part to me. Did I tell you I hexed her?'

'Hexed her?' Lazzaro frowned—he was pushing the stroller now, guiding it down the bumpy steps as Caitlyn clipped alongside, and this time he wasn't pretending not to understand—he honestly didn't.

'I wrapped her name around a piece of garlic and stuck it in the freezer—she's getting her just deserts!'

'You're telling me that you put a spell on her?'

'Just a little one.' Caitlyn pouted. 'Wishes do come true, you know.'

'Then make one.'

They were back at the Trevi Fountain and Lazzaro was rummaging in his pocket for loose change. Only Caitlyn didn't need to waste a wish—didn't need to wish on a coin or a star, or cut up pictures—because she knew without wishing that they'd be back for more, knew without question that they were in this for ever.

'Go on,' Lazzaro prompted, holding out a coin, but Caitlyn shook her head.

'I've got all my wishes—how about you?'

'Just one…' He tossed the coin into the fountain, then pulled her towards him as only Lazzaro could. 'A girl.'

'A girl?'

'Or a boy.' Lazzaro shrugged. 'I want another mini-you.'

'It might be a mini-*you* this time.'

'I don't care.' Lazzaro laughed, as he did often these days. 'Let's just go and make another baby.'

* * * * *

One Magical Christmas

CAROL MARINELLI

For Bob and Glynn
Love you lots
xxx

CHAPTER ONE

'HI THERE! I'm Imogen.'

Accident and Emergency Consultant Angus Maitlin looked up from orders he was hastily writing as, wearing a smile and not a trace of unease, the woman walked towards him.

'Sorry?' Handing his orders to his intern, Angus frowned at the unfamiliar face.

'Heather said I should come introduce myself to you,' she patiently explained, and Angus picked out an Australian accent. 'I've been sent down from Maternity to help with the emergency you're expecting in...'

She watched him glance at her ID badge.

'You're a midwife?'

'And an RN.' Imogen added, without elaborating. Something told her that this good-looking package of testosterone really wasn't in the mood to listen!

'Have you worked here before?' His hands gestured to the frantic Resuscitation area. The five beds were full and one was being cleared for a burn victim trapped in a car on a busy London motorway. 'Do you know the layout?'

'Not yet,' she said, looking around her. 'I've only been in the country two days. Still, I'm sure—'

She didn't have a chance to finish so she just stood there as he stalked off, no doubt to complain to the nursing unit manager. Well, let him complain, Imogen thought—she didn't want to be here and he clearly didn't want her here either! With a bit of luck she'd be sent back to Maternity.

'Heather!' Angus barked, not yet out of Imogen's earshot. 'When I said that I urgently needed more help in Resus I didn't mean you to send in a midwife!'

Angus rarely lost his temper but he was close to it now. The department was full, Resus was full, and his request for more staff had been met by this rather large, grinning woman in a white agency nurse's uniform who had only just set foot in the country!

'I'll come and help if need be,' Heather responded calmly. 'But the nursing co-ordinator did tell me that not only is Imogen a midwife, she's also advanced emergency and ICU trained. Though,' she added sweetly, 'I do have a grad nurse in the observation ward. I can swap her over if you think that would be more—'

'I'll manage,' Angus cut it in curtly, and then changed his mind, closing his eyes for a second and running a hand through his dark blond hair. 'I'm sorry, Heather—I didn't think to ask about her qualifications. It's just when she said that she'd only just arrived here…'

He glanced over to where Imogen stood where he'd rudely left her, and gave a small wince of apology. He expected to receive a rather pained, martyred look back—it would have been what he deserved—only, clearly amused, she merely shrugged and smiled. The strangest thing of all was, given the morning he was having, Angus actually found himself smiling back.

'I'm sure people suffer from burns in Australia!' Heather's sarcasm soon wiped it from his face, though.

'I get it, OK?' He reached for his water bottle at the nurses' station and took a long drink. The patient they were expecting was still being extricated from the car and there was plenty he could be doing in that time, but from the brief description of the horrific injuries that would soon present, Angus guessed a minute to centre himself was probably going to be time well spent.

'Is everything OK, Angus?' Heather Barker also had plenty she could be getting on with but, used to priorities shifting quickly in this busy London accident and emergency department, she took a moment to deal with the latest category one to present. Angus Maitlin, the usually completely together consultant, the utter lynchpin of the department, seemed for once to not be faring so well.

Not that he said it.

Not that he ever said it.

Impossibly busy, he was usually infinitely calm and dependable. Not only did Angus help run the accident and emergency department, he was also married to a successful model, a proud father to two young children *and* had, in the past few years, become something of a TV celebrity. Angus had been asked, by the local television station, to give his medical opinion on post-traumatic stress syndrome. His deep, serious voice, his undeniable good looks, combined with just the right dash of humour, had proved an instant hit, and the cameras, along with the audience, had adored him. Which meant he had been asked back again, and now Angus Maitlin was regularly called on to deliver his particular brand of medicine on a current affairs show. Yet somehow his celebrity status hadn't changed him a jot—Angus still had his priorities well in place—his family first, the emergency department a very close second, or, when the situation demanded, Emergency first, family second, and then, somehow, everything else got slotted in.

Just not today.

Not for the past couple of months, actually.

'Angus?' When he ignored her question Heather rephrased it. 'Is there a problem?'

'Of course not.'

'Anything that you might want to talk about?'

'I'm fine.'

Sitting on a stool, muscular, yet long limbed and elegant, his thick fringe flopping over jade eyes, his immaculately cut suit straining just a touch to contain wide shoulders as he drank some water, Angus Maitlin looked better than fine—the absolute picture of relaxed health, in fact—only everyone in the department knew better.

'It's not like you to snap at the nurses.'

'I'll apologise to Imogen. I really am fine, things are just busy.'

'It's not just Imogen…' He could tell Heather was uncomfortable with this discussion and he was too. 'I've had a couple of grumbles from staff recently. And we always are busy—especially at this time of year.'

They were. It was a week before Christmas and London was alive. The streets were filled with panicked shoppers, parties, cold weather, ice, families travelling, people meeting. Combine all that with alcohol in abundance and December was always going to be a busy time—only it had never usually fazed him.

'What's going on, Angus?' Heather pushed. 'You just haven't been yourself lately. Look, I know it's not a great time to talk now, but once we get the place settled...or we can catch up for coffee after the shift...'

'Really, I'm fine.' Angus said firmly. Heather was the last person he wanted privy to his problems. Oh, she meant well and everything, but some things were just... private. 'I hate burns, and this one sounds bad.' He gave her a tight smile, picked up the phone when it trilled and spoke to Ambulance Control. Then took another quick drink of water and stood up from his stool. 'They've just got the victim out of the car—ETA twelve minutes...'

For someone who hadn't been shown around, Imogen *had* done a great job of setting up. Burn packs were opened on a trolley, sterile drapes were waiting, and despite his rather abrupt walk out earlier she gave him a roll-of-the-eye smile as Angus returned.

'Couldn't get rid of me, then?'

'Believe me, I tried!' Angus joked, surprisingly refreshed by her humour.

'Given that we're going to be spending the next few hours together, I'd better introduce myself properly—I'm Imogen Lake.'

'Angus…' he offered back, 'Angus Maitlin—I'm one of the consultants here. Look, I'm sorry if I was curt with you earlier.'

'That's OK.'

'No, it's not…' He was washing his hands, but he looked over at her as he spoke. 'I completely jumped the gun—when you said that you'd been pulled from the maternity ward, that you were a midwife, I thought the nursing co-ordinator had messed up.'

'They often do!' She was smiling even more readily now—his rather snooty English accent along with his genuine apology making it very easy to do so.

'You weren't in the middle of a delivery or anything?' Angus asked, wincing just a touch as she nodded.

'And I was enjoying it too.' Imogen added, just to make him feel worse. 'So what do we know about the patient?'

'The victim coming in was the driver of a motor vehicle heading onto the M25.' Angus told her the little he could. 'According to Ambulance Control, the car lost control at the junction, hit the sign and exploded on impact, a fire truck witnessed the whole thing and the crew were straight onto it, putting out the fire as quickly as they could…'

'Is the patient male or female?' Imogen asked.

'We don't know yet.'

'OK.' It was her only response to the grim answer—that the victim's gender hadn't been immediately identified was just another indication of the direness of the situation.

Imogen truly didn't want to be here.

She had spent the last hour in a darkened delivery room, coaching Jamila Kapur through the final first stages of labour and into the second stage. Jamila had just been ready to start pushing when Imogen had been called to the phone.

When the nurse co-ordinator had rung and asked if she'd help out in Emergency, Imogen had immediately said no and not just because she didn't want to go down there. Continuity of care with labouring mums was important to Imogen, and just as she wouldn't have walked out on Mrs Kapur if she had been at that stage of labour when her shift ended, in the same way she hadn't wanted to walk out on her then.

Then the co-ordinator had rung again, reading off her qualifications as if Imogen mightn't be aware that she had them! Telling her that her skills would be better deployed in Emergency and that was where they were sending her.

Her first shift, in a different hospital, in a different country and an agency nurse to boot, she really wasn't in any position to argue.

Imogen felt as if she'd been pulled from the womb herself—hauled from where she had been comfortable and happy then plunged into the bright lights of the busy department, to be greeted by unfamiliar faces, chaos and noise. But—as Imogen always did—she just took a deep breath and decided to get on with it.

It wasn't the patient's fault that she didn't want to be here!

'Where are the gowns?' She answered her own question, pulling two packs down from the rack on the wall. She handed one to Angus before putting on her own, her ample figure disappearing under a mass of shapeless paper, and Angus felt more than a pang of guilt at complaining about her earlier. She seemed completely undaunted by what was coming in, and by all accounts it would be horrific, yet from the organised way she'd set up for the patient, from the qualifications he now knew she had, her unruffled manner wasn't because of ignorance—she was clearly a very experienced nurse.

'The anaesthetist should be here.' Angus glanced at his watch. 'You paged him?'

'Twice.'

On cue he arrived and Imogen handed him a gown too as Angus gave the information they had.

Her fine red hair was already scraped neatly back in a ponytail, but she popped on a paper hat, as Angus did the same, to maintain a sterile field as far as possible and minimise the risk of infection.

The wait was interminable and Angus glanced at his watch, the delay in arrival possibly meaning that the patient had died en route. 'What the hell's keeping—?' His voice stopped abruptly, the short blast of the siren warning of the imminent arrival.

Even though it was still only nine a.m. the sky was so heavy with rain it was practically dark outside. The blue light of the ambulance flashed through the high windows, and Angus gave Imogen a grim smile as they waited those few seconds more. This time, however, her freckled face didn't return it, blonde eyelashes blinking on pale blue eyes as instead she took in a deep breath then let it out as the paramedics' footsteps got louder as they sped their patient towards Resus.

'I hate burns!' Imogen said, catching Angus still looking at her.

It was the only indication, Angus realised, that she was actually nervous.

CHAPTER TWO

It was organised chaos.

The type where everyone worked to save a life—and not just in the emergency department but in so many unseen areas of the hospital. Porters running with vital samples up to Pathology, who in turn raced to give baseline bloods and do an urgent cross-match—as the radiographer came quickly around to take an urgent portable chest film.

The patient's name was Maria. That was all the information they had so far. Her bag carrying all the details that would have identified her had been lost in the furnace of the car. But in a brief moment of consciousness as they had extricated her from the car she had given her name.

The paramedics were dripping wet—a combination of rain, sweat and the dousing of the car, and smelt of petrol and smoke. Their faces were black with soot and dust from the fire. Two of the firefighters were being triaged outside, one with minor burns and one with smoke inhalation.

By every eye-witness account that had been given, Maria should have been dead.

'Core temperature?' Angus snapped as he viewed the young woman in front of him.

'Thirty-four point eight,' Imogen responded.

And it seemed bizarre that someone who had been severely burnt might be suffering from hypothermia, but the dousing, the exposure, the injuries just compounded everything. The thermostat in Resus was turned up, the staff dripping with sweat in the stifling warmth as the patient's burnt body shivered.

'She put up her hands...' Angus was swiftly examining her, and the little bit of hope that had flared in Imogen as they'd wheeled her in was quashed. The beautiful face that she'd first glimpsed was, apart from the palms of her hands and some area on her forearms and buttocks, the only area of her body that wasn't severely burnt.

'TBSA, greater than 85 per cent.' Angus called, and Imogen wrote it down. The total body surface area that had suffered burns was horrific and for now intense Resuscitation would continue. Maria would be treated as any trauma victim, airway, breathing and circulation the first priority, and they would be assessed and controlled before a more comprehensive examination would occur, but things didn't look good. Even though the depth of the burns still needed to be assessed, with every observation, with every revelation the outcome for Maria was becoming more and more dire.

'There was one more victim at the scene—deceased,' the paramedic added quietly. 'No ID.'

'They were in the car together?' Angus checked. 'Is the deceased male or female?' The paramedic gave a tight shake of his head. 'We don't know at this stage. Adult,' he added, which couldn't really be described as consolation, but when the paramedic spoke next, Angus conceded, it was perhaps a small one. 'The child car seat in the rear of the vehicle was empty.'

There were many reasons that no one liked burns—the rapidity, the severity and the potential for appalling injuries, the sheer devastation to the victim's life, the long road ahead, both physically and mentally if they made it through. It took a very special breed of staff indeed to work on a burns unit, and most emergency staff were grateful that they only dealt with this type of injury relatively occasionally and for a short time only.

The golden hour—the hour most critical in determining the outcome for the patient—was utilised to the full for Maria. Despite her appalling injuries, as the fluids were poured in and oxygen delivered, she began to moan.

From the firefighters' accounts and the police officers' initial assessment, the skid marks on the road indicated Maria had struggled desperately to regain control of the car. When it had crashed the nature of her injuries suggested that she had put up her hands instinctively to shield her face, and in doing so she had protected her airway too. Still, she was being closely monitored by the anaesthetist, delivering high-concentration humidified oxygen as well as generous amounts of morphine, ready to intubate earlier rather than later if her airway declined. The paramedics had managed to insert one IV at the scene, but it was insufficient for the volume of fluids required and further access proved impossible.

Instead, Angus delivered the vital fluids she desperately needed via intra-osseous infusion. This was a quick procedure, which needed strength to execute and involved puncturing the bone and delivering the fluids straight into the bone marrow. As Angus did that, Imogen, with great difficulty, inserted a catheter, and watched with mounting unease as Maria's urine output dropped down to zero.

'Can we roll her again?' Angus ordered, and with Heather's help Imogen gently held Maria on her side as Angus, assisted now by a fellow emergency consultant, examined her.

'It's OK, Maria…' Through it all Imogen spoke to her patient, focussing on her face, actually trying not to look at anything else. 'The doctors are just taking a look at you.'

As Maria groaned, Angus nodded and gestured impatiently, telling them they could roll her back. This time neither Heather nor Imogen took any offence at his brusque manner.

'Can I leave you for five minutes?' Heather pulled off her gloves and cursed the ringing phone on the wall and the doctor calling her from the other side of the curtain. 'Press the emergency bell if you need anything at all.'

Now that the patient was relatively more stable, another RN was floating between two patients and assisting where she could, but, for the most part, Imogen was nursing Maria one on one.

Angus now confirmed that most of the burns were full thickness—the most severe kind. It took everything Imogen had to deliver a smile as for the first time and just for a second Maria's eyes briefly opened.

Imogen lowered her head nearer to the patient's. 'It's OK, Maria, you're in hospital, we're looking after you.' It was all she got to say before Maria's eyes closed again.

He'd apologise to Imogen again.

Talking on the telephone to a burns specialist at another major London hospital, and taking a quick swig of water as he did so, Angus looked over and saw Imogen pause for a second to lower her head and talk to the unconscious patient again. She'd done this every couple of minutes or so since Maria had arrived in the department and Angus knew it would be helping as much as the morphine if Maria could hear her.

Angus was proud of the team he had helped build at this hospital, considered them absolutely the best, and yet there was no one who could have done better than Imogen had this morning. Through it all she had been quietly efficient. Everything he had needed had been handed to him and not once had she flinched in assisting Angus in a procedure so vile that even an intern, who had asked to observe had at one point had to walk out.

A vile procedure in a vile, vile morning.

When the burns consultant, Declan Jones, arrived Angus ushered him over to the far wall to discuss the patient privately in greater depth. The stench in the warm room matched the loathsome diagnosis that Angus was just so reluctant to come to.

'I respect your opinion, Declan...' As Imogen walked over to the huddle she could hear the restraint in his voice. 'More than respect it—you know that ...'

'She's talking,' Imogen said.

'Is she orientated?' Angus asked, swallowing down a sudden wave of bile.

'Fully. She's Italian, but her English is very good, though she has a strong accent. She's struggling obviously, but she's conscious now. She's confirmed that her surname is Vanaldi. Her husband Rico was the passenger in the car.' He watched those blonde eyelashes blink a couple of times before she continued. 'She has a son called Guido, he's fifteen months old and at day care…'

Till this point information had trickled in in dribs and drabs. The police had managed to ID the vehicle and registration, which had given them an address. They had then been and spoken with neighbours and were now on their way to the day-care centre her child was attending.

'That matches what the police said,' Angus nodded. 'Are there any other relatives we can call?'

'She said not.'

'There must be someone!' Angus insisted, because there just had to be. Maria was a young woman, for goodness' sake, with a child, and she'd just lost her husband. She couldn't be expected to face this alone. 'She needs someone with her.'

'I'll ask her again.'

'Is there any urine output yet?' Angus called as she walked off, his jaw clenching closed when she shook her head.

'Still zero.'

Usually it was good news that the patient was talking. For a patient so ill to now be alert and orientated, in practically every other scenario it would be reason to cheer, but not today.

Maria Vanaldi had awoken probably to be told that she would inevitably die—her calamitous injuries simply incompatible with life.

And it was Angus who would have to be the one to tell her.

'Is there anyone else I can discuss this with?' It was always exquisitely difficult, questioning a colleague, one who actually specialised in the field and whose expertise Angus had called on, but etiquette couldn't really come into it and Declan understood that.

'I'll give you some names.' He let out a sigh. 'Though I've already called two of them. I'm sorry, Angus.'

'There's an older brother,' Imogen stated as a policeman came over, clearly just as drained from it all as the rest of them, and his news wasn't any more cheering.

'We've contacted the day-care centre, they're open till six tonight. The husband's the only other point of contact on their forms.'

'Bring the child to Emergency,' Angus interrupted. 'She'll want to see him and hopefully we'll have some relatives arriving soon.' He turned to Imogen. 'You say that she's got a brother?'

'He's her only relative.' Imogen gave a troubled nod. 'But he's in Italy and Maria doesn't know his phone number. She says it's on her mobile, which is in the car…'

'Can I talk to her?' the police officer asked. 'We can enter the house and go through her phone book or whatever to try and locate the contact number for him, but it would make it quicker if she could tell us where to look.'

Angus shook his head. 'I'll talk to her.'

He approached the bed and smiled into two petrified eyes. 'Hi, Maria, I'm Angus, I'm the doctor looking after you.'

'Guido!'

'Your son?' Angus said. 'He's being taken care of.'

'He's at day care.' In the few minutes since he'd left her side, Maria's degree of consciousness had improved, but even generous amounts of morphine couldn't dim her anguish as adrenaline kicked in and her mind raced to recapture her world. 'He will not know! They will not know...'

'We know where he is,' Angus said gently. 'The police have contacted the day-care centre and are bringing him in here. You'll be able to see him soon.'

'He's not well...' She was choking on her tears, each word a supreme effort. 'He has a cold—I should have kept him at home...'

If only she had, Imogen thought, then checked herself. It was a futile exercise, one patients went through over and over when they or their loved ones landed in Emergency. The recriminations and the reprimands, going over and over the endless, meaningless decisions that had brought them to that point and wishing different choices had been made. As Angus caught her eye for a moment, she knew he was going through it too—if only. If only she had left him at home, or left later, or earlier, or stopped for a chat, or not stopped...

It truly was pointless.

'You couldn't have known,' he said firmly. 'You couldn't have foreseen this. This was not your fault.'

'I wasn't speeding...' And Imogen watched as Maria

thought things through. 'Rico?' Her eyes fled from Angus's to Imogen. 'How is Rico?'

'Who's Rico?'

'My husband.'

'Was he in the car with you?' Angus checked, because he had to.

'How is he?'

And then came the difficult bit, where he had to tell this young woman that there had been another fatality in the car. It was hard when the identity hadn't been confirmed, hard because there was absolutely no point in giving her false hope, and he delivered the brutal news as gently as he could, watching as her shocked, muddled brain attempted to decipher it then chose not to accept it.

'No.' Her denial was followed swiftly by anger, her Italian accent more pronounced, her eyes accusing. 'You've got it wrong. It might not be him.'

'Someone needs to be here for you.' Angus said, choosing not to push it. 'Imogen said you have a brother in Italy. Are there any family or friends closer?'

'Only Elijah.'

'What about Rico's family?'

'No!'

'OK.' She was getting distressed, alarms bleeping everywhere, and he hadn't even told her the hardest part. 'The police are near your house, they can break in and get your brother's phone number. Do you know where it would be?'

'No…' She closed her eyes, swallowed really hard and then gave an answer that only a woman could understand. 'By the phone—but it's a mess.'

'Is it in a phone book?'

'The place is a mess.' Angus frowned just a fraction. People's bizarre responses never ceased to amaze him. Here she was lying in the Resuscitation bay, her husband was dead and she was worried that the house was a mess.

'You should see my place,' Imogen said as she watched Angus's expression, her calm voice reassuring the woman. 'I can promise you that they've seen worse. In fact, I can promise you that they won't even notice the mess. They won't even bat an eyelid.'

It had taken him a moment to get it, but he realised then that it was easier for Maria to focus on the pointless for a moment.

'It's a mess…' The morphine was taking over now, or maybe Maria just didn't care any more as she closed her eyes.

Despite the closed eyes, still Imogen chatted easily to her and Angus could see they had already built up a rapport, which Maria was going to need. 'Just tell me where the number is—his name's Elijah. What's his surname?'

'My surname…' Maria answered.

'Have you got a lot of pain still?' Imogen checked, turning up the morphine pump as soon as Maria nodded wearily. 'We'll keep turning it up till we get on top of it.'

Sometimes, Angus thought to himself, you had to face up to facts. As he desperately did the rounds on the telephone, calling as many people as he knew to ask for a second opinion or for some objective advice, Angus realised that, despite extenuating circumstances, despite supreme effort, despite so much potential and no matter how much he didn't want it to be so, Maria's life would soon fail.

'Her lactate levels alone will kill her.' Imogen met him at the soft-drink machine in the corridor. Heather had taken over for five minutes, giving Imogen a chance to dash to the loo and to get a quick drink. 'You haven't got any change for the machine?' he asked as he ran his hand through his hair.

Imogen emptied her pockets, handing over some coins, and he popped them into the machine, too distracted to ask what she wanted and she too distracted to care. He punched in the same number twice and they gulped icy, fizzy, sweet orange which proved a great choice, sitting in a relatives' interview room for a couple of minutes, before heading back into hell.

'Would you want to know?' Angus looked over to Imogen. 'I want to give her hope—I mean, we'll follow the burns protocol, she'll go up to ICU, but…'

'They moved here from Italy two years ago apparently.' Imogen didn't immediately answer his question. 'The neighbours told the police that they kept themselves pretty much to themselves. They found the brother's number too…' Her voice trailed off as she thought about it, really thought about it, and Angus waited. 'Yes,' she said after the longest time. 'I'd want to know, I'd want to use whatever time I had to make arrangements for my son.'

'Me, too.' He rubbed his hand over his forehead and Imogen could see his agony, could see the compassion behind the rather brusque facade, and knew that this was tearing him up too.

'A little bit of hope is OK, though,' she added.

'There's going to be no Christmas miracle here.'

'I know.' Imogen nodded. 'But Maria's not me and she's not you and if she doesn't want to know…'

'I'll play it by ear.' He stood up, turned to go and then paused. 'Thanks, by the way.' They both knew he wasn't thanking her for the drink. 'I'll go and ring the brother,' Angus said, grateful that she didn't wish him luck, grateful that she just nodded. 'God, I hope he speaks English.'

'I'll send someone to get you if there's anything urgent.'

'Thanks.'

Ringing relatives was never easy and Elijah Vanaldi proved more difficult than most. Hanging up the phone, Angus dragged his hand through his thick mop of hair and held onto it, resting his head in his hand for the longest time, trying to summon the strength to face the *most* difficult part of this vile day: to tell the beautiful, vibrant woman herself that her life would soon be over— that not only had her son lost his father but that, in a matter of, at best, hours, he would lose his mother too.

He flicked off the do-not-disturb light and almost instantaneously someone knocked at the door to his office. Imogen's face was grim as she stepped into the unfamiliar terrain and Angus wondered whether or not it would even be necessary to tell Maria now.

'She knows…' Swallowing hard, Imogen's pale blue eyes met his. 'She knows that she's dying.'

'You told her?' Angus barked, his voice gruff. It was *his* job to do that, and as much as he was dreading it he wanted to ensure that it was done right, but as Imogen shook her head, he regretted his harsh tone.

'Of course I didn't tell her—I'm not a complete idiot!'

And just because they were both snapping and snarling, they knew that there was no need for either of them to say sorry. In the short but painfully long time they'd worked together, they'd already built up a rapport.

'Maria worked it out for herself,' Imogen explained, and he watched as she chewed nervously on her bottom lip for a moment before continuing. 'She said "I'm going to die, aren't I?" And I didn't tell her she was wrong, I simply told her that I'd come and get you to talk to her. I'm just letting you know that she's already pretty much aware…'

'Thank you for telling me.' He gave a weary smile. 'You've been amazing this morning.'

'Not bad for a foreigner?' Imogen gave her own weary smile back, just letting him know that she'd heard all of his earlier complaint to Heather.

'Yes, not bad.' Angus smiled. 'I guess we might have to keep you.'

'How was the brother?' Imogen asked, and neither smiled now.

'Brusque, disbelieving, angry…take your pick. He's on his way.'

'That's good…' Imogen found herself frowning, and couldn't quite work out why. Angus Maitlin had every right to look grim. As gruelling as Emergency was at times, this morning took the cake. Yet she could see the purple stains of insomnia under his eyes, the swallow of nervousness over his perfect Windsor knot, remembered the short fuse he had greeted her with, and knew there had to be more, knew, because she'd been there herself. 'Gus could talk to her…'

'Gus?'

'The other consultant.'

'I know who Gus is,' Angus snapped. 'Don't worry, I can be nice when I remember. Look...' He stopped himself then and forced a half-smile. 'It's just with it being Christmas and everything, my wife's the same age...'

'I know.' Imogen nodded her understanding, but a smudge of a frown remained, not for her patient but for him.

'Come on.' Angus stood up. 'Let's get this over with.'

As they reached the nurses' station, quietly discussing the best way to go about it, Angus became aware that Imogen had more insight into Maria's personality than he did and absorbed her words carefully.

'She's going to be terrified for her little boy, for Guido and his future. I guess the main thing I'd want to hear is that—'

'Angus.' Heather's interruption halted Imogen's train of thought. 'Gemma's on the phone for you.'

'Tell her I'll call her back.'

'She says that it's urgent.'

'It always is with Gemma,' Angus snapped, and Imogen knew that he just wanted to get the unpleasant task of speaking with Maria over with. 'Tell her I'll ring her back when I can.'

'She says that it's to do with the kids.'

'What's the problem, Gemma?'

Imogen frowned as with a hiss of irritation Angus took the telephone. Of course Angus was busy, and of course he didn't want interruptions, but if it had been

Brad ringing to say there was something urgent going on with Heath, Imogen would have been tripping over her feet to get to the phone—no matter how busy she was at work.

'What do you mean—you sacked Ainslie?'

Imogen's glance caught Heather's, and they both shared a slightly wide-eyed look.

'The nanny!' Heather mouthed for Imogen's benefit.

'Oh!'

'The morning I'm having and you ring to tell me you've sacked the nanny. I couldn't give a damn if you've got a photo shoot tomorrow, Gemma.' Pinching the bridge of his nose with his finger and thumb, Angus closed his eyes. 'Frankly, I couldn't have cared less if Ainslie *was* stealing the odd thing—she was the best thing to happen to the kids and to get rid of her one week before Christmas…' He went to hang up then changed his mind. 'No, Gemma, you sort it out for once!'

He aimed the receiver in the general direction of the phone but missed spectacularly, then as he strode towards the Resuscitation area he stopped, dragged in a huge breath and leant against the wall for a moment. Imogen was glad he did, glad he took a moment to compose himself before he went in to see Maria—she deserved calm and his full attention.

'Sorry about that.'

'No problem.' Imogen smiled, because it wasn't. Oh, she didn't have a nanny, of course, but had Brad rung her with something so trivial, she'd have no doubt put on a similar show herself.

'It's just sometimes…' He stopped himself then, just

as she had so many times in another lifetime. And even if she had only just met him, even if they were from opposite sides of the globe and even though he was stunning looking and she was rather, well, plain, Imogen knew that they had one thing in common: both of them had had to work, to function, to keep on keeping on through the rocky part of a failing marriage—even if Angus wasn't ready to admit it.

'Impossible?' she offered, watching his eyes jerk to hers, seeing that flash of surprise that someone might just possibly understand. 'Brad used to ring me all the time with some perceived drama, or I'd be ringing him with one of my own...'

'Brad's your husband?'

'Brad's my ex-husband.'

'Oh!' He pulled away from the wall then, clearly deciding that she didn't understand at all, that the flash of recognition that he'd thought he'd seen actually didn't apply to him in the slightest.

'It isn't actually a *perceived* drama,' he said tartly. 'Gemma was right to ring, she just caught me at a bad time.'

'Sure.'

'Really,' he insisted. 'Gemma and I are fine. It just wasn't the best time to call, that's all.'

'Good.'

He was about to insist again that nothing was wrong, but Imogen decided it wasn't her business anyway, the fleeting moment of connection long since gone. It was time now to get on with the unpleasant task in hand— and it was Imogen who concluded the conversation.

'Let's go and speak with Maria.'

CHAPTER THREE

IMOGEN HAD nursed since the age of eighteen, and now at thirty-two years of age and with most of her experience in either Intensive Care or Emergency, she had seen more than her fair share of tragedy and dealt with many unbearably sad situations. Most stayed with her enough to be recalled when required, some would stay with her for ever—and some, like Maria, would actually change her.

Despite his cool greeting and sometimes brusque demeanour, still Imogen had liked Angus. She had worked in Emergency long enough to form a very rapid opinion, and generally she was spot on.

And now, listening to him confirm Maria's darkest fears, Imogen knew that she was right. Understood even why he wanted to be the one to tell her. Lacing compassion with authority, he led her through the news, tender yet firm he let her find her own route, which was, for Maria, to face the truth. When many others would have left, Angus stayed, reiterating when needed and sometimes just quiet as Maria had to grieve for her own short life too. Yet somehow she rallied, maternal instinct kicking in, knowing that in the little time that remained she had to make plans for her son.

'I have to speak to my brother.' Her blue eyes were urgent. 'I cannot die before I speak with him.'

'He said the same thing,' Angus said gently. 'He's flying in.'

'I need to speak to him about Guido—about what must happen to him.'

'I'll also get Social Services to come and speak to you—' Angus started, but Maria was having none of it.

'I just want Elijah.'

'Do you have a will, a lawyer?' Angus asked, but Maria simply wouldn't go there. Her brother was the only one she would consider talking to, the only person she wanted now apart from her son.

'Your brother's on his way,' Angus said.

'How long does a flight take from Rome to London?' Imogen asked.

'About three hours,' Angus answered, but there was also getting to the airport, booking a flight and realistically they were looking more at five or six hours, and no one was sure Maria had that.

'I think I want to see Guido.' Maria screwed up her eyes with the agony of it. 'But I'm worried that I'll scare him...'

'Your face is fine,' Imogen said softly. 'I'll give it a wash and we'll make sure everything else is covered. I'll turn down all the machines so that they don't alarm him.'

'I won't be able to hold him,' Maria croaked.

'I'll hold him for you,' Imogen said. 'I'll put his face right next to yours and you can feel him and smell him...'

'I don't want to start crying. I don't know if I want him to see me like this.'

'OK,' Imogen soothed. 'You let me know.'

'How's her pain?' Angus checked a little while later. Maria was calmer, lying with her eyes closed but not sleeping as Imogen sat quietly by her side.

'I'm OK.' She opened her eyes to let Angus know she wasn't sleeping. 'Any word from my brother?'

'Not yet.'

'Then I'll wait.'

'Don't try and be brave,' Imogen said. 'We can keep increasing your morphine, make you more comfortable...'

'No more till Elijah is here—I want to be conscious when my brother comes.'

Imogen had long since learnt that people were people, women still women even in the most dire of times— even when they were dying. Friends and just a bit of a smile were always needed. Suddenly Maria was asking for her face to be washed and if she could be tidied up a bit—as she emotionally prepared herself to see her son. A healthy dose of morphine combined with a good measure of denial meant that Maria managed a little chat as Imogen gently tended to her.

'I forgot to bring my make-up.' It took a second to realise that Maria had managed a joke and they shared a smile. 'I am never without it.'

'I've got some lipstick,' Imogen offered, 'if you want to use it.'

'Thank you. You know, I thought I was imagining things when I saw Angus.'

'I thought I was, too, when I came on duty,' Imogen grinned, glad to be Maria's friend today, glad that for a little while more Maria could be Maria. 'Bloody gorgeous, isn't he?'

'He's on the television, too.' Maria said, her eyes almost crossed as she tried to focus.

'Angus?' Imogen frowned.

'A lot—he's a TV doctor or something.'

'I'll have to remember to set my DVD to record him.' Imogen winked. 'A little memento to take back to Australia. Hey...' Imogen frowned for the first time at her patient. 'How come your eyeliner's still on?'

'It's a tattoo!' Maria coughed as she tried to laugh.

'Wow!' Imogen was genuinely impressed. 'I've always wanted to get my eyelashes dyed—I've just never got around to it.'

'Do it!' Maria said, managing to focus her eyes on Imogen. 'Go and do it!'

'I will.'

'Have a proper break.' Heather was insistent. 'I'll go in and stay with her. I want you to go and have a coffee and a sandwich and catch your breath for a little while. You, too!' Heather added to Angus.

There really was no point being a martyr—Imogen had learnt that long ago. Sure, there were times when ten minutes for a quick drink and a sit-down *were* impossible to find, but today Imogen knew that a quick refuel would help not just the doctor and nurse but the patient too. Maria was being reviewed by the anaesthetist now, the team ensuring that everything possible was being done to keep Maria pain free and to respect her wishes to remain conscious for as long as possible until her brother arrived.

Peeling off the dirty gowns and paper hats, it was a relief to be out of them. Imogen was aware she must look a sight, her red hair damp with sweat and stuck to her head. Looking at Angus, there was no doubt that she too had a nice big crease around her forehead where her hat had been, only her uniform, she was sure, wasn't quite as fresh looking as his crisp shirt.

And though she had joked with Maria about it, now that she was alone with him, away from the horrors, for the first time Imogen *really* noticed how gorgeous he was.

His beautifully cut hair had recovered from the cap just a little better than hers, and as she walked behind him to the staffroom she saw how it tapered into his neck, saw the wide set of his shoulders and caught a whiff of his gorgeous scent as he held the door open and they walked inside. He was so tall and broad he actually made Imogen feel slender as she stood beside him and loaded four slices of bread into the toaster and he made two quick coffees. He had nice hands too, Imogen thought, noticing how he stirred sugar into her coffee. But seeing his wedding band glint, she chose not to go there.

Wouldn't do to others what had been done to her— not that a man as divine as Angus Maitlin would even deign her that sort of a glance!

Still, he wasn't just nice to look at, he was a nice guy too, and after the morning they'd so far shared, it was nice to actually *meet* him.

And it felt so-o-o good to sit down.

So good not to be in that room where death was present. So good that, despite the horrors, despite the fact it was the foremost thing on both their minds, for most of their break they chose not to talk about it.

'So you're from Australia?'

'Queensland.' Imogen nodded.

'And you only just got here.'

'I didn't intend to start work quite so quickly. I was supposed to be finding somewhere to stay, but when I checked into the youth hostel there were already four messages from the hospital asking if I could ring them—I'd sent in all my paperwork and references a few weeks ago.'

'So what brings you here?' Angus asked. She didn't look like the regular travellers they got here—young nurses just qualified and ready to party. His eyes narrowed as he tried to guess her age—late twenties, early thirties perhaps. 'You said you've got a son?'

'I do...' He watched as her face brightened. 'Heath. He's here with his dad. Brad's working in London, so I thought I'd come over for Christmas.'

Angus's narrowed eyes were joined by a frown now and he fought quickly to check it. So what if her child lived on the other side of the world with his father? It certainly wasn't his place to judge.

'I was hoping to work just a couple of nights a week to cover the rent in a serviced apartment,' Imogen continued, 'but having seen the prices of temporary rentals that I *can* afford...' Imogen pulled a face. 'Well, let's just say they're not exactly the places I'd want to bring Heath back to! So it looks like I'm going to just have to take him sightseeing when I see him.'

'You're separated from your husband?' Angus checked.

'Divorced.'

'And he's English?'

'He's Australian.' Imogen laughed, enjoying his confusion. 'Brad's just working here.'

'So what does he do for a living? If you don't mind me asking.'

'He's an actor!' Imogen rolled her eyes. 'And not a very good one either—if you don't mind me saying.' Angus's frown was replaced by a grin as she smiled at him.

'Maria said that you're on television too!'

'She recognised me?' He could feel his cheeks redden. It was the one thing in his life that embarrassed him. He took his television appearances seriously, saw it as an excellent means for education, but lately personal questions had been creeping into the show, a sort of thirst for knowledge about him was being created, a celebrity status evolving that, unlike Gemma, he didn't aspire to. 'I have a regular spot on a current affairs show, discussing current medical trends, health issues… It's no big deal.'

'It is to Maria! She thinks you're marvellous!' Imogen winked. 'Says you're quite a hottie.'

'A hottie?' Angus queried then wished he hadn't, working it out before Imogen could answer.

'Cute!' Imogen grinned. 'But, I told her the camera *always* lies, and given I was married to an actor for years. I speak on good authority.' He couldn't quite make her out. She was very calm, laid back even, but she had this dry edge to her humour he liked.

'Anyway…' Angus went to bite into his toast '…I'm going to give it up soon.'

'Had enough?' Imogen said casually, but Angus, though apparently calm, was actually reeling inside! He hadn't told anyone that, had only *just* broached the subject with Gemma. It was just the sort of careless comment that he shouldn't be making. He hadn't even told them at the show, and he moved quickly to right it.

'I'd rather you didn't say anything.'

'About what?' Imogen asked.

'About what I just said.' Angus cleared his throat. 'It wouldn't look good if it got out.'

'I'll say!' Imogen grinned. 'We can't have everybody knowing that the amazing Dr Maitlin doesn't even know what a hottie is!'

In a morning where there should have been none, somehow she'd brought just a touch of laughter, and not just to him, Angus noticed, but to their patient too. Imogen Lake, the only shred of good fortune Maria Vanaldi had had today.

Emergency's gain, Maternity's loss, Angus thought, thinking back to his obstetric rotation. She'd be great at that too.

'So you're a midwife too?'

'I am.' But suddenly she wasn't quite so forthcoming.

'You're emergency trained, though—clearly!'

'Yes.'

'And Heather said you had ICU qualification,' Angus pushed. 'So which do you prefer?'

'I don't know. I've been doing emergency for years now—since I qualified. I love it and everything, but…'

He watched as she shrugged. 'Midwifery never really appealed to me till I had Heath. I've kept my hand in and I generally do a shift a month at the birthing centre at the local maternity hospital back home. I'm thinking of applying for a full-time job there when I get back. Actually...' she gave a tight smile '...I'm thinking about a lot of things.'

'Won't you miss Emergency?'

'That's a bit of a daft question to ask this morning,' she answered, and Angus would have loved to have spoken to her some more, was actually sorry when the quick reprieve was over when she drained her cup and stood. 'Speaking of which, I'd better get back to Maria.'

'I'll be there in a moment.'

'Thank you—' Maria held Imogen's eyes '—for being there today. I'm so glad it was you.'

'I'm glad it was me too...' Imogen answered, and even though today had been one of the worst shifts in memory and she'd have given anything to have missed it, would far rather have been bringing a gorgeous life into the world than helping one come to an end, somehow she was glad she had been there too, because she had helped. Imogen felt safe in the knowledge that she had done her job well—and Maria deserved that today.

She was a good nurse—Imogen knew that—and a good woman too, and today Maria had needed both. As painful as it might be, Imogen was actually glad that she *could* help this woman on her final journey.

'I don't want to die!' Loaded with morphine now,

Maria's eyes were like pinpricks as she tried to focus on Imogen.

'I know.' Imogen stroked her cheek.

'I'm not ready.'

'I know.'

She could feel Angus, fiddling with the morphine, checking Maria's NG tube, lifting up the catheter and checking that there was still no output, and Imogen knew somehow that he was there for her. And as Imogen removed her mask, knowing it was pointless now, she felt him in the room as she did the hardest bit of nursing and gave a bit more of herself to her patient.

'I'm scared.'

And she could say I know again, only Imogen knew she had to give more, had to ask her patient for more, and Angus's hand on her shoulder was very gratefully received. The stab of his fingers in her shoulder actually hurt a touch as they dug in, but they were very welcome—that someone was standing silently beside her, supporting her as she tried to support Maria and tie up the loose knots in a life about to be taken too soon.

'What are you most scared of, Maria?' Imogen asked, because until she knew she couldn't possibly understand the most vital bits in Maria's life. 'Tell me and if I can help I will.'

'I'm scared for Guido. I'm scared that Rico's family will get him...' Maria screwed her eyes closed. 'Elijah knows.'

'Your brother?' Imogen checked.

'He knows what they're like. I don't want them raising him.'

'What about your brother?' Imogen asked. 'Can he raise Guido?'

'I don't know…' Maria sobbed. 'I don't know if he can, if he'll want to. He doesn't have children, he's not married… I need to talk to him. He knows how it is…' Maria's eyes pleaded for understanding that Imogen failed for a second to give, but thankfully there was a man behind her who stepped right in.

'Elijah will be here soon.' Still Angus gripped her shoulder as he spoke. 'And I promise you that we will come up with the very best solution we can for your son.'

Elijah rang his sister from the plane, and Imogen held the telephone while Maria spoke to him, but it was too much for Maria, sobbing into the phone despite her brother's attempts to calm her.

'She's getting more distressed…' Imogen took over the call, speaking to the man whose Italian accent was thick and rich. He sounded incredibly together, given the circumstances, but Imogen could hear the pain behind each word. 'She just needs to see you. I know you're doing your best to get here.'

There were no thank yous or goodbyes from either of them, nothing the other could say, both just dealing with it the best that they could.

Maria's condition continued to worsen, so much so that when Elijah rang again to check on his sister and to say that his plane would be landing soon it was becoming ever clearer that he might not get here in time. Angus wearily closed his eyes for a second before he began speaking on the phone. Maria was sobbing in earnest now, scared to see Guido and scared not to, and finally Imogen made the decision for her.

'You need to see your baby.' Imogen said softly. 'I'll go to the ward and get him.'

'Will you stay with me?'

'Of course…' Imogen soothed.

'Not just while I'm with Guido… Till Elijah…'

'Of course,' Imogen said again, because she would.

'Are you OK?' Angus asked as Imogen blew her nose at the nurses' station. She was waiting to be put through to the charge nurse on the children's ward to say that she was coming up to fetch Guido.

'Not really.'

'Do you want me to ask Heather if she can swap nurses? You've been in with Maria for ages, it must be—'

'I don't think Maria needs a fresh face appearing at the moment.'

'If it gets too much…' Angus offered, but she just rolled her eyes and the conversation was terminated as the charge nurse on the children's ward came to the phone and offered to bring him down herself. But Imogen declined.

'I'll come and get him. I'm going to hold him while he sees her, so it might be better if I introduce myself to him up there on the ward.'

First, though, she went back into Maria to let her know that she'd see Guido very soon then arranged cotton sheets around Maria to hide the worst of her burns.

'How do I look?' Maria managed a brave feeble joke.

'Like his mum,' Imogen said gently. 'He'll cry because of the machinery, not you. Your face is fine.'

* * *

Guido didn't cry, just whimpered to get closer to his mum, and Imogen held him carefully, doing her utmost not to cry herself as Maria, aching for contact, pressed her cheek against her son and told him she loved him over and over. Even Angus was glassy-eyed when he came in to check on her, and finally when it was too much for Guido, when his mum wasn't holding him as he wanted, when the pain and emotion were just too much for Maria, Imogen made the horrible decision and took Guido back up to the children's ward, treating Guido as she could only hope someone would treat Heath if the roles had been reversed.

Stepping into the children's ward was like stepping into Santa's grotto—reindeer pulling sleighs lined the walls, snowflakes were sprayed on the windows and a wonderful tree glittered behind barriers at the nurses' station, only they didn't put a smile on Imogen's face.

Dangerously close to tears, irritated by the nurses' chatter at the desk, she told them that she was back and walked to Guido's room. He was too confused to cry now, the police, the hospital, his mum, these strangers all too much. Utterly exhausted and bewildered, Guido almost jumped out of her arms and into the metal hospital cot, clinging to a teddy bear, curling up like a little ball and popping his thumb in his mouth. Imogen quietly stroked his hair as his eyes closed and waited till he was asleep before heading back down to Maria.

As Imogen stepped back into Emergency she was greeted by a Santa Claus being pushed on an ambulance trolley and writhing in pain. 'Strangulated hernia—

where do you want him?' the paramedic said, trying his best to sound serious.

'I'll take him.' Heather grinned. 'You're finished now, Imogen.'

Imogen glanced at her watch, surprised to see that it was already nearly one o'clock—the end of her shift. 'What's happening with Maria?'

'She's going up to ICU. They just rang to say they're ready.'

'I'll take her up,' Imogen offered. 'I'll go and get my time sheet. Just sign me off for one.'

'Imogen...' Angus called her as she headed out of the doors with Maria. Security was holding a lift for her, and the porters had sent an extra person along to ensure that the path was clear for a speedy run up to ICU. It really wasn't a ideal time to stop for a chat.

'Thanks for this morning.'

'No problem.'

'No, really, Heather or I should go over it with you. Come back down after ICU—'

'I don't have time.' Imogen shook her head.

'You have to make time.' Angus pushed.

'Really, I'm fine.' Imogen said, gesturing to the porters to get going, and there really wasn't much else Angus could say.

Speeding along the corridor and then handing over the patient to the ICU staff, Imogen sat down beside Maria, not as a nurse this time but as a friend.

At least until Elijah got here.

CHAPTER FOUR

WITH his entire day almost taken up with Maria Vanaldi, by the time his patient was wheeled up to ICU, a lot of things had piled up for Angus.

And not just at work.

Grabbing a coffee, he headed to his office for five minutes to ring Gemma, hoping that whatever the latest crisis was to blow up at home, it had somehow been diverted. 'Hey, Gemma.' He heard the cold silence of her answer, but still tried. 'Sorry about before and taking so long to get back to you—it's been hell here.'

'Well, it's not exactly been a barrel of laughs here!'

'We had this woman in,' Angus attempted. 'She's the same age as you, her husband died, they've got a toddler…' Only he could tell she didn't want to hear it, which made it impossible to share it. Oh, he knew he couldn't take it all home and, yes, it annoyed him too when she droned on and on about her own career, but sometimes he listened, sometimes he tried, and he really needed her to at least try today.

It just wasn't going to happen.

'Can we talk about *your* family for a moment, please, Angus?'

He didn't bother to tell her that he'd been trying to.

Instead he heard, rather sharply, how they were still minus a nanny a week before Christmas and how Gemma *had* to work tomorrow. And if there wasn't already enough to deal with, there was something else gnawing at Angus.

'It just doesn't make any sense. I can't believe that Ainslie would steal.'

'She's got money problems,' Gemma pointed out. 'Ainslie told you about that loan she had with her ex-boyfriend, well, maybe it was starting to catch up…'

'None of that was her fault, though.'

'Angus, whose side are you on here? I caught the nanny stealing—what the hell did you want me to do? Give her a pay rise?'

Frankly, yes! he was tempted to answer, if it avoided all this!

'So where is she now?' Angus asked instead.

'I don't know and I don't care,' Gemma huffed. 'She's hardly our responsibility.'

But to Angus she was.

Ainslie had been with the family for three months now. She had lined up the job with his family from her home in Australia and though at twenty-eight years old she wasn't some naive teenager, he didn't like the idea of her being kicked out onto the street with no money, no reference and just a week before Christmas. She was way too old to be his daughter, but if, heaven forbid, Clemmie ever loaded up a backpack and headed to the other side of the world, he could only hope that someone, somewhere, would feel equally responsible.

Just as he did now.

And not just for Ainslie.

Imogen was from Australia, had landed here just a day or so before and had walked into a nursing shift from hell. In mid-conversation with his wife, Angus watched the red light on his phone flash, indicating that someone else was trying to get through, then his pager began to beep and the balls that Angus juggled, as he always did, suddenly all paused in mid-air.

Just this tiny pregnant pause as for a second everything just seemed to stand still.

Gemma's voice came as though from somewhere way in the distance as whoever it was on the other line gave up and the red light went off. Angus snapped off his pager before the second shrill and there was just stillness as the only thing on his mind was the woman he had worked with that morning. He could see her so clearly it was as if she was standing in front of him, those pale blue eyes blinking back at him, her freckly, kind face full of understanding, and he knew that she knew.

Knew, even though he'd denied it, that for him things were hell right now.

'Angus.' Gemma's voice snapped him to weary attention. 'You're going to have to take the day off tomorrow or ring your mother and ask her to come down. I simply cannot miss this shoot—you know how important—'

'Gemma…' His voice was supremely calm, but there was an edge to it, enough of an edge to tell Gemma that she'd better listen carefully. 'We've got more important things to worry about than a photo shoot, or whether or not I come in to work tomorrow, or finding a new nanny. Yes, I will see if I can get cover for tomorrow, but not so that you can go on your photo shoot. I'm going to ask my sister to watch the kids and then…' He took a deep breath and made himself say it '…we need to do some serious talking.'

'Hey!' Lost in thought, Angus nearly collided with Imogen as he headed for the staff lockers. 'I thought you finished ages ago?'

'I did!' Imogen nodded. 'I just didn't like to leave Maria on her own. I know the ICU nurses are fab and everything but, well, I got to talk to her, I guess I was there when she first came in, it just seemed wrong to leave her…'

'How about a drink? I'm sure I owe you one.'

'No thanks.'

'I can have a word with Heather,' Angus offered. 'I'm happy to speak to Admin about your hours…'

'I sat down all afternoon.' Imogen gave a watery smile. 'I made it very clear to the ICU nurses that I was there as a friend for Maria and nothing else. I don't want to be paid for it.'

'How is she?' Angus said slowly. He'd been asked to be kept informed but, given Imogen was here, he wondered if he was just about to hear the news they all expected.

'Not good. Her brother arrived half an hour ago. She's spoken to him, but she's starting to get distressed…' Imogen's eyes filled up, 'I brought Guido in again and she's had a good dose of morphine. The anaesthetist is going to intubate her soon. To be honest, I couldn't take it much more.'

'What will you do now?' Angus asked, not that it was his concern, of course, but he was worried about her, knew the toll today would have taken on her. The thought of going back to the cheerful, carefree world of a youth hostel certainly wouldn't appeal to him today and he doubted it would appeal to Imogen.

'I don't know.' She gave a tight shrug, blew her fringe skywards, and then said it again. 'I don't know.'

'Maybe see your son...' Angus suggested, though it wasn't his place, but with what she'd had to endure today, with all that she'd taken on, it was surely right that he was concerned, surely right that he didn't want her heading off alone. 'Do you talk to your ex?'

'Not about important things.' She gave a tight smile. 'I'll be fine.'

'Look, maybe—' Angus's voice stopped as quickly as it had started. The most stupid idea had come to mind, that maybe she could stay with him and Gemma for a few weeks, help out with the kids while Gemma went on her shoot and while they found a new nanny, but as her eyes darted to his, for reasons he didn't even want to fathom, he quickly changed his mind. 'Come and have a coffee—I've got time.'

'No, you haven't.'

'You're right,' Angus admitted. 'But I'm already so far behind today that I'm never going to catch up. Have a drink...'

'I'd really rather not…' She gave a pale smile. 'I'm not very good company.'

'I don't expect good company.' He frowned at her pale face and lips and was really quite worried now. 'You need a debrief, Imogen. I make sure our regular staff get to talk things through when there's been a difficult patient. It's hard enough for them, never mind agency staff, especially ones who have just landed in the country…'

'I'm fine.' She wouldn't accept his smile and she wouldn't accept his help. Except she wasn't fine, tears were filling those pale blue eyes now, the tip of her snub nose red, and all Angus knew was that he didn't want her to go, didn't want her heading off onto the wet London streets, with no one to unload to. 'How about you?'

'Me?' Her question confused him. They were supposed to be talking about her!

'This morning didn't upset you?'

'Of course it did, but I'm used to it—it's a busy hospital…'

'You can never get used to that.' She shook her head. 'I've been doing this for years and, believe it or not, we do get our fair share of trauma in Australia, even the occasional burn. But *that*, by anyone's standards, was awful.'

'Yes.' Angus admitted. 'It was.'

'So?' She demanded. 'Who debriefs the boss?'

'I get by…' Angus shrugged. 'I speak to the other consultants sometimes and Heather's pretty good. Mind you, I try not to…' His voice trailed off for a moment. 'Well—as you said, I'm the boss.'

'What about your wife?'

A short, incredulous laugh shot out of his lips before

he could stop it and it was all evident in his bitter, mirthless laugh.

'You're fine too, then?' Her ironic words were the kindest, most honest he'd heard in a long time and Angus stood there. They both just stood there for the longest time, the moment only broken when Heather walked past.

'Oh, there you are Angus. There's a baby I'm moving over to Resus—not quite sure what's going on but very listless…' She gave Imogen a kind, tired smile. 'I'm glad to see you, Imogen. I was actually going to ring you. ICU just called—Maria's just passed away. Her brother wanted to thank you both for all you did for her…'

There was a long silence. Heather bustled off, Angus telling her he'd be there in just a moment, and still he stood and watched as a fat tear slid down Imogen's cheek and she quickly wiped it away with the back of her hand. Angus cursed how times had changed, how it was impossible these days to comfort a colleague with a quick cuddle, unless it was one you really knew well, as it could so easily be construed as inappropriate. He didn't even have a hanky to offer her, just a paltry 'I'm sorry'.

'She was never going to live…' Imogen sniffed and then wept just a little bit more, before pulling herself together. 'Told you I hated burns,' she said, hitching up her bag up and wishing him a good evening.

Inappropriate. As Angus checked over the baby, as he listened to its chest, checked the depressed fontanel, took bloods and started an IV, his mind was completely on the job, but later, filling out the lab forms and waiting to be put through to Pathology, his mind wandered back to

Imogen. Oh, yes, it *would* have been inappropriate to hold her—because it wouldn't have just been about work.

The last year of his marriage had, by mutual agreement with his wife, been a loveless, sexless pit, but not once had he been tempted. Oh, sure, there had been offers and he wasn't blind enough not to notice a beautiful woman, only Imogen wasn't a classic beauty, Imogen wasn't his type at all.

But, then, what was his type?

God, but he'd wanted to hold her…

He actually shook his head as he sat there. He wasn't going to go there—even in his head. They'd shared the shift from hell, there was bound to be some sort of connection between them and anyone would be worried about her heading off alone. But even after speaking to Pathology and hanging up the phone, despite not a single rustle of paper, as he sat there Angus could feel the winds of change whistling through the department. He could feel the unsettling breeze swirling around him and knew, just knew, that things couldn't go on the way they were.

CHAPTER FIVE

'HI THERE!'

Walking through the car park, cursing the snow that had started to fall, lost in thought, dread in every cell of his body and grey with tension, Angus did a double-take as the vibrant woman greeted him.

Oh, my! was his first thought.

She should never wear white! was his second.

Wearing long, flat black boots, black stockings, black skirt and the softest grey jumper under a cropped black jacket, Imogen was somehow a blaze of colour with her red hair. There was a rosy tinge to her pale cheeks and those once fair eyelashes were now black too, a slick of mascara bringing out the blue of her eyes, and her soft smiling mouth was certainly pretty in pink.

'Sorry,' Angus blinked, 'I didn't recognise you without your uniform. How are you?'

'Great.' She smiled. 'Well, I'm starting to get over my jet-lag anyway! I just popped in to Admin to hand in my time sheet—I forgot yesterday. Oh, and I nipped in to see Mrs Kapur.'

'Mrs Kapur?' Angus frowned.

'She had a little girl, six pounds four and doing beautifully. She even let me have a little hold!'

'That's right, you were in the middle of a delivery…' Now the surprise at seeing her out of uniform was rapidly wearing off, Angus regretted prolonging the conversation. He had merely been trying to be polite, but now all Angus wanted to do was head into Emergency and do what he had to. He really didn't want to be standing in a car park, making idle chit-chat, only Imogen didn't appear to be in a hurry to go anywhere.

'How were things when you got home?'

'Fine.' Angus nodded and moved to go, before politeness forced him to ask, 'How about you?'

'Well, I'd hardly call the youth hostel home. I lasted about twenty minutes!'

She *had* been great yesterday, Angus reminded himself, and like him would have had no one to talk to about it so it would be rude now to cut her off, not to ask the question she was waiting for.

'So, what did you do?'

'I went and got my eyelashes dyed and then took a gentle spin on the London Eye and cried my eyes out. I must have looked a fright! I'm surprised the other passengers didn't press the emergency bell. What about you?'

'Me?'

'How are you?'

'I told you, I'm…' He was just about to make the usual polite response that meant nothing, just about to move on and get on with his day, but something stopped him. Whether it was the events of the last few hours that had him acting out of character, or whether it was her that made him change his mind, Angus wasn't sure and could hardly believe he said the words that slipped out of his grim mouth. 'Well, since you ask, I'm feeling pretty crap actually!'

And still she smiled, still she didn't move, just blinked those newly dyed eyelashes back at him and stared at him with those blue eyes. There were bits of snow in her hair now, Angus thought, one flake on her eyelashes, and just this…something. Something that made him stand there, that made him speak when perhaps he shouldn't, made the morning's events real when till now it had felt like a bad dream.

'My marriage just broke up.'

'Just?' A smudge of a frown was the only change to her expression.

'About four hours ago…' What the hell was he doing? Here he was standing in the car park and telling an agency nurse his problems, yet it was as if a ticker-tape parade was coming out of his mouth! Words just spilling out! All he could do was wait for the procession to pass as it all tumbled out. 'I'm just about to go into work—tell them I can't come in over the next few days. I've no idea who's going to fill in for me over Christmas…'

'How are the kids?' She dragged his mind back to the important part of the problem.

'My sister's watching them.'

'They're not with their mum?'

'No, she's gone.' She was frowning now and Angus didn't like it. He neither needed nor wanted her concern.

'She's just gone?'

'It's all under control!' Angus snapped, only it wasn't. He had a horrible feeling that there was a tinge of panic in his voice, it sure as hell sounded like it. He was an emergency consultant, for heaven's sake, was used to dealing with drama and problems, only it wasn't that his marriage was over that had him reeling—he'd dealt with that ages ago. No, now it was the thought of facing the kids, of telling them—what? He didn't know.

'Come and have a coffee.'

Was that her answer? Was she mad?

Angus certainly looked at her as if she was!

'I don't have time...' He didn't. He had to go into work and give them the news that the dependable Angus, one of only two emergency consultants covering the Christmas break, actually couldn't cover it. The thought of sitting in the canteen or the staffroom and talking, instead of doing, was incomprehensible.

'Come on...' She gestured with her head, and started to walk away from the hospital, offering the same wise words he had offered yesterday. 'You have to make time.'

'I don't have sugar...' Irritated, but not at her, he snapped out the words. His life was down the drain, he had a million things he *had* to get on with, yet here he was sitting in a packed café, surrounded by Christmas shoppers. Carols were frying his brain from the speakers overhead as she calmly came over with two big mugs of sickly, milky coffee and proceeded to load them with sugar.

'You do today.' Imogen shrugged as a strange sort of grin came to her lips. 'You're in shock!'

'Shut up!' He actually laughed. On a day when he

never thought he would, when there was nothing, not a single thing to smile about, he started to laugh. Maybe he *was* in shock, Angus thought. Maybe this strange euphoria, this sort of relief that was zipping into him, was some sort of shock reaction, which a mug of something hot and sweet wasn't ever going to cure. But, as he took a sip, it somehow did. Not a lot, not even a little bit, but it sort of did do something.

'I'm not in shock,' he said finally when he'd taken a drink and put down his mug, 'because it really wasn't a shock—I just didn't think it would be today that it ended.'

'And certainly not the day after she sacked the nanny.' Imogen, as she always seemed to, Angus was realising, got right to the very point. 'How old are your children?'

'Jack's five, Clemmie's four.'

'Are they at school?'

'Jack is.' He nodded. 'Clemmie starts in September. Not that it makes any difference at the moment, they're on holiday and I'm rostered on all over Christmas. She sacked our cleaning lady last month as well,' Angus added gloomily. 'The house is like a bomb site!'

'Can you ask her to come back?' Imogen asked.

'Who—Gemma or the cleaning lady?'

'The nanny.' Imogen grinned, assessing him as she would a patient and glad to see he had his sense of humour intact.

'Don't think so…' He shook his head. 'I went to see her this morning; I gave her her holiday money and a reference. She's actually already found another job—you'll never guess who for.'

'Who?' Imogen frowned.

'Guess.'

'I don't know anyone in London.'

'Guido!' He watched as her jaw dropped. 'As dire as my situation is, I think Maria's brother needs help more than I do right now—and Ainslie's great. It's good to know that Guido's being taken care of.'

'By a thief?' Imogen pointed out.

'No.' Angus took a long drink of his coffee. 'I'm pretty sure that I was right about that too…' He gave a tight smile as she sat there bemused. 'And I'd hazard a guess that the cleaning lady wasn't guzzling our gin either.'

'You've lost me.'

'Never mind. My loss is Elijah Vanaldi's gain…' Angus said evasively, 'that's all you need to know. Guido will be well taken care of by Ainslie.'

'So what happened?' Imogen asked. 'With you and Gemma?'

He gave a tight smile. He certainly wasn't going to go there—and certainly not with a stranger. 'I'm sure you'll understand, given that you've been through it yourself, if I don't want to talk about it.'

'No.' Imogen shook her head. 'Talking about it is the only way to get through it.'

'For you perhaps,' Angus clipped, but Imogen wasn't fazed.

'I'll show you mine if you show me yours.'

Why was he grinning again?

'Brad had an affair.'

'I'm sorry.'

'Oh, no.' Imogen gave him a startled look. 'Don't be sorry—it was absolutely my fault!'

'Pardon?'

'He had needs, you see...' Imogen said. 'Very Special Needs. He's very good-looking, he's an actor, you know...'

'Oh.'

'I mean, what was I thinking, Angus?' She shot him a serious look. 'I should have been at the gym if I'd cared about him, really cared about him. I'd have lost my weight straight after I had Heath, now, wouldn't I? And I certainly wouldn't have had a baby guzzling on my boobs at all hours of the night. I would have asked about his day more, wouldn't I, Angus?'

She was like icy water on an impossibly hot day, just this refreshing drench that stunned him. He didn't get her, yet he was starting to want to—never knew when she opened her mouth where it was going, yet every word gave him something, like this join-the-dot picture, as she revealed herself.

'If I had really wanted to keep him,' she continued, not lowering her voice, not caring who might hear, just utterly at ease with herself she carried on. He was half smiling, but very sad too as he stared at this amazing woman—sad for all she had been through, but smiling at the way she shared it. 'I would have stroked his ego more, I would have been tidier, remembered to put on my make-up before he came home, perhaps dressed a bit better. You see, Angus, I didn't understand how demanding his career was, but *she* did. *She* appreciated him, she understood his Very Special Needs—whereas I was fat, lazy and lousy in bed!' She ticked them off one by one on her hands. 'So, you see, it was absolutely my fault that he had an affair.'

'I'm sorry.'

'For what?'

'For what you must have been through. I'm sure you didn't deserve it.'

'I didn't,' Imogen said without even a trace of bitterness. 'And I'm not, by the way!'

'Not what?'

'Fat.'

'No,' Angus politely agreed, 'you're not.'

'I mean, I'm not supermodel material—I accept that—and, yes, I do like to eat, but I think there are better words to describe me than fat!'

'You're not fat.' Obviously getting hot now, she'd taken off her jacket, big boobs jiggling under her jumper. Her skirt was biting into her waist over her soft, round tummy, and Angus felt a terribly inappropriate stirring under the table. 'You're...' *Gorgeous* was what he'd been about to say, but that seemed too much. *Fine as you are* sounded patronising and just way, way too little, so he settled for 'lovely' instead, which seemed sort of safe and couldn't be construed as flirting, because he wasn't flirting. Well, he didn't think he was.

'And I'm not lazy.'

'I know that!' Angus answered, 'I worked with you yesterday—I know that you're far from lazy!'

'And...' Imogen gave a cheeky grin as he reached for his mug '...Brad was wrong on the final count too!'

'Quite!' He took a gulp of his coffee.

'Just in case you were wondering!' She winked.

He wasn't going to answer that one!

So she tried another question instead. 'Was she

worried, Gemma?' Imogen flushed just a little as she fished. 'About you and the nanny?'

'Ainslie!' Angus shot her an incredulous look.

'Just wondering.' Imogen shrugged. 'Just you said that you went to see her this morning…'

'Because she was thrown out of my house!' He didn't even hide his annoyance at her suggestion. 'Because, like you, she's from Australia, and in the same way I was concerned about you yesterday…' He stopped in mid-sentence, because for the first time in the entire conversation he was veering from the truth. His concern for Ainslie had been as an employer, whereas his concern for Imogen… Angus swallowed hard. 'Look,' he said brusquely, 'I can assure you Gemma wasn't, neither did she have any reason to be, jealous.'

'Then consider me assured!'

'In fact—' Angus bristled with indignation '—it's Gemma who's been having an affair.'

'So things weren't happy at home?'

'You don't know that,' Angus started, but she was right, because the facts spoke for themselves. Eventually he nodded. 'She says she didn't intend to have an affair, but she fell in love.'

'Well, you can't plan for that,' Imogen said.

'You can when you're married.' Angus argued then gave in. 'OK, yes—things weren't good at home. We were both holding on till Clemmie went to school—it was over a long time ago. Gemma's a model,' he explained. 'She stopped working when we had the children, then when Clemmie was one she went back to it. Till that point, even before we had kids, it had been pretty low key, catalogues, brochures that type of thing. Then suddenly things just took off for her in a way neither of us expected really. I supported her at the start, well I hope I did. That's how I got into this blasted celebrity doctor spot—I was at a television studio where she was being interviewed and they needed an expert opinion…'

'Do you like doing it?'

'Sometimes,' Angus said. 'It's certainly a good forum for education—just sometimes…' He gave a tight shrug, not noticing her slight smile at the rather formal description. 'It started to take over and I pulled back. Gemma wanted me to do more of the celebrity stuff and wind things down at the hospital, but for me that wasn't an option. I guess, in the end, we just wanted different things.'

'Like what?' Imogen asked, but Angus didn't answer. 'Like what?' she pushed, but Angus just shook his head.

'I don't know,' he admitted. 'We've got great kids, a great home, we love our work…' He blew out a breath of frustration. 'I don't know.'

'Tell me about it…' Imogen sighed then perked up. 'Except Brad's and my home wasn't actually that great and I wasn't particularly happy at work either, but we did have the great-kid bit!'

'Are you always so open?'

'No!' Imogen grinned. 'But given I'm not going to be here for long, and after yesterday I have no intention of working back down in your emergency room again, I think I can afford to be. You can be too!'

'We agreed last year things weren't working…' He gave a pensive smile. 'That makes it sound like we drew a neat conclusion, but it was the toughest thing we'd ever done. We both decided to stay together till Clemmie was at school.'

'In September?' Imogen checked.

'Yep.' Angus nodded. 'I'd signed up till then with the TV station, knowing that once they were both at school, I was going to give it up anyway and become the primary carer.'

'Not Gemma?'

'She figures she's only got a few years of modelling left—as I pointed out to her, the kids only have one childhood...' He drew in a deep breath then let it out. 'For the kids I could live a year or so in a marriage that was over, just not an unfaithful one. Gemma, it would seem, couldn't. After I got back from speaking with Ainslie this morning, we had an almighty row and the truth came out. Gemma did what I always knew she would in the end...' His eyes were two balls of pain. 'She walked out on the kids.'

'Do they know?'

'They know that she'll be away for a few days. I've told them she's away on a photo shoot, they're pretty used to that... I'm hoping that she'll see sense.'

'That she'll come back?' Imogen checked, but Angus shook his head.

'That we can work out properly what we're going to tell them—*then* tell the kids together. But, no—she's not coming back.'

'So what now?'

'Don't know...' he admitted. 'My mum's in Scotland. I'll ring her tonight, ask her to come and help out for a couple of weeks...'

'Will she be terribly upset?'

'I don't know,' Angus said. 'I'm going to have to ask her though...' He gave a small grimace as he realized how many other busy lives would be disrupted by his. 'She's going to visit friends for a few days for Christmas. I'll ask her to come after that—at least till I find a new nanny. My sister, Lorna, lives nearby. I'm sure she can help out sometimes, although she is working...'

'So you have got a plan!'

'Sort of.'

'Good.'

'Which doesn't help now.' He took another mouthful of coffee then screwed up his face. 'This is cold—do you want another?'

She didn't, but she nodded, and Angus idly watched from the counter as she sat and checked her phone as he ordered a couple of coffees and two mini Christmas puddings, surprised himself at how much better he felt now just by talking.

'Don't you miss Heath?' Angus asked Imogen, though he was still thinking about Gemma. 'When he's with his dad?'

'All the time!' Imogen answered. 'I feel like I've permanently forgotten my keys when he isn't around. I confess to being the world's most overprotective mother—Brad always said he'd turn out to be a mummy's boy if I didn't back off, but he's turned out quite the opposite...'

'So how...' Angus frowned '...can you stand for him to live in London and you in Australia?' This time it was Imogen looking at him as if he'd gone stark raving mad in the middle of the café! 'You said he was here with his dad.'

'He is,' Imogen answered slowly, 'because I brought him here.'

'Oh!'

'Brad doesn't live here!' She smiled at his confusion. 'Brad and I pretty much share care back home in Queensland,' Imogen explained. 'Though, given the nature of his work, it tends to fall on me. When he got offered this role, well, it was huge for him. They've got time off over the Christmas break, but it would have been practically impossible for him to get home and he didn't want to be apart from Heath for Christmas. It's just a one-off—you see, he's got terminal cancer.'

'Oh, my God!'

'Not Brad!' Imogen grinned at his appalled expression. 'His character—Shane. He only took the part because it was short term—just three months. Brad would never come and live here and leave Heath. He's only going to be in England for a few more weeks, but even though I really wanted Heath to have some time in London, and some real quality time with his dad, I just couldn't stand to be away from him over Christmas. So I said that I'd bring him over, but that I'd stay pretty much in the background. I mean, Heath's having a ball, I've just taken him over to the studio now—he's watching his dad and all the cast are spoiling him. I don't want to interrupt that…'

'You're amazing,' Angus said.

'Amazing and broke!' Imogen admitted. 'This little

jaunt to support my ex-husband's rising career has cost an absolute fortune—the airfares, the accommodation, my mad moment on the London Eye—'

'Worth it?' Angus broke in.

'Very much so!' Imogen smiled. 'I took Heath to see Buckingham Palace this morning, which was just amazing. Mind you, I'm already sick of taking him to cafes for lunch. I don't want him staying with me at the youth hostel—but I can't afford to stay anywhere else...' Her voice trailed off as she caught him frowning. Their eyes locked for just a fraction of time, then both rapidly looked away concentrating on their mini Christmas puddings.

'You could always...' Angus broke the sudden silence then blew out a breath, before looking at her again. Serious, practical, yet somehow terribly hazardous, she offered a taste of a solution. 'Look, I'm minus a nanny. The nanny's empty room might not be the best on offer, but I'm sure that it would beat the youth hostel...'

'I don't want to be a nanny.' Imogen gave a polite smile. 'I am trying to have a bit of a holiday, believe it or not.'

'I'm not asking you for that.' Angus cleared his throat. 'Just helping out a friend and you'd be helping me too. It makes sense.'

'Why would you do that?' Imogen asked, and he opened his mouth to respond only Angus couldn't, because if it had been anyone else at work in her predicament, he wasn't sure that he'd make the same offer. In fact, he wouldn't even be having this conversation, would never dream of telling anyone at work so much about him and Gemma. There was just no point of reference—nothing familiar—and not a hope of answering her question.

'It would be bliss to actually have Heath stay over with me for a couple of nights during the week, and that's not going to happen at the youth hostel.' Her voice dragged him out of his introspection. 'I could juggle my shifts around yours... Are you sure about this, Angus?' Imogen asked.

'Absolutely.' Angus answered, without thinking, but when his brain caught up the conclusion was the same. 'Absolutely.'

'Just till your mum gets here?'

'Whatever suits you.'

'How soon...?'

'When can I...?'

They both laughed as they spoke over each other.

'Why don't I go home and speak to the kids?' Angus suggested. 'You go and pack up your stuff. Then, if it's OK, I'll dash over to the hospital and tell them....'

'Tell them what?'

'That I...' He opened his mouth, closed it, then opened it again. 'I'm on all day tomorrow... Are you sure?'

'Works perfectly for me!' Imogen answered. 'I'm on a day off.'

CHAPTER SIX

PACKING up her things at the youth hostel didn't take Imogen long. Angus had assured her his house was easy to find and was a mere two minutes' walk from an underground station. She had his address and phone number in her pocket, but as Imogen sat on the tube, her heart was hammering.

It had all made perfect sense at the time.

Sitting in the café with him, talking to him, confident and relaxed in his company, it had seemed an obvious solution for both of them. The last night at the hostel had been hell—the noise, the laughter, the sheer energy of the place just too much to deal with, when all she'd wanted was to flop in front of the television and *not* think about her day. It was also no place to bring Heath and although she was desperate to cram in as much sightseeing as possible with him, she was already tired of sitting in cafés with him. A homebody by anyone's standards, at the end of the day Imogen wanted to be in rather than out, wanted to just be with her son rather than think up things to amuse him.

It just didn't make perfect sense now.

Coming out from the underground station and finding Angus's street easily, Imogen was tempted to turn and run in the other direction as she wheeled her suitcase towards yet another destination unknown.

And how she hated them.

Hated the chaos her life had been plunged into when Heath had been just a baby. She had spent the last three years extricating herself from it.

Sensible might just as well be her middle name. She never took risks, never did things on impulse, well, hadn't done in a long time. As *amazing* as Angus thought she was for coming to London, he hadn't known the angst it had caused her to be hurtled out of the comfort zone she had created for herself and Heath back home in Australia. He wouldn't have a clue how out of character it was for her to have asked him for coffee, to sit in a café with a man she'd only just met and *then* agree to move in with him!

And he couldn't possibly have known how much courage it took for her to knock on his door and smile widely as he opened it.

'This is Imogen…' Angus introduced her as he led her through to the lounge. 'She's a nurse from the hospital and she's going to help out for a little while.'

'Will Ainslie come back?' Clemmie, her hair thick with curls and her eyes as green as Angus's, gave Imogen a bored glance then spoke to her father.

'No, Ainslie's got a job with a new family now,' Angus answered.

'Ainslie was fun!' Dark eyed and dark haired, Jack looked directly at Imogen as he threw down a challenge.

'I can manage fun.' Imogen smiled, unfazed. 'I like your Christmas tree!'

Actually, she didn't. On the positive side, at least it was a *real* Christmas tree, but it was so tastefully decorated it surely belonged in a department store. Large silver ribbons and not a lot else dressed the lonely branches, and several, beautifully wrapped silver boxes lay strategically underneath, causing the children to stand to rigid attention when Imogen strolled over and picked one up.

'You're not supposed to touch!' Clemmie warned.

'Whoops! Are they for display purposes only?' Imogen smiled, replacing the empty box.

'I made a decoration at school…' Jack scampered out and returned with several pieces of pasta stuck on a card and sprayed gold.

'That's fabulous!' Imogen beamed, placing it on the tree and standing back to admire it. 'Maybe we can make some more tomorrow when your dad's at work—if that's OK with you guys!'

'Imogen is *not* the new nanny,' Angus warned his children. 'She's a friend, helping out for now, so remember that.

'Come on.' He smiled. 'I'll show you around.'

The children didn't follow, and now, back in his company, chatting easily as he showed her around his home, it all made perfect sense again. Even though it was an enigma to Imogen, from the two busy schedules that were pinned up on the fridge the Maitlin family was obviously used to having staff, used to having people living in their home, cleaning their things *and* looking after their children.

'The children have a separate menu?' Imogen frowned as she looked at a piece of paper attached to the fridge.

'I'm not expecting you to follow it.' Angus laughed. 'That was for Ainslie. Anyway, the children have already had tea...' Which did nothing to fade her frown. 'At my sister's.'

'You mean dinner?'

Still, apart from the endless lists, the house was gorgeous.

Well, apart from the endless photos.

For the most part she was comfortable with her body. Sure, Brad's words had hurt at the time and for a good while after that, but, as her mother had pointed out, her whole family might be curvy, big bosomed and big bottomed, but they weren't unhealthy. Imogen's sister had also pointed out, furiously jabbing at a magazine to reiterate the point, that no woman who had had children could possibly, without a lot of airbrushing, look like that!

'When was that taken?' Imogen paused at a particularly spectacular image of a woman rising from the ocean in a man's white shirt.

'The year before last...' Angus frowned. 'When we went to Thailand, supposedly to try and make things work.'

'It's lovely,' Imogen said, deciding to take a photo of her own to send as a postcard to her sister!

Used to airy, open-plan houses, painted walls and floorboards, Imogen adored the old house. The carpets were thick and cream and the bold choices of colour on the wallpapered walls were so different to their own house—even the stairs would be a novelty for Heath.

She could practically see him surfing his way down them head first. There was even a little box bedroom, which at first Imogen assumed was for her but was actually a spare that, Angus told her, she was welcome to use for Heath.

'This is yours.' He led her up yet another set of stairs to the 'nanny's accommodation', which translated to a converted attic decorated in white and yellow, with a skylight that had blinds and even a little kitchenette with a microwave, fridge and kettle.

'Does anyone actually eat together in this house?'

'I don't expect you to hide away in the attic,' Angus said. 'There's no bathroom facilities up here, though…'

'I wasn't expecting there to be.'

'Getting and keeping a good nanny is a serious business here,' Angus explained to a thoroughly bemused Imogen. 'Ideally they should have their own self-contained accommodation.'

'So you don't have to see them!'

'It's the other way around.' Angus laughed. 'They don't want to see us on their time off. Honestly, it's like a minefield.'

And one she had no intention of walking through!

Especially when at seven p.m., Clemmie informed Imogen that she'd forgotten to put her pyjamas out on her bed for her.

'Ainslie always did!' Clemmie said tearfully when Angus scolded her.

'Imogen is not the new nanny. I've told you she's a friend who's helping us out. Imogen's got a job at the hospital and her own little boy to look after.'

'How old is he?' Clemmie asked, suddenly interested.

'Four—like you. He's called Heath.'

'Well, my dad's on the television!' Clemmie said proudly.

'So's Heath's dad!' Imogen said, equally as proudly, then glanced at her watch. 'May I?'

'Help yourself,' Angus answered, somewhat bemused as the three of them piled on the sofa and proceeded to watch what was surely unsuitable viewing for a four- and a five-year-old, but from the squeals of recognition it wasn't the first time they had seen the show and from their rapt expressions it wouldn't be the last.

'Shane's Heath's dad?' Jack checked, clearly impressed.

'Cool!' Clemmie chanted.

And when surely he should be frantic, should be ringing round relatives, thinking about lawyers, trying to contact Gemma, for the moment at least he paused.

'Ten minutes,' Angus warned the children, 'then it's time to get ready for bed.'

Not that they were listening, all eyes in the room drawn to six feet two of bronzed Australian muscle, Shane's sun-bleached blond hair long and tousled on the pillow of his hospital bed. As if on cue Imogen's mobile began to ring.

'Hey, Brad!' Absolutely at ease, she grinned into the phone. 'I'm watching you now—tell them to go easy on the blusher next time...' Then she spoke with her son and Angus wondered if he and Gemma could ever get there, could chat and grin and even manage a laugh. Right now that world seemed light years away. Later, when Clemmie and Jack were in bed, and Imogen was rather expertly pulling a cork out of a bottle of her duty-free wine, Angus thought that perhaps now was the time he should be overcome with emotion, grief, panic, when *surely* now he should be thinking about tracking down his errant wife, or ringing his family, or getting started the million and one tasks that surely lay ahead. Instead, he pulled two steaks out of the freezer and watched as their dinner defrosted through the glass door of the microwave, watched as Imogen chopped onions and mushrooms and added a dash of wine to the sauce for the steaks, and it seemed incongruous how good he actually felt.

'To you!' Imogen tapped his glass and took a sip. 'To getting through.'

'I don't know how I would have, especially with it being Christmas…'

'You would have.'

'I would,' he agreed, taking another sip, 'but it would have messed up a lot of people's plans. This is really nice wine, by the way.'

'We do a good red.' Imogen smiled. 'I've got five more bottles upstairs!' Then she was serious. 'The kids seem OK.'

'They're used to people coming and going, and they're used to Gemma being away. They seem more upset that Ainslie's gone at the moment… though they'll be devastated when I tell them about their mother and me.'

'Just wait till Gemma's calmed down,' Imogen said wisely. 'Things might look different.'

'We won't be getting back together.' The slight raise of her brows irritated him. 'Once I've made up my mind, Imogen, I don't change it.'

It was a nice dinner—a *really* nice dinner—just talking about work, and about Angus trying to cram in an eighty-hour working week at the hospital and also look after a family. They talked about Imogen's life in Australia and her colossal mortgage, how she missed midwifery and how she juggled her shifts around Heath and Brad and she told him how much easier things would be in a few weeks once Heath started school.

'Are you seeing anyone?'

Oh, so casually he said it—well, she knew so much about him, surely it was right to ask?

'No.' She frowned over her wineglass at him. 'You?'

'I've only been separated for…' he glanced at his watch '…oh, ten hours now.'

That wasn't what she'd been asking, but from the way he'd answered she didn't need to clarify the question. Somehow Imogen knew that the man sitting at the table, leaning over to top up her glass, was as decent and as nice as he appeared.

As he went to fill her glass, both shared a quick yikes look when they realised the bottle was empty.

'I'm going to bed.' Imogen stretched as she stood.

'It's not even nine o'clock.'

'Perhaps, but I'm still jet-lagged.'

'Sorry—I keep forgetting you've only just got here. You just seem so….' His voice trailed off, not sure himself what he had been trying to say. ''Night, Imogen, and thanks, thanks for all your help today.'

''Night, Angus.'

Familiar.

As he stacked the dishwasher Angus shook his head, unhappy with the description.

Comfortable.

Only that didn't fit either, because at every turn she shocked him, shocked himself too—he'd told her things he never thought he'd share.

She'd been right about so many things, though, Angus thought, and it had been good to talk, to be honest, to share some of what he was going through.

Though there was one thing that she'd got wrong...

Picking up the phone, he rang his mother, took a deep breath and paused for the longest time when she answered the phone.

'Is anybody there?'

'It's me, Angus.'

Yes, Imogen was wrong, because his marriage to Gemma really was over. Angus knew that for sure, or he'd never have made that call.

Imogen stared at the ceiling as she listened to the low murmur of Angus's voice drifting up the stairs as he spoke on the telephone. Suddenly she found she was holding her breath too.

In three years she'd barely even glanced at another man—let alone flirt.

Oh, and she had been flirting. Not deliberately—in fact, only now, lying in bed and going over the day, was

Imogen blushing as red as her hair as she recalled some of the things that she'd said. They'd been the sort of cheeky, flirty things the old Imogen would have said a million years ago when she and Brad had been happy.

What *had* she been thinking? Imogen scolded herself.

Angus Maitlin was married to a model, for heaven's sake, or had *just* broken up with her. As if he'd even *think* of her in that way. And he was only being nice because he was glad she was here, that was all. Without her, a lot of people's Christmas plans would have been messed up and he would have had to fly his mother down from Scotland or try and arrange rapid child care just a week before Christmas. Yes, he was just glad she was here.

She was glad she was here too!

Everyone had said she was crazy, zipping over to London when she could least afford it, and had told her that she was being too soft on Brad, that he was taking advantage of her, but it was actually the other way around.

She needed this, Imogen thought. Lying in a strange bed, in a strange house, in a strange country, in the middle of an English winter—she actually felt as if she was thawing out.

As if the Imogen that had been placed in cold storage when her marriage had broken down and she had struggled just to survive was making itself known again.

So what if she had been flirting? She was testing her wings, that was all.

As the phone pinged off, as the rumble of pipes through the house stilled, as she heard the heavy creak of the stairs, never had a house been more noisy, but as quiet filled her little attic Imogen stared up at the skylight, too tired to close the blinds now, a streetlight outside illuminating low clouds as they drifted past, the sky lighter than it had been at nine that morning, which didn't make sense, but she was too tired to work it out.

Yes, she needed this, Imogen realised, turning on her side and letting delicious waves of sleep wash over her.

Needed to be where no one actually knew her, so that maybe, just maybe she could find herself again.

CHAPTER SEVEN

AN EYEFUL of grey and the thick sound of nothing woke her up.

Staring at the skylight, struggling to orientate herself, the snowflakes falling was nothing like she'd dreamed of. The wad of grey slush peeled away from the edge of the skylight and slid down the glass and as Imogen climbed out of bed she found out for the first time what it *really* meant to be cold. She was tempted to tell Angus why he couldn't keep a nanny!

'Sorry!' Grinning, just back from a run, Angus looked as warm as the toast he was buttering. 'The heating timer's not working. I meant to put it on before my run. The house will warm up soon.'

'You run in snow!'

'It's not snowing!' Angus refuted. 'Though it is trying to. It's turning to slush as soon as it hits the ground.'

Handing her a cup of tea, Imogen wasn't sure if it was her breath or the steam that was coming out of her mouth. Disgustingly healthy, brimming with energy, Angus joined her, but she started to forgive him when he proceeded to spread thick marmalade on a mountain of toast. He *did* have nice hands, large yet neat, with short white nails and a flash of an expensive watch. Imogen noticed his left hand was now minus a wedding ring.

'Did you want marmalade?' He checked when he caught her looking.

'Thanks!' Imogen said, and forgave him completely when he didn't moan that she ate more than half of the toast.

'Any plans for today?'

'None as yet…' The whole day stretched out before her—three kids and the whole of London waiting to be explored, and she'd take her time deciding. 'I want to do the Duck Tour…' She misread his frown. 'I saw it on the Internet—this bus takes you around London then straight onto the river.'

'I know what it is—are you really going to do that?'

'Maybe…' Imogen shrugged. 'Or I might wait for a warmer day.'

It irked her that he laughed.

Imogen Von Trapp she was not, but with accommodation sorted, and her three little charges marching beside her with maps in hand, Imogen felt close. She snapped away with her camera as Heath, Clemmie and Jack teased the solider at the Horse Guard Parade—Clemmie furious she couldn't extract a smile. There was so much to see, and while she was here Imogen fully intended to see it all, but by mid-afternoon her charges were sagging. Cracking a bar of chocolate on the tube, she tried to inject some enthusiasm as they headed for Knightsbridge.

'I don't want to go shopping!' Heath moaned.

'Not even if you get to see Santa?' Imogen checked.

'It's not the real one!' Jack scolded. 'Everyone knows that they just send a helper to the shops!'

'Oh, no!' Imogen cajoled. 'Everyone knows that the *real* Santa only goes to Harrods!'

Every time he saw her she was more beautiful.

As if the first image of her had been in black and white, and not so gradually the colour was being turned up. She was wearing her black skirt and flat boots again only with fishnet stockings this time and a sort of dusky pink jumper that was clearly too warm for her in the kitchen, because there was a pink glow to her cheeks. He noticed this because she was wearing long silver earrings that caught the light as she smiled up at him from the table where she was sitting.

'Angus, this is Brad.' Imogen introduced them as Angus walked in the kitchen after an extremely long day.

'Hi, there!' Blond, long limbed and utterly at ease, Brad grinned up at him from the kitchen table, where they sat with two mugs of tea. Then Brad looked at Imogen, saw the tint that spread up to her cheeks, saw the slight flurry of her hands, the rapid way she blinked when she was suddenly nervous—and knew it was time to go.

'Hello!' Angus said politely, pulling out a chair and joining them, only his heart wasn't in it. There was this niggling pain in his stomach now, causing him to wonder if the stress might be catching up with him and he was getting an ulcer.

'And this...' Imogen said as six little feet charged down the stairs and into the kitchen, skidding to a halt, 'is Heath.'

'Hi!' Bold, confident and a mini-version of his father, Heath grinned up at him, showing a spectacular gap where his baby teeth had once been.

'Hi, there!'

Clemmie was dancing on the spot and thrusting a photo at him, 'Imogen took us to see Santa!'

'It's not the fake one!' Jack warned. 'Imogen took us to see the real one.'

'Fantastic!' Angus duly said, only it was a great photo—three beaming faces and one very flustered-looking Santa. Suddenly Angus was grinning too, 'Wow!' he added. 'You really did meet the real thing.'

'The food hall was fabulous too!' Imogen said, heading to the kettle to make Angus a drink. 'I thought I'd died and gone to heaven. I'm worn out now, though!'

'I'd better get going.' Brad smiled as the kids all scampered off to the lounge.

'Don't rush off on my account!' Angus offered, but Brad was already on his way out, standing at the kitchen door and calling for Heath to hurry up and say goodbye.

'Think about what I said, Imo,' Brad added as he waited. 'It might be nice for Heath to wake up on Christmas morning with us both there.'

'It would be too confusing for him,' Imogen called. 'I'll come over about ten.'

And even though Brad's voice was laid-back and casual, as Angus watched Brad watching Imogen, he knew he was anything but. Knew, that the, oh, so laid-back Brad, still fancied his ex-wife.

'Think about it!' Brad said, again calling for Heath and getting the little guy into his coat, then giving Imogen a bit more than a friendly kiss on the cheek. He ought to think about eating, Angus decided, because his stomach was really starting to hurt now.

'Come and see the tree!' Clemmie declared, once Brad and Heath had gone. 'Santa gave us glitter-glue and paper...'

'Oh, my!' Angus whistled through his teeth as he walked into the lounge. The once tastefully decorated tree was now a blaze of multicoloured stars and angels and some other shapes he couldn't quite decipher. 'It's brilliant!' Angus declared to the kids, and then added under his breath for Imogen's benefit, 'Gemma will have a coronary!'

'I did think about that!' Imogen admitted, 'but when Santa gives you glue and glitter pens and there's a tree just begging for colour...'

'You've got glitter in your hair.'

'I've got glitter *everywhere*!' Imogen responded, pushing the arms up on her V-neck jumper and revealing some glittery forearms. 'I'll never get it off!'

'You and Brad are friendly,' Angus commented a little while later, frying up chicken that was generously dressed with tarragon, while Imogen made a vast salad.

'We are now!' Imogen answered, pulling a mango out of the fridge.

'Where the hell did you get that?'

'The food hall at Harrods,' Imogen laughed, 'I told you it was fabulous. I just couldn't resist—it reminded me of home.'

'So, you're just friends now?' Angus prolonged the conversation, not the one about the fruit, which she was expertly slicing, instead broaching the other things that reminded her of home.

'Brad's a great guy and he's a wonderful dad…' Imogen shrugged. 'He's just a lousy husband!' She poured the hot chicken and oil over the cold salad, added the mango and tossed it all in together as the four of them sat down to eat.

'What's this?' Jack, who did his level best not to eat anything green, let alone salad in December, frowned at his dinner.

'Imogen's warm chicken salad,' Imogen announced, as if she'd lifted the recipe from a book. 'And it's bliss!'

It was, just the thing his grumbling ulcer needed, Angus decided, slicing a crusty bread stick, stunned again at the normality of it all, or rather the abnormality of it all, as for the second time in as many days he sat down to a nice home-cooked dinner.

'The agency rang, they asked if I could do a late shift tomorrow.' Imogen took a big gulp of water. 'I said I'd get back to them, but I just saw your roster on the fridge and it's got "OC" written over tomorrow—am I right in assuming that's "on call"?'

'It just changed to "OAN"—or "on all night".' Angus grinned. 'Gus has a do to go to, but it's not a problem—I've already rung Lorna and she's going to have the kids tomorrow night, so take the shift.'

'You're sure?' Imogen checked. 'I can always ring the agency.'

'No need.' Angus said, helping himself to seconds. As easily as that it was sorted, no histrionics, no 'What about *my* career?'—just a simple solution to a simple problem, and for the first time in the longest time Angus actually felt as if he could breathe!

Until she stood up and leant over to load Jack's already empty plate with some more of the nicest warm salad imaginable on a cold December night and treated him to a glimpse of two very freckly, very glittery breasts.

'It gets everywhere, I tell you!' Imogen laughed as she caught him looking then blushed and looked away. 'I'm never going to get it off.'

Later, with the kids in their pyjamas, and the living room beginning to look a lot like Christmas, with the four of them watching Shane kissing a nubile blonde under the mistletoe, Imogen shot him a look.

'Are you OK?'

'Not sure…' Angus said, uncomfortably massaging his stomach. 'You know, I think I might be getting an ulcer.'

'Stress!' Imogen said, turning her head back to the television. 'Have a glass of milk.'

'How many times do I have to say it?' Angus responded, only she wasn't listening. 'I'm fine!'

'I've never seen so many Colles' fractures!'

'It's par for the course on this side of the world.' Heather grinned, as Imogen massaged her aching back.

After Maria, Imogen had never intended to go back to

Emergency, but the agency had rung a few times, and comparing Heath's 'to-do' list in London alongside her bank account, a full late shift, even if it was in Emergency, was one Imogen couldn't really justify declining.

Thankfully it had proven far less eventful that her first shift in London. Oh, it had been busy, but dramas had been few and far between and heading towards her supper break, Imogen had just one more wrist to help plaster.

Colles' fractures often occurred when people put out their hands to save themselves from a fall, and the slushy, icy streets had meant that Imogen had seen more in one shift than she usually would in a year in Queensland. She was happily explaining this to Ivy Banford as she held up her hand while Owen Richards, the intern, plastered it.

'Well, I still feel like an old fool!' Ivy scolded herself. 'As if I'm not enough trouble to everybody already.'

'Trouble?' Imogen frowned, taking in the neatly done-up blouse and smart shoes, the powdered nose and the lips that still held a smudge of coral. 'Since when were you any trouble to anyone?'

Ivy Banford wouldn't know *how* to make trouble. She'd been sitting patiently in the waiting room since eleven a.m., called for an x-Ray at three, and only now, as the clock edged past seven, was her wrist finally having a cast applied. And all she had done was apologise.

'I'm supposed to be at my son William's for Christmas. I wanted to have it at mine, but they all insisted...told me I should relax and let them do it. Now all I'm going to do is get in the way.'

'So there will be no stuffing the turkey?' Imogen

smiled. 'No laying the table or peeling a mountain of potatoes…'

'I said I'd get the parsnips,' Ivy fretted, pointing to her shopping trolley, 'and I said that I'd do the stuffing—'

'Ivy,' Imogen interrupted, 'I'm sure your son's wife is dying to impress you with her Christmas dinner.'

'She just wants to show me she can do it better.' Ivy pouted. 'She fancies herself as a gourmet chef—she's been waiting to get her hands on that turkey for years…'

'Give the baby her bottle!' Imogen said, her smile widening when she realised Angus had come into the plaster room.

'Meaning?'

'Let her do it all,' Imogen explained. 'Your job is to sit there with a big glass of sherry, play with the grandkids and let everyone spoil you for once. And,' Imogen added, 'even if the parsnips are burnt and the turkey's pink, you're to tell her it was the best Christmas dinner ever!'

'I will not,' Ivy thundered. 'What would that achieve?'

'Could be the start of world peace!' Imogen was holding her back now, grateful when Angus came and took the heavy arm from her as Owen continued to work on Ivy's wrist. 'Try it!'

'Huh!' Ivy huffed, but a small smile was forming. 'She'd get the shock of her life, mind!'

'And she'd know you didn't mean it!' Owen chimed in, as Imogen popped Ivy's arm into a sling.

'Just because you act like a sweet old thing…' Imogen winked '…doesn't mean you are one!'

'Your relatives are here,' Heather said as she ushered in a worried-looking man followed by his grim-faced wife.

'Oh, Mum, what have you been doing?'

'I'm fine, William!' Ivy said, refusing his help with her coat. Catching Imogen's eye, she relented and let him help her put it on. 'I didn't manage to get the parsnips.'

'Doesn't matter a scrap, Mum!' William soothed. 'Elise has got everything under control.'

'Such a relief...' Ivy smiled warmly at her daughter-in-law. 'I've a feeling this is going to be the best Christmas yet. Elise, dear, would you pass me my purse?'

But even before she'd pried out a note with one hand, Imogen was on to her.

'Don't you dare, Ivy!'

'Buy some sweets for your little boy!' Ivy insisted, pressing the note into Imogen's hand.

'I'll buy his sweets!' Imogen stuffed the fiver back in the purse and snapped it closed. 'You put it towards your sherry!'

'You're incorrigible.' Owen grinned as the trio shuffled off.

'I'm thirsty too!' Imogen smiled. 'I'm going for my break.'

'Good idea!' Owen agreed, following her out and telling Heather he'd be back in fifteen minutes. The sound of their laughter drifted down the corridor and Angus felt a kick in his stomach again.

'Everything OK?' Heather checked, as she noticed Angus rubbing his abdomen.

'Everything's fine!' Angus nodded then changed his mind, 'Actually, Heather, you couldn't get me some Gaviscon or Mylanta...?'

'For who? Did I miss someone?'

'It's actually for me.' Angus pulled a face. 'I think I've got an ulcer. I'm going to get some milk.'

It was a quiet evening—'The lull before the storm,' Heather warned, pouring out a dose of antacid then handing it to Angus. 'Better?' Heather checked, as Angus downed the chalky brew.

'Thanks.'

But walking into the staffroom, to find Imogen and Owen giggling as *Celebrity Doctor* calmly discussed some rather intimate issues, didn't exactly help.

'Do we have to watch this?' Angus snapped. 'It's actually a serious subject if you bothered to listen.'

'Sorry!' Imogen smothered a smile and though clearly not remotely sorry she did change the channel. However, this meant that he had to sit and watch a certain blonde head, *again*, writhing on the pillow, only this time in pain as the doctors battled to save Shane.

'He's gorgeous!' Another nurse, Cassie, had joined them now, gaping at the screen then over at Imogen, clearly unable to comprehend that someone as gorgeous as *Shane* could ever have married someone as plain and as overweight as Imogen. 'And he's such a good actor.'

'Do you think so?' Imogen sounded surprised. 'He's a complete hypochondriac. He carried on exactly like that when he had toothache.'

The storm didn't eventuate. The lull stretched on and when the night staff started to arrive, Heather had sent most of her regular staff home, knowing the night shift would dash around if there was an emergency. A few nurses milled around what patients there were and

Imogen filled in the time by doing a restock as Heather and Angus chatted.

'Ready for Christmas?' Heather asked Angus as she updated the whiteboard.

'Hope so.'

'Don't worry—I'm sure Gemma's got it all under control.'

'Actually, Heather…Gemma and I broke up.' Imogen watched as Heather's hand paused over the whiteboard, her face aghast as she turned around. 'It's fine, Heather.'

'It's not fine!' Heather looked as if she was about to cry. 'Angus, why didn't you say?'

'I just did.'

'But…'

'Look!' Angus gave a wry smile. 'I'm just letting you know in case something unforseen happens—Gus has offered to help out if need be.'

'So where are the kids?'

'At home.'

'Where's Gemma?' As Angus gave a small eye roll, Heather sagged. 'When did all this happen? Oh, Angus…'

'It's all under control.'

'But how?' Heather asked. 'Who's helping with the kids?'

Imogen swallowed hard, her cheeks darkening a touch, wondering if Angus would say anything, and how Heather would react if he did. There was no need to worry, Angus's next comment making it spectacularly clear that his home and work lives were kept very separate.

'I've got some temporary help for now and my mother is coming down to stay after Christmas.'

He smiled over at Imogen, only she didn't smile back. In fact, she looked away.

Temporary.

Strange how much that word had stung her to hear.

Temporary.

Funny that the same word buzzed like a blowfly around Angus for the rest of his night shift.

And when she said goodnight, when the quiet department suddenly seemed empty without her, when he joined Owen later in the staffroom and had to listen to his junior tell him how great that red-headed agency nurse was, two weeks suddenly seemed too short.

His marriage was over, his life was supposed to be in chaos, Christmas was just a couple of days away and yet he was coping, would make sure that the kids coped, knew that they'd all get through.

The only thing that daunted him at this moment was the prospect of Imogen leaving.

That temporary solution he had found raised an entirely new set of problems all of a sudden.

CHAPTER EIGHT

ON SHEER impulse Imogen had purchased a red bikini and sheer silver sarong at the departure terminal in Queensland.

She'd had absolutely no intention of wearing them until she got home, and they'd nestled in her case with the labels still on. But, waking at the crack of dawn, her sleeping pattern still horribly out of whack, finally she had a reason to put them on.

Angus had point blank refused to take rent.

Admittedly she hadn't pushed the point, but the bliss of having a nice roof over her head for her time in London and as much work as she wanted meant Imogen could pay him back in other ways—like mangos—and at 5.30 a.m., when restless legs started twitching, she decided she could give the bathroom a rather overdue clean, because Mrs Gemma Maitlin certainly hadn't picked up the cleaning baton when she'd fired the cleaning lady!

Wrinkling up her nose, Imogen peered into the shower. Housework wasn't exactly her forte, but occasionally the urge hit, and it was hitting now. Turning up the heating and grabbing the radio as she located the cleaning gear, she padded to the bathroom, dropping her sarong in the hallway and frowning at her reflection in the bathroom mirror.

'Diet!' she warned herself, turning round and grimacing at her bottom, but at least it was tanned—brown fat was certainly more attractive than white! Yes, in the new year she was definitely going on diet.

'But after we get back!' she promised her reflection. Then she promptly forgot about it as she bopped along to the music, glad by the time that she'd finished and jet-lag had hit that Angus's kids were at his sister's and Heath was with Brad, so that she could now head down to the kitchen, grab a cup of tea and crawl back into bed before Angus came home.

Then she heard his key in the front door.

Eyes wide, her face red from exertion, Imogen wondered what she should do. She could just stand in the bathroom and hope he didn't notice or she could make a dash to her room. But if he looked up he'd see her running across the landing and she could hear his foot on the bottom step now so, not wanting to stink of bleach, she sprayed a generous dash of perfume and forced a smile on her face as she headed out to meet him.

Tired, grumpy and freezing, all Angus wanted to do as he put the key in the front door and headed up the stairs was to fall into bed.

Tired, because he'd been up all night.

Grumpy, because his shirt, suit and tie had lasted till seven a.m. but were now in a plastic bag, awaiting a trip to the dry cleaner's. Tossing the bag in the corner, he decided to deal with that unpleasant task later.

Freezing, because hair wet from a quick shower at work and dressed now in threadbare theatre gear, he'd found out five minutes from home that he really should have stopped for petrol at the last garage.

The heat hit him as soon as he stepped into the hall—the place was like a sauna!

He didn't have the energy to work out why—all he wanted was bed.

Till he saw Imogen standing on the landing.

'Morning!'

'Morning!' Angus gave what he hoped was a normal smile as he stood at the bottom of the stairs, trying not to look surprised or to comment on the fact that she was wearing nothing other than a red bikini. He failed miserably on both counts. 'Imogen!' He gaped. 'Why are you dressed like that?'

'I was just cleaning the shower…'

'You wear a bikini to clean the shower?'

'No!' She gave him a very old-fashioned look. 'Normally I wear *nothing* to clean the showers, but given this is your home…'

Picking up a sliver of silver fabric from the floor, she wrapped it around her rather magnificent bosom. 'Do you want some breakfast?'

'Nope!' Funny that he had to feign a yawn now. 'I'm going straight to bed, I want to grab a few hours before I pick up the kids.'

'I'll pick up the kids,' Imogen offered. 'You should have something to eat and then you'll sleep well.'

He'd sleep well without something to eat, Angus was about to say, but she was walking down the stairs and was passing him now, and it would seem rude just to head on up. So Angus followed her into the kitchen, yawning again, but for real this time, as he sat on a barstool and poured some muesli into a bowl as Imogen screwed up her nose.

'I'll make you some pancakes.'

'Muesli's fine.'

'Not after a night shift!' Imogen said, tipping the lot into the bin and, Angus realised, refusing to look at him. 'It will only take a moment.'

'Great,' Angus said.

'There's some mango left…' She pulled it from the fridge, holding up half a fruit, and without waiting for his reply ran the knife along the plump fruit, scoring it into little crosses, then pushing her fingers onto the soft skin and inverting it so that all the fruit poked up into little squares and it felt strangely erotic.

She probably walked around like this at home all the time, Angus frantically reasoned. Wandering around the house in a bikini was probably the norm where she came from. Only there were kangaroos in Australia too, but he didn't expect to see one when he looked out of the window. Still, Angus told himself, she no doubt spent her entire day wearing as little as possible—only that thought wasn't exactly helping matters either!

The huge kitchen was claustrophobically tiny now, and he could see her freckly breasts jiggling before his eyes as she whipped up the batter.

'Won't be long!' Imogen smiled.

'The heating's high...' Angus said gruffly.

'Is it?' Imogen shrugged.

He could hear the batter sizzling as it hit the frying pan. Her back was to him and it was brown, this gorgeous brown that was so rare these days. Her tan not perfect because he could see the straps where another bikini must have been, could see the freckles that showered her back, only it looked pretty perfect to him...

'Here.' Leaning over the bench, she handed him breakfast and as she leant forward he could see the white of her breast as her bikini shifted, saw a little bit of Imogen that had never seen the sun. He knew she'd caught him looking because she was looking at him too, knew because the already hot room was stifling now. The bubbling steam from the kettle nothing compared to the cauldron sizzling between them. Three days after one's marriage ended was arguably the best or worst time to act on impulse—only Angus wasn't actually thinking about that.

For ages his marriage had been over and there was this assumption, from his mother, from Gemma, even from Imogen at first, that he must, in that time, have been seeing someone else. As if coping with the demise and subsequent end of his marriage couldn't have been enough to keep him occupied. Oh, they hadn't come right out and said it, but he could sense they thought there had to be more.

Well, there hadn't been anyone.

But, yes, there was more.

Pushing a plate towards him, loaded with pancakes and mango and syrup, Angus's mouth should have been watering, only it was a touch dry as he realised that there was way more to it than anyone knew.

And he was looking right at her.

Only now Imogen wasn't looking away, as she always had before. In fact, she was looking right at him. For the first time in the longest time, the first time for ages, the woman Angus wanted was looking back at him…

And with want in her eyes.

He *was* beautiful.

She'd known that from the start.

And he was nice.

She'd known that too.

But that this august yet tender man might actually want her in the way she wanted him was, for Imogen, a revelation.

Embarrassed at being caught in her bikini, she'd attempted casual—had, oh, so casually covered herself with her sarong and wished, as she often did, that she'd kept to her diet, or even considered that he might come home early. There were so many things Imogen hadn't factored in, and seeing the want in his eyes as she'd come down the stairs had been one of them.

Oh, she'd dismissed it, told herself she was imagining things.

But, standing in the kitchen, attempting to be normal, she could hear the fizz of arousal sizzling around them. She tried to tell herself over and over that she was misreading things, that it was her want that she could sense and not his.

Only it was everywhere.

She could feel his eyes on her, burning into her back as she turned away, could feel his need in the stifling air she dragged into her tight chest. Awareness in every jerky movement, she was scared to turn around, scared that he might see the tumble of emotions that were coursing through her.

Because, as the kettle rattled to the boil, as she slid the plate she'd prepared towards him, Imogen knew it was impossible, knew that Angus Maitlin could have any woman he wanted...

Only he wanted her.

Watching him stride towards her, she could taste him almost before he kissed her. His mouth on hers had been the last thing she'd expected on awakening, yet it was everything she needed now. Angus made her feel like a woman again, one who had come alive.

For Angus it was the easiest walk of his life.

Used to making difficult decisions in an instant, this one was actually incredibly easy. Oh, he'd wrestled with it for days, had gone over every argument in his head as to why it would never happen, why it could never work, had told himself that he was imagining things, that this vibrant stunning woman saw him as nothing more than a colleague and a friend...

Till she looked up and he saw the pink flush that was ever present in her cheeks spread across her neck and down her chest. He registered the tiny swallow in her throat, and for Angus, walking round the bench and over to her came as naturally as breathing—in fact, more naturally, because breathing was proving difficult right now, his lungs taut. His hands rested on the tops of her arms and he felt her tremulous body beneath them, a body that didn't want soothing, her skin soft and smooth beneath his fingers. He noticed a bergamot note to her perfume as his face neared hers, and it would have been so easy to kiss her then, but haste would have deprived him of seeing those pale blue eyes, black now with pupils dilated with lust. The scent of her skin filled his nostrils and the arousal between them intensified as the feel of her soft cheek grazed against his. He wanted to taste her mouth now so he did, placing his lips on hers and closing his eyes at the exquisite sweetness of ripe flesh that wanted to taste him too—and taste him she did, sucking on his bottom lip. Her hands on his shoulders, fingers kneading lightly as thoroughly he kissed her back.

'Oh, God, Imogen...' He moaned her name as he pulled back, knowing that at this point it should stop, should merit discussion, acknowledgement, something...but the bliss of wanting was here and now and the bliss of being wanted was mind-blowing. She kissed him back, her response moist, lingering, slow, like a river inevitably rolling. He could feel her hands slipping under his theatre top, inquisitive fingers exploring his stomach. He didn't want it to end, wanted also to explore this woman who wore a bikini and sarong on a freezing December morning—who had brought sunshine and warmth into what should have been the bleakest and coldest of winters. His hands, without guidance, were undoing the knot of her sarong, watching two red triangles strain against the gorgeous flesh of her breasts. He wanted to taste the woman who fed him fruit when he wanted bed, and pushing aside the bikini top he lowered his mouth. Her nipples were as hard as hazelnuts swelling in his mouth as he tasted her, his hand on her skin, her back, her waist, feeling the delicious, unfamiliar curves, the generous flesh that was for him, tasting the feel of want on his mouth, these myriad sensations as she kissed him back. And it felt so right—he'd come home this morning and it felt as if he were coming home to her now, to a kiss that had been waiting patiently, to a kiss that was almost *familiar*, because he'd been there before.

He may have said goodnight to her from the day she'd moved in, but he'd met her only a couple of hours later in his dreams. And dreams didn't match up to the real feel of her mouth on his, sucking him, kissing him, devouring him. Imogen, alive in his arms, and he was coming alive again too. In one easy shift she was sitting on the kitchen bench, sliding his theatre top over his head, and the moan of delight as she saw his torso had him so hard he had to slow himself down. Her fingers pressed harder into his shoulder, her hungry lips tasting his nipples now. Angus noticed there were still the last remnants of glitter on her nipple, this little glimmer of gold where there shouldn't be, and he sucked at it, yet still it stayed. He flicked at the fleck again with his tongue, willing himself to slow down, but she was playing with the ties of his theatre bottoms now, pulling them down with some difficulty over his erection as he dealt with the far easier task of her bikini bottom ties.

Alone in the kitchen, not a wedding ring between them, but there was a whole lot else. Staring into her pale blue eyes, seeing her blink, Angus knew she knew it too.

'We shouldn't...' he half heartedly attempted, kissing her again.

'We should,' Imogen purred as she kissed him back.

'You'll be gone soon...'

'I'm here now.' She guided his hands to her sweetest place and as the pad of his thumb took her most intimate pulse, he tried one last attempt at reason.

'It's too soon...' But her ankles were round his back and it felt like he'd been waiting for ever.

'Not for me.'

'I'm crazy about you, Imogen,' Angus gasped, hovering at her entrance, seeing the golden curls that beckoned him and desperate to enter, her breathless response all the invitation required as he plunged in blissfully.

'Me, too!'

It was like stumbling into paradise, feeling her legs coil around him as she dragged him in, smelling her, tasting her, feeling her. This stunning, beautiful woman was somehow as into him as much as he was into her. It *was* too much, and certainly *too soon*, and just as Angus tried to slow himself down, just as he forced himself to think about tax receipts and spreadsheets and anything mundane, she dragged him in deeper, her ankles coiling around his back, her head arching backwards, and he kissed the hollows of her throat. Angus knew that nothing was going to distract him now, and better still, as he felt her tighten, and heard these little throaty gasps come from the throat he was kissing, distraction was as unnecessary as it was impossible. He could feel the rhythm of her orgasm beating for him to join her in this heady place, and the only thing Angus was concentrating on was her, was Imogen, and how she made him feel. Then the heaven of his climax and the sheer pleasure of hers when it happened had his heart thumping a tattoo in his chest. As he held her after it all should have dimmed as reality invaded, as they were back in the kitchen having taken the biggest most reckless step of their lives. But, if anything, the world looked better.

'Oh, Angus.' Still inside her, still holding her, as blue eyes met his, there was no place he would rather have been. 'What do you do to me?'

'I could ask the same thing.'

And it should have been awkward, only it wasn't.

And guilt was curiously absent as he kissed her again.

There was not even a hint of uncertainty as she popped the pancakes in the microwave for all of thirty seconds, grabbed a fork and they both headed upstairs, just a tiny pause at the landing as he steered her to his bedroom.

'My room,' Imogen insisted. 'I can't do anything in there.'

'I can't do anything in the nanny's room!' Angus grinned. 'Anyway, it's a single bed!'

'Brilliant!'

'I thought I was getting an ulcer.'

'You need to eat more regularly.'

They were lying naked on her tiny bed, blinds closed on the skylight, the heating still up high and the radio still blaring, feeding each other mango in golden syrup, both discovering again what it felt like to be happy.

Not fine, or OK, or getting there, but actually happy.

Absolutely at ease, lost in the moment and just, well, happy.

'I keep getting this pain, you see….' Angus tapped his stomach. 'Well, not a pain as such…right here… right here in my solar plexus.'

'You poor baby!' Imogen soothed, bending her head and kissing it better.

'Every time I see your ex, either in the flesh or on the television, every time I hear Owen tell me how bloody fantastic that red-headed agency nurse is…' He blew out a breath. 'I didn't realise it at the time, but this little network of nerves, that really don't do much, scrunches into a ball every time…'

'Oh.' She looked up at him. 'Are you jealous?'

'I don't know.' Angus grimaced, because he'd never really been jealous before.

'Well, don't be!' Imogen frowned. 'Brad's like one of your boxes under the tree—beautifully gift wrapped, but sadly empty. There's nothing between us, nothing at all.'

Tired now, he watched as she slipped under the sheet, watched her lovely face on the pillow, those blue eyes smiling at him, and it felt utterly right to join her and spoon his body in behind her, to place his hand on the curve where her waist met her bottom and just hold her, and utterly wrong that in two weeks she'd be gone.

'Gemma's boyfriend's not Australian, by any chance?' Imogen said, much later in that time before falling asleep.

'Afraid not. Brad might get more work here…?'

'He's been offered a job on a children's show back home.'

'Oh.'

He wasn't remotely tired now. Too used to sleeping

alone, he had been trying to accommodate to the feel of her in his arms, trying to fathom out that this was real, as his mind, which was used to coming up with them, raced for a solution, for something, some way to hold on to what they had only just found. Only at every twist of his thoughts he was thwarted…

Kids, careers, exes, schools—oh, and a tiny matter of ten thousand or so miles.

And she waited, stared at the wall and waited for him to say that they'd work something out, waited for him to tell her that it would all be OK, that somehow it might work.

Only he couldn't.

'We should keep it quiet,' Angus said instead.

'I wasn't going to rush into work and put up a poster.'

'I know.' He felt her body stiffen, could hear the irritated edge in her voice, especially when she continued.

'Don't worry, I won't damage your perfect reputation.'

'Imogen.' He put his hand up to her cheek, tucked a stray strand of hair behind her ear and tried to voice what he was feeling. 'It's not just about my reputation—you go home soon, all it will look like to others is a fling… It's about your reputation too.'

'I know.' She was glad she was facing away from him. Tears were stinging her eyes, knowing he was right and wishing it wasn't so.

'And it would be just so confusing for the kids….'

'Of course.' She gave a big sniff. 'They don't need to know anything.' Which was right and everything, but it just made it seem like a dirty little secret. As if all they shared, all that had felt so right, was seemingly wrong.

'You know…' Imogen gave a pale smile. '…I always wondered what Heath would be like, you know, if I met someone…'

'He hasn't met any of your boyfriends?'

'There haven't been any boyfriends.'

'But you and Brad broke up ages ago.'

'I wasn't ready,' Imogen said, and he rolled her towards him then, didn't want to talk to her back when he could see her instead, and he stared deep into those eyes that had entranced him from the second they'd locked with his. He knew then that he didn't really know her at all, only *how* he wanted to. He wanted to know everything about the shy but provocative, gentle yet sexy, completely stunning woman that had greeted him on the stairs, and who had just been his. 'I don't share my mango with everyone!'

She was attempting a joke, only he wasn't smiling, the seriousness of their situation hitting home. Serious, Angus realised, because this deep, beautiful woman had trusted only him with her patched-up heart, and that was something he could never take lightly.

'Come here,' he said, as if the two centimetres that separated them in the bed was as vast as the distance that separated their future. Pulling her towards him, he kissed her deeply, though tenderly, blotting out the many questions with slow, deep answers, because for now there wasn't any rush. They didn't have to think about anything right now.

Imogen wasn't going anywhere today and neither was Angus.

CHAPTER NINE

'WHAT did you guys do today?'

'Nothing!' Looking up from smiling, pyjama-clad people mulling over a vast jigsaw, Imogen's smile was arguably the widest when Angus came home from work the next day. 'We just flopped.'

'Flopped?'

'Flopped around and didn't do much. We didn't even get dressed—did we, guys?'

'We brushed our teeth!' Jack said.

'I didn't!' Heath grinned, but one look from his mother and he hurtled up the stairs to the bathroom. Also in pyjamas, Imogen wandered into the kitchen where Angus was serving up some wicked-looking noodles.

'Thanks for this!'

'They're just noodles!'

'I mean this...' She gave a sigh of contentment as she looked around and beyond the kitchen. 'You have no idea how much it means to just do *nothing* with Heath. It's just been so nice to have a quiet day, instead of thinking up things to do or sitting in a burger bar, which is what I would have been doing today if I wasn't here.'

'Thank you too...' Angus smiled. 'It's been so nice to go to work and know the kids are happy and not have to worry about what I'm going to find when I come home. Have they asked about Gemma?'

'Clemmie has.' Imogen nodded. 'Gemma rang this afternoon and spoke to them for a couple of minutes, but Jack's asking when she's coming home. Have you spoken to her?'

'I've rung her,' Angus said, 'but I just got her voice-mail. I've sent her a few texts—told her that we need to sort things out as to what to tell the kids. I've told her too that she needs to see them...' He raked a hand through his hair. 'I'm just in this holding pattern—till I see her, till I speak to her, I don't know...'

Which left Imogen in a holding pattern too.

Knowing that at any minute Gemma could come back, that with one phone call everything would change.

And it was selfish of her to not wish that for him.

How could she not wish that his relationship with Gemma was salvageable? How could she not wish that Clemmie and Jack's mum might suddenly come home—after all, home was where she would be heading soon.

'Have you sorted out the boxroom for Heath?' His question dragged her out of her introspection. 'There are spare pillows in the hall cupboard, I think.'

'I had hoped he'd want to sleep in with me, given we haven't spent a night under the same roof for a while, but times have changed apparently—he's got new friends now!'

'There's a trundle bed under Jack's,' Angus suggested.

'All options examined...' Imogen rolled her eyes.

'They want to camp out.' She gave a little wince. 'In the lounge.'

'Of course they do!' Angus grinned and she was so happy he did—so happy that a little bit of chaos didn't matter to him. 'Why would you want a soft warm bed when there's a cold hard floor?'

'They're planning a midnight feast too.' Imogen giggled. 'Though we don't know about that.'

And she loved it that he lowered all the crisps and treats to a lower shelf, loved it that he put a few cans of usually forbidden fizz in the fridge and pulled the ice cream to the front of the freezer. Loved it that he couldn't just *get* the blankets for the kids to make the fort, but *had* to help them too. And with growing amusement Imogen came back from a long soak in the bath to find some rather impressive-looking tents, all of which Angus had to go in and check for size and comfort.

'Mine's the best!' Clemmie demanded. 'Isn't it, Imogen?'

'It's fabulous!' Imogen declared, checking it out for herself. 'I might sleep here myself.'

And later, when the living room was a no-go zone, and Imogen had eaten the last of the noodles while Angus finished off the crossword in the newspaper, when she was sitting in a dressing-gown at the kitchen table as Angus headed off to the shower, when his mother called and she had to knock for him to come out of the shower, it was just too much.

Standing in the kitchen dripping wet with a towel around his hips, trying to find a pen to write down his mother's flight arrival time, Imogen knew that if she spent a second longer in the same room with him and didn't touch him, she'd surely self combust, and she could take no more.

'I'm going to bed.'

'It's only nine o'clock!' Angus said, cursing as the crayon he was using to write, suddenly snapped. 'What did I say the flight number was?'

Only she couldn't answer. Simply couldn't tell him how much she wanted him, or how it was killing her inside to know that this magical evening doing *nothing* with the kids, this slice of heaven they had found, couldn't be shared with others and certainly couldn't last.

'I'll make you a cup of tea…' He was halfway to the kettle and she'd half decided to stay up a bit longer when the phone rang. She watched the set of his shoulders stiffen, watched his free hand rake through his damp hair and even before he said her name, Imogen knew that it was Gemma.

Knew she wouldn't be getting her cup of tea.

Closing the kitchen door, she checked on the kids—smiling at their excited faces and joining in the fun, leaving him to it, because his marriage ending had nothing to do with her.

But it was hard.

Especially when the phone in the living room clicked off and she knew the call was over, but he still didn't come out.

Especially when later, much later, the kids charged into the kitchen, with Imogen racing to stop them, only to find Angus with his head in his hands at the table.

'Are you crying?' Clemmie said accusingly.

'Don't be daft!' Angus grinned but looked distinctly glassy-eyed. 'I've got a cold.'

And later, lying in bed, she could hear the commotion downstairs, kids giggling, the fridge door opening, and as the bedroom door pushed open and he sat down on the side of her bed, she hated the tears that greeted his hand when he stroked her cheek.

'Sorry!' She shuddered the word out.

'For what?'

'You were right....' Imogen gulped. 'It is too soon.'

'Not for me.'

'You miss her—and it's right that you miss her...'

'Imogen, have you any idea how unbearable the last few days would have been without you?' Still he stroked her cheek. 'And have you any idea how unbearable my life was before I met you?'

'No.'

'She's coming over tomorrow. We're going to tell the kids—that's what's beating me up.'

'It's nearly Christmas,' Imogen croaked.

'Which gives us a little time to get our act together for Christmas Day.' Angus screwed his eyes closed. 'Couldn't she have waited?' Then he cursed himself. 'I shouldn't have pushed things—'

'No.' Imogen interrupted. 'Angus, you can't plan these things and Gemma couldn't either. She didn't just *decide* to fall in love...'

'Don't expect me to forgive her...' Angus shook his head.

'Would it have been any easier in September?' Imogen

asked. 'With Clemmie all excited about school... Or maybe you could have held out till Easter...'

'Imogen, don't...'

But she did.

'Or last year when you knew things were over...'

'No,' Angus admitted. Gazing down at her, the muddied waters cleared a touch as he realised in many ways that time had actually been kind, because somehow she was here beside him. 'What would I do without you?'

'You'll find out soon enough.'

His mouth was gentle. A kiss so tender, so kind, so merited that for that second, even if the kids had rampaged up the stairs and caught them, it would have surely been justified.

So justified that when the crisp packets were empty, when the carefully built tents had long since collapsed and three little people lay curled up on the floor, with Angus and Imogen tucking blankets around shoulders, it seemed right that he take her hand as they headed up the stairs to bed. Somehow it would be wrong to sleep alone tonight.

'Put the chair against the door.' Imogen gulped, shy all of a sudden, hating the body he seemed to adore, not as bold as before and wishing he'd turn the lights off or would turn around long enough so that she could jump under the covers without him seeing her.

But see her he did.

One touch and she was comfortable.

One kiss and he soothed her.

Chased away the insecurities with every caress.

And never had his love been as sweet as it was bitter.

The depth of his kiss almost annulled by its sheer impossibility. Like a barnacle on a rock, she clung to him, couldn't bear that soon they would be ripped apart. Her single bed was just so much better for the intimacies they shared, to feel the muscle of him beside her, every roll, every kiss, every tumble bringing them closer until he was where he belonged—inside her.

And it was the saddest, sweetest love she had ever made. Every stroke, every beat of him pushing them to a place they'd never been, to mutuality, affinity, to a space in the world that was solely for them.

Sweet to have visited.

So sad to leave.

Her single bed huge when later, much later, he crept from the room.

CHAPTER TEN

OH, YOU can smile and distract, you can make soothing noises, you can ignore and deny and you can really try to hide things, but children always know.

Especially at Christmas.

'Mum's coming in an hour.' Clemmie was sitting on the stairs, watching as Imogen pulled her boots and coat on. She was taking Heath on the London Duck Tour, would ride around Central London then plunge into the Thames in the same amphibious vehicle.

Heath had been bright-eyed with excitement when Imogen had told him about it.

Jack and Clemmie hadn't even asked if they could go.

'That's good,' Imogen said, looking at her little angry face and truly not knowing what to say.

'I'm going to play in my room.'

Imogen didn't call out goodbye to Angus and didn't call it out to the children, relieved just to open the front door and escape the oppressive atmosphere.

'Hello, Imogen.'

The camera did lie. Because standing on the doorstep, close to six feet tall in high-heeled cream boots and a soft cream coat, dark hair billowing around her pale face, Imogen hadn't braced herself for Gemma's absolute beauty, or that she might know her name.

'Angus said he'd arranged some temporary help…'

Oh, she needn't have worried, Imogen realised, because not for a second would this stunning woman ever consider her a threat. It wouldn't even enter her head that Angus might want someone as dowdy and as plain as her.

'The children have raved about you on the phone… Thank you so much for taking care of my babies,' Gemma continued in a flurry, and Imogen realised the woman was actually beside herself with nerves, still standing on the doorstep of her own home, as if it was up to Imogen to ask her inside.

Truly not knowing what to say, Imogen was saved from answering as Angus came down the hallway.

'Hello, Gemma.'

'Oh, Angus.'

Of course she didn't need to be asked in, Imogen thought as she stepped out into the street. Of course, when Gemma burst out crying, Angus would comfort her as together they faced the most appalling task together. Only she had never expected to like her, had never expected to be moved by the raw tears that had spilled from her eyes, the throaty sob that had come from her lips. And if it moved her, then what must it have done for Angus?

Maybe they might make it work, Imogen thought, huddled up with Heath, freezing as they sped through the streets taking photos and quacking at passersby.

Heath whooped with delight as they plunged into the river and even though it was fun and brilliant and a day she'd remember for ever, Imogen felt as if her heart was being squeezed from the inside.

Especially after she dropped off Heath at Brad's and went back to a house that felt different somehow, no matter how Angus tried to act normal.

A new normal.

A new normal where Angus went into work for a few hours and Gemma came over on Christmas Eve to take the children out and Imogen attempted some last-minute Christmas shopping. Heath was easy to buy for and Jack and Clemmie were too. Brad? Well, thankfully, given it was December, sunglasses were drastically reduced in price, which took care of that.

If only Angus was so easy.

Along with the last of the frantic last-minute shoppers she wandered around vast department stores, trying to find the perfect present for the perfect man—and knowing she had one chance to get it right.

That this could be their only Christmas.

And it would take more than a miracle for it to be a happy one. There was just way too much hurt all around.

'Get everything?' Angus asked, when laden with bags she nearly fell through the door.

'If I didn't, it's too late now! How are the kids?' Imogen added, as he helped her stuff the bags in the stair cupboards.

'They seem OK...' His jacket and tie were off, his shirt coming untucked at the hips, but he was still the most impressive man she had ever seen, Imogen thought as he waited till they were alone before discussing it again. 'They really do seem OK. You know, we clung on for a year, thinking we were doing the right thing, but I'm starting to wonder if we—'

'My tooth fell out!' Clemmie burst into the kitchen, dripping blood and smiling at the same time.

'That's what happens if you keep tugging at it.' Angus grinned, getting a wad of kitchen roll and dealing with the casualty. 'She's hoping for bonus points if Santa and the tooth fairy both come on Christmas Eve!'

Clemmie grinned her gappy smile and it reminded Imogen so much of Heath it hurt. Oh, she adored Clemmie, adored Jack, only they weren't her babies.

Her first Christmas Eve without Heath beside her and surely no one in the world knew how she felt.

Except one.

'Mum's on the phone!' Angus called later as he was putting two excited children to bed. Imogen sat in a room bathed with fairy lights, feeling sick on her third mince pie, missing Heath so much it hurt. As she watched a rerun of Shane, all Imogen could wonder was how grown-ups got it so wrong.

How did they mess up so badly—and who was it that suffered the most?

And then she thought of Maria.

Tears sliding down her cheeks, she thought of how, even if it was a difficult life sometimes, she'd so much rather live it. She thought of little Guido, and prayed he was OK without his parents to love him. She barely looked up when Angus walked into the lounge, laden with boxes that *weren't* empty for underneath the tree.

'Still hurts, huh?' Angus asked, staring for a minute at the TV and Shane, then back at her.

'Always,' Imogen answered, as his pager trilled.

And because he was a consultant, because the pubs were turning out and because Gus had promised to come in at six next morning if he could just have Christmas Eve undisturbed, she nodded and took over.

Lugging the presents under the tree as he sped into the night.

She left the Christmas lights on and took bites out of four mince pies then bit on the carrot that had been left for Rudolph. Then she headed up the stairs and quietly filled their stockings, before having to go back down because she'd forgotten that the tooth fairy was coming tonight too. By the end it was a relief, just a blessed relief, to finally close her bedroom door.

It would take more than a miracle to make this Christmas a happy one, Imogen thought, staring up at her little skylight, hearing the wail of sirens in the distance and the swoosh of cars as they sped through the night. Finally she gave way to the tears she'd held in as she'd hung Clemmie's stocking and fiddled with Jack's; as she'd kissed two little faces goodnight, and had done all the right things for Gemma's children…

While all the while missing her own.

CHAPTER ELEVEN

THERE was one advantage to putting two overexcited children to bed on Christmas Eve.

It was actually past eight when the ringing of the phone pierced the house. Sitting up, blinking through swollen lids, Imogen *just* had time to grab her sarong and wrap it around her before two thoroughly overexcited bundles burst into her room.

'Mummy's coming!' Jack yelped. 'She's coming over!'

'Santa's been!' Clemmie chimed in.

Various squeals pierced her brain as two mini-tornadoes spun out of her room and charged down the stairs, leaving Imogen to ponder that things really did seem better in the morning as she was greeted by one tired unshaven sexy blond in a pair of hipsters.

'They seem OK with it.' She could hear the relief in his voice. 'Gemma called me at work. We're going to do Christmas dinner here.'

'That's great.'

'I'm not so sure...' Angus frowned. 'Won't it be too confusing for them?'

'They don't seem confused!' Imogen said, and then

looked at him, really looked at him, because Angus didn't seem confused either. The tense man she had met that first day, the strained man she had seen on the day everything had fallen apart, seemed light years away from the one who stood before her now. 'Merry Christmas, Angus.'

'It looks like we might just manage to scrape one together,' Angus answered. 'Merry Christmas, Imogen.'

Standing on the landing with a lovely soft mouth that thoroughly kissed her, and a morning erection that had them both wondering if they could leave it to the kids to find out what Santa had bought them, while Daddy and Imogen concentrated on being naughty and nice, it actually started to look like it might be.

'When did you get back?' Imogen asked directly into his mouth.

'Seven.' His mouth answered into her kiss.

'Daddy!' Clemmie wailed from downstairs.

Christmas really was magic.

Imogen had seen it in her training when she'd worked a shift on the children's ward—seen how, no matter how dire, everyone pulled together and made the impossible work on that day. She'd seen it in her own family a few short years ago and was seeing it now with Angus's.

Angus, with an hour's sleep to his name, trying to work out what parcel Santa had left for whom, because he'd been sure when he'd wrapped them that he'd remember! Smiling and holding it together and doing his very best for the two little people who mattered most.

Or rather three little people.

Imogen pulled out her phone and chatted excitedly

to Heath, who was ripping open parcels of his own, and then to Brad, instructing him to turn down the turkey and telling him that she'd be there by ten.

And Gemma must be feeling the same, because she rang again, laughing and talking to the kids and reminding them she'd be there by eleven.

And by the time the kids were whizzing around the room, building Lego castles and playing with dolls, Angus had his little pile of presents left to open and Imogen was blinking at her rather big pile.

A big pile she truly hadn't been expecting.

'Go on, then!' Angus prompted.

'You first,' Imogen replied, just wanting to get it over, kicking herself at the choice she'd made, of all the stupid, soppy, romantic things to go and buy him.

Not that Angus thought it was.

'A waffle-maker?' She could hear the sort of bafflement in his voice as he stared at his kitchen appliance.

'It's going to be your new best friend.' Imogen smiled. 'Brilliant for a quick lunch, or a nice breakfast for the kids...sort of like a pancake mixture...' She saw a smile flare at the side of his mouth as he examined his gift rather more closely.

'Heart-shaped waffles!' Angus said.

'And they only take a few moments to make!'

She saw his tongue roll in his cheek, saw the shake of his head as he got it—all the hours searching for the perfect gift more than worth it now, her humour his.

His loss hers.

'It looks like I'm going to be eating a lot of waffles when you're...'

He didn't say it, he didn't have to—they both knew what lay ahead. And Imogen actually got it then—she'd been waiting, waiting for the wave of grief to hit him, and she realised then that it already had. That hellish year he had lived through had been his mourning time, and Angus really was ready to move on.

It nearly killed her that it wouldn't be with her.

'From the kids!' Angus said, as she opened her smellies.

'From me...' he said gruffly, as she pulled back the wrapper on a vast silk bedspread. 'I'll pay the excess baggage—figured if I can't be with you...'

And it was so nice...too nice, just a whole world away where she'd have to cuddle up to this instead of him, it was easier to open her next present than to think about it.

'From me too...' Angus said as she unwrapped a beautiful glass snow globe, shaking it up and watching the snow fall on Knightsbridge.

'I can see the food hall!' Imogen joked, pretending to peer into the tiny windows. 'Ooh, mangoes!'

'Keep opening.'

'There's more? Angus you shouldn't have...'

'I didn't. You seem to have built up quite a fan club since you've been here.'

'Lollies?'

'Sweets in England!' Angus grinned. 'Read the card.'

Dear Imogen,
I asked Elise to drop these off for you and your lovely little boy.

I felt awful at first being so helpless, but Elise said she doesn't mind a bit!!!
Enjoy being spoiled.
I do!
Ivy Banford

'Cheeky old thing!' Imogen grinned, but her eyes were brimming. 'What's this?' she asked, turning over a silver envelope.

'I'm not sure. I saw Heather putting it in the agency nurse's pigeon hole and I swiped it for you.'

'Probably just a card from Heather…'

But it wasn't. She barely made it past the first line…handing it to Angus who after a moment read it out loud.

'Dear Imogen,

'You spent time with my sister when I could not. Maria worried about her house, she told me you understood—that meant a lot to her—to be understood on that day.

'Forgive me if you find this gift offensive—my hope is to make you smile as you think of my sister.

'With deepest thanks,

'Elijah and Guido Vanaldi'

'That's quite a fan club you've got there,' Angus said, his voice just a touch gruff, reading the gift card more closely. 'You have a cleaner for a year.'

'A cleaner?'

'Actually, you have the crème de la crème of cleaners, to do with what you will for a year... What sort of a present is that?'

'The perfect one.' Imogen crumpled. 'Only I won't be here...'

And she truly didn't know if she was crying because she'd miss him and the children or crying because right now she missed Heath, or crying for Maria, or for the fact that the one time in her life she had the crème de la crème of *everything* lined up and at her service and raring to go, she was in absolutely no position to take what was on offer.

'Come on...' Angus summoned her to the kitchen. 'We've got cooking to do.'

Jack, wearing reindeer ears, poured the batter, and Clemmie insisted on being chief taster. Breakfast really was delicious, but as wonderful as it was to be with Angus, Jack and Clemmie on Christmas morning, there was somewhere else she needed to be.

Wanted to be.

'I'm going to go.'

It was barely after nine, but long before that he had sensed her distraction, knew she wanted to be with Heath. Watched as she applied mascara, lipstick, pulled on her boots, hugged the kids and told them to have a great day.

Watched as she left.

Then waited for Gemma to arrive.

And Christmas really was magic, because somehow he wasn't quite so angry. Somehow he managed to just put it all on hold.

He had understood when he'd seen Gemma's puffy

eyes and nervous face that she had been scared—scared of facing him, scared of telling the kids, scared of the future too, no doubt.

So they had one thing in common at least! And now they had two, both wanting to give their kids a good Christmas to remember.

'Wow!' Gemma beamed as the kids showed her the graffiti job they'd performed on the tree. 'You two have been busy!'

'Imogen helped us make them.'

'Imogen?' She glanced over to Angus. 'The kids do seem fond of her. Can she stay on?'

'Afraid not!' Angus busied himself picking up wrapping paper. 'But Mum's coming in a couple of days and I'll put an ad in in the new year.'

'Well, between us all…' Gemma was picking up paper too, holding a garbage bag for the first time in years and actually cleaning up the mess so they could enjoy the day '…we'll work it all out.'

Yes, magic, because when, after a vast Christmas dinner and a couple of very welcome glasses of Imogen's red wine, he didn't explode when Gemma asked if she could have the children with her that night where she was staying.

'You're staying with him?'

'Yes, but he's not there tonight—he's going to visit his family. I thought it might be better for the children to see where I'm staying for the first time without Roger being there…' She swallowed hard as she voiced his name. 'I think that would be too confusing for them.'

Oh, and there was such a smart retort on the tip of

his tongue, but he swallowed it down with another swig of wine and managed a curt nod.

Magic, because later, when the house was unbearably quiet, when the living room was littered with toys and no kids, and all the beds upstairs were empty, when for a second he didn't think he could stand it, there she was. He watched from the window as Brad dropped Imogen off, grimacing just a touch as she kissed her ex goodbye. In turn Imogen sniffed Gemma's perfume in the air when she walked through the door.

'How was it?'

'Great!' Imogen beamed, depositing a large amount of bags, not noticing the set of his jaw as she opened a box and pulled out a pair of soft suede boots. 'He remembered my size.'

'How's Heath?'

'Asleep!' Imogen giggled. 'Not for long, though. With the amount of cake and drinks he's had, I wouldn't be surprised if he's up a few times in the night. But we had a great day. I was so worried how it would be, but it turned out to be wonderful. How about for you?'

'It went pretty well,' Angus said, 'given the circumstances. We just put everything on hold and tried to give the kids a great day—which I think we did.'

'Are they in bed?'

'They're at Gemma's.' He saw her eyes widen just a fraction. 'They really did seem to have a good day. They're going to stay again in a couple of nights if all goes well. They went about half an hour before you came home.' She watched him flinch at his choice of words and gave a soft smile.

'It feels like home.' Imogen said, because it did. Getting out of the car and walking up the steps, for the first time in the longest time she actually felt as if she was coming home. This peace to her soul that he brought, a connection that was blissfully familiar. 'And well done, you.'

Yes, it felt like home and it felt like Christmas when, full from the day's excesses, they still managed to gorge on Ivy's presents as they sat cuddled up on the sofa beside the twinkling Christmas tree, watching the same slushy movie that was surely on the world over on Christmas night. It felt like home and it felt completely right.

So right it hurt.

CHAPTER TWELVE

'I'M SCARED.'

At three in the morning and after a long and exhausting labour, Roberta Cummings had every reason to be scared. Her labour hadn't progressed but, determined to deliver naturally, she had held on. Imogen had come in often to check and finally the resident had sent for his registrar when, at still only five centimetres dilated, the baby's heart rate had started to dip during contractions and an emergency caesarean had been decided on.

'You're going to be fine.' Imogen assured Roberta.

'What about the baby?'

'Hey!' Imogen held the terrified woman's hand and it was such bliss to be able to reassure her, 'We've been watching you closely all night and we're doing this now, *before* the baby gets into too much distress... When you wake up, you'll have your baby!'

There was a quiet assuredness in Imogen, which she imbued in her patients. Here on Maternity, even though things could go wrong, even though they did, Imogen was confident in the process of birth, even when it was a complicated one. With the right team and the right approach, this emergency would turn into something wonderful and *that* for Imogen made it the place she wanted to be.

'Now, do you understand what's happening?' Smiling down at his patient, despite the flurry of activity going on in the theatre, the obstetrician, Oliver Hanson, was calm and unruffled. 'We can't wait for the epidural to take effect, so the anaesthetist is going to put you to sleep...'

'Think baby thoughts.' Imogen smiled as the anaesthetist placed a mask over Roberta's face, and Imogen held her hand, watched her relax and then stiffen. Then, as medications were slipped into her IV, she jolted as her body resisted, and then relaxed again as the anaesthetist swiftly intubated.

'Let's get this little guy out,' Oliver said. Only now, with the patient safely asleep, did he show the haste this procedure required if the baby was to be born safely. Making his incision, strong arms had to work hard as the baby's head was deep into the birth canal. A wrinkly purple bottom followed by two floppy legs was delivered onto the drapes, and even though it was the third delivery Imogen had seen that night, still it never ceased to amaze her. She watched as he was expertly lifted, a theatre nurse receiving the precious bundle and heading over to the cot as the team vigorously rubbed the baby, his navy eyes open, not even blinking.

'Let's cover that ugly head before Dad sees you!' Rita, a senior midwife said with a laugh as the baby's head was elongated from his difficult attempt at birth.

They all knew it would all settle down soon, but could often scare new parents. 'Right, Imogen, do you want to take him to the nursery?'

Which was the best bit for Imogen, introducing the little fellow to his dad, who sat and held him as they waited for his mum to be ready to meet him too. Oh, and she could have bathed him and dressed him up in one of the little outfits his mum had brought in for this day, but she chose to wait and let Roberta see him all sticky and messy and covered in vernix.

'Imogen?' Rita popped her head in just as Imogen was introducing a very tired but elated Roberta to her son. 'The nurse co-ordinator's on the telephone. Now that we've quietened down here, she wondered if you'd mind popping down to Emergency for the last couple of hours of your shift.'

'Sorry about this!' Heather apologised the moment Imogen hit the department and she walked her over to Resus. 'The place is steaming. I had to send two staff home at midnight with this wretched flu that's going around—that's why I'm stuck on nights too—then we had this one bought in…

'Gunshot wound!' she added as they walked briskly. 'To the right upper chest, and from what the police say there might be a couple more on the way!'

'Can we roll him over?' Angus didn't acknowledge her and she didn't expect him to as she joined the rather sparse trauma team and helped to roll the patient over so that Angus could examine the exit wound. She knew she was just another pair of efficient hands as they raced to put in a chest drain and push through blood in the hope of getting him up to Theatre before he bled out. For the second time that night Imogen hit the theatre doors, running alongside Angus, the thoracic team having run ahead and already scrubbed and gotten in place.

'Sorry!' Both slightly breathless from the run and adrenaline, it took a while for Imogen to answer.

'For what?' Imogen stopped at the water cooler and took a long drink. 'I don't expect you to kiss me hello!'

'For telling Heather to get you from Maternity.'

'You told Heather that I was working?' Imogen frowned.

'I said that I'd bumped into you in the car park.' Registering her frown, he spectacularly misinterpreted it. 'It was hardly the place to say that I knew you were at work.'

'I'm not worried about that.' Stopping midway in the corridor she angrily confronted him. 'I was actually enjoying my shift. I assumed that the nurse co-ordinator had requested me. You had no right to tell them to pull me off Maternity.'

'Imogen, a guy was bleeding out. We had staff dropping like flies and Heather frantically trying to call people in. I *knew* that there was an experienced emergency nurse up on Maternity. We needed you—'

'Needed me?' Imogen furiously interrupted. 'Or was it just terribly convenient that I happened to be there?'

'Well done, guys!' Heather's weary face greeted two stony ones. 'Thanks so much for that, Imogen—I don't know what we'd have done without you.'

'Survived, no doubt!'

'Probably.' Heather yawned. 'But you made things a lot easier. Hey, Angus, I was going to drop round this afternoon when I woke up. I've made up a few meals…'

'You don't have to do that.' Angus smiled and shook his head. 'Anyway, I'm going to the airport to pick up Mum.'

'Well, tomorrow, then,' Heather pushed. 'I can pop them over—'

'And offend my mum!' Angus's smile froze in his face as he met Imogen's eyes. 'Honestly, Heather, we're fine. You don't have to worry.'

'You were right.' Angus arrived home a couple of hours after Imogen, and she could have pretended to be asleep but couldn't be bothered with games. Instead, she just lay there as Angus placed a mug of tea on her bedside table and nudged her knees just a little bit to make room for him when he sat down. 'I shouldn't have told Heather that you were working— I should have left it to the co-ordinator to work it out. I just didn't think. The department was bursting and we needed help quickly…'

'I get all of that,' Imogen said, staring up at the skylight, 'but don't…' blue eyes snapped to his '…choose when it's convenient to know me.'

'I don't.'

'Come on, Angus. You're not leaving for the airport till five—don't tell me if I wasn't here that Heather wouldn't be welcome to drop over.'

'I don't need food parcels, Imogen.'

'Perhaps, but if Heather drops by and sees me here,

then work will know, which wouldn't look too good for you, would it?'

'What do you want me to say here?' Angus asked. 'That we should tell everyone? Tell them at work, tell Gemma, tell my mother, tell the kids... And then what? You'll go. You'll be on that plane and back to your life in Australia and I'll still be here. Surely it's better if it's just between us.'

'Which is why I think I should go. I don't think it can work with your mum here. I think it might be awkward...' Imogen gulped. 'I mean, it's hard enough keeping it from the kids.'

'She doesn't still tuck me in at night.' Angus attempted a joke, only she didn't return his smile.

'It's not about that...' Tears were welling in her eyes. 'It's about us. I mean, she'll know I'm not the nanny or just a friend helping out. She'll see what we're like....'

'Like what?'

'Like this.'

And she answered the question that he hadn't been able to back at the café. When she'd asked him what the different things had been that he and Gemma had wanted, he hadn't known how to answer, but *this* was what he wanted and *this* was what he couldn't have.

'Stay.' He didn't know if he was asking for the next few nights or for ever, but he knew her answer covered both.

'I can't.'

'Don't go.' His eyes closed on the impossibility of it all, then opened again, his voice firmer now. 'Look, I've got to pick up the kids at three. Come to the airport, stay for a couple of days, at least till after New Year. You can't stay at the hostel for that…'

'I might want to go out partying!' Imogen tried, but they both knew she wouldn't.

'Stay a bit longer and let the kids get used to the idea of you going…'

'They're not going to miss me….'

'Oh, they will.' Angus insisted. 'I can assure you my mum won't notice a thing. And if by some miracle she does…' he blew out a breath '…then I guess I'll have to just deal with it.'

'You're so pretty!' Clemmie sighed as, feeling anything but, Imogen peered in the mirror at her puffy face and dragged a brush through her hair.

'Really? Well, so are you.'

'Oh, I will be,' Clemmie nodded assuredly, 'when my teeth stop falling out.'

They were just adorable.

Used to dealing with kids, it still took her by surprise how quickly she'd come to *like* Clemmie and Jack. Oh, all kids were cute and all kids were nice and funny if you stopped to look, but too many years in Emergency had knocked some of that sentiment out of her.

Till she'd had Heath and till she'd met Clemmie and Jack.

Jack, as direct and as serious as his father could be.

Clemmie, as offbeat and as funny as her father could sometimes be too!

And she adored them both for it—for the way they'd made Heath feel welcome, for the tiny moments like this one as Clemmie stood in the bathroom and told Imogen she was wonderful then promptly steered the conversation back to herself.

'I wish I could look pretty for the party tomorrow.'

'That's right.' Imogen smothered a smile as Clemmie worked her way up to whatever it was she'd be asking. 'You and Jack have got a party to go to.'

'I don't want Nanny to do my hair.' Clemmie came over and fiddled with her hairbrush. 'She hurts when she brushes it and she doesn't do it very nice—she always puts it in bunches. But if you're my nanny too…'

'I'm not really a nanny, and your Nanny's a different sort of nanny…' Imogen attempted, but it was too hard. 'But, yes, I am helping look after you and, if you want, I can do your hair.'

'With that sparkly stuff that was in my stocking?' Clemmie checked, finally getting to the point she had been wanting to make all along!

'Sure.' Imogen grinned.

The drive to the airport was pretty fraught, the traffic moving at a snail's pace, giving Angus and Imogen plenty of time to pause for thought as they watched the planes take off and land. Three weeks had stretched endlessly ahead, when Imogen had first landed. A long, long holiday then she'd go back home with Heath. At first it had felt like for ever, only now, as all good holidays do at the end, the days were starting to fly by fast. New Year's Eve was just around the corner and then just a few days after she would be on her way home.

She'd made so many plans, there had been so many

things she'd wanted to do in her time here, and she'd achieved them all—just never when she'd made those plans had she expected to fall in love.

Yes, love.

Oh, she'd told herself it was a holiday romance, only that didn't quite fit.

Holiday romances didn't work, apparently because you were lying on a beach by day getting nice and tanned and out at night sipping cocktails, which didn't translate to the real world.

Yet they'd lived in the real world.

Through the rain and the gloom they'd still managed to find laughter, so it couldn't be a holiday romance. And it certainly wasn't a fling…at least not for her.

Heathrow was as daunting as it had been when she'd arrived with Heath—people everywhere, trolleys, noise, tension, and that was just the car park! But standing in Arrivals she couldn't help but get caught up in the excitement. Clemmie, dancing on the spot, arguing with Jack as to what presents Nanny might bring. Imogen wondered what Angus's mother would be like. She imagined some stern, serious, forebidding-looking woman and reeled a touch when all four feet eleven of Jean was introduced to her. Imogen realised before they'd even made it back to the car that Angus's mother was completely potty and really quite lovely.

'Could you make me a cup of tea?' She smiled sweetly at Imogen as they stepped into the house and Angus baulked.

'I told you, Mum, she's not a housekeeper. Imogen's a friend who's helping out.'

'Then she won't mind making me a cup of tea!'

'I don't mind at all,' Imogen answered, smothering a smile as she filled the teapot.

'She'll be back soon!' Jean said, as if Gemma had gone on day trip.

'It's over, Mum.'

'Marriage takes work, Angus.'

'And we did work at it.'

'It wasn't all perfect for your father and I. But we worked at it.'

'Mum, Gemma's met someone else.'

'Maybe she's got that postnatal depression or something.'

'Give me strength!' Angus gritted his teeth as Jean headed off to the bathroom. 'Clemmie's four!'

'She just doesn't want it to be over.'

'But it is.' Angus gave a wry shake of his head. 'Why am I the only one who believes it?'

Still, as delightful as Jean was, as nice as dinner was, as Imogen lay in bed that night she knew there'd be no getting up for a glass of water. Knew Angus was right, that it would be unfair on Jean to tell her, unfair on the kids…. It was just unfair all round.

That glimpse of Heathrow airport, just too real to ignore, meant she couldn't pretend it wasn't happening any more.

CHAPTER THIRTEEN

'SORRY, no, I've actually got plans for New Year's Eve!' Imogen snapped off the phone just a little pink in the face as Angus knew she was lying.

'What are they?' Angus asked.

'Bath and bed!'

'Go on,' Angus pushed, 'I'm working it. It would be fun.'

'New Year's Eve in Accident and Emergency really isn't my idea of a fun night. Now, if they offered me Maternity, I might consider it.'

'Morning! Anything I can do?' Not quite so potty, Jean had retired to bed when it was time to do the dishes, had woken only after the children had eaten breakfast and was now pouring a drink from the pot of tea Imogen had just made.

'Did you hear the kettle, Mum?' Angus grinned, as Imogen's mobile shrilled again.

'Go on.' He smiled. 'It will pay for Madame Tussaud's.'

He wasn't smiling a moment later when he saw her face pale.

'Talk about what, Brad?' Imogen said as she stood up and left the room. For Angus it was almost impossible to carry on chatting to his mother as if nothing was happening. It was hell for him to just sit there and drink tea and pretend it didn't matter that for the first time since he'd known her she'd left the room to take Brad's call.

'I have to go out,' she said when she came back.

'Problem?' Angus asked, his face as strained as hers and both trying not to show it. 'Is Heath OK?'

'Heath's fine.' Imogen gave a tight shrug. 'Brad's got something he wants to discuss. I should only be a couple of hours—I'll be back in time to do Clemmie's hair.'

'Who's Brad?' Jean frowned, the second Imogen had gone.

'Imogen's ex-husband.' Funny, that of all the new phrases he'd been getting used to these past couple of weeks, that one came out the hardest.

'Nice that they're civil.'

She must be becoming a local, Imogen briefly thought as she raced up the escalator instead of just standing. She hadn't even noticed the other passengers on the tube, had just sat there staring blindly out of the darkened windows, trying to fathom what Brad could possibly have to say. Oh, he'd pulled out more than a few surprises in their time together, and a few in their time apart. She'd considered herself quite unshockable where Brad was concerned, till now.

She'd never heard him so nervous.

Laid-back Brad, suddenly supremely polite and, yes, definitely nervous.

He'd met someone, Imogen decided, taking the lift up to his apartment, just like she had... Only that wouldn't faze Brad! But maybe this one *was* serious... Maybe, Imogen gulped, this one was pregnant and there was going to be a brother or sister for Heath.

Knocking on his door, Imogen blew out her breath, sure she'd covered all options.

'Hey!' He kissed her on the cheek, just as he always did, and she played with Heath for a few moments, just as she always did, then Brad asked Heath if he'd play in his room for a moment because Mum and Dad had something they wanted to talk about.

'I don't know how to say this...' Brad wasn't his usual laid-back self as, instead of lounging on the sofa opposite he stood up and paced. 'Actually, I don't even know if I should say this. But if I don't tell you...'

Oh, she hadn't covered all her options, Imogen realised, sitting on the sofa, listening to what he had to say and realising that even after all this time Brad still had it in him to surprise her.

They were *extremely* civil, Angus thought darkly, sitting in an empty lounge, trying not to notice the semi-darkness, trying not to care that two hours had turned into six.

Only he did care.

A lot.

To ring or not?

For the hundredth time he picked up the phone, and for the hundredth time he replaced it and stared out of the window as if willing her to appear.

She'd gone to see Brad for a couple of hours, six

hours ago. She'd told Clemmie she'd be back to do her hair for the party—but she hadn't been. Clemmie was at the party wearing Jean's bunches, though Angus had managed to avoid tears by spraying them silver.

Would it look like he was checking up on her?

Was he checking up on her?

But what if she was hurt?

What if something had happened and he hadn't rung, hadn't rung because he didn't know if he was allowed to check up on her.

Seeing Brad's car pull up, seeing her pale face as she climbed out huddled in her coat, Angus's load didn't lighten. He could see the set of her shoulders, could see as she came up the steps the tension in her pale face, and as she turned the key in the door, somehow he knew it wasn't going to be great. Even before he saw her tear-streaked face and eyes that couldn't quite look at him, he knew that she had something difficult to tell him.

'I'm sorry I didn't get back earlier.'

'It's fine.'

'Was Clemmie OK?'

'She's fine too. Mum's taken them to the party...' He managed a smile. 'I had a go with the sparkly stuff.'

'I wanted to ring...' Still she couldn't look at him. 'Only I didn't know what to say.'

'That's OK...'

'Brad kind of sprang something on me, something I wasn't expecting...'

And it was Angus who didn't know what to say now, Angus who really just didn't.

'I need to think, Angus.' Now she did look at him, tears pooling in her eyes. 'I know you must think—'

'I don't know what to think Imogen.'

'We were just talking about things.'

'What things?' His candid question was merited, and she looked up into those questioning jade eyes and it would have been the easiest thing in the world to tell him, to reveal to him her quandary, to ask this knowledgeable, strong man if maybe, just maybe he could show her the way. Only Imogen knew she had to find the answer herself, had learnt long ago that the easy option often turned out to be hardest in the end.

'What would you call this?' She saw his perplexed expression at her strange response. 'Us,' she elaborated. 'A fling, a relationship, a holiday romance? I mean, if you had to describe it…' The pause was interminable. Watching, waiting for him to answer, seeing the hesitation, the indecision gave Imogen the first taste of bitterness. 'But, then, you wouldn't have to describe it, because no one knows about us, do they?' She stared at him for the longest time. 'Is there any chance for you and Gemma?'

'I've already told you.' His answer came readily this time. 'We're finished.'

'Because if there is a chance,' Imogen said, ignoring his response, 'then you need to explore every option and I don't think you can do that while we're together…'

'Who are we talking about here, Imogen?' Angus asked. 'Do you really think I would have embarked on this if my marriage wasn't completely over?'

'This what, Angus?'

And he didn't know what to call it because it wasn't a fling and it wasn't some knee-jerk response to freedom either and it certainly wasn't a holiday romance, because he was right here at home and Imogen had been there for him during the most difficult of times.

Yet it couldn't be love, because if this was love, then very soon he was going to lose it, and out of all of this, it was the thing he couldn't stand losing the most. Couldn't risk loving her, only to lose her.

'Brad and I have some things that we need to sort out, and so do you and Gemma.'

He didn't even have it in him to be angry, even when later Brad's car pulled up to collect her, because as Heath thundered in and Brad waited in the car for her, though Imogen wasn't crying, she was the saddest, most confused he'd ever seen her.

It should have been easy too, for the kids to all say goodbye. Used to comings and goings, surely people who'd been in their lives for only a couple of weeks shouldn't hurt so much to lose. But they'd been through a lot together, and three tearful children didn't help matters.

'You can write...' Angus attempted.

'I can't write,' Clemmie wailed.

'Well, you can ring then.' His eyes met Imogen's. Maybe she was right to just go, because if two weeks hurt like this, imagine what it would be like in three?

'Ring me!' He fiddled with the buttons on her coat. 'I might see you at work.' He managed a weak smile. 'I promise not to haul you off Maternity again.'

'You can!' Imogen said. 'I'll call you—before I go back, I mean.'

'Do.' He didn't care if his mother was there and if he might have to explain later, didn't really care about anything, except that she was going, and he pulled her into him. Despite her bulk when he held her close, because he couldn't bear to let her go, never had someone felt more fragile.

'He's not worth it.' For the first time he crossed the line, entered a discussion where he didn't belong. 'He'll let you down.'

'I have to think,' Imogen mumbled into his shoulder, then pulled away, 'and so do you.'

CHAPTER FOURTEEN

'READY for action?'

Smiling, even though it was false, Angus walked into the staffroom at ten minutes to nine, depositing a couple of cakes and bottles of fizz on the table as he greeted the team that would witness probably the busiest of nights on the Accident and Emergency calendar year.

Oh, Christmas Eve was impossible once the pubs closed, and Christmas Day always managed to pull a few unpleasant surprises out of the hat, but the fireworks that heralded the new year weren't exclusive to the London skies. Come midnight the department, or rather the patients, would, no doubt, put on a spectacular display of their own, and extra security guards had been rostered on along with the most experienced medical staff.

'Ready!' Heather grinned—a true emergency nurse who was actually looking forward to the night. 'I've bought in a vast turkey curry—it's in the fridge, just help yourself!'

'Oh, I will!' Angus agreed, doing just that and picking up a couple of mince pies to get him started. The mood was festive almost, and although he'd brought food in and would join in with the crazy, alternative New Year's Eve party the staff would have—every breath hurt.

Hurt because a year that needed to end was about to.

Another year was starting, only he didn't quite feel ready.

He would have, though.

If Imogen hadn't entered his life.

If she hadn't waltzed right in and given him a taste of how good, how wonderful, how normal and just delicious being good and wonderful and normal could be.

He was supposed to be busy getting divorced at this point.

Not nursing a broken heart for someone else.

'Have a slice now.' Barb, one of the nurses misread his watery gaze and pushed a massive pavlova towards him, lashings of meringue laced with sugared mango. 'Imogen gave me the recipe.'

How long would it last?

How much longer would her name pepper the department? She'd worked a few shifts and it was as if she'd left a flurry of glitter wherever she'd been.

And he didn't want it to diminish.

Didn't want to take down the Christmas tree, even though Jean kept telling him to.

Didn't want to forget, even though it hurt to remember.

'Go on, have a piece—you know you want to.'

Oh, he did want to. Wanted to ring her up and tell her to get the hell away from Brad. That he didn't deserve her, had hurt her once and would do it again. But what right did he have to do that?

Except that he loved her.

Right there and then Angus admitted to himself what he didn't want to. Didn't want to love her, because he knew he was going to lose her.

They'd both known from the start that it could never go anywhere, that circumstances, geography would keep them apart but, apart or not, Angus knew he didn't need her name to be mentioned to remember the morning they'd found each other. In fact, kneed in the groin with longing, Angus knew that he'd never look at another morning without remembering her.

'Hi, guys!'

Her voice was just utterly unexpected, like some auditory hallucination as he bit into the pavlova.

'Imogen—thank heavens!' Heather practically fell on her as she walked in the staffroom just as the team headed out for handover. 'I begged the agency to send you—I had two of my senior staff ring in sick for this shift just before I went home this morning. I was desperate.'

'The agency said—the *third* time they called!' He watched as she smiled, as she deposited a vast tray on the coffee-table, kebab sticks spiked with pineapples, strawberries, kiwi fruits and mango—bringing summer into the room in so many ways. As she gave him a tight smile, blinking rapidly a few times, he knew that this was hard for her too.

Knew she didn't want to be here—but he was so glad that she was.

'Grab a drink and bring it round,' Heather ordered. 'We'll be having our coffee breaks at the nurses' station tonight. And I am sorry,' she added, 'for pestering you.'

'It worked.' Imogen smiled.

'Still, I shouldn't have asked them to ring you at the hostel when you wouldn't answer your mobile.'

And for a minute it was just the two of them. Imogen dunking a tea bag in her cup and heaping in sugar as Angus fiddled with his stethoscope.

'How have things been?'

'Good,' came her noncommittal answer.

'I didn't expect to see you tonight.'

'I didn't expect to be here, but the agency kept ringing…'

'You're staying at the youth hostel?'

'Where else would I be?' Imogen started, and then paused, two little spots of red burning in her cheek, not from embarrassment but anger. 'You think I'm back with Brad?'

'Well, you did go to him.' All the anger, all the hurt and the bitterness was there in his sentence.

'To talk…' Her words were as laced with anger and bitterness as his. 'I told you that we had things to discuss. Do you really think I'm so available that he could just snap his fingers and I'd run back?'

'Of course not.'

'That I'm so lucky to have him want me—'

'Imogen…' Angus broke in, but she didn't want to hear it.

'I told you it was over with him. I don't change my mind about things Angus…' She gave a twisted smile. 'Except when the blasted agency keep ringing and I end up doing a shift in the last place I want to be.'

'I'm sorry things are so awkward between us.'

'It's actually not all about you, Angus...' She gave a pale smile as Angus frowned. 'I'd better get round there.'

The department was fairly quiet, as it often was early on New Year's Eve, almost as if everyone saved their dramas for later. Heather made sure that her staff took themselves off for extended breaks and filled themselves up on the mountain of food they had brought, while they still had the chance. Imogen wished they were busy, wished the lull would end so the night would be over more quickly.

Wished she knew what Angus was thinking when she caught him looking at her.

'We've got a paediatric arrest coming in!' Angus's face was grim. 'Drowning.'

'Now?' It was a stupid comment. People didn't plan their dramas, didn't know that they were supposed to be quiet till midnight, and it certainly wouldn't enter the family's head that their desperately ill child was the very last thing Imogen wanted to deal with right now.

'New Year's Eve party...' Heather came off the phone from a further update from Ambulance Control. 'The bath was filled with ice for the drinks, and he fell in. Dad found him—it was his party. They can't get hold of his mum—apparently she's working tonight. We don't know how long he's been down.'

'How old?' Imogen croaked.

'Three or four,' Heather answered, 'I can't get a clear answer, it sounds pretty chaotic.'

'It's not Heath.' He could see her hands shaking as

she pulled out the leads for the cardiac monitor and opened the pads for the defibrillator, knew exactly what she was thinking.

'You don't know that.'

And he put his arm around her and gave her a squeeze, because now he could, Imogen realised, because now she'd been there a little while longer, now she was considered one of them, it was deemed appropriate.

Only it wasn't.

A friendly cuddle from him was the last thing she needed tonight.

'I'm going to wait for the ambulance,' she said, slipping his arm off and heading outside, shivering as she heard the sirens draw closer, trying to make small talk with a chatty security guard as the nine hours left of her shift stretched on endlessly.

It wasn't Heath.

The second the ambulance doors opened, her mind was put at ease, but the dread stayed with her as she took over the cardiac massage as the paramedics unclipped the stretcher and ran in. Drowning she was more familiar with than burns—nearly every garden in Australia had a pool, and sadly, and all too often, this type of patient presented.

'He's in VF…' The paramedics reeled off the list of treatment and drugs that had been given at the scene and en route, and even though it looked dire, the news was actually as good as it could be.

He was two, not three or four, Imogen heard as she pressed the palm of her hand on his sternum, and an ice-filled bath a far better option for an unsupervised toddler to tumble into than a hot one. He'd have been plunged into hypothermia, which meant the demand for oxygen to his brain would have been rapidly diminished, which gave him a better chance of being left without brain damage. He was still in VF, which meant there was some activity happening in his little heart too.

All of this went through her head as she continued the massage, stepping back every now and then as Angus shocked the little body...blocking out the cries and shouts of his family from the other side of the doors and focussing on the little boy who was clinging to life.

'Do you want to swap?' Barb offered to take over the massage, but she was getting a good rhythm on the monitor and Imogen shook her head.

'I'm fine.'

'Let's go again...' The defibrillator was whirring and Imogen felt as if she were watching from above, could see the warmed fluids dripping into his veins, could see herself going through the painful motions, and later saw the relief on everyone's face when they got him back. And, yes, she had said the right thing when she comforted the parents as Angus gave them the tentative good news and, yes, she did all the right things as she took the little boy up to the Intensive Care and handed him over. But as she walked out of the paediatric section and past the adults, she could see the bed where Maria had been, only with another person in it. And as she walked down the corridor and back to Emergency, all she knew was that she didn't want to make that walk again.

'You look exhausted!' Heather grinned as she came back. 'The night hasn't even started!'

'Fifteen minutes till lift-off!' Imogen glanced at her watch and smiled back.

'Why don't you have a break?' Heather suggested kindly. 'Take the lift and go out on the fire escape…'

'The fire escape?'

'You'll get a good view of the fireworks—if anyone deserves to see London at its best tonight, it's you.'

'This is my last shift in Emergency.' She didn't turn her head when Angus walked out onto the fire escape to join her, had seen him look up when Heather had been talking, had known that he would come.

'Your last?' The cold air caught in his throat, making it hard to keep his voice light. 'So you're ready for home, then?'

'I meant…' Her face was pale, her eyes like glass in the darkness as she turned to him. 'It's my last ever shift in Emergency. I can't do it any more. I'm going back to midwifery. I know you can't always guarantee the outcome, but I'm going to work with the lowest-risk mums and hopefully spend the rest of my nursing time bringing in lives instead of watching them end. I just can't do it any more. I can't go home and cry myself to sleep, I can't stand all the violence and the death, I just…' She shook her head. 'I just haven't got it in me any more.'

And Angus realised then, that no matter how much he might love her, he didn't really know her. That as close as they had been, there hadn't been time to get close enough, because this beautiful, talented, consummate professional actually bled inside every day she came to work.

'You're burnt out,' Angus said softly. 'It happens. Maybe take a break, do something else for a while.'

'I was hoping to do that here, only once they find out you're emergency trained...' she gave a tight smile '...well, you've seen first hand what happens.'

'I'm sorry.'

'Don't be,' Imogen answered. 'It's helped in a way. I know I've had enough of it. I know the money's going to be less—I'm at the bottom rung in midwifery and at the top in Emergency, but some things are just more important. I'm going to apply for a full-time job in maternity.'

'You might change your mind.'

'I already told you, Angus, I *don't* change my mind.'

She was telling him something and it hurt to hear it— any relief he'd felt earlier that she wasn't with Brad countered by the agony of the future she was mapping out without him.

'Look Imogen...' It was Angus's turn now to open up. 'I haven't been completely honest with you.'

'Did you sleep with Gemma?' There, she had been brave enough to say it, a few years older and brave enough to confront what she hadn't been able to a few years ago.

'Why do you always do that, Imogen?' Angus asked. 'Why do you have to dash to the worst-case scenario all the time?'

'Because it usually is.'

'Was,' Angus said gently. 'Imogen, it's over between me and Gemma. Even my mum's starting to believe it. We went out for lunch last week, but that was more to see if we could handle the divorce without lawyers.'

'Can you?'

'Nope!' Angus gave a half-grin.

'So when weren't you honest?'

'When I said why I didn't want anyone at work to know.' He blew out a breath, and she knew it was a long one because the freezing night made it white and it went on for ever. 'Everything I said, I meant—I mean, I did feel uncomfortable about people knowing, especially given how soon after Gemma it happened and how long you'd be here, especially that you were leaving... But that wasn't entirely the reason...'

'Just say it Angus.' Her eyes brimmed with tears that she hoped he couldn't see.

'I didn't want Heather to know. I felt it would be unfair to her.'

'Heather?' Imogen did a double-take.

'I'm trusting you with this...'

'You and Heather?' She saw him frown. 'I'm sorry—of course you can trust me not to say anything.'

'She's got a bit of a thing for me...' He said it only with kindness. 'She had too much to drink at one of the work Christmas parties a couple of years ago and out it came. Nothing happened, of course,' Angus said, and she was grateful she had bitten her tongue to refrain from asking. 'And I told her nothing ever would happen, you know, that I was flattered and everything, but that I was happily married... She was mortified the next day—rang me in tears, even offered to resign, but look...' He gave an uncomfortable shrug. 'I sort of pretended that I'd had too much to drink and couldn't really remember all she'd said. It made it easier for her…' And that he would do that for Heather made her eyes fill with tears for entirely different reasons.

This, one of the many reasons she loved about him.

Loved him.

Which was why she'd shown him all of her—or most of her.

'I just think it would be a bit of a kick in the teeth for her,' Angus explained further. 'She's rung a couple of times, I've tried to put her off.'

'Maybe she just wants to be friends now.'

'She is a friend.' Angus nodded. 'Which is why I don't want to hurt her.

'Imogen…' She knew what was coming, knew what he was going to ask, knew he wanted the rest of her that she was so very scared to give. 'Why do you think I don't want people to know?'

'Because it's too soon…' she attempted.

'Why else?' Holding her hands, even if he wasn't looking at her, Imogen knew that he'd seen her, not just here and now and not just naked, but that he could see inside her very soul, see the bits she thought she had long ago dealt with and never wanted to show again. And the bits she'd sworn she'd never let another man see.

'Brad was embarrassed to be seen with me.'

'Then he's a fool.'

'Look at Gemma and look at me…'

'I'm not comparing.'

'Of course you are.' Imogen snapped. 'I do! I look at Brad and I look at you and you're both good-looking, all the women adore you, you're both on television—'

'How's this for a comparison, then,' Angus broke

in. 'We're both crazy about you and while Brad, I'm sure, is regretting losing you, I know that I'm about to face the same…'

'Then do something about it.'

'Like what?' Angus asked, only there wasn't an answer. 'I hated geography at school,' Angus said. 'Now I know why.'

She didn't smile at his joke and neither did he—just stood in endless silence, wanting the agony over but never wanting it to end. 'A couple more minutes…' he glanced at his watch and tried to lighten things up. 'Hey, it's already New Year's Day for you! What's the time difference in Australia?'

'No, it's New Year's Eve for me too,' Imogen corrected him, her voice utterly steady, her eyes holding his as she conveyed the seriousness of her words, 'because everything I love most in the world is here, right now, in London.'

It could never be wrong to kiss her.

Even if it could never last, never work, even if in a few days she'd be gone, it could never be wrong to kiss her, and it would never be pointless to prolong it.

Because pulling her into his arms, feeling the sweet taste of her as he parted her lips with his tongue, every second, every minute that he kissed her, held her, adored her was another minute he could remember for ever.

'Hey…' Ever the chameleon, she pulled back just a fraction, their warm breaths mingling. 'If you make love to me here, at least we won't have to say we haven't had sex this year…'

'As much as I might want to…' Angus grinned even

though his eyes were glassy '...I am not going to have sex on the fire escape at work!'

'Spoilsport,' she teased.

'Imogen...' He kissed her again, but was adamant. 'It's a measure of how much I love you that I'm not going to.' He stopped then, stopped because he'd never meant to say it, had never really let himself feel it. Love wasn't supposed to come along just yet.

Love was something in the distance, something that would maybe happen in his life later, much later, but love was what it was, right here, right now, and he was holding it in his arms.

'I love you, Imogen.'

Only she didn't say it back. Instead, she stared back at him for the longest time, then blinked a few times before she gave her strange answer and turned to go.

'Then you'd *really* better do something about it.'

'How were the fireworks?' Heather asked as they returned to the still quiet department.

'Spectacular.' Imogen grinned, picking up a fruit kebab and making Angus's stomach fold over on itself as she licked the tip of a strawberry. Then she added for Angus's benefit, 'But they fizzled out at the end—not quite the big bang I was hoping for!'

'Could you hurry up and see her, please?' Heather said as she handed Angus a chart. 'The husband's getting a bit worked up.'

'Sorry?' Angus frowned.

'Louise Williams, the abdo pain in cubicle four. Oh, sorry.' She gave an apologetic smile. 'It was Gus I spoke to about her—she's twenty weeks pregnant, had a miscarriage earlier in the year, oh, it's last year now…'

And Imogen saw it then.

Saw how often Heather called for Angus if there was a problem, how Heather arranged her breaks around his and probably her shifts too—and saw how hard it would be, not just for Angus but for Heather too, if the truth came out.

Not that she had time to dwell on it, not when at fifteen minutes past midnight on New Years Day the fireworks went off again.

CHAPTER FIFTEEN

'WE'VE GOT multiple stabbings coming in.' Heather had to practically shout as a group of young men spilled out of the waiting room, security men quickly onto them as the waiting room started to fill. 'Gus is onto it and the surgeons are coming. Imogen,' she called out, 'can you take the abdo pain?'

The noises in the department did nothing to soothe the terrified woman and Imogen held her hand as Angus gently probed her abdomen, Louise's anxious husband hovering.

'You've had no bleeding?' Angus checked.

'None. Just this pain. I'm losing my baby, aren't I?'

'Let me take a look at you,' Angus said firmly, 'before we rush to any conclusions. Now, have you had any nausea or vomiting?'

'I feel sick,' Louise said, 'but I haven't been sick.'

'How's your appetite?'

'I can't eat.'

'OK…' Angus checked the card which had her observations recorded. 'I'm just going to get the Doppler.'

'Doppler?' Louise's eyes darted to Imogen.

'It's just a little machine, so he can listen to the baby's heartbeat.'

'Oh, God!'

'Just try and take it easy,' Imogen said gently, but even though she was calm and reassuring, Imogen did let out a breath when, after only a few seconds of trying to locate it, the delicious sounds of a strong, regular foetal heartbeat was picked up.

'OK…' Angus gave a thin smile at the heartbeat. 'That's certainly good news. You're a bit dehydrated. I see Heather put in a drip and took some bloods—I'm going to get those sent straight to the lab and I'm going to get some IV fluids started on you…'

'Aren't you going to examine me?' Louise flushed. 'I mean…'

'I'm not going to do a PV,' Angus said, 'because the obstetrician is going to want to do one and if your uterus is a bit irritable, I don't want to disturb things. I'm just going to speak with a colleague and then I'll come back and talk to you.'

'What do you think is wrong?'

'Let me just have a quick word with the surgeon and then I'll be back.'

'The surgeon!' Louise startled, but Angus was already gone, leaving Imogen to deal with a less than impressed husband.

'What?' he demanded. 'Are we too menial to even be told what he's thinking?'

'We've got a surgical emergency in Resus,' Imogen said calmly. 'I suspect he wants to catch the team before they race off to Theatre.'

'Oh.'

Which was exactly the case, as it turned out. The surgical consultant made a brief appearance and examined Louise, then went outside the cubicle to talk to Angus as the couple became more agitated. Once Louise had been for an urgent ultrasound, Imogen did her observations regularly and tried to reassure them, only she was practically running between patients as the waiting room filled fit to burst, nurses, doctors everywhere calling out for assistance. If they'd had double the staff on tonight, it still wouldn't have been enough.

'Will someone please have the decency to tell us what the hell is going on!'

Imogen, wearing gloves and holding up an inebriated patient's tea towel–wrapped hand that contained a partially severed finger wasn't really in a position to calm the furious Mr Williams as he stormed out of the cubicle. 'My wife's in bloody agony and all you lot keep saying is that you're waiting for blood results.'

'The obstetrician's on his way down,' Imogen said, 'just as soon—'

'I don't want to hear how busy he is!' Mr Williams roared, coming up to her, shouting right in her face. 'I don't want to know about other patients, when my wife…'

As his voice trailed off Imogen actually thought he was going to hit her, could do nothing to defend herself as she held on to her patient. She could see the hairs up his nose and the veins bulging in his forehead, could hear her patient slurring obscenities in her defence, and then she realized that he *was* going to hit her. She could see his fist, and behind that Angus dropping the phone and racing over, but Security got there first, grabbing his hand before it made contact, coming between the relative and the nurse, taking control of the situation, as they often did.

It was a non-event really—something that happened, something she was more than used to dealing with. She was just utterly weary to the bone of being *used* to dealing with it.

'I'll take him for you.'

Cassie saw Imogen's pale face and relieved her of her drunken patient as Imogen peeled off her bloodied gloves while Angus read the Riot Act.

'If you ever threaten or verbally abuse my staff again I will have you removed from the department and arrested!' There was no doubt from his voice that he meant every word.

'I didn't threaten her!'

Even though Angus was completely in control, his anger was palpable, contempt lacing every word as he responded to Mr Williams.

'When a six-foot man gets in the face of a woman and shouts, believe me, sir, it's extremely threatening. And when that same man raises his fist…'

'I wasn't going to hit her!'

Debatable perhaps—only there simply wasn't time.

'Now…' Angus let out a long breath. 'Even though it seems you have been here ages, it has, in fact, been an hour. In that time your wife has been examined by myself and the surgeon, she has had an IV started and bloods taken and has been sent for an ultrasound. I was actually on the phone just now getting some results and was about to come in and talk to you.'

'Hi, there.' Whistling as he walked, grinning as he came over, Oliver Hanson, incredibly laid-back, dressed in theatre scrubs and oblivious to all that had occurred, joined the little gathering. 'Hi, there, Imogen—good to see you.' Then he raised his eyebrows to Angus. 'I hear you've got a suspected appendicitis for me to see— twenty weeks gestation.'

Which wasn't the best way to deliver the potential diagnosis, but then the whole exercise had been a bit of a disaster. A touch pale in the face and a bit grim-lipped, Imogen followed the doctors and Mr Williams into the cubicle as Security hovered outside.

'I'm sorry!' Mr Williams glanced over at Imogen, who nodded.

'He didn't mean to scare you.' Louise was in tears. 'He's just worried about me.'

'Let's listen to the doctors.' Imogen forced a smile, told herself that it wasn't Louise's fault she was married to this man. It was simply her job to put the patient at ease, only it was getting harder and harder to do.

'We think you have appendicitis,' Angus started. 'It's difficult to diagnose in pregnancy as there are some tests we can't do because they may affect the baby. Some of the changes in blood that happen during pregnancy make the lab findings more difficult to interpret too. The ultrasound of your abdomen appears normal, which has ruled out some other tentative diagnoses and I've spoken again to Mr Lucas, the surgeon who saw you, and he agrees that appendicitis is the most likely diagnosis. However, until you have the operation, we won't know for sure.'

'But isn't that dangerous for the baby?'

'It's far more dangerous for the baby if your appendix ruptures,' Oliver explained. 'That's why we'd prefer not to wait. Yes, there is a chance that the surgery might cause premature labour, but I'll start an infusion that should hopefully prevent that, and we'll work closely with the anaesthetist. We all want your pregnancy to continue.'

'So there's no real choice?' Mr Williams's voice was gruff.

'No.' Angus spoke to his patient. 'Mr Lucas is in Theatre and he'll be ready for you soon, so the best thing we can do is get you up as quickly as possible. You've had some IV fluids so you're better hydrated now and the anaesthetist is going to come down and talk to you but, yes, we'll get you up as soon as possible.'

'You'll be OK.' Imogen smiled once all the doctors had gone and she prepared Louise for Theatre, collecting all her notes and going through the endless check lists.

'I never even thought it could be appendicitis—I thought I was losing the baby.'

'It's always your first thought when you're pregnant, but appendicitis is just as common during pregnancy as it is at other times—just more complicated. You'll go up to Maternity after the operation so they can watch the baby closely.'

'You've seen this before then?'

'I'm a midwife.' Imogen nodded. 'So, yes, I've seen it before.'

'A midwife?' Louise frowned. 'So what are you doing working here?'

'Earning a living.' Imogen answered, as the porter clicked off the brakes on the trolley and they headed through the bedlam of the emergency department, tears stinging her eyes as she gave the wrong but honest answer.

'You've been marvellous as always, Imogen!' Always generous with praise for her staff, Heather thanked Imogen profusely as she signed her time sheet at seven-thirty a.m. The place was still full, patients everywhere, linen skips and bins overflowing, but order was slowly being restored. 'Have a look at the roster before you go and take your pick—there are plenty of shifts to be filled this week.'

'No, thanks!' Pulling off her hair-tie, Imogen hoisted her bag on her shoulder. 'I'm done.'

'I thought you were here for a little while longer?'

'I mean with Emergency.' Oh, so casually she'd said it, but Heather quickly noticed the wobble in her voice. 'I'm calling it a day.'

'Imogen!' Heather's voice was full of concern, causing a few nurses to turn round. 'Did that incident with Mr Williams—?'

'I'd made up my mind before that,' Imogen interrupted. 'I'm just...' she gave a helpless shrug '...tired of it, I guess. Burnt out—isn't that what they say? I love Emergency and everything. It's just getting too much, since I had Heath.'

'Excuse me!' Looking nothing like the angry, raging man from earlier, Mr Williams appeared at the nurses' station. 'Louise had her operation and the baby seems fine.'

'That's good to know,' Imogen said, and the smile she gave was genuine because it *was* good to know.

'About before.' He was red in the face again, but for different reasons this time. 'I really am sorry for what happened.'

His apology was genuine, Imogen knew that.

And she was about to open her mouth, to tell him it was OK, that he had been stressed and worried about his wife and the baby and that it didn't matter.

Only it did.

It mattered a lot.

Mr Williams wasn't the reason she was giving up a job she loved, but the Mr Williamses of the world were a big part of it.

And somehow sorry wasn't enough for Imogen this morning.

His apology, no matter how genuine, just one she couldn't accept any more. Without a word she walked off and left him standing there, tears streaming down her face as she exited through the ambulance bay, before finally she said the words she'd really wanted to.

'So you should be!'

CHAPTER SIXTEEN

SHE so did not need this.

Stamping through the slush, Imogen wished she'd been more assertive, wished she'd just stuck to her guns and refused to take the shift.

OK, they'd assured her that she wouldn't actually be in Emergency, that the nurse unit manager had agreed that she could stay in the observation ward. Only that made it worse somehow—being there and not doing anything, hearing the buzz of Emergency and not being a part of it.

Seeing Angus again.

The only thing worse than that was the thought of *not* seeing him again.

It had been four days since they'd last kissed, four days since she'd, cryptically perhaps, laid her heart on the line and four days when he hadn't done a thing about it.

No phone call.

No text.

Nothing.

So what if he'd said he loved her? For all he knew she could be on a plane already winging her way back to Queensland with Heath, which was probably what he wanted, Imogen thought, her face stinging as the heat of the hospital hit her frozen cheeks. Yes, once she was safely out the country there would be no chance of their embarrassing little interlude coming out, no explanations necessary.

The heat had nothing to do with the tears that suddenly pricked her eyes.

'Hi, Imogen…' Cassie greeted her warmly. 'Go and grab a coffee before handover.'

'I'm in Obs.' Imogen forced a smile. 'I'll just head straight round there.'

'You've got time for a coffee,' Cassie insisted. 'Actually, I'll join you. I never got my break this morning, the place was bedlam as usual…' She chatted away as they walked, two nurses heading off to the staffroom. Cassie could never have known how much it hurt Imogen to glimpse Resus, see the machines, the patients, the buzz of Emergency that she loved but which didn't love her back, that just hurt too much to stay.

She actually wanted to turn and run—she could turn and run. She was an agency nurse, easily replaced, could plead a migraine, anything, as long as she didn't have to put herself through it.

'Surprise!'

Opening the staffroom door, it really was one.

Colleagues and friends she had only just made all standing there to greet her, the table laid with Chinese take-aways and cola and crisps. Emergency staff only ever needed a teeny excuse to throw a party, but that they might throw one for her—an agency nurse who had done just a very few shifts—was unfathomable.

'Now...' Heather handed her a cup of cola and took the floor. 'We don't do this for everyone, but we're not losing an agency nurse—the nursing world's losing a good emergency nurse and we figured she deserved a bit of a send-off! How long have you been one of us?'

'Ten years?' Imogen gulped.

'Then you've more than earned a party.'

They'd signed a card and her eyes blurred as she read the messages, especially Angus's. Short and sweet, he'd wished her luck in her new career, thanked her for her hard work here and signed it without love, and with very best wishes for her future—just not theirs.

Which was to be expected, of course.

It just hurt.

Hurt too that he couldn't make it, Heather explained, because he was recording his TV show.

And when the party was over, sitting in the obs ward, her one head injury patient snoring his head off, Imogen knew that ten cardiac arrests and a few stabbings would be much easier to deal with than her own thoughts.

Sitting in a busy department in a busy city, never had she felt more alone.

'Why don't you have your break?' Heather bustled round. 'I'll watch Mr Knight.'

'I've been sitting down for three hours!' Imogen pulled her head out of the book she was desperately trying to concentrate on. 'I don't need a break.'

'Well, I do!' Heather said, sliding into the seat beside her. 'I really am glad you came in today.'

'I am too. It was really thoughtful of you all...' Imogen flushed. 'I wasn't expecting it.'

'Not just for that. That incident with Mr Williams...I didn't want you leaving on a bad note...'

'He's not the reason I'm finishing up.'

'I know that, but it did upset you.'

'It didn't used to,' Imogen explained. 'I used to be able to shrug it off. I just can't any more. So now it's either get upset or get hard and cynical—and I don't want that to be me.'

'That isn't you,' Heather agreed. 'I do know how you feel, after the week we've had here, what with Maria Vanaldi and everything...'

'Maria?'

'You haven't seen the news?'

'They don't have televisions in the rooms at the youth hostel—what about Maria?'

'It wasn't an accident.'

'The car lost control...'

'It had been tampered with. It was her husband's family apparently.'

And Imogen closed her eyes, knowing in that moment that the choice she'd struggled so hard to come to had, for her, been the right one.

'Go and have your break,' Heather said again, and this time Imogen didn't refuse.

His voice in the room hurt.

Imogen was glad that even though she'd joked with Maria about it, she'd never actually thought to record

Angus's show because, seeing him, hearing him and not being able to have him hurt in a way it didn't when she watched Brad.

She knew that if she did have a recording, she'd torture herself over and over, watching his beautiful, proud face, slightly defiant as the carefully scripted interview commenced.

She put more bread in the toaster and stood in the empty staffroom, tears streaming down her face as she rammed the lovely buttery toast into her mouth and waited for the next round to toast, wishing it would fill the hole in her soul. She listened as they spoke about viewers who were lonely and ill over Christmas, listened as they talked about the miracle that should be Christmas but in reality how incredibly hard it was for some people at this time of year.

And then came the difficult part.

Imogen could hear the shift in tone from the interviewer and watched Angus's chin lift a fraction, ready to face the public music. Only it wasn't quite the tune she was expecting to hear.

'A lot of our viewers are going to be sorry to hear that this is to be your final regular appearance on the show.'

'That's correct.' Angus nodded.

'We've seen in the newspapers this week—' his colleague, no doubt his friend, cleared her throat just a touch '—that your own marriage just ended.'

'It did.' And because he was a so-called celebrity, because part of his job was asking people to bare their lives, Imogen screwed her eyes closed as Angus, this private, beautiful man, was forced to open up—if not for the good of himself, then for the good of all.

'Did that have any impact on your decision to leave the show?'

'Of course,' Angus answered brusquely, and Imogen could only smile at his closed-off expression, the same one she'd seen when they'd sat in the café that first time together.

'It must be a painful time.'

'It's a…' There was a pause, just a beat of a pause that had her open her eyes, that had the interviewer frowning just a touch, as maybe, just maybe, Angus deviated from the script. 'It's a *searching* time,' he said carefully, but on behalf of so many, so, so eloquently he added, 'For all involved.'

'It's been reported that there was another party involved—do you have any comment you'd like to make to that?'

And she went to bite into her toast but changed her mind, her throat so thick with tears that there wasn't room for anything else. She waited for his polite rebuttal, for his clipped 'No comment', for his request for his family's privacy—only it never came.

'My wife, without malice or intent, fell in love with someone else.'

'Oh!' Imogen saw the slight, frantic dart of the interviewer's eyes. She smiled, despite her tears, as with candour, honesty and integrity he reached into living rooms everywhere and showed the world a little bit of why he really was so special.

'And you don't fall in love with someone else if things are good at home,' Angus continued, borrowing Imogen's script for a moment then reverting back to his own. 'And for that I take my full share of the responsibility.'

'That's very forgiving.'

'You don't choose with whom, when and where you fall in love,' Angus responded coolly. 'I didn't understand that, but now, thanks to a very special person, I do.'

'So...' The interviewer was shuffling her papers now, staring at them as if willing something to leap out and tell her what the hell to say. 'You're saying that you too—'

'Absolutely.' Imogen's gasp came as the staffroom door opened, knew without turning it was him, could feel his arms wrap around her as he held her from behind and stared at her from the screen. 'There is the most wonderful woman in my life at the moment and I intend to keep it that way. I'm going to learn from my mistakes, which,' he added, 'we actually do all make.

'Gemma and I decided to be honest.' His words were soft and low in her ear. 'She doesn't deserve to be portrayed as the guilty party in this. We both just want it over, so we decided to be upfront and just get it all over and done with. Gemma has my support, even if it nearly killed me to give it on national television...'

'I'm so proud of you.'

'I'm proud of me too,' Angus said. 'And I'm proud of you too.'

'For what?'

'For being you. For making me see.' And he didn't add '*sense*' or '*things more clearly*.' He didn't need to, because his eyes were open. Now he really could see that there was so much more than two sides to a story, that the two sides had other sides, and those other sides had other sides too. People were people and that was OK. That was what made them real.

'You didn't call me.'

'I didn't know what to say,' Angus admitted. 'I knew I had to offer you something, only I didn't know what. And then things got busy... Maria Vanaldi...'

'I heard it wasn't an accident.'

'It got nasty—the police contacted me to ask if Maria had said anything, and I went round to see Ainslie. I was worried about her being caught up in it all and not knowing what was going on. I spoke to Elijah...'

'Guido's uncle?'

'He's his guardian now. And that sounds simple, only this man lives in Italy, a rich playboy who hops on planes the way we take the underground and he didn't even know if he wanted to do it—and then he fell in love with his nephew. A few days with Guido and he's turning his life around if it means that he can keep him.'

And that Guido was safe, that he would be loved and looked after was the nicest thing she could have hoped to hear, or, Imogen admitted, gazing into jade eyes that adored her, almost the nicest.

'You were never the easy option,' he said, turning her to face him. 'You were never a quick fling or convenient or not good enough or any one of those things you beat yourself up with. You were the most difficult option possible, Imogen.'

'Why?'

'Because you live on the other side of the world,

because in a few days you'll be back there with your Heath and I'll be here with Clemmie and Jack. You were absolutely the last person it made sense to fall in love with.' He pulled up her chin to make her look at him. 'You were never a threat to my marriage—it was over long before you came along. The only threat you were was to my sanity. The craziest thing I could do was fall in love with you, but I did. I love you. I absolutely love you. And I don't know how, but I know it can work.' She opened her mouth to talk, but it was Angus's turn still. 'I can't bear the thought of you on the other side of the world without me there beside you every day, but it's a far better option than losing you. I don't care if people say long-distance love can't work, because those people don't know me and they don't know you…

'I don't change my mind either and I won't change my mind about this. If I have to spend every minute of annual leave flying to see you, if I have to work every shift I can so I can fly you back to see me just as much as you can, if we can't properly be together till the kids are much older—we'll still be together, if only you'll have me.'

That he would give her his heart, and let her go with it, that he trusted her enough to return with it whenever she could was the greatest gift of them all—a miracle really, Imogen thought, smiling through her tears as he kissed her swollen buttery mouth till it was she who pulled away.

'It's a Christmas miracle!'

'It is…' Angus grumbled, not caring that Heather had just walked in, not dropping Imogen or pulling back, just wanting to kiss and taste her again, because she was his—she really was.

'No...' Imogen gave a giggle. 'Shane's going into remission.'

'Shane?'

'Shane!'

'But he's only got two weeks to live!' Heather's shocked gasp had Imogen giggling. Heather loved the show—loved, loved, loved it, taped every episode and was always pumping Imogen for inside info. 'It's completely incurable—Dr Adams said so last night.'

'It's a miracle, I tell you!' Imogen said, waving her hands like a gospel singer, then as Angus watched on, bemused, the two women doubled over in a fit of laughing.

'Don't breathe a word!' Imogen warned. 'If the story line ever gets out...'

'Praise be!' Heather said, grinning, slipping out and, unbeknown to them standing guard on the other side of the door so that no one could possibly disturb them.

'She knows?' Imogen checked.

'I told her.'

'So the party...'

'The party was their idea. Heather just told me that you'd be back today. Imogen, when did you find out about Brad?' Puzzled eyes frowned down at her. 'Is that what you two had to discuss?'

'Brad and I had to talk.' She was suddenly serious and always, always beautiful. 'He's been offered another year's work here and he wants to take it.'

'And you couldn't tell me that?' He didn't get it.

'Imogen, have you any idea what I've been through, trying to think of ways we could be together, trying to come up with a solution? And all the while you had one.'

'I had a temporary solution, Angus, and we both deserve a lot more than that. Brad just dropped it on me—his character proved popular and they offered him a year's contract. Of course, my first instinct was to say yes, but it wasn't a solution. What happens in a year when his contract's up, what happens if I hate it here? And why should I leave a home and family I love because Brad's been offered a job? If you and Gemma got back together or if you and I didn't work out, I needed to be sure I was staying for the right reasons…'

And he got it then, got what a huge decision it must have been for her. 'It took a glass or two of wine and a lot of tears but we actually managed some very grown-up talking—something neither of us are very good at. He had to get it that I can't just follow my ex-husband around the globe, and I had to get my head around the fact that you couldn't come into my decision either.' She saw him frown. 'This had to be about Heath and I.' She took a big breath. 'Whether I could stand to be in London without you.'

'Could you?'

'I can stand anything, Angus.' She gave him her soft smile. 'But I'd rather do it with you.'

'Then you will.'

'But what about next year…when his contract…?'

'Who knows?' Angus hushed her with his lips. 'This, I do know, though, we'll work it out.'

'Will we?' And he saw her blink a couple of times, just as he had that first day. He saw again that this soft, utterly together woman sometimes got nervous, sometimes got scared, and it thrilled him that he could read her, could comfort her and could love her.

'Always!'

EPILOGUE

'I FEEL so fat!'

Angus looked over to where Imogen lay.

'I could think of so many better ways to describe you.'

Oh, and he could.

Dressed in her favourite red bikini, they'd been enjoying a gentle dip in the pool after a massive Christmas barbecue and now Imogen was on the lounger, her belly ripe with their baby, her skin freckled by the hot Queensland sun. It was still as if each day the colour in his world brightened.

What could potentially have been the worst year of his life had been the best.

Clemmie and Jack thriving, as their parents did the same.

Thanks to Imogen.

Thanks to this funny, complicated, beautiful woman who had stepped into the path of an oncoming train and somehow made them all change track.

Christmas in Australia!

Who'd have thought?

Hauling himself out of the pool and lying on the

lounger next to her, dripping water as he went, Angus watched the three kids splashing and playing in the water, then grinned over to where Imogen lay. 'They're having a ball.'

'They're killing me,' Imogen groaned. 'They've been up since five!'

'It's been a long day, having all your family over and everything, but we can go to bed soon,' Angus pointed out. 'Brad will be here soon and Gemma and Roger just texted to say they were on their way.'

'Good!'

Who'd have thought?

Angus lay back as Imogen heaved herself up again and then joined the kids in the pool for one last play before they headed off to enjoy the rest of Christmas Day with their other families.

She'd wanted to have their baby in Australia.

Which should have been impossible as they'd all wanted Christmas with the children.

But because, through it all, Imogen had been consistently nice and kind and infinitely understanding, somehow that sentiment grew and somehow, when needed, the universe gave back.

Taking some long overdue leave, Angus was even doing the odd stint in Australia, realising in years to come he might well do many shifts more. The home she'd struggled so hard to keep for Heath was now a furnished rental that the hospital used, only not these past weeks. Tentative plans put forward had been made so much easier when Gemma and Roger had decided that bringing the children for a holiday in Australia might be rather nice. Brad too had taken time off from his very busy schedule and was even planning to negotiate four weeks off each Christmas.

Impossible almost, yet they'd worked it out.

For Imogen.

He was quite a nice guy really, Angus conceded as, sunglasses on, long hair so blond it was white now, Brad sauntered into the back yard and the kids leapt out of the pool to greet him.

Yes, quite a nice guy for a thickhead, Angus thought as Brad knelt down and kissed Imogen on the cheek.

Oh, his solar plexus still got the odd workout, but nothing too major. And a bit of jealously was OK, Imogen had pointed out, if it kept him on his elbows!

'Hey, Angus!'

'Merry Christmas, Brad,' Angus responded, just a touch formally.

'Do you want me to watch them?'

'Watch them?' Angus could see his frown in the mirrored sunglasses.

'Till Gemma gets here.' He nodded in Imogen's direction and Angus was on his feet in an instant. Her forearms were resting on the edge of the pool, a look of intense concentration on her face. Suddenly Brad wasn't the thickhead here, because a doctor and a midwife they may be, but it had taken the actor to first realise what was happening. Irritable, restless, Imogen wasn't tired and cranky—she was in labour.

Imogen had worked it out, though, by the time he got poolside.

'I wanted a water birth...' Imogen stopped talking

then, her face bright red and screwed up in agony for a long moment till finally she blew out. 'But I'm not having it in the pool!'

'Heath took for ever,' Brad drawled, 'but doesn't the second one usually come quicker? At least, that's what you used to say…'

'Thanks, Brad!' Angus snapped. 'Just watch the kids, bring the car round…'

'Just get me into the house,' Imogen groaned through gritted teeth. 'Brad, call an ambulance.'

This was so not how she'd planned it. A full-time midwife practically till the moment they'd flown back to Australia, she'd worked out her birth plan, and being hauled up the pools steps and led to the house, her ex-husband the one ringing for an ambulance and watching the kids as Angus steered her inside, wasn't a part of it.

'Let's get to the bedroom.' Angus was trying to be calm, but Imogen could hear the note of panic in his voice and it panicked her. Nothing fazed Angus, nothing medical anyway.

'The bathroom…' Imogen gasped. 'I don't want to ruin my silk bedspread…'

'Never mind the bloody bedspread.'

'But I broke the snow globe.'

The silk bedspread wasn't ever going to be an issue, the living-room floor having to suffice, Angus sweating despite the air conditioner on full blast as he pulled off her bikini bottoms.

'I wanted drugs.'

'I know.'

'I wanted to go in the spa.'

'I know...' Angus gritted his teeth. 'Just try and breathe through it. The ambulance will be here soon.'

'Angus...' As another contraction hit and she just really, really had to push, she also really had to ask. 'There's something wrong.'

'There's nothing wrong.' Angus tried to steady himself, attempted a reassuring smile. 'It's got red hair!'

'Poor thing.' Imogen tried to smile back but started crying, because she could see the panic in his eyes, see the grim set of his jaw, knew that he was seriously worried. 'I've worked alongside you—I know when something's going wrong.'

'Nothing's going wrong,' Angus said, only it didn't soothe her. 'It's just never been you before.' And in her panic it didn't make sense, but in that moment between contractions, that last moment between birth and born, the mist cleared.

He loved her.

Absolutely loved her.

And love made things a bit scary sometimes because the stakes were so high.

'It's all good.' Angus said. 'All looks completely normal.'

And it was.

Scary but good. Agony sometimes, but completely and utterly healthy and normal—this thing called living.

Imogen got to deliver her herself, with a bit of help from Angus, lifting their daughter out together and watching in awe as blue eyes opened and she screamed her welcome. A blaze of red, from kicking feet and fists that punched in rage, right to her little screwed-up face and tufts of red hair.

'She's perfect...'

'She is,' Angus said, because it was all he could manage, actually relieved when the paramedics arrived and he could just be a dad.

'Born under a Christmas tree,' the paramedic greeted them. 'You're going to have some fun picking names.'

'Do I have to go to hospital?'

'You need to be checked,' the paramedic said. 'The little one too.'

'You can have that spa,' Angus said temptingly when her face fell. 'And champagne and...' He grinned. 'I can ask Gemma if she minds cleaning up the mess!'

And they were the nicest paramedics, Angus thought, high on adrenaline and loving everyone. They were in absolutely no rush, even happy to let her freshen up a bit once they'd got her on the stretcher and Imogen had decided that she really didn't want Gemma to see her coming out looking quite this bad!

'I want Heath.'

So Angus got him. His usually happy face, pinched and worried, but relaxing into a smile when he saw his new sister. Jack looked pretty chuffed too and Clemmie burst into tears because she'd desperately wanted a boy so that she'd still be the only girl. And then Heath looking worried again when it really was time to get them to the hospital.

'He'll be OK.' Brad assured them, and Angus had to swallow, not jealousy now, maybe even a tear as he saw a slightly wistful look on Brad's face as he gave Imogen a fond kiss goodbye. 'I'll bring him up to see you later tonight.' He looked over at Angus. 'If that's OK with you guys.'

'That'd be great.'

'Us too?' Clemmie asked.

'Yes, you too!' Gemma smiled but her eyes were a little bit glassy, a wistful look on her face as for the first time she met Imogen's eyes. 'Congratulations!'

'Congratulations!' Brad shook Angus's hand and Roger did the same.

Yep, just a bit painful sometimes, Imogen thought as they wheeled her off—for all concerned—but worth it.

And what better way to spend Christmas night? Tucked up in bed, champagne in hand, choosing from a massive chocolate selection with Angus cuddled up beside her, choosing names for a certain little lady who didn't have one yet.

'Holly?' Imogen said again.

'Natalie?' Angus frowned. 'You know, there really aren't that many to choose from.'

'I know!' Imogen breathed, staring over to her daughter, her hair all fluffy after her first bath, her complexion creamy now, fair eyelashes curling upwards, her little snub nose covered by her hand as she sucked on her thumb.

'Summer!'

'Summer?' Angus creased up his nose. 'That's not a Christmas name.'

'She was born in summer.'

'But Christmas is in winter in England, it won't make sense.'

'It will to us.'

'A December baby called Summer!' Angus looked over to his sleeping new daughter. A little ray of sunshine, a little bit of summer, no matter how cold the winter, and, yes, he conceded happily, Imogen was right and he kissed her to tell her so.

'Summer Lake...' Imogen sighed, coming up for breath.

'Summer Maitlin,' Angus corrected, kissing her again.

'Summer Lake-Maitlin.' Imogen said, and then she smiled. 'We'll keep working on it.'

Hired: The Italian's Convenient Mistress

CAROL MARINELLI

CHAPTER ONE

WHERE?

Jammed closely between rush hour commuters, her backpack hopefully still by the door where she'd left it, Ainslie didn't even need to hold the handrail to stay standing as the London Underground jolted her towards a destination unknown and her mind begged the question: where could she go?

There was Earls Court, of course—wasn't that where all Australian backpackers went when they were in London?

Only she wasn't backpacking. She had come to London to work. She'd had a job and accommodation already secured, and had been enjoying her work and life for three very full months—until today.

Her thick blonde hair was still dripping from the rain shower she'd been caught in, and beads of sweat broke out onto her brow as another surge of panic hit.

What on earth was she going to do?

Oh, she had friends, of course. Or rather other nannies she'd first met at playgroup, then at weekly get-togethers with the children. Later, on their time off, they'd discovered together all that London had to offer.

Friends who right now would be sitting in a bar. Sitting and listening, aghast, to the news that Ainslie had been fired, had been accused of stealing from her employers. And whether they believed she'd done it or not didn't really matter—their bosses moved in her ex-boss's circles, and if they wanted to keep their jobs the last thing they needed was a branded thief arriving homeless at their doors.

'*Scusi.*' A low male voice growled in her ear as the tube lurched, and the baby the man was holding was pressed further against her.

'It's okay,' Ainslie said, not even looking up, instead trying to move back a touch as the tube halted in a tunnel between stations. But there was no room to manoeuvre, and she arched her back, trying hard not to disturb the sleeping child in his arms.

God, it was hot!

Despite the cold December conditions outside, here on the tube it was boiling. Hundreds of people were crammed together, dressed in winter coats and scarves, damp from the rain, turning the carriage into an uncomfortable sauna, and Ainslie took a grateful gulp of air as someone opened an air vent.

The baby looked hot too. Bundled into a coat, he was wearing gloves and a woolly hat with earflaps—like an old-fashion fighter pilot—and his little cheeks were red and angry. But he didn't seem distressed. In fact he was asleep, long black eyelashes fanning the red cheeks.

Cute kid, Ainslie thought for about a tenth of a second— before her eyes pooled with tears at the thought of Jack and Clemmie, the little charges she hadn't even been allowed to say goodbye to.

'Sorry!' It was now Ainslie's turn to apologise, as she was pushed further against the baby. She saw his little face screw up in discomfort, and she pressed herself back, to try and give him more room, looking up at his father to briefly express her helplessness. Only suddenly she was just that...

Helpless.

Lost, just lost for a moment, as she stared into the most exquisite face she had ever witnessed close up. Glassy blue eyes that were bloodshot briefly met hers. His thick glossy black hair was unkempt, and his black eyelashes were as long as his son's. His mouth was set in a grim line as he nodded his understanding that it wasn't her fault, before his eyes flicked away down to his son, trying to soothe the now restless, grizzling baby back to sleep, talking to him in Italian. But his rich, deep voice did nothing to soothe the child. The babe's eyes fluttered open, as blue as his father's, but it was as if the child didn't even recognise him. His wail of distress caused a few heads to turn.

'Hush, Guido, it is okay...' He was speaking to him in English now—English that was laced with a rich accent as he again attempted to calm the baby. Now that he wasn't looking at her, Ainslie could look at him more closely. Though stunning, he was clearly exhausted, his skin pale, huge violet smudges beneath his eyes, and he needed to shave. The stubble on his jaw was so black it appeared blue.

'Guido, it is okay...' His voice was louder now, as the tube lurched back into motion, but it only distressed the baby further. His back arching like a cat trying to escape, he clawed his way up his father's chest, flinging himself backwards. But there was nowhere to go, and his little face pressed into Ainslie's as his father struggled to contain him.

'It's okay…' Ainslie didn't know if she was talking to the father or his child as he apologised, gained control and pulled the babe tightly in. But Ainslie could see the child's panic, had felt his burning cheek against hers for just a fraction of time—it had been boiling. Instinctively, as if at work, she put her hand to his head and felt him burning beneath it.

'He's hot…' For a second time she looked into the man's eyes, only this time her mind was on the child. 'He has a fever…'

'He's sick…' The man nodded, and Ainslie didn't know if he would have elaborated further because just then the tube pulled into a station, and as commuters piled off and piled on they were separated.

She should have put it out of her mind. Heaven knows she had enough to think about at the moment—like finding somewhere to stay for tonight, finding a job with no reference, clearing her name, telling her mum—only she couldn't. The little boy's screams, though muffled, still reached her; the look on his father's face, the wretched exhaustion, his voice, his eyes, stayed with her. This stranger had whirred her senses. He was wearing a heavy grey coat, but she'd caught a glimpse of a collar and suit. Maybe he'd picked the little boy up from daycare? Perhaps they'd just come from the doctor's…?

What did it matter? Ainslie told herself as the tube pulled into Earls Court station.

According to her guide it was *the* descending place for Australians in London—now all she had to do was find a youth hostel. Pushing her way through the slowly moving masses, relieved that her backpack had amazingly still been where she'd left it, Ainslie stood on the platform, taking a deep breath, glad to be out of the stifling crowd.

She could hear her mobile trilling and sat on a little bench, nervous when she saw that it was Angus, her old boss, calling. Wondering what he had to say, she let the call go through to her message bank, grateful she wouldn't have to come up with an instant answer to any difficult questions he might pose.

Angus Maitlin might be a famous celebrity doctor—one who appeared regularly in magazines and on television—but he was also a consultant in Accident and Emergency and a wise and shrewd man. Living with him for three months, Ainslie had worked that out quickly, and in the evenings when he had been at home, listening to him as he read a book to one of the kids, half watching the evening news Angus had always made her smile.

'There's more to it!' he'd often say at the end of a report—or, 'He did it!' as an emotional plea was read out.

But the memory wasn't making her smile now, as Ainslie wondered how she could possibly lie and get away with it to this wise, shrewd, and also terribly kind man.

'Ainslie—it's Angus. Gemma just told me what happened. I don't know what to say. Look—I don't like that you're out there with no money or references—I hope you're at a friend's. If you needed money...we could have sorted something out. I'm working till late, but I'll ring tomorrow...'

Clearly Angus was finding the situation difficult, because his voice trailed off then, and Ainslie felt tears tumble out of her eyes for the first time since it had happened. Sadly she realised that he believed her to be guilty. She could hear the disappointment in his kind voice.

Well, of course he believed Gemma—she was his wife! A wife who had told her husband that things had been going missing since Ainslie had started. A wife who had told him she had caught the nanny red-handed, having found her ring and necklace in Ainslie's bedroom drawer. Better that than admitting that it was the nanny who had actually caught *her* red-handed.

Or rather red-faced, beneath her lover, when Ainslie had brought the children home unexpectedly early.

Slumped against the wall on the busy platform, Ainslie began crying her eyes out—not loud tears, just shivering gulps as she gave in and wept. She'd been counting on her Christmas bonus—had needed the money desperately, thanks to Nick and the mess that was unfolding back home. It was the first time she'd actually cried since she'd picked up her mail two weeks ago and found out that her ex-boyfriend had, unbeknownst to her, taken out a joint loan while they were together. The deceit had been almost more upsetting than the financial ramifications, and the tears she had held back spilled out now, as she faced the bleakest of Christmases. Not that anyone noticed. Not that anyone even gave her a second glance. Surrounded by people in one of the busiest cities in the world, never had Ainslie felt more alone.

She could hear the baby crying again too, and his loud sobs matched how she felt…

Guido.

The fraught cries snapped Ainslie out of her own introspection, her eyes scanning the platform until she found him.

He wasn't a baby, more a toddler—eighteen months old, perhaps. He was standing—no, sitting. No, now he was lying on the platform floor and kicking his legs, throwing a spectacular tantrum. His less than impressed father was half kneeling, a laptop and briefcase discarded on the platform beside him, holding his child with one hand as with the other he attempted to open a pushchair with all the skill of someone who'd never opened a pushchair in his life—and certainly not while trying to hold onto a frantic toddler.

And just as the crowd had ignored her tears, so too did they ignore this man's plight. Heads down, they just hurried past, and either didn't see or pretended not to notice; everyone was too busy to offer help.

Wiping her cheeks with the back of her hand, Ainslie walked over. 'Can I help?'

She watched him stiffen momentarily. His head was almost automatically shaking in refusal, highlighting that this was clearly a man who wasn't used to accepting help. Then in almost the same instant he let out a reluctant breath and conceded, picking up the little boy and standing to his impressive height.

'Can you open this pushchair?'

'Of course.'

'Please,' he added as a very late afterthought, as with two easy motions Ainslie did just that.

'Thank you.' He dismissed her then, and really she should have turned and gone. But Ainslie knew that an open pushchair was only half the battle. She watched and wondered with vague amusement how he'd manage to get this stiff, angry child into the chair.

With great difficulty he tried to buckle Guido in. Failing on the first effort, he undid his coat, and Ainslie was treated to a glimpse of impressive suit, a shirt unbuttoned at the neck. Even Ainslie could tell that suits and coats as exquisite as the one this man was wearing didn't often belong to a daddy who spent a lot of time at home.

This daddy, Ainslie guessed as Guido's shrieks trebled, must have spent so much time in the office that his son hardly recognised him. There were no easy motions, no practised ease, as he tried to get the unwilling, resisting arms of the child into the straps of the pushchair.

'I can manage!' he growled as she hovered.

But he couldn't. The angry little bundle continued kicking and thumping.

Just as Ainslie had decided to let him do just that and deal with her own problems, Guido caught them both by surprise…

Staring at his father, his screams stopped for a second, a second that allowed him to draw breath, and Ainslie stood open mouthed as the little boy, very deliberately, very angrily and very directly, spat in the face of his father.

'Puh!'

It was no accident—he even added sound—and Ainslie's eyes widened in horror, staring at the shocked expression of the man, who didn't look as if he'd take too well to being spat on. Then he did the most unexpected thing and grinned; that crabby, exhausted, haughty face was actually breaking into a laugh, and it caught the little boy by surprise, because he relaxed just long enough for the pushchair strap to be clicked into place.

The man stood up and, still grinning, pulled out a very smart navy silk handkerchief and wiped his face.

'Little gypsy tramp—just like his father!'

Which wasn't the best of introductions!

'Oh…' Ainslie nodded.

The last remnants of his smile were fading, and, after wrapping the child in a blanket, he took off his coat and wrapped that around the little boy too. But even though it was freezing outside, it was way, way too much for a little boy who was boiling up.

Ainslie couldn't help herself. 'He has a fever!'

'So I keep him warm.'

'No…' Ainslie shook her head in exasperation. 'I work with children, and what he needs is to cool down…' She looked at his bemused expression and knew he didn't have a clue. 'He's *very* hot.' When still he didn't seem to understand, she spoke more loudly, more slowly. 'He might fit…have a convulsion…' she explained.

'I am neither deaf nor stupid! You do not have to speak pigeon English.'

'Sorry…' Ainslie blushed.

'I have just seen a doctor with him, and he has been prescribed some medicine.' He pulled a rather scruffy bag from his pocket, along with a rolled-up tie. 'When I get him home I will give it.'

'But they're antibiotics—what he needs…' Oh, what was the point? Turning on her heel, she gave a shrug. The sooner this arrogant know it all got home to his wife the sooner his boiling, ill-mannered baby could get some paracetamol in him and hopefully cool down.

'He needs what?'

A hand grabbed her arm, and Ainslie felt her throat tighten. He had just *sooo* done the wrong thing. Only he didn't let go, and even though she had a jacket on the inappropriate touch burned through the thick material, just a trickle of fear invading. But she was on a busy tube station, Ainslie reminded herself, and turned around to confront him.

'What is it he needs?'

'Could you remove your hand?' Angry green eyes met his, watched as he blinked and stared down at his hand as if it didn't even belong to him.

'I am sorry!' Instantly he let go—his apology absolutely genuine. 'I am worried about him—and I don't know what to do.'

'Get him home…' Ainslie's voice was softer. 'He needs some paracetamol. Once he's had that he'll settle…'

'Paracetamol?' He checked, and Ainslie nodded.

'And he needs his mum.'

This time she really was going. This time she knew he wouldn't grab her. Only he didn't have to. His voice stilled her as she started walking, his words halting her before she disappeared for ever into the heavy crowd.

'She died this afternoon.'

CHAPTER TWO

His words seared into her. Aghast, she swung around, looked from father to son and back to the father, at the identical blue eyes that stared back at her.

And it was horrible.

That no one knew. That all those strangers had stood on that tube, had tutted at the baby, at the pushchair, had walked past as he'd struggled on the platform—and not a single one knew the misery that was taking place.

There were just a few days until Christmas.

The date didn't matter—it would have been terrible on any day—but that it was so close to Christmas, that this beautiful little boy would be without his mother, that she would be without him, just made it worse somehow. And it made her own problems pale in comparison.

'Can you help me?' His voice was low but there was a thread of urgency.

'Me?'

'You said you work with children?'

'I do, but—'

'Then you must know how to stop his fever? How to take care of him?' There was a plea in his rich voice, a tinge of fear, even panic for his son. 'I don't know what to do. I do not know children; I do not know what this boy needs...' He dived out of his own hell just enough to glimpse her confusion, just long enough to interpret it. 'He is not my son—he is my nephew. There was a car accident. I came from Italy this morning as soon as I hear the news.'

Heard the news. Ainslie opened her mouth to correct him, and then stopped herself—working with people who were usually under three feet tall gave her a tendency to do that! His story certainly explained his visible exhaustion. Dressed in a suit, juggling a laptop and a briefcase along with the stroller, he must have literally left in the middle of whatever it was he was doing and stepped onto a plane.

'Where's his father?' The platform was full—again they were being pushed closer. Only this time they *were* together, sharing this appalling conversation.

Her eyes closed for a second as he answered, 'He died instantly.'

When Ainslie opened them again, he was waiting for her, strong but desperate. His eyes held hers.

'Can you tell me what he needs…help me with him?'

You don't read out a list of questions when you witness someone drowning.

You don't ask their name or age, or if they're worthy of saving. You don't ring for references or ask for a police check—instead you do what you can.

'Yes,' she said simply, because to Ainslie it was just impossible to even think of walking away, of not helping someone who so clearly needed it.

'His home is close by—there is a pharmacy on the way.'

The platform was packed now. Another tube was pulling

in and spewing out its contents. People walked fast as they left the platform, and the station was a blizzard of people, rushing to get home or to go out, stopping to buy their paper, chatting into their phones, arranging dates, parties, meetings—getting on with living.

Getting on with life.

A blast of icy December air hit them as they stepped out onto the busy street. It was the strangest walk; he took her backpack and Ainslie pushed the stroller. Christmas was everywhere—the shops ablaze with decorations, people tipsy from pre-dinner drinks heading for a work party—and it just seemed to magnify his loss. Even the chemist was full of cheery, piped music, chiming Christmas songs, and lazy shoppers were grabbing easy gifts as they stopped to buy Guido's paracetamol.

'Should we get nappies, wipes...or do you have plenty?'

'I haven't been to the house since I arrived—I have no idea what my sister would have. We'd better get them—get whatever you think he might need.'

So she did—put whatever she thought might be needed into a basket and stood trying to hush the little boy as his uncle paid, watching the checkout assistant chatting happily away to her colleague, briefly asking the man if he had had a good day, not noticing that he didn't respond, his face a quilt of muscles as he handed over his credit card.

'I don't know your name.' It was the first thing she said as he made his way back to them.

'Elijah...' He gave a tight smile. 'Elijah Vanaldi. And you?'

'Ainslie Farrell.'

And that was all they said. They walked along in silence

till they came to a quieter street and stopped outside a vast four-storey residence.

But somehow, for now, it was enough.

It was surreal—Elijah working out keys as she stared at the wreath on the door, stepping into someone's house, someone's life, someone you didn't even know, and being entrusted to take care of their most treasured possession. And though it was a beautiful towering white stucco home, as she stepped in, walked along polished floorboards and glimpsed the vast lounge, though her eyes took in the high ceilings and vast windows and expensive furnishings, they didn't merit a mention. The only thing Ainslie could really notice was the collection of shoes and coats in the hall, the scent of pine in the air from the Christmas tree, and the half-cup of cold tea on the granite bench when she walked into the luxury kitchen. Sadness engulfed her when she saw the simple shopping list on the fridge and the breakfast dishes piled by the sink.

Elijah undressed an exhausted Guido.

'Has he had dinner?'

'He had some biscuits, he doesn't seem very hungry.' Elijah held his hand to his forehead. 'He still feels hot. Should I bathe him?'

'I wouldn't worry about it tonight. Let's just get him changed for bed and give him his medicine.' As she wandered upstairs to find pyjamas for Guido, Ainslie could tell that this elegant house with its lavish furniture and expensive fittings was first and foremost a home—a home with a book by the unmade bed, and hair staighteners still plugged in. In the bathroom a tap drizzled, and piles of damp towels and knickers littered the floor, reminding Ainslie that this was a family home that had been left with every intention of coming back.

'She rang me last week to say she was giving in and finally going to get a housekeeper...' His voice behind her made Ainslie jump, and she felt the sting of tears behind her eyes as he walked over and turned off the tap. 'She was never very good at tidying up.'

'Mess doesn't matter.'

'She'd die if she knew we'd seen it like this...' Elijah halted, grimacing at his own words. 'You always had to ring Maria to warn her you coming over—she hated it when people dropped in. She'd hate that she didn't do one of her infamous quick tidies—she'd be embarrassed at someone seeing the place like this.'

'She thought she was coming home.'

'He has an ear infection.' Elijah watched as she easily measured out the antibiotics. 'The doctor said that was why he was miserable and so naughty, but—as I explained to him—from what my sister tells me, and what I have seen of him, he is always trouble!'

'He's got croup too,' Ainslie said, as Guido suitably barked. 'Poor little thing. The medicine should help his pain, though, and the antibiotics will hopefully kick in soon.'

'Hopefully.' Elijah sighed. 'For now I will make him some food, then he can go to bed.' He pulled a piece of paper out of his pocket and looked at it for a moment, then headed to where Guido was sitting on the couch, his eyes half closed, half watching the cartoon that Elijah had put on for him.

There were people who had no idea about children, and people who had *no* idea about children, and Ainslie watched as he peeled a rather overripe banana and handed it to the little boy, who just blinked back at him, bemused.

'Maria said he liked bananas.'

'He's not a monkey…' Ainslie's grin faded. 'Let me,' she said instead, and headed to the kitchen. She found some bread in the freezer and gave it a spin in the microwave, then took off the crusts and put some mashed banana in. She arranged it on a plastic plate and offered it to Guido, who this time accepted it.

Later—when he was falling asleep with exhaustion—Elijah carried his nephew upstairs and Ainslie followed, tucking the little boy, unresisting, into bed.

'He has a night light.' Elijah was looking at his bit of paper again. 'He wakes up, but all he wants is his blanket put back on.'

Watching his strong hands tuck the blanket around the little boy's shoulders, Ainslie could feel her nose running, and had to turn her head quickly away as he straightened up. She headed down the stairs and into the lounge, sniffing away tears as a short time later he came back in, holding two mugs of coffee.

'Thank you.' He handed one to her and sat down, took a sip of his drink and held it in his mouth before talking again. 'I am not a stupid person…'

'I know.' Ainslie gulped. 'I'm sorry about what I said about the banana thing…' She managed a little smile, and he did the same.

'I have nothing, *nothing* to do with children. Nothing!' he added again, in case she hadn't heard it the first or second time. 'And my sister said that she wanted me to have him. That she wanted me to be the one who raises him.'

'What happened?'

For the first time it seemed right to ask—right that she should know a little bit more.

'There was a car accident—it ran off the road and caught fire on impact.' He gave a hopeless shrug. 'I was at work when the hospital called—in the middle of a meeting. Normally I would not be disturbed, but my PA called me out, said this was a call I needed to take. I knew it would be bad. I had no idea how bad, though—a doctor told me that Rico, Guido's father, was already dead, and that my sister was asking for me. I came straight away. Guido had been at a crèche and they'd brought him to the hospital.'

'I'm sorry.'

'She knew she was dying—she had terrible burns—but she was able to talk. She waited for me to get there so she could tell me what she wanted, so she could tell me herself the things Guido likes…'

'That was the list you were reading?'

He nodded, but it was a hopeless one. 'I love my sister, I love my nephew, but I have no idea how they really lived. I saw them often, but I have no clue with day-to-day things, I've never even thought of having children…'

'Is there anyone else?' Ainslie blinked, glimpsing how impossible it must be for him—for his whole life to be turned around, to be so suddenly plunged into grief and told you were to be a father.

'There was just my sister—our parents are dead.'

'But her husband's family…' It was never going to be

the easiest conversation to have—sitting with a stranger who was engulfed by grief and exhaustion—it was always going to be difficult. But, watching his face harden, hearing his sharp intake of breath, even if she didn't know him at all, Ainslie knew she had said the wrong thing.

'Never!' The venom behind the single world had Ainslie reeling.

'Soon they will be here. Already they are making noises about taking care of Guido, and noises are all I will let them be. They are not interested in him.'

'But they say they want him?' Ainslie frowned, her mouth opening to speak again, and then she got it. As he flicked his hand at their impressive surroundings, she answered in her head the question she hadn't even asked yet.

Elijah answered it with words. 'They want this. And the insurance pay-out—and the property Maria and Rico had in Italy…' He glanced over to her. 'And in case you are wondering—I do not need it…' He drained his mug. 'Neither do I need a toddler. Especially one who spits!' In the pit of his grief he managed to smile at the memory, and then it faded; his voice was pensive when next it came. 'I hope Rico knew that I did actually like him.'

She didn't understand, but it wasn't right to ask—wasn't right to demand more information from a man who had lost so much, a man who had just been plunged into hell.

'You should try and sleep,' Ainslie offered instead.

'Why?' He stared back at her. 'Somehow I do not believe that things will be better in the morning.'

'They might…' Ainslie attempted, but it was pretty futile.

'Thank you…' He said it again, only it was more determined now. He was back in control and, ready to face the challenge of what lay ahead, he stood up. 'Thank you for explaining about the medicine and for helping me to get him to sleep. I will be fine now. Can I get you a taxi…?'

'Actually…' Ainslie ran a worried hand through her hair. She had been so consumed with his problems that for a little while she'd actually forgotten her own.

'Do you know a number?'

'Sorry?'

He was picking up the phone. 'For the taxi—do you know a number?'

'I can walk.' Ainslie's voice was a croak, but she cleared her throat. Surely a youth hostel would still be open? Surely?

'You're not walking!' Elijah shook his head. 'I will take…' He must have remembered at that point the sleeping toddler upstairs, because his voice trailed off. 'I insist you take a taxi.' Which was easier said than done. First he had to find a telephone directory, and then, as Ainslie stood there, he punched in the numbers and looked over. 'To where?'

'The youth hostel.'

'Youth hostel?' He frowned at her skirt and boots, at her twenty-eight-year-old face and glanced at his watch. In those two small gestures he compounded every one of her fears—she wasn't a backpacker, and nine p.m. on a dark December night was too late to start acting like one. 'How long have you been staying there?'

'I haven't.' Ainslie gave a tight shrug. 'I was on my way there when we met. I'm actually from Australia…'

'I have just come from Italy—first class,' he added, 'and I looked more dishevelled than you when I got off the plane.'

Somehow she doubted it, but she understood the point he was making.

'Well, I've been here for three months. I have a job—*had* a job…'

'Working with children?'

'That's right.'

'But not now?' She shook her head, loath to elaborate, but thankfully he sensed her unwillingness and didn't push.

'Stay.' It was an offer, not a plea. The phone rested on his shoulder as he affirmed his offer. 'Stay for tonight—as you say, tomorrow things may seem better.'

Ainslie opened her mouth to tell him why she couldn't possibly—only nothing came out.

Even if a hostel was open, even if she could get in one, the thought of registering, the thought of starting again, of greeting strangers, lying in a bed in a room for six, held utterly no appeal.

'Stay!' Elijah said more firmly. 'Guido is sick—it makes sense.'

It made no sense.

Not a single scrap of sense.

But somehow it did.

CHAPTER THREE

THOUGH he never voiced it, Ainslie knew and could understand that he didn't want to be alone. Jangling with nerves after the day's events, while simultaneously drooping with exhaustion, she sat on the sofa, tucked her legs under her and stifled a yawn as Elijah located two glasses and poured them both a vast brandy. Even though she didn't particularly like the taste, she accepted it, screwing up her nose as she took a sip, the warmth spreading down her throat to her stomach. She knew there and then why it was called medicinal—for the first time since she'd caught Gemma in between the sheets the adrenaline that had propelled her dimmed slightly, and she actually relaxed a touch—till he asked her a question.

'You said you worked with children?'

'I'm a kindergarten teacher—well, I am in Australia. Here I've been working as a live-in nanny.'

'Why?' Elijah frowned.

'Why not?' Ainslie retorted—though he was hardly the first to ask. Why would she give up a perfectly nice job, walk out on her perfectly nice boyfriend, and travel to the other side of the world to be paid peanuts to live in someone else's home and look after their kids?

'What were you running away from?'

'I wasn't running...' Ainslie bristled, and then, because he had been honest, somehow she could be more honest with this stranger than she had been with her own family. 'I suppose I *was* running away—only I didn't know from what at the time. I had a nice job, a lovely boyfriend, nice everything, really...'

'But?'

'Something wasn't right.' Ainslie gave a tight shrug. 'It was nothing I could put my finger on, but it turns out my instincts were right.'

'In what way?'

Shrewd eyes narrowed on her as she stiffened, and Elijah didn't push as, with a shake of her head, Ainslie stared into her glass and declined to elaborate. 'Everyone said I was crazy, that I'd regret it, but coming to London was the best thing I've ever done—I've loved every minute.'

'So why were you standing on the platform crying?' Elijah asked, and her eyes flew back to his. She was surprised he'd even noticed. 'And why are you checking into a youth hostel so late in the evening?'

'Things didn't work out with my boss...' Ainslie attempted casual, but those astute eyes were still watching her carefully. 'I'll find something else.'

'You already have,' Elijah answered easily. 'I don't know how long it will be for, but I'm certainly going to be here till after Christmas...'

'You don't know me...' Ainslie frowned.

'I won't know the girl the agency sends tomorrow either!' he pointed out. 'The offer's there if you want it.'

'Won't his father's family want to help out?' She could see him bristle—see him tense, just as he had before when they were mentioned.

He was about to tell her it was none of her business—about to snap some smart response—but those green eyes that beckoned him weren't judging, and there was no trace of nosiness in her voice. Elijah realised he didn't want to push her away, didn't want to be alone. For the first time in his life he actually needed to talk.

'Our families have never got on. When Maria started going out with Rico I didn't talk to my sister for two years.'

'Were you close before that?'

'We were all the other had. I was five when my mother died; Maria was only one. Our father turned to drink, and he died when I was twelve.'

He'd never told anyone this—could scarcely believe the words were coming out of his own mouth. Her jade-green eyes hardly ever left his. Every now and then she looked away, swirling her brandy in her glass as he spoke, but her gaze always returned to him. Her damp blonde hair was drying now, coiling into curls on her shoulders, and for the first time he walked through the murky depths of his past in the hope that it would guide him to the right future, that the decisions that must surely be made now would be the right ones for Guido.

'We brought ourselves up,' Elijah explained. 'Did things that today I am not proud of. But at the time...' He gave a regretful shrug. 'There was a family in our village—the Castellas. They were as rough as us, and after the same thing—money to survive. You could say we were rivals, I guess. One day Rico's older brother Marco came on to Maria.' His eyes flinched at the memory. 'She was still a child—thirteen—and she was an innocent child too. I had always been the one who did the cheating and stealing while Maria went to school; she was a good girl. Maria always hated Marco for what he did to her; she would not want him near Guido.'

'So this isn't about revenge?'

'I had my revenge the day it happened,' Elijah said darkly. 'I beat him to a pulp.'

'So the hatred just grew?' Ainslie asked, but Elijah didn't answer directly.

'When I was seventeen I was outside a café, watching some rich tourists. It was a couple, and I was waiting till it was darker, till they'd had a few more drinks and wouldn't be paying close attention to their wallets. They spoke to the waiter. Their Italian was quite good—they were looking to retire, wanted a property with a view…' He smiled at the memory. 'There was no estate agent in our small village in Sicily then—it wasn't a tourist spot. I knew, I just knew, that I didn't want to be stealing and cheating to get by any more. Finally I knew what I could do to get out of it.'

She didn't comment further, didn't frown at the fact that he'd stolen, didn't wince at his past, and that gave him the strength to continue.

'I sold them my late grandfather's home—to me and to my friends it was a shack, just a deserted place we hung out in. It had been passed to us, Maria and me, but till then it had been worth nothing. But we cleaned it painted and polished it, and Maria picked flowers for the inside. I could see what they wanted, and knew that this villa was it.'

'*You* sold it to them?'

'They dealt with the lawyers, they had the papers drawn up.' Elijah nodded. 'Then, after that, I sold our own home. With every bit of money I made I bought more properties, then I moved out of our village and on to bigger things—and the Castellas were still there, thieving on the beach. With every success that came our way they hated us more—just as we hated them.'

'You're a real estate agent?' Ainslie checked, wondering why that made him smile.

'I'm a property developer. I buy homes like this one—beautiful homes the world over—and I retain the exterior, gut the interior, and turn them into flats.'

'Ouch!' Ainslie winced, staring around at this vast lounge, the size of a ballroom, at the ornate cornices and the marble mantelpiece over the dreamy fireplace, loath to think of it being destroyed.

'Of course we try to retain as many original features as possible!' He gave an ironic smile.

'Philistine.'

'Perhaps!' Elijah conceded. 'Maria, too, fell in love with this place.'

'And she fell in love with Rico too?'

After the longest time he nodded, that single gesture telling her he would reveal more.

'Not till years later. I was furious—so too was his family. None of us went to the wedding...' He closed his eyes in regret. 'She still worked for me, supported her husband. I kept pointing out that he wasn't working, but slowly I started to see that they were for real. They had to be real. Because in spite of what had happened—with all that his brother had done—still she loved Rico. So we started speaking again, and then I realised how hard things were for them. Rico's family blamed Maria for what had happened to them, for the slur to Marco's name. They said that she had asked for it, that it had been her coming on to him…'

'She was thirteen!'

'Easier for them to blame her than change him. Rico is a mechanic, and his family ran the car repair place in the village, so he couldn't work. I knew they couldn't stay in the village—there was too much bad blood, too many slurs for them to ever make a real go of it. I suggested they move in here for a while—Maria spoke some English. I had purchased the place furnished, and I said she could oversee the plans, help with the architects and inspections till it was ready to get off the ground. It never did.' He smiled as he said it. 'The renovations started—only not the ones I had intended—Rico found work straight away, and they settled right in. I would often come to visit…'

'You were living in London?'

'No, I am mainly in Italy. But I am here once or twice a month, and every time I came here I noticed it had become more and more their home—a few new cushions for the couches, a rug here and there. And then when she got pregnant Maria started talking about a mural in the nursery. I gave in when Guido was born. I knew that they loved each other completely, and as a belated wedding gift I decided to sign the place over to them.'

'Some wedding gift!'

'Oh, it was to be their Christmas present too!'

Ainslie smiled at the faint joke. She knew nothing about property prices, save that London was fiercely expensive. She'd thought Gemma and Angus lived in luxury, but this house, right in the heart of London, was just stunning. Under any other circumstances she'd have paid to enter and be gazing at this lounge from behind a red rope! Ainslie gulped, staring over at the man sitting beside her on the couch. And under any other circumstances she'd be gazing at him on the silver screen, or in a glossy magazine.

Effortlessly stunning, he was quite simply the most beautiful man she had ever witnessed in the flesh. The features that had first dazzled her on the tube merited closer inspection now.

His jet hair was thick and glossy, and there was a slightly depraved look to his piercing blue eyes—but that could, Ainslie conceded, be more born of exhaustion than excess. His very straight Roman nose was a proud feature. All his features were wonderful in their own right, yet combined they were stunning. But what moved Ainslie most, what exalted him from good-looking to stunning, were the full lips of his mouth—the curve of them when he smiled. It was a mouth that softened his features, a mouth that flexed around his expressive language, a mouth that drew you closer, that held your attention when he spoke.

'It felt right that she have this house. Right that I could take care of her still. She's my sister—*was* my sister…' His voice husked, his mouth struggling with the correction.

'She still is…' Ainslie said softly. 'Always will be.'

'This place was their home. It is right that it's Guido's home now.'

'What will you do?'

'I don't know.' He stared into the bottom of his near-empty glass as if he were trying to gaze into a crystal ball. 'Marco and his wife, Dina, have never seen him, have played no part in his life, and yet now Rico and Maria are dead they say they want to be involved.'

'Were *you* involved?'

'I've never babysat, never changed his nappy...' Elijah answered. 'But I spoke with my sister on the phone most days. As I said, I'm in London once or maybe twice a month, and I normally stopped by. I was—am—a part of his life. It just never entered my head it would be to this extent.'

'It might be the same for Marco and Dina,' Ainslie offered. 'Maybe they've had a shock? Maybe they've realised...?' Her voice trailed off as he shook his head.

'I don't trust them.' He drained the last dregs before continuing, 'I don't want that man near my nephew—he is the last person Maria would want for him. I know people can change, and I know that it was a long time ago. But some things—well, they are too hard to excuse or forgive.'

'There's no one else?'

'No one apart from one reprobate uncle who likes to burn the candle at both ends and has an appalling track record with women.'

'Oh!' Ainslie blinked, rather liking the sound of him. 'Where's he, then?'

'You're looking at him.' He even managed to laugh, but it faded quickly. 'The trouble is, as wrong as I think Marco and Dina would be for him, I don't trust that I am right for Guido either. I don't have a lifestyle that really fits in with raising a child. I can provide for him, I can give him the best of everything...'

But he deserved so much more than that, and they both knew it.

'It might be time to grow up, I guess!' Elijah said, putting down his glass and standing. 'Either that or try and find a way to put aside lifelong rivalries and remember it isn't a patch on the beach we're fighting over any more.'

'You'll work it out.'

'Just not tonight…'

They shuffled through the house and up the stairs.

'This is a guest room,' Elijah announced. 'And there's another one here.' Elijah pushed open another door. 'You can choose.'

'I don't care…'

Ainslie shrugged, so he chose for her, depositing her backpack in a pretty yellow and white room that was to be her home for tonight.

'I'll just check on Guido.'

They both did.

Stood in his parents' bedroom and peered into his cot. His flushed face was paler now, his thumb was in his mouth and his bottom was in the air, and tears welled in Ainslie's eyes as she stared down at him. Safe and warm but suddenly alone, without the two people who would have loved him the most. The vast bed in the room looked horribly empty as they crept out.

'Will we wake up?' As he turned to go he thought better of it. 'Who will wake up to Guido?'

And it was a very sensible question. Babies who woke in the night wouldn't usually be factored in to Elijah Vanaldi's agenda. Little whimpers of distress wouldn't necessarily jerk a man like him from slumber.

'I'll wake.' Ainslie smiled softly at his exhausted face. 'You should try and get some rest.'

She'd wake if only first she could sleep.

Her head was racing at a million miles an hour as she lay in the strange bed, listening as Elijah showered. Familiar sounds in an unfamiliar place, and for the first time since she'd put the key in the front door this afternoon she was able to draw breath.

To actually think about what she should do with her own situation.

If she pleaded her case Gemma had made it clear that without warning or hesitation she would call the police, and Ainslie knew that no one would employ a childcare worker who was being investigated. Even if she could prove her innocence, the slur alone would be enough to ruin her time in England. Elijah had offered her a position, but for how long? A day? A week? How long would it be till he went back to Italy?

Ainslie blinked into the darkness. He was trusting her to help him—what would he say if he knew that she had been accused of theft?

As the shrill screams of Guido pierced the night Elijah sat up, gulping in air as he awoke from a nightmare...

His sister had been dead—no, she'd been dying—her body horribly disfigured, her voice a strained, hoarse whisper as she'd tried to speak through her swollen and damaged windpipe, imploring him to listen, warning him of the Castellas descending, claiming her baby, taking what they considered theirs. He'd gone to hold her hand, to tell her it was all okay, that he would take care of things. Only her hand... He could feel bile rising in his throat as he replayed the image.

It was just a dream, Elijah assured himself, sheathed in sweat, and trying to pull himself out of it. A nightmare. The horrible panic, the utter dread with which he'd awoken should be abating now, should be dimming as reality filtered in. Instead, Elijah could feel his heart quicken as he took in his surrounds. Another shot of adrenaline propelled him out of bed in panic. He grabbed a towel and wrapped it around his hips, dashing to his nephew as he realised he hadn't awoken *from* a nightmare—he was living one.

'He's okay!'

It was like falling off a cliff into soft outstretched arms. Ainslie was leaning over Guido's cot, pressing her finger to her lips to tell him to be quiet, dressed in vast, shapeless pyjamas that were covered in some pattern he couldn't make out. Guido's little night light caught the gold in her blonde hair as briefly she looked up from the child she soothed, her voice soft and calming—not just to Guido, but to himself.

Only Ainslie herself wasn't soothed. Clemmie and Jack had both regularly woken in the night and, used to sleeping light, she'd woken when Guido had first whimpered. She had been stumbling down the hall by the time his screaming had started, and had been able to quickly soothe him— deliberately not turning on the light, so her strange presence wouldn't alarm him. Instead she'd replaced his blanket, as Elijah had mentioned, and patting his back had gently hushed him. And then Elijah had come to the door, breathless, as if he'd been running.

'He's nearly back to sleep,' she whispered as he came over quietly. Ainslie lowered her head back into the crib.

Suddenly she was glad for the dim lighting in the room, because her face was one burning blush at the sight of Elijah wearing nothing more than a towel, and she was absolutely aware of his presence as he stood beside her till she was happy that Guido was asleep.

Of course he'd be wearing nothing, Ainslie scolded herself as they crept out of the bedroom. He hadn't exactly had time to pack, and she couldn't somehow see a man like Elijah rummaging through his dead brother-in-law's clothes to find something to wear.

But that wasn't the problem and she knew it—hell, she'd caught Angus, her old employer, on the landing in nothing more than a pair of boxers loads of times, and it had done nothing for her, nothing at all, had barely merited a thought. But walking along the landing behind Elijah, seeing the taut definition of his muscled back, the silky olive skin, inhaling the soapy masculine scent of him, well, it merited more than just a thought.

'Goodnight.' He turned to face her, his hair all rumpled from falling asleep with it wet, still unshaven, his incredibly beautiful eyes dark wells of anguish as he hesitated to go. 'Do you think he knows? Do you think he knows that they are gone?'

'On some level, perhaps.' She was helpless to comfort him—had been wondering the same thing herself as she'd soothed the little boy back to sleep. 'He'll know things are different, he'll be unsettled and he'll want his parents. But so long as his little world is safe he'll be okay.'

'Will he remember them?' He delivered a slightly mocking laugh to himself. 'Of course he won't.'

'I don't agree,' Ainslie said gently, because it was up to

Elijah now to turn the fragile images Guido held and somehow merge them into his life. 'I mean, there will be pictures, DVDs with them on it that he can watch over and over. I don't know much about child grief, but I think…'

'I can hardly remember,' Elijah said, explaining the mocking laugh. 'I can hardly remember my mother at all—and she died when I was five. Guido is not even two. He's only fifteen months old.'

'Did your father talk to you about her?' Ainslie pushed, but she already knew the answer. 'You can make it different for Guido.'

'Can I?'

Her hand instinctively reached out for his arm, touching him as she would anyone in so much pain. Only the contact, the feeling of his skin beneath her fingers, the hairs on his arm, the satin of his skin against her palm, the touch that had been offered as comfort, shifted to something else entirely as her eyes jerked to his.

At any point she could have reclaimed her hand. At any point she could have said goodnight and gone back to her room. Only she didn't—couldn't. The air thrummed with the thick scent of arousal—grief and shock a strange propellant, one that forced a million emotions into the air in one very direct hit, accelerating feelings and blurring boundaries. The day that had left them both reeling, forced them to go through the motions, to run on sheer adrenaline, was at an end now, and now they paused—paused long enough to draw breath before the impossible race started again. A race neither wanted to resume.

Just easier, far easier, to ignore the pain for a moment, to stand and instead of facing the future face each other.

Elijah stared into her eyes as he tried to picture the last few hours without her in it. Always he had a solution—another plan to initiate if things didn't go his way. There was nothing that truly daunted him. But walking out of that hospital, holding his nephew in his arms, he had felt the weight of responsibility overwhelm him. Gripped with fear, not for himself but for Guido, he had had no glimmer of a plan, no thought process to follow, had just clung on to his nephew as he'd clung to *him*. And then she had come along—an angel descending when he'd needed it most. And he needed her now.

'Why did you stop?' His voice was low, his question important.

'Why wouldn't I stop?' Ainslie blinked. 'You needed help.'

'But no one else did.'

Hundreds had passed him that day—had jammed against him on the underground, hadn't made room as he'd lifted the stroller, had squashed into Guido as if they didn't even notice he was there. At the platform before he'd met her many had seen him struggle, and out of all of them she was the only one who had tried to help. He didn't want to picture how this night would have been without her kind concern. Didn't want to envisage stepping into this house alone with Guido. Didn't want to think about any of it for even a second longer…

His breath was getting faster now, the nightmare coming back, and he struggled to surface from it, to drag in air and escape. He needed her now just as much, if not more, than then. He drew comfort in the only way he knew how. He lowered his mouth and claimed hers, the bliss of contact fulfilling a craving, a need for escape—such a balmy escape—the medicine so sweet, the feel of her in his arms like a haven.

For a second she resisted, fought the urge to kiss him back. The speed of it all, the inappropriateness, flitted into her mind, then flitted out—because maybe she craved oblivion too. As his tongue parted her lips and his skilled mouth searched hers Ainslie thought that maybe it was because she'd never been so thoroughly kissed before. The wretched, wretched day was fading—the sting of Gemma's accusations, the panic and fear that had gripped her when she'd found herself alone in a strange city—all was abating as with his mouth he soothed and excited.

In this crazy day he had helped her too—was helping her now.

This heady, blinding kiss was frenzied almost—like an anaesthetic, dousing pain, dimming thought. His hands knotted in her hair as he drank from her mouth, his mouth so hot on hers there was a delicious hurt. Deep lusty kisses both claimed and bestowed, and each breath she took was his, each breath she gave he gulped in. It was a dangerous kiss that could only lead to more. Yet somehow he made her feel safe, his strong arms holding her, his hands clutching her to him, his lips grazing her neck, the scratch of his chin on her sensitive skin making her weak. She'd never been kissed like this before—never been wanted or wanted so badly herself. The heady rush fizzed in her veins, racing around her body—stroking her pelvic floor like an inner caress. And it had to stop, because if it didn't then they wouldn't.

Pulling back her head, though his arms still circled her body, she called a reluctant halt. Both were staring, both breathing as if they had run a mile. The delicious shock doused her, her own body's response astonished her—

every encounter in her life laid end to end didn't come close to matching this.

'Don't…' He husked his response to her unvoiced statement—disparity evident as her body thrummed in his arms.

'I have to.' She could hardly speak, her whole body so drenched with arousal, so utterly opposed to her mind, that it took every ounce of effort she possessed to walk from his room, to lie on her bed…to walk away from his.

It was just a kiss. She told herself. *A kiss because…*

Only she couldn't answer that one. Ainslie's fingers moved to her mouth, feeling it swollen where his lips had been. She could still feel the tender flesh of her neck where his chin had made her raw.

And it wasn't just a kiss—kisses had never left her weak like that; kisses had never left her lost. Which she had been, completely lost in the moment with him.

She tried to put it out of her mind, to focus on her problems instead of letting her imagination wander, to tell herself to let it go.

But her body said otherwise. And the slightly open bedroom doors channelled their want as they both lay alone in the oppressive silence. Ainslie, her body twitching with desire and thick, greedy need, lay there rigid, almost in desperation for the escape they had briefly found, willing herself to relax, to sleep. Trying to ignore the man who lay just metres away, who was, after one kiss, the only man who had utterly moved her.

CHAPTER FOUR

'WHEN did all that come?' Exhausted, dishevelled, and still coming to terms with yesterday, Ainslie had tripped over a pile of luxury luggage in the hall.

'While you were sleeping,' Elijah said, not looking up. Dressed only in a pair of grey hipsters, unshaven and tousled, he still managed to look absurdly sexy as he shared a bowl of cereal with Guido—one spoon for his nephew, then a larger one for Elijah. 'I arranged some belongings to be couriered over yesterday.' He glanced up at her raised eyebrows—raised because, with all that had taken place, how could he even think about clothes? 'I couldn't face putting on my suit again today.'

'Oh!' Ainslie said, feeling horribly small all of a sudden, as she tried to work out the kitchen. She knew how adrift *she* felt without all of her belongings—but at least she had clean knickers.

Elijah turned to face her. 'I've also arranged a driver—Tony. He's going to be staying in a room on the third floor, so he's available whenever you need him—that is if you stay.'

'A live-in driver!'

'It's impossible to park in London.' Elijah shrugged, lying easily. She didn't need to know he'd actually arranged a bodyguard for Guido—there was no way he was risking the Castellas coming to take him. 'And I don't like walking. Actually,' he conceded slightly, 'he's just broken up with his wife and he needs a live-in job. It was either him or rely on taxis.'

'You've been busy.'

'I always am.' Elijah waited till she came over before continuing. 'Look, I really don't want to push, but I need to know if you are willing to work for me.'

His eyes met hers when finally she joined him at the breakfast table. There had been no mention of what had taken place last night. He'd shown not a trace of awkwardness when he'd greeted her. In fact he was so cool, so completely together, Ainslie even wondered if she'd imagined the whole thing—like some strange erotic dream that made her blush to think about it. She was actually starting to wonder if anything *had* happened, because Elijah didn't look at all fazed or embarrassed.

Or maybe he was just used to it, Ainslie mused as she sugared her coffee. Perhaps he was so used to snogging the hired help whenever it took his fancy it didn't merit a second thought.

It had merited more than a second thought for Ainslie. Problems like finding work and somewhere to live in a strange country just a few days before Christmas, like coming up with some quick money to pay off her debt, had all become mere irrelevancies as she'd lain in bed and relived his kiss over and over.

And now he was asking for an answer as to whether she

would work for him—an answer that, on several levels, she was hesitant to give.

'Can I have some time to think about it?'

'Unfortunately, no—I have already received a rather irate call from Guido's case worker. It would seem that I should not have taken him without the Social Services department's approval.'

'Well, that would have gone down well!' Ainslie couldn't keep the note of sarcasm out of her voice.

'It didn't.'

'So how did you respond?'

'I said that perhaps they should question their procedures rather than me!' He gave a tight smile. 'That didn't go down too well either! And Marco and his wife, Dina, have arrived, and have made it clear that they will be applying for custody. Guido's case worker is coming to meet with me here this morning—it would be helpful to say that I already have arranged childcare, and if you can't work for me I can at least call an agency and be able to say that I have lined up some interviews.'

'I understand that...' Ainslie stirred honey into some porridge and attempted to feed a less than impressed Guido, who was far happier sharing his uncle's bowl. 'I just don't think it's going to be possible for me to work for you.'

'Because you have another job to go to?' She could hear the sarcasm in his voice.

'No.'

'Because you would rather spend Christmas in a youth hostel?'

His arrogance didn't faze her.

'Maybe because I'd prefer to have a few days off over

Christmas and New Year rather than being treated like dirt while I mind some rich family's child!' She gave him a sweet smile over Guido's porridge, but it didn't meet her eyes. They both knew that wasn't the reason.

'I would not treat you badly. And there would be no repeat...' He didn't elaborate. He didn't have to. The colour roared up her cheeks as for a dangerous second they both revisited last night, as her erotic dream was confirmed as reality. 'The top floor is self contained—you could have that. We could draw up a contract...'

'That's not the only issue...' Ainslie swallowed hard, her face burning as she wondered if a lie was a lie if it was by omission. It would be so, so easy to accept his offer. The thought of spending Christmas at a youth hostel, of searching for work at the most impossible time of the year, was daunting to say the least. She knew Elijah was desperate, that he probably wouldn't get around to checking her references for a while, but still integrity won, and Ainslie knew she had somehow to tell him her truth without revealing Gemma's indiscretion. 'You might not want me looking after Guido.' Two vertical lines deepened on the bridge of his nose, but that was the only reaction she took in before she quickly looked away. 'It wasn't a mutual parting of ways—I was actually sacked yesterday.'

'For?'

It was a reasonable question—a *very* reasonable question—and one Ainslie didn't know how to answer. To tell him the truth, the whole truth, felt disloyal to Angus and especially to the children—privileged information gathered when you worked in someone's home, whether good or bad, wasn't hers to divulge. Yet to be labelled a thief, to have her own reputation tarnished, posed for Ainslie an impossible conundrum.

The shrill of her mobile broke the strained silence, and Ainslie cringed when she saw it was Angus.

'Ainslie?' His voice was worried. 'Where are you?'

'I'm fine.'

'What happened?'

'Just leave it, Angus.' Her face was one burning blush. She was wishing, wishing Elijah would show some manners, would get up and leave the table so she could take this exquisitely difficult phone call in private.

'I can't just leave it. Gemma says things have been going missing for weeks...is that true?'

And here was the horrible junction one invariably came to when lying—to claw back from the pit and admit the painful truth, or to cross the point of no return and fully embark on a lie.

'Look, Angus...just give me a moment...'

Despite giving him a rather pointed look, it was clear Elijah wasn't going anywhere, so it was Ainslie who left the table and headed into the kitchen. Closing the door, she let out a long breath, wondering what on earth she could say to make things if not better for herself then no worse for him. For Angus to believe her she had to lie convincingly—it was that or let him know his wife was cheating.

'You know I needed money.' She screwed her eyes closed as she said it. 'Nick hasn't kept up with the loan payments. I didn't think Gemma would miss a few things.'

'Ainslie—this just doesn't sound like you—you're one of the most honest people I've met, and the kids just adored you. I thought you were happy working with them...'

He didn't believe her—wouldn't take the out she was offering. So, taking a deep breath, Ainslie attempted to be more convincing, tried adding a bit of spite to her voice as tears streamed down her face.

'Well, I wasn't happy, actually! And I got sick of seeing Gemma parading her nice things. I decided I wanted some nice things too. I'm surprised she even noticed the necklace was gone—it's not as if she's spoilt for choice.'

There was a horribly long silence, but that was preferable to hearing him speak—the disappointment evident in his voice as he bought her lie.

'Where are you now?'

'Don't worry about me.'

'Unfortunately I do.' Angus let out a tired sigh. 'We owe you some wages—and there's your Christmas bonus...'

'I'm not going to be working for Christmas.'

'You've been great with the kids these last three months—and you've done a lot of babysitting at short notice. I'd rather do this right.' Angus's voice was resigned. 'Look, can we meet? I'll bring the rest of your things and—I'm sorry, Ainslie—Gemma wants the phone back. And—well—the kids were pretty upset. They've made you a card...'

'I'm sorry, Angus...' Her voice was thick with tears.

'Meet me in half an hour.'

'That was my boss.' Red-eyed, Ainslie returned to the table, where Elijah was sipping on disgustingly strong coffee. 'My old boss,' she corrected. 'I have to go and meet him.'

'To obtain a reference?' Tongue firmly in cheek, Elijah looked at her—and she knew, just knew, what he was thinking. Her employment had ended because she'd been found having an affair with her boss. If only he knew the truth!

'I doubt it somehow.'

'Did your termination have anything to do with your work with the children?'

'No.'

He watched a salty fat tear spill down her cheek.

'His wife—well, she wanted me gone. She said that I...'

Her voice trailed off. She knew, just knew, what Elijah must be thinking and struggled to rectify it. 'It's not what it seems.'

'It never is!' Elijah said dryly, and she gave a helpless shake of her head. 'So what happened?'

'I'd rather not say.'

'You're behind with a loan?'

'You were listening!' Ainslie gasped, appalled not just that he had listened, but at how blatantly he'd admitted it.

Elijah just shrugged. 'I have no qualms listening through the door—not where my nephew's safety is concerned.'

'You had no right!'

'I don't see it that way—some of the best decisions I have made have been based on information others would rather I hadn't heard. So, I ask again—you are behind with a loan?'

Ainslie gave a miserable nod. 'I was relying on my Christmas bonus to make some payments.'

'And Nick is your ex? You have debts with him?'

'Debts I didn't know about...' Ainslie was struggling and failing not to cry. 'I found out a couple of weeks ago that he'd taken a loan out while were together—in both our names. I didn't know anything about it till I got some forwarded mail. He hasn't paid the last two payments, and I've rung him a few times and it doesn't sound as if he's got any intention of meeting them.'

'So now you've found out why you left him…' His insight halted her tears. 'Something really *wasn't* right. Have you contacted a lawyer?'

'A lawyer would probably end up costing more than the loan…' Ainslie gave a worried shake of her head. 'It's easier to just keep paying it for now. I've spoken to the bank, but they haven't been very helpful…'

'So you have a motive, and you've admitted to something you didn't do. The question remains, why would you admit to something you didn't do?'

Her eyes shot to his, her face colouring under his scrutiny. 'What do you mean? If you were listening properly you'd have heard me say that I did steal.'

'Thieves never admit, though.' Still he stared. 'I know because I was one—and I know that you are not.'

That he believed her, that somehow, despite all evidence to the contrary, he believed her, brought a fresh batch of tears to her eyes.

'So why did you just lie?'

'It's complicated…' His interrogation flailed her—his insight, his questions, confused her. She was tempted, so tempted to tell this stranger her truth, yet even knowing she couldn't, but that he believed her, brought strange comfort.

'Angus—he's a doctor. He's quite famous, actually; he's on television, in the news. When I took the job I signed a contract… I promised them that…' Ainslie shook her head. It was hopeless. 'Look, I'm sorry that I can't answer your questions, and understand that you may want to reconsider your offer. I have to go and meet Angus now—if I could leave my things for a couple of hours…?' God, why didn't he just say something—anything? Ainslie thought. His scrutiny was unnerving her.

But even when he answered he left her hanging.

'Guido's social worker will be arriving soon—I will let you know my decision on your return.'

He'd already made it. Whatever had gone on, or was still going on between herself and her old boss, at least she was discreet. For a man in Elijah's position, a female with discretion was a rare commodity—and one, amongst other things, he was going to need to win Guido's case worker over.

He'd met Ms Anderson at the hospital yesterday, and had disliked her instantly. Normally Elijah could charm any woman. He had flirted from the cradle, and quickly worked out that with the right flash of those blue eyes he instantly got his way—not with Ms Anderson.

'Your lifestyle really isn't suited to such a young child.' Ms Anderson got straight to the point once he'd shown her in. 'While I appreciate you can afford the best in childcare, what we are seeking for Guido is a more nurturing family environment for him to thrive. His uncle Marco and his wife, Dina, already have two children, and understand more what they are offering to take on…'

'My sister was explicit in her wish—and that was that *I* had custody of Guido.'

'Your sister was dying when she made that wish. She was no doubt in pain and emotional too…' Ms Anderson said, slightly more softly. 'And while of course her wishes must be taken into consideration, there are Guido's father's wishes to consider too.'

'His would have been the same.'

'Without a will, we'll never know.'

'*I* know!' Elijah flared, but fought it. He knew he had to keep his emotions in check if he was going to put across his point. 'Rico didn't talk to his family—that is why they were here in London. They wanted to be away from them.'

'That's not what the Castellas told me.' As he opened his mouth to argue, Ms Anderson overrode him. 'I am not getting into a pointless debate of "he said, she said". In the absence of a will, all we can look after is the best interests of the child—that is our primary concern.'

'It is *my* primary concern too!'

'It wasn't yesterday!' Ms Anderson was resolute. 'You walked out of the hospital yesterday evening with Guido—you just took him…'

'There was no reason for him to be there. He wasn't involved in the car accident. He has an ear infection and croup! It hardly merits a hospital bed!'

'His immediate care was supposed to be discussed *prior* to his discharge.'

'He is my nephew.' Elijah glowered. 'You speak as if I kidnapped him, as if I am depriving him of medical care, when in fact, I told a hospital doctor my intentions, and he himself prescribed medicine.'

'You waited till the Social Services department was closed, though, and you spoke with a very junior doctor! I'm sure you can be quite intimidating when you want to be!' Ms Anderson held his glare. 'The department wants Guido's passport…'

'Well, they can't have it. I have no idea where it is.'

'Then it looks as if I might be here for a while. Do you want me to help you look?'

Of course it was in the second drawer she opened—there in the dresser, amongst wedding photos, birth and marriage certificates. Elijah's lips pursed. His clothes arriving, employing a supposed driver and a nanny, were all intended to make it look as if he were planning to stay—yet his intention *had* been to leave straight after the funeral. Back to his lawyers, his contacts, to the power he held in his home town—power that would cut through this senseless red tape in a matter of days. For a second Elijah rued the fact he hadn't headed straight for the airport this morning—but that wasn't going to get him anywhere. So instead of dwelling on a past that couldn't be altered, Elijah treated it as a business problem, handing over the passport without comment as he was forced to move swiftly to Plan B—or rather quickly come up with a Plan B.

'Surely he should be here…?' Elijah said, his hands gesturing to the impressive lounge. 'Here amongst familiar things? At least for now, till a decision is made…'

'It's a big house…'

Ms Anderson gave a nervous cough as Elijah's face hardened. Clearly the cosy family scenario she had just mentioned was not going to eventuate *here*.

'It is *my* house,' Elijah clipped.

'Your house?' Ms Anderson frowned, peering down at her notes. 'The Castellas said that it belonged to Maria and Rico—that they had just taken possession of the title.'

He was about to deliver a smart reply, but something halted him.

'They said that?' His mind was whirring at the fact that they would even *know*—but then his home town was small, and even if his lawyers were discreet, who knew about their secretaries, or the typist, or whoever was cleaning the desk? 'Don't you think it strange that within weeks of Maria and Rico—?'

'Mr Vanaldi…' Her voice bordered on the sympathetic. 'The police have said that the accident wasn't suspicious, and the Castellas were in Italy when it occurred.'

He was sounding irrational, Elijah knew that—but she didn't know the Castellas, or the levels they'd stoop to. Instead of arguing his point Elijah chose to play his cards close, to stay one step ahead just as he always did.

'I'm just tired…' he quickly retracted.

'Of course you are.'

'But our families really do not get on…' he said carefully. 'It would not be in Guido's best interests to have two feuding families taking care of him at this time.'

'Well, if you're not prepared to put aside your differences, then I'm going to have make the choice for you, and frankly, Mr Vanaldi, I have looked into your lifestyle…' She pulled a face as if she were sucking on a lemon. 'Yachts, international trips, homes all over the place, partying…' She gave another uncomfortable cough. 'And it would seem you have rather a lot of lady-friends. It really doesn't sound like the most stable of environments—but the Castellas have said that they are prepared to relocate to England, if necessary. They are willing to do whatever it takes to give Guido a proper, loving home.'

'To live off him—' Elijah sneered.

'Mr Vanaldi!' Ms Anderson broke in. 'Affluence doesn't come into it. It's not a question of being able to provide materially for Guido—it would seem that for this child that's the only thing I *don't* have to worry about.'

She was right—silently he stared over at her—affluence had *nothing* to do with this. His money, his lavish lifestyle, wasn't what was needed here. Elijah knew that, and he also knew it had nothing to do with pride or possession... His gaze drifted to the photos on the mantelpiece, to the smiling faces of his sister and her husband.

How he'd hated Rico when Maria had confessed she was dating him.

Hated that Maria had got involved with the Castellas.

Gypsies.

As he had once been.

Rough, tough survivors—ruthlessly knocking over anyone who stood in their way. But the incident between Maria and Marco had changed Elijah, made him realise that the life he was leading was not one he wished to pursue. His ability to survive, to thrive, to read people was put to better use now. Elijah was the one who had pulled himself up by the bootlaces from a dirt-poor upbringing and made something of himself.

And how the Castellas hated him for it.

Had hated Maria too.

Hated Rico for crossing to the other side.

And yet now suddenly they wanted Guido.

It would be so much easier for him to let Ms Anderson make the wrong decision... He could hear Guido stirring on the intercom system, and his jaw tightened at the mere prospect of the screams that would follow. Elijah Vanaldi was a man with not an ounce of paternal instinct. Yes, it would be infinitely easier to nod to the social worker, to say yes, Guido *would* be better off with a ready-made family—better off with his aunt and uncle and cousins—

only Elijah had never taken the easy option in life before, and he wasn't about to start now.

'I'm not going to go away, Ms Anderson. I am not going to give up on my nephew. You can do your research, you can rake as much dirt as you like on me—or I can save you the effort and tell you myself. I have a criminal record, mainly for petty theft and fighting—though there have been no further convictions since I turned seventeen. I'm sure that's not the case with Marco Castella. I have a lavish lifestyle that, yes, is probably not geared to raising a fifteen-month-old—but, given I didn't know I was going to be raising one, I trust that won't be held against me. And, yes, there have been many women. But, as I just pointed out, that was when I had no commitment to Guido. I will not step aside from this fight...'

'You do actually *want* what you're fighting for, don't you?' Ms Anderson angrily interrupted. 'Because if this is about winning a battle or proving a point, please remember that there is a child in the middle.'

He did—at every turn of his thoughts he did. He was honest enough with himself to know he wasn't perhaps the best choice as a parent for his nephew, but if it came down to him or the Castellas, like it or not, want it or not, he was the *only* choice.

Maria had never been able to stand Marco to be near her—there was no way on earth or in heaven she'd want him near her only child.

All he could do was his best for Guido.

Buy a little piece of time and use it to work out what was best.

Guido was crying now, waking from his nap and demanding a mother who wasn't there. Without excusing himself Elijah walked upstairs, into his sister's room, and stared over to where his nephew stood in the cot, coughing and crying and stinking to high heaven. Guido's outstretched arms pulled back when he saw it was his uncle, then the baby changed his mind and held them out again to be picked up.

What do you want me to do? Elijah didn't say it, just stared back into suspicious blue eyes, and he felt something twist inside, saw himself unwanted, ignored, told to clear off and play. And though he didn't want Guido to be used as a meal ticket for the Castellas, what he could offer was only the same in the extreme. With him, Guido's lifestyle would be peppered with nannies and first-class travel, and he knew that wasn't what this little boy needed.

'Che cosa lo desiderate fare?' This time he did say it out loud, only there could be no answer.

Picking up the little boy, feeling him rest his hot little head in his neck, the weight of responsibility in his arms was so heavy he almost buckled. Elijah wanted so badly to give his nephew the upbringing Maria would have chosen for him, wanted him to have always what Maria and himself had known only for a short while.

His eyes scanned Maria's dressing table, fixing on a shallow glass dish. Reaching out, he picked up a ring—his mother's ring—cheap Italian gold dotted with seed pearls and little bits of red glass. Despite what he'd told Ainslie last night, despite what he actually had believed, for the first time in the longest time he remembered—remembered his mum cooking, laughing, singing, remembered the short time when his life had been easy.

'*Da!*' Guido wriggled in his arms, pointing to the window, and Elijah gave a rare smile as he saw the first snow of winter whirring in the air and taking for ever to fall. He headed over to the window and looked at the billowing white flakes, melting into water before they even hit the ground.

And there was Ainslie—shivering in her flimsy jacket, pulling it down over her splendid bottom, dragging a vast case behind her. Her blonde hair was dark now, it was so wet, and something else twisted inside him—because despite the cold words he'd heard her say to Angus, she didn't look like the cool, calculated gold-digger he'd heard on the phone this morning.

And he didn't want her lost and alone in London at Christmas either.

'Lesson one,' he said lying Guido down on the change mat and trying not to look as he changed his first nappy. 'Sometimes you have to make things work your way, Guido.'

Ms Anderson listened as Elijah's thick Italian words came over the intercom, then got back to her notes. A good-looking playboy he might well be, but he was persuasive too. She'd had every intention of telling him that for Christmas at least Guido should stay with the Castellas—a charming family. She'd spoken to them at length before coming here, had helped them find the apartment they were renting, and was meeting them back at her office this afternoon. But hearing Elijah Vanaldi's surprisingly tender voice crackle over the speakers, then hearing him curse when he attempted to hold kicking legs still while he put on a nappy, Ms Anderson knew he wasn't playing to an audience. He would have forgotten about the intercom the second he left the room, and she knew that she really was listening to him interact with his nephew. Now, hearing the baby laugh, hearing Guido giggle and shriek as his uncle playfully scolded him for the *odore,* it was how it should be—a baby giggling and laughing, utterly oblivious to the tragedy unfolding around him. Something inside her shifted.

Her already heavy schedule was weightier now.

This wasn't going to be as cut and dried as she'd first hoped.

'Blasted snow!'

Since her trip to England had been but a glimmer in her eyes, Ainslie had dreamed of the proverbial white Christmas—had actually planned her trip so that she would arrive here in time for winter. Had it worked out with the Maitlins she'd have been heading off with them on her first ever skiing holiday in the New Year, but as snow swirled around her, soaked through her jacket, fell on her face, already raw and red from crying, all it did was sting... Angus had been lovely, which had made it worse somehow. He had given her more than a month's pay, plus her Christmas bonus, and had even, probably against his better judgement, given her a reference.

But what good was a reference a week before Christmas?

She'd checked out the local youth hostel and it looked as busy and exciting as her guidebook promised. She'd been told that a shared dorm *should* be available later in the day—only it was the last place she wanted to be right now. After the hell of the past two days she wanted somewhere quiet, where she could lick her wounds and regroup...but where? On a limited budget, and with not much chance of getting immediate work, she wasn't exactly spoilt for choice.

Lugging her case up the steps, Ainslie decided to be brave, to ask Elijah if his offer still stood—just for a few days at least.

Rehearsing her speech, Ainslie stood on the doorstep, but before she'd even knocked the door was flung open.

Elijah pulled her into the warm as Guido ran down the hall in a nappy that was falling off and a T-shirt that was on inside out.

'You've been gone ages...'

'Really? Was I?'

'And you're frozen...' His hands were pulling at her jacket, taking off the damp garment as Ainslie spun in confusion at his effusive greeting. 'You're soaked.'

'Elijah, what on—?' She never got to finish, never got to say another word, because his mouth was on hers, his flesh pressing hers, his skin warm against her frozen cheeks. He was pinning her against the wall, kissing her cheeks, her eyes, as he took her icy hands. Then, just as she regrouped and opened her mouth to speak, his lips hushed her again. She could feel him pressing a ring on her finger. The whole intoxicating, dizzying contact took seconds, perhaps, but was utterly, utterly spinning her mind. This kiss was nothing, *nothing* like the one they had shared last night, and she pushed him back, her eyes frightened by his fervour—till they met his. She frowned at the silent plea she saw there...and then another presence was making itself known, a figure in the peripheries of her vision walking down the hall.

'Ms Anderson!' Elijah's hand gripped hers tightly. 'This is Ainslie…'

'Ainslie?' The middle-aged woman was picking up Guido. Maybe she was an aunt Elijah had discovered? Maybe Rico's relatives had arrived and they were talking? Or a neighbour, perhaps? All these thoughts whirred through Ainslie's head as she offered her hand to greet the woman.

'Is this the nanny?' Ms Anderson asked.

'The nanny?' Elijah let out a slightly incredulous laugh. 'Heavens, no—didn't I tell you? Ainslie is my fiancée.'

CHAPTER FIVE

'YOUR fiancée!' The wary, slightly sour expression on the prim, middle-aged face, faded in an instant. 'You're engaged? But why on earth didn't you say?'

'I didn't think to...' Elijah was still holding her hand, his eyes catching Ainslie's, almost daring her to refute him. 'I'm sorry—of course you would need to know these things. I just never thought. I've had so much—we've had so much on our minds.'

'And how does your fiancée feel...? I'm sorry.' She frowned over to Ainslie. 'I didn't introduce myself. I'm Rita Anderson, Guido's case worker—we were just trying to sort out Guido's short-term care, while we make a decision for the long term.'

'Ainslie Farrell.' Her eyes darted to Elijah, then back to Ms Anderson, her head whirring as Ms Anderson's eyes fell on the ring Ainslie now had on her finger.

'My—that's unusual!'

It certainly was, Ainslie thought as for the first time she eyed 'her' ring. Elijah's improvisation skills were rather lacking, because he might not have pulled it out of a

Christmas cracker, but it came close—certainly not the usual choice of ring for a billionaire's fiancée!

'It was my mother's.' Elijah explained, which actually made Ms Anderson's first smile even bigger.

'How lovely. So, how long have you two been engaged?'

'A few weeks.' How easily he lied.

'And how does your fiancée feel about all this?' Ms Anderson's gaze fell directly on Ainslie as she asked Elijah a question. 'Have you two spoken about taking on Guido?'

'There hasn't been much time for talking,' Ainslie answered in truthfulness. 'In fact…' she shot a look at Elijah '…I'm a bit stunned by it all.'

'Naturally she is overwhelmed.' Elijah took over the conversation. 'We both are. Ms Anderson, this has been a shock to us—we are trying to adjust, trying to work out what is best for Guido. For now surely that is for him to be here, in his own home, amongst his own things—?'

'Perhaps you could both show me around while we talk,' Ms Anderson interrupted. 'I do have to meet the Castellas again soon. I really had no idea, Mr Vanaldi, that you were engaged,' she added as she headed, uninvited, up the stairs.

'Nor did I…' Ainslie muttered, taking Guido in her arms. 'Elijah, what on earth is going on?'

'Just go along with it…' Elijah's voice was low. 'Please.'

'The paternal uncle and aunt naturally want to see Guido…' Ms Anderson said, pausing to frown as she passed the room Ainslie had slept in, her shrewd eyes taking in the backpack on the floor and the noticeably single bed.

'This is your room, Ainslie?'

'Yes,' Ainslie started, then, feeling his hand tighten around hers, realised the trap she'd unwittingly walked into.

'We were not comfortable sleeping in my sister's bed,' Elijah said smoothly. 'So Ainslie suggested she take the room closest to Guido on his first night.'

'And do you have experience with children?'

'She's a kindergarten teacher in Australia.' Elijah smiled like the cat who'd got the cream as he answered for her, and Ms Anderson jotted it down. 'Well, she was until she met me!'

They were in Maria and Rico's room now. Guido was running around and picking up his toys, holding them out to Ainslie and showing her his things.

'Well, it would be nice for Guido to have some consistency during these early days...' Ms Anderson said. 'But the Castellas really—'

'Surely,' Elijah pushed, 'it is better for now that he stays at home—at least for Christmas?'

His blue eyes met Ms Anderson's, and if Ainslie hadn't known better he'd have had her convinced too. He was so assured, so persuasive—and, Ainslie thought with a sudden flurry of nerves, a truly excellent liar!

'If the situation was different I would invite them to stay here. But there is, as I said...' he snapped his fingers as he impatiently summoned suitable words '...bad blood between the families.'

'They have a right to see him.'

'Take him now...' Elijah said easily, but a muscle flickered in his cheek. He thanked his lucky stars for his foresight in hiring Tony for the ease it gave him to make the offer. 'You are meeting with them; let them have some time with Guido. My driver will take you...'

'I can drive myself.'

'His car seat isn't transferable—Tony fitted it this morning—and, given what has just happened, naturally safety is my first concern. Take Guido to see the rest of his family and then—' still he stared at Ms Anderson '—bring my nephew back to his home while the department makes its decision.'

And it sounded reasonable—so reasonable.

Ms Anderson blinked rapidly. 'Do you have help?' She sniffed at the pile of linen still on the bathroom floor.

'Housework was never my sister's forte...' Elijah shrugged. 'She refused to get a housekeeper, and I'm afraid it shows, but I will arrange help in the New Year—there is no chance of getting anyone now.'

'I'll manage...' For the first time since she'd messed up with the sleeping arrangements Ainslie spoke.

'But surely you should be spending time getting to know Guido? This house is huge...' Her eyes swivelled to the next flight of stairs. 'How many levels are there?'

'Four—I have my driver using a room on the third level, but the top is self contained—it would be perfect for a nanny or housekeeper. I'm sure there will be no trouble hiring someone in the New Year.'

'Can I see it?'

'Of course.' Elijah shrugged. 'I will get the keys.' Which took for ever.

When he eventually returned Ainslie was one burning blush, having had to make small talk with an incredibly nosy Ms Anderson. Elijah led them both up the thickly carpeted stairs to the self-contained area.

It was vast—the entire top floor was converted into a three-bedroomed flat, with a huge lounge and tasteful furnishings, but from the thick layer of dust and the cobwebs it must have been closed off for years.

Ms Anderson spoke. 'My sister Enid is actually looking for live-in work—she's extremely qualified…'

'Have her forward her résumé to me,' Elijah said. 'As I said—we'll be looking for someone once we've got this place cleaned up.'

'She's available now.' Her eyes held a challenge as they met Elijah's. 'And I'm sure she'd be happy to clean it to your liking. She's done housekeeping and has childcare qualifications. She's got no family apart from me. Of course you may not want anyone here, getting in the way of you and your lovely new fiancée, but…' Her voice trailed off but her intent was clear, and Elijah met the challenge with a tight smile.

'She sounds perfect.'

'What on earth have you done?' The second Ms Anderson left with Guido, Ainslie confronted him. 'You can't just pass me off as your fiancée!'

'I agree…' Elijah ran a disapproving eye along the length of her body and Ainslie burned with humiliation and anger. 'Hopefully she will think you look such a fright because you got caught in the snow.'

'Well, excuse me!' Ainslie retorted, but her sarcasm was entirely wasted.

'You don't have to apologise. They are not back till four—I can take you shopping…do something with your hair…'

'I'm not talking about how I look,' Ainslie spat, once she'd lifted her jaw from the floor. 'You can't just play around with people's lives like that—you can't just tell me what to do, what to say, what to wear! What on earth made you think I'd say yes!'

'You have no job, no home, and no reference!' Elijah retorted. 'And, as you said to your lover this morning, you like the nice things in life—well, now you get to sample them!'

'How dare you?' Shaking, gibbering with rage, she grabbed an envelope out of her bag, ignoring Elijah's raised eyebrows as she pulled away the wad of notes Angus had given her and thrust the reference under his nose. But Elijah just laughed mirthlessly as he read it.

'I see there is no home number to contact...' His cruel grin widened. 'And so carefully worded too! You know, I admit to knowing nothing about children, but were I considering employing you on the strength of this I would be asking myself why the mother of the children is not so gushing in her praise—why I can only contact the father on his work number...' His eyes challenged her to answer—only Ainslie couldn't. Instead she spoke up.

'You can't railroad me into pretending to be your fiancée.'

'You don't know me.' Elijah shrugged. Maybe he was going about this the wrong way, he conceded to himself. Maybe he should have sat her down, told her just how desperate he was. But panic was taking over at the thought of Guido with the Castellas, of them holding him this very minute, of them *taking* him. And they knew about the house transfer. It all blurred his sentences, until every word, every gesture, was driven by a panic no one must see. 'I can be extremely persuasive when I have to be.'

'I don't mind helping out,' Ainslie retorted. 'I don't mind working for you for a few days...'

'You don't *mind*?' Elijah checked. 'Don't pretend you have options, Ainslie.'

'Oh, but I do…' She wouldn't be spoken to like this. Snatching back her reference, she stuffed it in her bag, then headed up the stairs, taking them two, three at a time. 'I've already booked a place at the youth hostel, and if I can't get another job in the New Year then I'll go back home to Australia.' She was grabbing her clothes, shoving them into her backpack. 'I helped *you* last night, Elijah, not the other way around!' She turned to face him. The heating in the house had brought colour back to her face now, and two angry red spots were burning on her cheeks. 'I might have been in a bit of a pickle, but I'd certainly have managed if you hadn't come along—and, frankly, twelve hours in your company really hasn't changed anything.'

Only it had.

Lugging her backpack down the stairs, Ainslie crashed past the pushchair, the jumble of toys, Maria's and Rico's shoes, and wrenched open the front door. The snow was really falling now. Earls Court Square was pretty in white, but far more attractive-looking through the glass window of a warm house. But anger kept the cold out—anger gave her the strength to somehow drag her backpack and case down the steps and onto the street. And hopefully it would propel her all the way to the youth hostel, away from this pompous, presuming man. Sure, he had problems—and, sure, she felt wretched for Guido. But it wasn't her problem to solve—she already had enough of her own.

'Ainslie.'

The snow seemed to catch the word, seemed to hold it in the air like a snowflake, soaring it, whirring it, circling it, till it landed wintry and lonely on her soul as he walked down the steps to join her.

'You've got staff now—you've got someone to take care of Guido. Your things have arrived, and things are starting to sort themselves out.'

'I am *expected* to have staff!' Elijah retorted. 'If I am to show this woman I am serious about staying here till Guido's future is decided, then I need to have staff!'

'And a fiancée too?'

'Yes!' His voice was urgent. 'Yes, because that woman was two minutes away from deciding I was not suitable. Ainslie, I divide my time between cities, I have properties all over Europe, I fly first class the way most people take a bus. I dine in the best restaurants each night, with the world's most beautiful woman...' And so hopeless was his voice, so abject his misery, Ainslie knew that his impromptu list of credentials had nothing to do with showing off—quite the reverse in this case. 'There are a lot of women who would be only too happy—'

'I get the picture!' Ainslie put up her hand to stop him. She didn't actually want to think about his appalling reputation and the numerous women waiting in the wings. 'If that is your life, Elijah, how on earth do you think you're going to slot in Guido?'

'I don't know.' His honesty touched her. 'I don't know if I am what he needs. I don't even know if that is what I want. From the moment the hospital called me nothing in my world has made sense. All I know is that I have to give it a try. Maria died yesterday, and her last words were that she wanted me to take care of him—if I hand him over to his aunt and uncle now then that will never, ever happen.'

'It won't work.'

'We can make it work,' Elijah insisted. 'If you help me I will help you too. I will give you a reference for anywhere—I don't care if I have to say you worked for me all the time you have been in England...'

'That would be a lie, though.'

'So?' He was standing in front of her in black jeans and a black jumper, his full mouth the only colour in his pale face. Flakes of snow had settled on his black hair and as surly as his response was, she actually understood. This man, who had come out fighting, would continue to fight—because he had everything to lose. 'I need time. Time to think. If it is better for Guido to go with Rico's family, if I see they would be better for him, I will accept that. If adoption is better than the home I can provide, then I will accept that too—but I have to do this for my sister, for Guido, for me. I will lie, I will cheat—I will do whatever it takes. But I ask you to believe my intentions are honourable.'

'I'm not a good liar...' Her teeth were chattering now.

'I can lie for two.'

'And—contrary to what you might think—I don't cheat either.'

He gave just a hint of an ironic smile, his eyebrows raising just a fraction—but, staring down at her, Elijah didn't care if she was actually a very good liar or was just deceiving herself. All that mattered was that she stayed.

'I will pay you well—I will sort out that loan for you.'

It was irrelevant.

As they stood there staring, somehow both knew money wasn't the issue here—that whatever force had first pushed them together was bigger than a pay cheque or a reference.

'If her sister stays—' she was shivering violently now as she spoke '—we're going to have to share a bed...'

'We will put pillows down the middle...' His hands cupped her cheeks, a lazy smile blushing his lips as he eked out the same from her. 'So that you don't take advantage of me.'

He could have kissed her then—it felt as if he *was* kissing her. The caress of his words, his hands on her cheeks, the warmth between them—all defied the bitterness of winter. An outlandish pact was silently made as they stood there—as she glimpsed something, something indefinable, an almost intangible kindness behind that ruthless guarded face. A foretaste of how this man could be. And as he lifted her backpack, and took her case just as easily, and with the other hand held hers and led her up the steps, it was so much more than duty or money or fear that led her back to the house.

It was him.

'Quel sembre volgore!' Drumming his fingers on the couch, not only did Elijah run a bored eye over Ainslie— he spoke over her too.

In the middle of an exclusive London department store he had somehow found what was surely a Milan supermodel masquerading as a shop assistant, and the two of them had absolutely no qualms speaking in Italian and loudly tutting at Ainslie's choice in clothes.

'Vulgar?' Dropping her jaw, Ainslie confronted him. 'Did you just say that I looked vulgar?'

'Those boots!' Elijah flicked his hands at the offending leather. 'And that coat, *would*, at a funeral, look vulgar!'

Staring at the ceiling-to-floor mirrors that showed her from *every* angle, reluctantly Ainslie conceded that he did have a point. The black coat with its nipped-in waist and the long flat leather boots had looked so tasteful, but combined... Well...Ainslie gulped as she caught her reflection from behind—despite being fully dressed, somehow she looked as if she had nothing on underneath.

Unbuttoning the coat with a sigh, for a crazy second she forgot why they were there, forgot the hell of the last twenty-four hours, and forgot where she was, who *he* was. With a cheeky grin Ainslie turned and flashed her fully clothed body at him.

He didn't get the joke.

Ainslie stood as the personal service continued, as a woman dressed like a dental nurse came over and introduced herself as the manager of the beauty salon—only she spoke with Elijah.

Ainslie continued to stand and listen as Elijah told the woman what he wanted to happen with Ainslie's hair.

'I *can* talk!' Ainslie interrupted furiously.

'You don't know what I want done, though.' And he proceeded to dissect her eyebrows, her complexion, openly criticising *everything*, really, as if she were some donkey that needed to be groomed into a glossy racehorse.

'What about the clothes?'

'I'll take care of that with Tania,' Elijah answered, 'now we've worked out what *doesn't* suit you! And despite what she might say to you, my fiancée does *not* just need a trim!' Elijah flashed Ainslie a quick warning smile as he spoke with the manager. 'She needs it properly cut and styled—and please...' He held up a wad of curls and examined the rather sun-bleached ends. 'Can you do something with the colour too?'

She was determined to hate it!

She sat bristling with anger as her eyebrows were waxed, a face mask was applied, along with a hair dye, and her finger and toenails were simultaneously pummelled and painted—as half the salon set to work to transform her into a woman deemed worthy enough to wear his cheap ring.

'The colour's marvellous!' The chief colourist beamed at the final unveiling. 'It really suits you.'

Her naturally honey-blonde hair, which had spent way too long in the ocean and being dried by the harsh Australian sun, was now a much softer ash-blonde. The cut was just superb and, despite her best efforts not to, Ainslie couldn't help but lean forward in her chair, pulling at one heavy curl and blinking her newly dyed lashes as it popped back into perfect shape beside a perfect eyebrow. As the make-up therapist pointed out, the dark grey eyeshadow and charcoal liner really *did* bring out the green of her eyes— and what was more, Ainslie realised, sucking in her lips, contrary to what she'd previously thought she *did* have cheekbones!

'That's better!' Elijah barely glanced up from the newspaper he was reading as she came out of the salon.

'I pass, do I?' Ainslie retorted. But as always the last word went to Elijah.

'Once you get some decent clothes on.'

And, loathsome as he was, he was right. In soft grey wool trousers, topped with the palest pink jumper which felt as blissful to touch as it was to wear, sitting in the lounge as they awaited Tony and Guido's arrival, she felt horribly awkward, but really rather good.

Ainslie was appalled when Elijah caught her peering in her compact mirror, flicking back her hair, but he didn't comment, just stared moodily out of the window till the rest of his waifs and strays arrived. Ainslie joined him to watch as they all spilled out of the car. Ms Anderson, carrying Guido, who was closely followed by a woman who must be her sister—and Tony, an absolute brute of a man, his chauffeur uniform way too tight for his huge frame, taking up the rear.

'I should put up a sign to tell people I've had a change of career...' Elijah sighed, and despite herself Ainslie giggled. 'Let everyone know that I'm running a refuge for the homeless and displaced.'

Enid was nothing, *nothing* like her rather prim sister.

With a booming Northern accent she introduced herself, ruffled Guido's hair and then headed for the kitchen.

'Would you like me to show you your accommodation?' Ainslie offered.

'I'm sure I'll find it!'

'Or a cup of coffee, perhaps?'

'I'll bring you one through in just a moment.'

Elijah just laughed at her burning blush when Enid stalked off to the kitchen.

'I was offering to make *her* one!'

'Then don't.' He grinned. 'Remember your place—and that is up here, with me!'

Loathsome snob, Ainslie thought, but didn't say it.

As Tony dragged suitcase after suitcase up the stairs, assuring Elijah he'd soon be out of their way, Enid buttonholed Ainslie and asked to be taken through her routine.

'We don't actually have much of a routine.'

Ainslie's eyes darted to Elijah, who was too busy playing with a grizzling Guido to notice.

'I understand you haven't established one with Guido yet,' Enid said kindly. 'I was talking more about meals, what sort of things you and Mr Vanaldi like to eat.'

'We tend to dine out, though obviously we won't be as much now...' Ainslie said helplessly, praying he wasn't allergic to nuts or had celiac disease or something dire. 'Anything, really!'

'I'm quite a plain cook,' Enid warned her, standing up. 'And there's not much in the kitchen. I'll see what I can manage to rustle up for tonight.'

'This is like a nightmare,' Ainslie whispered when she'd gone. 'I don't even know how many sugars you have in your coffee.'

'Three.' Elijah shrugged, watching as Guido stood on two fat legs and tottered over to Ainslie, holding his arms out to be lifted, which she did. Scooping him up in her arms and instead of, as she had been, trying to cheer him, she calmed him down, pulled him right into her and stroked his hair, soothed him with assurances after, Elijah realised then, what must have been another daunting day for Guido—meeting strangers, missing his parents.

'You're good with him.'

'It's my—' Ainslie started, but didn't finish. And it wasn't because Enid came back into the room that her voice trailed off. Holding Guido, feeling him relax against her, Ainslie knew in her heart that this was so much more than a job.

Bravely, Ainslie thought, Enid had made spaghetti bolognaise for her and Elijah. But he simply fell on it. He mopped his plate with bread when he'd finished, then proceeded to tell her the plans for the funeral.

'It was either Christmas Eve, or wait another week.'

'What would you prefer?'

'Neither…' Elijah admitted. 'But I chose Christmas Eve. It's going to be hell either way, and I think it is better we get it over with, then do our best for Guido on Christmas Day.'

'What did Rico's family want?'

'To know who was paying for it. Naturally Ms Anderson tried to rephrase it, but that was their main concern. I've booked a hotel for afterwards, and I've rung all the friends in Maria's diary and replied to a few of her e-mails. One of the mothers from Guido's playgroup rang by chance today, to speak with Maria…' He faltered for just a second. 'She had no idea what had happened.'

'That must have been awful for you.'

'I would prefer it if you didn't answer the house phone. I will tell Enid also. I don't want to put either of you through it. I ended up consoling her…' He buried his face in his hands, the sarcasm, the jibes, the whole mask slipping as he let out a low rumble of a moan. 'This is so wrong—it just all is so wrong. Like a mistake has been made.'

'It has!' Ainslie could hear his pain, feel it from across the table.

'I went to ring her earlier.' He looked up, strong features

now hopeless. 'I went to dial this number—to ask her what flowers she liked... That is crazy...'

'It's not crazy...' She couldn't just sit and watch him sink. On reflex she went over to him, stood where he sat, rested her hands on his strained shoulders. 'You're not crazy—it's normal, I'm sure.'

'I want to ask her what I should do...' His anguish was there in each word, beneath her fingers his shoulders were rigid in her hands. 'I want to know what she would want.'

She could see her own fingers, pale against his black jumper, digging in and massaging the knots of tension, could see them moving against her will, as if they belonged to someone else. Instinctively her hands moved, working each taut bundle of tension till she felt the release.

'She already told you what she wanted.'

He nodded, taking solace in her words, taking solace in her touch—only for both of them it wasn't over. She was aware now that she was touching him. Some bizarre out-of-body experience had seen her cross the room, only now her mind was back, registering the change of surrounds and her fingers that had worked his flesh so easily were moving clumsily now...she jerked away when Enid came in the room.

'Ainslie...?' The question in Elijah's voice faded as he saw they had company.

'Don't mind me!' The housekeeper smiled, taking the plates as, awkward, blushing, Ainslie stepped back.

But later, lying in the bath, staring at the still water as she lay motionless, Ainslie knew her blushes, her awkwardness, had had nothing to do with Enid entering. It had been the contact that had her reeling—her own boldness, her own *knowing*, which had propelled her like iron ore to a magnet. And it wasn't a question of pleasing, Ainslie realised as still she lay. It wasn't a question of being good enough. It was knowing that you were.

That with him, kissing him, touching him, it wasn't about Elijah's skill or experience, or any of the stuff she'd read about as she'd muddled through the maze of dating.

It all came down to *her* and how he made her feel—the woman he brought out in her.

And now they had to share a bed.

CHAPTER SIX

'OH, PLEASE no!' Pulling acres of purple satin out of tissue paper, Ainslie stared at him aghast as she held up the offending garments. 'Do men actually like this stuff?'

'Tell me what I should have said!' Elijah snapped from his vantage point on the bed, a wad of pillows dividing the battlefield. 'Should I have told the assistant who was selecting your wardrobe that this particular billionaire's fiancée actually prefers flannelette pyjamas that are covered in monkeys?'

'I'm not wearing this!'

'Fine!' Elijah snapped. 'I'm sure Enid has seen naked ladies in the hallway at midnight; she probably won't turn a hair. I am telling you—you are not wearing those pyjamas.'

'I am!'

'Actually, you can't!' Elijah sniped as she unzipped her backpack. 'Because I threw out all your tat!'

He had!

'Don't you *ever* go through my things again!'

'That's a fine thing to say—given your current circumstances!'

He did feel a twinge of unfamiliar guilt as she flounced

out. Today had been hard for her too, and he had seen the flash of tears in eyes as she'd raced for the door—but, hell, what did she expect? Elijah consoled himself. If they were going to pass her off as his fiancée she could hardly walk around in high street clothes and fake handbags!

She was a funny little thing, though. Despite his hell, Elijah found himself smiling inside when she returned from the bathroom, her skin clashing violently with the satin and her whole body one burning blush. Despite the fact that this man actually *didn't* like that sort of stuff, he felt a stirring beneath the sheet that said otherwise. He couldn't help but notice the unfamiliar sight of a round bottom and the curve of a stomach the nightdress clung to—such a contrast to the reed-thin women he was used to bedding—and he couldn't help but notice a glimpse of pink areola as she leant to pull back the covers. What she lacked in sophistication she repaid tenfold in femininity. She slipped into bed beside him, then slid halfway down the sheets—a waft of toothpaste the only scent to greet him. Never had spearmint been more refreshing... Or, Elijah thought, hands bunched into fists above the sheet, never had the scent of spearmint been more sexy!

He could feel her twitching with nerves beside him, feel her vulnerability, and it moved him—he knew she was expecting him to pounce. But that would only complicate things. He'd assured her there would be no repeats.

'Goodnight!' he barked, flicking off the light, willing himself to sleep. But every time he closed his eyes all he could see was her. Not the image of her tonight, or even today. Instead the image of her last night was the one that danced before his eyes, the feel her in his arms, the soft balmy escape of her lips.

No repeats.

Blowing out his breath, he willed sleep to come, but knew it would evade him. He resigned himself instead to a long, sleepless night.

Ainslie wasn't faring much better. Staring into the sudden darkness, she felt her throat so constricted, her body so rigid, that she couldn't attempt to answer his brusque goodnight.

In the sexiest lingerie, next to the sexiest man, all she felt was stupid. The whole day had been one awful lesson in humiliation. And, lest she forget, she recalled him at the department store, holding up her hair as if it were a rag, replayed over and over in her mind every sarcastic barb he had uttered. The fact that he was lying utterly unmoved beside her reinforced that she was nowhere near the type of woman Elijah Vanaldi dated.

So why had he kissed her?

Her blush was back. She stared unseeing at the ceiling as she felt him restless beside her, his uneven breathing telling her that he wasn't asleep.

And thank God for the pillows between them—because just at the memory of his kiss she wanted to curl towards him. Her whole body seemed to be leaping like a salmon in an autumn river—defying her wishes to settle and heading upstream as Elijah blew out a breath beside her.

He had kissed her because he could, Ainslie decided. Because his sister had just died and she had been there.

She could feel her hands on his shoulders again, feel the velvet of his skin as she'd stroked his neck, the bit of flesh at the nape of his neck she'd wanted to lower her head to and kiss...

She breathed out into the darkness. The air was so thick, so warm, it was an effort to drag a breath back in. Her skin was too warm from the bath, the covers a heavy weight as Elijah lay restless beside her.

'I'm sorry—I need to go to the loo!' Her voice was a croak as, with an almost weary sigh, Elijah reached over and switched the light back on. 'It's static…' A slightly hysterical giggle wobbled in her throat as she slid off the sheet and peeled the nightdress from her body. Her hair crackled as it left the pillow 'It's ruining my hair!'

He didn't even deign to smile.

God, she looked a sight.

Staring in the mirror at her hair sticking up everywhere, and her flesh spilling out, Ainslie was about to tuck one wayward bosom back safely into her nightdress when Elijah came in behind her. Such was the blaze in his eyes, so heavy was her want, she didn't even pretend to scold him for not knocking.

'I would never have chosen this for you to wear.'

His hand caught hers, cupping her breast, and she watched in the mirror as he lowered his noble head to her neck, as he kissed her there deeply. Her own hand slipped, leaving his, and she watched with morbid fascination as her nipple lengthened, a whimper of regret escaping as he released her. All Ainslie knew was that she couldn't even try to fight it any more. The attraction, the intent, the presence that was there between them was just so overwhelming, so intense, it was as impossible to fathom as it was to ignore. She couldn't breathe—or rather, she could—but they were rapid shallow breaths that made her dizzy.

Standing frozen, watching in the mirror as he turned on the shower, she closed her eyes with giddy excitement as he returned a second later and led her, thousand-dollar nightdress and all, under the jets. The bliss of the water as it hit her stiff lacquered hair made her shiver. Wet satin clung to her as he poured shampoo and massaged it into her scalp, as his tongue stroked hers and his hands pulled at the fabric, pushing it down over her body, pressing her with his own body against the cold glass.

He was naked now too—and though she'd seen most of him, she hadn't seen this bit of him, and her equanimity was dimmed for ever as he revealed the splendid, terrifying sight of himself in full arousal. Whether from reflex or awe her knees went weak. She sank to the floor of the shower, kissing him intimately, tasting the soapy, wet maleness of him as the water kissed her eyes, as his fingers knotted in her hair—till he stopped her, till he held her face in the palm of his hands and forced her head up.

'This is how I want you…' Bedraggled, soaked, her eyes glittering with desire, face flushed despite the cool water, and utterly, utterly drunk on lust, he took in her every feature, then dragged her to her feet before he spoke again. '*This* is how you come to me at night.'

Impatient fingers were parting her thighs now, and his mouth was hungry at her breast, sucking, bruising, biting. It was delicious—as delicious as the hot pulse between her legs, beating for his fierce erection. Like a locating device he sought her. She could see him, full to bursting, wondered if he'd make it, if she'd make it, and was grateful his haste matched hers when he slipped inside her. Her orgasm was so deep, so intense, it made her sob with its power.

Everything dimmed as they centred, as for a minute she was lost to everything but him. Then came a dim awareness of her surrounds, and the cool water brought her round to a world that was different. Sensations were sharper somehow, the water too cool on her body, too loud in her ears. It must have been for him too, because Elijah turned off the taps, wrapped her in a towel and, placing another one around his hips, led her back to bed.

It was like getting up the first time after the flu—her legs weak, her body shivering, drained from the exertion, thrilled to be up but ready to slip back into bed.

But not till he'd dried her—and not just her skin, but her hair too. Then he pulled back the covers, and she lay there.

'Can we get rid of the safety barrier now?' He pulled the pillows away, but she couldn't smile, couldn't look at him—trying to make sense of a world that was the same only different from the one she'd left for a little while. She turned away from him.

'Don't run away from me as well.'

'I'm not.' His fingers traced the length of her spine, then over her bottom, tracing her contours, soothing her body as she struggled with her mind. 'I didn't.'

And she *hadn't* been running away, coming to London. She hadn't been walking out on her life. But she had been searching. Not for him, but for the bit of her that was missing—the something she had never been able to define but that she'd glimpsed tonight.

The wantonness he'd unleashed, this passion that had been untapped—it wasn't just sex. For her, at least...

'Look at me, then.' So easily he turned her over, and so hard was it to look at him.

'Have you any idea what you've done for me? Without you here I would be in hell—and instead…'

She could look at him now, could see the certainty in his eyes that chased away her doubts. This was as good and as right and as *necessary* as it had felt. In his arms she could feel the thick rope of connection that ran between them, that told her it was so much more than sex that had led her to his bed, that made her dizzy lying in his arms. His beauty astonished her—mesmerised her now that she could face him—and his words told her it was all okay, that she was safe to be the woman she was with him.

He confirmed it with a kiss. It was supremely tender, a long, languorous kiss now that the urgency was gone—a kiss to taste him, to explore him, and he let her take her time to relish in it. The need that had gripped them before was replaced now by a deeper want—a want to touch him, to allow her fingers, her mouth, to grow familiar with him, tracing his image with her senses, taking in details, like the swirl of hair around his areolae, the soapy taste of his flat hard nipple in her mouth, his moans as she licked it.

He explored her too, curves that he had once felt too generous entirely in proportion now as he revelled in her body. His pleasure was rising in her hands as he suckled her. A knot of legs as he entered her, and side on they faced each other. For the first time she didn't close her eyes, and neither did he, and she could have stayed like that for ever. Elijah was in no rush. His length was inside her and his eyes adored her. Rocking together, just locked in an unhurried pleasure. Relishing the slide of skin on skin and the delicious friction they created—hardly moving on the outside, but long, slow strokes stirred her deep within.

Each touch, each caress answered an unvoiced plea. She'd found her soul mate, like some glorious dance in the mirror, he echoed her thoughts and answered her wants.

It was a dance that couldn't go on for ever because the tip to transition had her crying, had him calling out her name as he filled her with his gift.

'Don't leave me.'

He groaned it out as he spilled inside her, and she dragged him in deeper in answer, so sure at that moment, so utterly and completely sure, that she never would.

CHAPTER SEVEN

'GUIDO, ritornato qui!'

But not even Elijah's stern order for Guido to come back could halt him. Giggling, running along the landing, Ainslie was awoken to the missile of a cheeky pre-dawn toddler, wide awake and ready to play, launching himself onto the bed as his exasperated uncle ran behind, just as he had the last few mornings. A strange glow of a routine, that was theirs, was forming out of the chaos.

'He escaped again!' Elijah explained, taking two kicking legs and trying to assert some authority *and* put on a nappy. But Guido, slippery with nappy cream, wriggled out of his strong hands, laughing and coughing and running across the bed to a grinning Ainslie.

'Here,' Ainslie offered, taking the nappy and tickling Guido on the tummy, making him laugh by blowing raspberries on his feet and managing to get his fat slippery body into the nappy as Elijah stretched out on the bed beside them, exhausted from his morning exercise with Guido.

'How can one person who is so small create so much chaos?'

'Very easily,' Ainslie grinned. 'They can smell fear too, you know.'

For a second he was about to refute her—Ainslie actually felt his body stiffen beside her, just as it had when she had first offered help—but then he laughed. This closed, guarded, stern man, who had so much on his mind, actually threw his head back and laughed. 'He terrifies me!'

And when Elijah laughed Guido did too, absolutely sensing weakness and crawling over the bed to his uncle, sitting on his chest and pressing fat hands into his face.

'You are trouble...' Elijah scowled to his delighted audience. 'Should we keep you?'

It sounded like the worst thing to say—so utterly open to misinterpretation that even Ainslie was jolted for a second—but lying there beside him, with Guido bouncing up and down, it was the nicest thing he could possibly have said.

Normal, almost.

Just the sort of thing one might say with absolute confidence because the answer wasn't in question—the sort of thing a parent might say to a child in all the certainty it was loved.

And he was.

'Always I tell Maria she is not strict enough with him.' He was holding Guido's hands now, and pulling him up to stand on his chest. 'She had no routine. I would come from the airport sometimes at ten at night and he would be still up playing—she couldn't say no to him... I tell her: that boy will be trouble...' He gave a wry smile. 'Had I known she was leaving the trouble for me, I would have insisted she was stricter.'

All of it he said with mirth, not a trace of pity, as Guido

played trampoline on his chest. But Elijah's words were so bittersweet they brought the sting of tears to Ainslie's eyes, as she watched this man who knew nothing about babies doing so very, very well—saw the genuine affection between uncle and nephew, the humour and history that bound families as the two of them became one. The ties that loosely bound them were tightening as she watched on—only it wasn't duty or obligation that was pulling the strings. There in the bed, sharing the dawn, Guido and his uncle were starting to become a family.

And—even if by default—Ainslie was a part of it too. She was scarcely able to comprehend that their chance encounter had been more than a meeting of minds, but bodies and souls too—that the passion that still taunted her with its recklessness, when she had a moment alone to dwell, made absolute sense when it was just the two of them...or three.

She'd worked with children since she was eighteen— had had her favourites too—but never had one captured her heart like Guido. It wasn't just his plight—the children in her care had had their traumas too—it was Guido's spirit that melted her. His eyes once as blue and as mistrusting as his uncle's that suddenly adored her when they smiled.

He was smiling at her now. Tired of being naughty, Guido had slid down his uncle's chest as the grown-ups planned his day, his thick lashes getting heavier by the minute as he lay between them, thumb in mouth, smiling lazily.

'He is still coughing.' Elijah frowned down in concern as Guido gave a croupy bark.

'Not as much...' Ainslie stroked the little dark curls. 'And croup can last for ages—he seems much better.'

'Still, maybe he should stay here today—it is the funeral

tomorrow...' Guido was supposed to be going to the Castellas for the afternoon. Ms Anderson had made it quite clear that regular contact was to be maintained with the Castellas while the Social Services department made its decision. Ainslie had pointed out on numerous occasions that it could only help Elijah's case if he showed willing, yet still he resisted. 'I will ring Ms Anderson—explain to her that—'

'You need to let him go,' Ainslie said softly. 'He'll be in a warm car, and Enid will be with him—there's no reason for him not to go.'

'Oh, but there is.' He was staring down at his nephew, his face colourless in the wintry dawn light as a chink in the curtain let in a grey slice of morning. The frost on the glass warned that it was cold outside, but it was so warm in here. 'Here—with me, with us—I know he is safe.'

He was. Little Guido, warm and asleep now between them, dreaming milky dreams and without a care in the world, was safe in the knowledge that he was loved, innocently trusting those who looked after him—and though Ainslie could see why Elijah didn't want to let him go, she also knew that he had to.

Despite their intimacy, Elijah's grief was his own—a private place she rarely glimpsed. His pain, his mistrust, the weight of the decisions he must soon make, were things he chose to explore alone, but there was no place as comfortable as the morning bed for exploring options. Bodies relaxed and minds refreshed from sleep, open to the gifts of a new day, brought a closeness, an ease, and for the first time they explored their new territory.

'Guido needs his family. Even if you don't like them, they are still his family. Maybe you have to try to put the past aside, for Guido's sake.' She watched his eyes shutter, watched his face actually grimace in resistance to her words, but instead of a clipped refusal to even listen to her reasoning, Elijah actually struggled to grasp it.

'Everything in me tells me not to trust them—that they are no good...' His eyes found hers then, and for once they were lost. 'I survive not just because I am clever but on *istinto*—on instinct. Now everyone tells me I am to ignore the thing that has kept me alive, that I must trust Guido to these people when it goes against everything I feel.'

'People do change, Elijah. What happened with Maria was years ago. I'm not making excuses—I'm not!' she said quickly again, when he opened his mouth to argue. 'I just think for Guido's sake you have to show good faith—you have to trust that his uncle and aunt want what's best for him too, even if it's hard for you to see it. Ringing Ms Anderson and making excuses, suggesting they might have had something to do with the accident—well, it's just making you look...' She didn't finish, just lay there staring over at him.

His head on the pillow, he was staring up at the ceiling, seemingly not listening. But he was. Racked with indecision, he lay there—he could feel the rise and fall of Guido's chest against his arm. His sister's most treasured possession. One she had entrusted him to take care of, to do his best for. And every fibre of his being told him to keep Guido by his side, that two minutes in the Castellas' company was two minutes too long. Yet his instinct had told him Ainslie wasn't a thief, intuition had told him he could trust her— and here she was, without agenda, telling him to let Guido go to the enemy, that everything would be okay...

Snapping his face to hers, Elijah surprised her with a smile as he finished her sentence for her.

'I look bitter?' he offered. 'Paranoid, even?'

'Just a bit.' Ainslie grinned. Suddenly he didn't look either of the two. The man smiling back looked ten years younger than the one she had first met. 'Do you want me to put Guido back in his cot?'

'Why?' Elijah asked, lids closing on his blue eyes, pulling his nephew into the crook of his arm and toying with Ainslie's hair.

She watched as he drifted off, watched for the first time this suspicious, mistrusting man actually relax. Only now it was Ainslie who couldn't.

He had listened to her.

The two men who had suddenly become so vital in her life both trusted her.

She just hoped she was saying the right thing.

'They've been gone too long.'

'It's only six…' Ainslie glanced at the clock on the mantelpiece for, oh, maybe the hundredth time. They'd had a busy day—first going to the undertakers, where Elijah had grimly gone through the difficult task of making the final preparations for tomorrow, then, taking a welcome pause from frantic last-minute Christmas shopping, Elijah had suggested somewhere nice for a late lunch.

'We'll never get a table there,' Ainslie had warned. 'Not at this time of year!'

Elijah had just frowned and pulled out his phone, and whatever the abracadabra word was that conjured up a table out of nowhere for the rich and the beautiful, somewhere in Italy his PA must have uttered it, because they had bypassed the grumbling queue, hadn't even been led to the bar! The beaming *maître d'* had greeted them by name and led them to a secluded table where a leisurely lunch had been taken.

Then they had parted for a couple of hours and hit the mad crowds. As busy and as crazy as the crowds had been, it *felt* like Christmas, carols blasting from record shops and brass bands adding to the seasonal feel.

Ainslie still found it hard to fathom that the sun set so early in England, but she was so glad it did. The gloomy afternoon had been giving way to dusk and the whole of Oxford Street was a canopy of lights, more magical and extravagant than she could have imagined, as she'd met up with Elijah and they'd jumped in a black taxi to head for home.

Only now it wasn't just the light of the day that had faded fast, but Elijah's easy mood as he waited for his nephew to return. 'I will ring Enid....' He was pulling his phone out of his pocket when the car pulled up. But the tension that had abated only slightly with their arrival returned as Guido, grizzling and miserable, entered the house. Enid was tight-lipped as she took off her coat, while Ainslie did the same for Guido.

'It's been a long day for him,' Enid said. 'I'll go and get him some dinner.'

'It's after six,' Elijah pointed out. 'Did they not give him any dinner?'

'They eat late.' Enid answered carefully, but Elijah was having none of it, and demanded to know what the problem was.

Enid remained tight-lipped. 'I don't want to make things any worse than they are.' Enid glanced to Ainslie for support. 'Nothing actually happened. They just weren't as friendly with him this time…'

'When your sister wasn't present,' Elijah pointed out.

'They don't know she's my sister…' Enid started, then her voice trailed off. 'It was just a difficult day. They were talking in Italian, and I didn't feel very welcome, that's all. Not that I'm complaining—it's important Guido sees his family…'

'Where was Tony?'

'Waiting outside in the car,' Enid huffed. 'They never even took him out a drink.'

'He comes in with you next time,' Elijah said. 'And if they have any problems with that, they can discuss it with me.'

'It's not necessary.' Enid shook her head. 'They were no doubt just upset—they're burying one of their family tomorrow too. It's a tense time for everyone.' She handed him an envelope. 'They asked me to give you this.'

Elijah face was black as thunder as he opened it. 'Their accommodation bill.' His lip sneered in distaste. 'It is clear they are after his money. You tell your sister—'

'I don't gossip to my sister about work.' Enid fixed him with a stern glare. 'If the Social Services department formally asks me, then of course I'll give my opinion. But I won't be running to my sister with every bit of gossip about the Castellas the same way I wouldn't discuss *your* dealings—you're my employer. Now, if you'll excuse me, I'm going to give Guido his supper.'

'Where does that leave me?' Elijah asked once they were alone. 'Even if she did put it in a formal report, Social Services would just disregard it.'

'There's nothing to *put* in a formal report,' Ainslie pointed out. 'Elijah, they're allowed to be upset and distracted today—they didn't do anything wrong.'

'Why would you be on their side?' His eyes flashed angrily. 'Guido comes home upset, having been ignored all day, and they send me the bill for their accommodation with a note saying that was it not for me they wouldn't be here... *Zingareschi*!' From the murderous look on Elijah's face as he tossed the note across the room, he hadn't just uttered a compliment! 'The peasants can't even spell in their own language.'

'Elijah, who is this helping?' Ainslie just wouldn't have it—refused to lose what they had found that morning. Walking over, she stood before him, stared up at his face, twisted and bitter with hate, and placed her hand on his cheek. 'You have to be the reasonable one here, for Guido's sake. Maybe they genuinely can't afford the accommodation...'

'So they expect *me* to pay? What is reasonable about that?'

'They're Guido's family—and if you can help now, who knows...?' She was loath to suggest it, but brave enough to do so. 'Elijah, what if they do end up with custody? Or what if you end up with shared care...?'

'No! I won't let it happen.'

'But it might!' Ainslie insisted. 'And anything you can do to forge a relationship with them now can surely only help Guido.'

'Even if it goes against everything I believe?'

He didn't get it, but she could see him struggling, could feel him wrestle with a hatred that was inbred, for the sake of his nephew.

There was nothing more honourable than what he did, this proud, strong man, after a moment's deep thought, nodded, actually backing down. 'I will try,' Elijah said. 'Tomorrow—I will try.'

CHAPTER EIGHT

NOT on Christmas Eve.

Standing in the cemetery, for a crazy second Ainslie wanted to shout it out. Tell the priest to stop.

Because someone somewhere had surely got it wrong?

Christmas was about love and laughter and magic. Not this—never this.

The coroner had released the bodies, and, as Elijah had wearily conceded, it was either today or wait till after the festivities—delay the agony a while longer.

She couldn't fathom his pain.

Couldn't fathom it because even though she'd never met them, as she watched two coffins being lowered into the ground, saw the dark mound of earth that would cover them rising out of the snow, heard Guido innocently sing and chatter to the shell-shocked gathering, Ainslie was overwhelmed with the horror of it all.

She understood exactly what Elijah had said—it was as if a terrible mistake had been made, as if the universe had, on this occasion, got it terribly, terribly wrong.

Yet somehow he held it together—as he had over the last few days, as he had during the service—his deep low voice breaking just once as he'd delivered the eulogy. Returning to her side afterwards he'd sat rigid, staring ahead, somehow doing what had to be done, getting through this most vile of days.

And she wanted to comfort, to offer support, but he neither sought nor accepted it. The hand that she had slipped into his when he came back to his seat had been quickly returned to her own lap unheld—and now, seemingly together but utterly apart, they stood at the graveside as the burial was concluded.

'I will talk to them now.' Holding Guido, instructing her to wait there, he made his way over to the Castellas—to the people he hadn't seen in years but had hated from a distance.

Ainslie's heart was in her mouth.

'How are things?' Ms Anderson was watching too.

'Difficult,' Ainslie admitted. 'But Elijah is making an effort.'

'As he should,' she said tartly. 'The Castellas are Guido's family too.'

But Elijah wasn't up to performing for the cameras, or rather for Ms Anderson. After the briefest of conversations he turned away, his black coat like a cloak billowing behind as he quickly marched. His face was a mask of rigid muscles as he reached Ainslie and Ms Anderson.

'Let's go.'

'You're supposed to—' Ainslie started, but he was already gone.

The undertaker was forming relatives into a line, on the premise that the mourners could shake their hands, or kiss as was the Italian way, and offer their condolences, but Elijah was having none of it.

'Come on!' he called over his shoulder.

'We can't...' He was in no mood to be argued with, but Ainslie tried. 'You're expected to line up—people want to see Guido.'

'They've seen enough!' Elijah retorted, stalking off. 'He's seen enough! I do not need their condolences!'

'That must have been extremely hard for you!' Speaking in her best social worker voice, but slightly breathless, Ms Anderson caught up with them as they reached the car. But Elijah clearly had more on his mind than winning favour with the social worker, because he didn't even deign to give a response. 'The Castellas are looking forward to spending some time with Guido back at the hotel.'

'He won't be there,' Elijah growled, his jaw tightening as the Castellas came over—and for the first time Ainslie saw the two families together, felt the simmering hatred.

'Mr Vanaldi isn't bringing Guido back to the hotel.' Ms Anderson's clipped voice was in stark contrast to the emotive protests of the Castellas.

'Voglio passare tempo con Guido.' Marco Castella put out his hands to his nephew, who clung tighter to Elijah.

'Non potere,' Elijah answered tightly.

'Voglio specialmente oggi essere con lui.'

'Would you mind telling me what's being said.'

Less than impressed, Ms Anderson confronted Elijah. Very much less than intimidated, he gave a surly translation.

'They say they want to spend some time with Guido. I tell them they can't.'

'Today—*specialmente*...' Marco's English was broken, his voice too as he pleaded to Ms Anderson for some time with his nephew. 'We are family.'

And no matter the bad blood between them, no matter that it was Elijah's side she should be on, Ainslie thought that Marco was right—a lavish spread had been put on at a luxury hotel. Surely it was right that Guido go along.

'Maybe we should bring him for a short while...'

Ainslie's suggestion was met with the filthiest of glares.

'Absolutely,' Ms Anderson flared. 'Mr Vanaldi—you have been granted *temporary* access only. Now, I shouldn't have to point out—'

'Then don't,' Elijah broke in, his eyes flashing angrily. 'Over and over you tell me that the best interests of the child are to be considered, that Guido must come first.'

'Of course!'

'You are the expert,' Elijah spat the words at the woman. 'So tell me, Ms Anderson, how Guido's interests are best to be served? My sister refused morphine in order to be able to tell me that he sleeps at two p.m. each afternoon. My nephew is recovering from a serious ear infection and croup, and his whole world has been turned around. How is it better that he goes to a hotel, where people will be drinking, where people will be emotional? Please—tell me now how it would be in his best interests to attend?'

She couldn't. Just stood rigid as Elijah awaited her response. But Guido was on his uncle's side, managing a timely croupy cough that broke the appalling silence.

'Quite!' Elijah said tartly. 'I will take my nephew home now—I will give him his antibiotic and settle him for his afternoon sleep. And when he is settled, my housekeeper—*with* childcare qualifications—will watch him for a couple of hours while my fiancée and I attend this circus.' He nodded to Tony, who opened the car door, and despite his anger, despite his palpable fury, Elijah was supremely gentle as he placed Guido in his car seat. Once they were all in, he wound down the window, his breath white as he hissed out his parting shot, pulling out an envelope from the glove box and thrusting it to Ms Anderson. 'The Castellas want their accommodation bill settled—I trust your department will take care of that?'

'You're right.' As Tony sped them home, it was Ainslie who finally spoke.

'I'm always right.'

'But...' Ainslie chewed her lip for a moment before continuing. 'If you want to appear the better option for Guido, surely it's better that you don't put Ms Anderson off side? I mean, perhaps you should try...'

'I *am* the better option, compared to them,' Elijah retorted. 'I do not need to *try* for anyone.'

'Then why am I here?' Ainslie snapped back. 'Appearances *do* matter!' She snapped her mouth closed, remembering that Tony was present, realising that this conversation couldn't take place here. But it would seem Elijah was past caring, all pretences dropped as he glared back at her and spat out his response.

'You are here because without a rapid fiancée I would not have been able to prevent them from taking him. Now I have time to properly sort out this mess—and I will sort it out! You are paid to appear supportive—remember that next time you contradict me in front of the social worker.'

If he didn't care that Tony was present, then neither did she. 'Am I paid to sleep with you too?'

'No—that's a privilege!'

If he hadn't been right in what he'd said to Ms

Anderson, she'd have told Tony to stop the car so she could get out. If it hadn't been his sister's funeral today, and if Guido hadn't been present, she'd have slapped his cheek. She had to settle for words instead.

'You bastard!'

'Consider it a perk of your job!' Elijah reiterated as they pulled up at the house.

Just in case she hadn't got the point. Just in case he hadn't humiliated her enough.

'How was it?' Enid's kind concern went unanswered as Elijah marched through the hall, the massive house a shrunken vacuum as tension consumed it.

Ainslie sat on the edge of the sofa, too stunned, too angry, too shocked to even *think* about acting normal.

But it seemed Elijah still could. He took the lunch Enid had prepared for Guido and fed the little boy, the vileness that had been on his lips absent as he spoke gently to his nephew. He shook his head at the cup of tea Enid proffered, while still Ainslie sat—ready to leave. Because how, *how*, after that, could she possibly stay?

'Let me put him to bed for you,' Enid offered.

'I'll manage,' Elijah answered, almost in a growl.

'This must be so hard for him...' Enid said as she sat on the couch beside Ainslie. 'For you too.'

And for a second Ainslie felt guilty. Enid's sympathy was utterly unmerited, given the charade they'd created, but tears stung the back of her eyes. The pain the day had inflicted was so raw, his words had been so acutely painful, it was enough to propel her from the sofa, to make a stand, to leave. But, hearing the slam of the bathroom door, hearing Elijah retch, hearing the spasms of pain that engulfed him, hearing some of the hell he held inside, she was overwhelmed too. Her own stomach tightened—doubling over, she sat back down, tears spilling out as she heard the depth of his grief—knowing, knowing at some level the pain he'd inflicted hadn't been aimed at her—yet he'd been too angry, too raw, just too detestable to pardon.

'We should go.' Grey, remote, and utterly not meeting her eyes, Elijah came into the lounge. 'Enid, you are to call if there is a problem.'

'Of course.'

'Come!' He summoned her, heading for the door, clearly expecting Ainslie to follow—only she couldn't. Couldn't just get up and meekly follow, no matter how much he was paying her.

'You really expect me to stand there and play—?'

'Would you excuse us, please, Enid?' he interrupted. 'It would seem my fiancée has something she wants to get off her chest.'

'Why bother?' Ainslie said when the door had closed behind her. 'Why get rid of Enid when we know Tony's going to tell her? There's no point pretending any more.'

'Tony won't tell her.'

'Of course he will!' Ainslie scorned.

'I employ Tony—he knows what is expected from him. I pay for his discretion!'

'Pay for him to sit quiet while you dare to speak to me like that?' Ainslie spat. 'Well, even a fake fiancée doesn't have to put up with that.' She was pulling at his ring. The sudden heat of the house after the cold outside made it hard to get it off, giving Elijah the second it took to cross the room and close his hands around hers—only it wasn't in apology.

'You will come with me this afternoon.'

'Or?' Ainslie challenged. 'You don't own me—I'll pay my own debts, Elijah, my ex's too, if I have to. But I'm not going to be spoken to like that—and I'm not coming this afternoon.'

'My PA told me this morning that the press are waiting to talk to me. Elijah Vanaldi considering fatherhood is quite a story to them. I told her that I have nothing to say to them, but perhaps I should reconsider…' Still his hands held hers. 'They might be interested to hear that I have a fiancée—interested in her story too…'

'Why would they be interested in me?' Ainslie countered. 'You're the one who'll come across badly if you talk to the press. Ms Anderson will find out for sure…'

'She'll find out about our little ruse this afternoon if you don't come.' Elijah shrugged. 'So really there is nothing to lose…'

'For me either.' Ainslie shrugged, attempted nonchalance, but her heart-rate was quickening. The hands that held hers were not ready to let her go, and a mirthless smile twisted on his mouth as he delivered his threat.

'I'm a bit worried about your friend Angus though. He might not fare so well…'

'You wouldn't.'

'Just watch me!' He wasn't even pretending to smile now. 'I told you when you agreed to this that I would do whatever it takes, use whatever means I had available to protect my nephew. And if that means digging the dirt on some *celebrity* doctor I've never even met, then consider it done!'

* * *

Standing, clutching her drink, Ainslie eyed the eclectic gathering. Waitresses moved among the crowd, offering finger food and drinks to young mothers from Guido's playgroup, who didn't quite blend with the suits of the finance and property world. Other friends of Maria and Rico's reminisced with each other, whilst Rico's family stood huddled together, drinking copiously, throwing the occasional dark look to the only person who, despite Ainslie by his side, despite making polite talk and absolutely doing his duty, somehow stood utterly alone.

'Mr Vanaldi!' It was a less confrontational Ms Anderson who came over. 'About before.' She ran an eye around the room, at the strained subdued gathering, at the simmering grief and tension beneath the surface, and gave an apologetic nod. 'You were right not to bring Guido.'

'Thank you.' Graciously he accepted her admission. 'I was also at fault...I went too far...' Stilted though it was, his own apology was genuine, and Ainslie realised as his hand sought hers that it wasn't exclusively aimed at Ms Anderson—that in his own strange way he was apologising to her too. 'I know your intentions are good.'

'What are your plans for Christmas Day—for Guido?' Ms Anderson enquired.

'We will keep it quiet—but in the afternoon, once he has had his rest, your sister has offered to take Guido to my brother-in-law's relatives for a few hours. My driver will take them, and they can spend the afternoon and evening with him, then Enid will bring him back to his home.'

'That sounds good.' She gave a sympathetic smile, first to Elijah and then to Ainslie. 'You two really do seem to be doing well with him—under the most trying of circumstances.'

Not that well, Ainslie thought, seemingly the perfect fiancée, standing sombre and loyal by her partner's side—only this time it was Ainslie's hand not holding his in return.

This time it was Ainslie who, after the polite exchange with Ms Anderson, claimed back her hand and her personal space and slipped to the loo.

As was her privilege.

Over and over he stung her with his words.

Little barbs of poison injected to her heart that couldn't merely be soothed with an afterthought of an apology.

Barely recognising herself, she stared in the mirror. It wasn't just the elegant hair that was unfamiliar, or the perfectly applied make-up that made her look different. Neither was it the black angora dress that could never be considered *vulgar* that altered her reflection. No, it was the troubled eyes she didn't recognise. The turmoil in her soul that had her wretched. The attraction she felt for him, the tenderness he displayed when he held her, was so at odds with the torment he inflicted at times.

Well, no more. Running her hands under the tap, Ainslie collected her many thoughts before she headed back out there. She'd see it through today—see it through till after Christmas for Guido. But then she'd go. And if he did go to the press about Angus… A surge of panic welled inside, but she quashed it. A hundred thought processes whirred at once as she washed her hands, then reached into her bag to retouch her lipstick. Her mind still buzzing with anger, she hardly noticed the woman who came up behind her.

'*Molto conveniente.*' Ten days of solid brushing wouldn't

take away the yellow of the teeth that met her gaze as she looked over her shoulder in the mirror. The snarl of the lips made Ainslie stiffen as Dina Castella confronted her, safe in the knowledge that they were alone.

'I don't know what you mean.'

'This is very *conveniente*.' Dina's English wasn't as good as Elijah's, but she had no trouble getting her point across. 'Suddenly the rich playboy has *una bella* fiancée!'

'We just recently got engaged.'

'Come…' she sneered. 'Since when did Elijah Vanaldi make a commitment to a woman? Any woman! You think we wouldn't have heard about this in our village? You think I am stupid?'

'Of course not.'

'So how much?' Dina glared. 'How much does he pay you?'

'This has nothing to do with money!' Ainslie said through gritted teeth, but Dina just gave a mocking laugh and picked up Ainslie's shaking hand, eying her ring with distaste.

'You come very cheap.'

'It was their mother's ring…' Ainslie flared. 'As I said, this isn't about money.'

'Why would you lie for him, then?' Dina countered, her face twisting with suppressed rage. 'Because we both know that you are…' She must have seen Ainslie's flush of colour, or the constriction as her throat tightened, because she was quick to pounce. 'If it's money you need walk away now. We will be able to take care of you. Unlike the Vanaldis, with all their lies and stories, at least the Castellas, good or bad, tell the truth.'

CHAPTER NINE

LA VIGILIA DI NATALE.

Christmas Eve. Only it didn't feel like it.

During her time in London Ainslie had never really experienced homesickness, but she felt it now. She ached, just ached for a hot Australian summer, for blue skies and the sun burning on her shoulders as she dragged an overloaded trolley through a packed supermarket car park. And for *Carols By Candlelight* booming on the television as friends dropped over, sniffing the aromatic air as they stepped out onto the decking, where her father would guard the barbecue. For the familiar traditions that were *her* idea of Christmas instead of the hastily amalgamated traditions they must somehow pull together now if they were to give this little boy any semblance of the Christmas his parents would have wanted for him. Ainslie and Elijah had to weave together an English and Sicilian Christmas—to somehow fill this house with love and laughter and hopefully let some magic into Guido's life.

Even if only for a little while.

'In Sicily we eat fish on Christmas Eve: seven fish dishes…' He actually managed a smile at Enid's rather pained expression and added that one would do. 'Also—' his voice thickened '—children do not write to Santa. Instead they write to their parents, tell them how much they love them.'

'He's too young...' Enid attempted, but Elijah shook his head.

'Maria wrote for Guido last year—it was something she wanted to happen—something she did not really have herself. It should be placed under the father's plate, and he reads it at dinner. Maybe we should do it for Guido...' His eyes turned to Ainslie. 'Till he is old enough.'

Which made no sense.

Oh, the tradition made sense—just not the *we*, and not the implication that there was a future, that there would be more Christmases.

'That sounds lovely.'

Enid's voice snapped Ainslie back to bitter reality—even when mired in grief Elijah played to his audience, and she had to remember that. *Had* to stop blurring the reality, had to stop believing that the tender words he whispered, that the love he made to her when he came to her at night, was anything more to him than a pleasurable interlude in a hellish journey—an escape.

Her throat tightened as she recalled his cruel words... a perk!

'Are you okay, Ainslie?' Elijah frowned over.

'Just tired.' Ainslie gave him a tight smile that didn't meet her eyes. 'It's been a draining day.'

She hadn't told him about Dina—had chosen to leave that little gem for later. She first wanted to work out her own feelings on what Dina had said, wanted to try and work out her own truth before she added fuel to an already raging inferno and voiced her misgivings to him.

'Mummmm-mummm-mummm...' Guido hummed the words as they sat at the table, screwing up his little face at the food Enid attempted to shovel into his clamped mouth.

'It's good for you, Guido,' Enid soothed, taking the opportunity when Guido opened his mouth to protest to quickly get a loaded spoon in.

But Guido's manners hadn't improved, and even Ainslie's strained face broke into a smile as Guido almost perfectly re-enacted his performance on the underground, spitting out his food in disgust.

'He will learn manners in time, I suppose...' Elijah started, as Enid carried the angry bundle upstairs for a bath, but his shrewd eyes instantly took in Ainslie's pursed lips. 'What?'

'Nothing.' Ainslie's voice was tight. She was quashing down her anger as she fiddled with the stem of her wine glass. Tonight of all nights was surely not the one to row.

'Say what you are clearly thinking!'

'I'd rather not.'

'Please share...' Elijah goaded. 'Better out than in.'

'Not always!' A flash of tears in her eyes was rapidly blinked away. 'Maybe Guido *won't* grow out of it—maybe it's hereditary?'

'What?'

'Spitting in people's faces—hurting someone who doesn't deserve it.'

'Ainslie... I have already addressed that.'

'Actually, you haven't!' Her voice was rising and she struggled to smother it. 'You delivered an apology to Ms

Anderson which cryptically I was supposed to accept as aimed at me too. Well, no. You've signed me up for the gig, and whether I want to or not I guess I've got to play, but…'

Her voice trailed off as Enid returned, a clean and smiling Guido in her arms, dressed in powder-blue pyjamas, his dark hair a mass of curls and a gorgeous sleepiness in the those blue, blue eyes that were so much like Elijah's. Holding out his arms to Ainslie, coyly almost, he nestled his head in her arms when she held him, clinging to her like a barnacle on a rock as she sat at the table.

How could she walk?

Merely drop him and go?

Inhaling his baby smell, holding onto this little bundle that could be comforted and soothed by her mere presence, both terrified and comforted *her*. In just a few days her presence had settled Guido. It was her arms he often wanted when Enid brought him into the room, her that he toddled to as he ran giggling out of the bath. At some deep level this little guy, in a very short space of time, knew that he could trust her.

'Guido…' Elijah cleared his throat, pulled out a piece of paper. 'You are too young to write, but I know you feel—I know you do not understand, but I know you are confused…'

If she was his *real* fiancée she should be dabbing her cheek, or smiling bravely at him to continue, but because she wasn't Ainslie's nose ran into the little shoulder that was hooked into hers. Guido's thumb bobbed into his mouth. He was safe in his little world as the lady held him and the man spoke. Guido had no comprehension of the future that had been buried today, trusting as only a baby could that it was all going to be okay.

'Your *mamma* and *papà* loved you—how many times they told me that I cannot count—and they would be proud, would want to be with you now. I hope they are. All I promise tonight is that I will always be there for you.'

She could feel the delicious, heavy, weightlessness of sleep in Guido's body—could feel his mass of muscle relax as she held him. The ribbons of tension that bound him tightened for a second as Enid peeled him from her arms—and she could feel the awful heavy silence when it was only they two.

'You realise that I needed you there this afternoon.' It was Elijah who broke the silence. 'And that if you leave...well, I lose him.'

'Well, you got your way,' Ainslie said coolly. 'For now.'

'Ainslie, I am trying to do as you suggest—I am trying to trust these people, trying to believe that maybe they have changed. But I went over there today and they didn't so much as look at Guido, just asked if I had the money for them. Everyone is telling me to make peace, that I have got it wrong.'

'Got *what* wrong?' Ainslie frowned, then gave a shake of her head. His problems were his own now. 'Let's just try and get through tomorrow.'

'You must both be exhausted.' Enid said later, when she brought two mugs of hot chocolate through to the vast lounge.

Elijah rolled his eyes at the offering and poured himself a rather large brandy. 'Today has been made much easier by having you here,' he said, and Enid flushed with pleasure. 'We were lucky to get you at such short notice. It has made a huge difference.'

'It's made a huge difference to me too! Christmas isn't a time to be on your own.'

And Ainslie watched as Elijah dispensed with formality and poured Enid a brandy too, asking her to join them, even teasing her about the humongous turkey that had commandeered half the fridge.

'I make a lovely Christmas dinner—you wait till you taste my chestnut stuffing!' Enid said proudly. 'I'll serve it at midday—so there's plenty of time for Guido to have his nap before he goes to his aunt and uncle's.'

'You must join us.' Elijah frowned.

'I'll feed Guido.' Enid nodded. 'And make sure he behaves. But I won't intrude.'

'Please do!' Elijah said. 'And Tony too. Ainslie and I—' he took her hand and she bristled, she just couldn't play any more today, but Elijah hadn't finished with her yet '—will need all the help we can to make it a happy day for Guido.'

'The more the merrier?' Enid gave a sympathetic smile. 'Well, don't worry—we'll make it a special day for him. Even if we're not...' she faltered. 'I'm sorry, of course *you're* his family.'

'Not the one that was meant for him,' Ainslie said, taking her hand back and drinking her chocolate, preferring to talk about Enid's world than lie about her own. 'What about your own family?'

'There's just my sister,' Enid answered. 'But I don't want to always land on her doorstep. I worked for a lovely family for twenty-four years. I looked after the house and the children. The parents both travelled overseas a lot with their work.'

'They became your family?' Ainslie asked.

'We're still close—even when the youngest had left home they kept me on to mind the house—but they've moved to Singapore now. He got this job offer out of the blue, and the next thing I knew the house was for sale. Which leaves me—' she took a sip of her brandy '—well, a little bit lost, I suppose. That's why it's nice to be here. I'm going to look for a house to buy in the New Year.'

'I could help with that. It looks as if I'm going to be here for a while,' Elijah offered easily. 'If you want me to.'

'Oh, I don't think it would be anything close to the grand scale you're used to dealing with.'

'I know a lot of people,' Elijah said, 'and I know who not to deal with.'

'Oh, well, that would be wonderful. Thank you.' Enid looked as if a huge weight had been lifted off her shoulders as she stood up and said goodnight. 'Before I go to bed, do you want me to help setting up the presents?'

Ainslie was about to accept when annoyingly Elijah declined Enid's offer, and for the first time Ainslie got a real glimpse of being a parent.

They soldiered on long after exhaustion had hit, placing Maria's lovingly wrapped presents under the tree. Ainslie added her own hastily bought gifts, but even with the smell of pine in the air and the fairly lights left on, when Elijah turned off the main lights and the room was bathed in the tree's glow still it felt a world away from Christmas. For little Guido it was far too late to hope for a miracle.

'What are you doing?' Elijah asked as she crept into Guido's room.

'Tying a stocking to his cot!' Ainslie hissed, trying to do just that, and wincing as Guido stirred at the intrusion.

'You're waking him up!' Elijah whispered from the doorway.

'Done!' Ainslie joined him in the hall.

'He won't know any different...'

'Of course he'll know,' Ainslie assured him. 'It's Christmas—he'll know it's a special, magical day.'

'Not for him.' There was a break in his voice, another dent appearing in the armour he had clad himself in just to make it through the day, and he looked so ragged, so weary, so exhausted, it took everything she possessed not to raise her hand and capture his tired face, not to press her lips against his tense cheek, to be the one to lead him to bed, to lay him down and somehow kiss away his pain. Only tonight she just couldn't—his callous words still rang in her ears, and anger, hurt and humiliation were a strong antidote to need.

No, miracles were sadly lacking in this house. Especially when Elijah pushed open the bedroom door and Ainslie carried on walking.

'Where are you going?'

'To find another room...' She gave a small, tight smile. 'Thankfully there's an inexhaustible supply in this house.'

'Ainslie...' He followed her, stood at the door to the guest room—utterly gorgeous, still in the suit he had worn to the funeral, his tie in his pocket, as it had been when first they'd met. 'I am sorry for before. Please, it is Christmas Eve. My sister was—' His throat tightened on words he couldn't say. Only she had no reserves left, no well to dip the bucket in and come to the surface smiling. She just stood there drenched in bitterness as, instead of pleading his case, he spoke about practicalities. 'What about Enid? She will know we are sleeping apart.'

'Couples fight,' Ainslie said. She had never once used her body as a tease, and even by undressing in front of him she wasn't tonight. She was just tired to the marrow, and if he wasn't going to leave, then he could stand there and watch her sleep. Slipping off her black stockings and pulling on the soft white silk pyjama shorts that she'd chosen for herself, Ainslie wriggled out of her skirt as he stood there. But she *did* turn away as she unhooked her bra and slipped the top over her bosom before turning around to face him. 'Even *real* couples fight.'

'At Christmas?' Elijah attempted, but it didn't move her. She didn't want sex that was an apology—she wanted the real thing.

'Especially at Christmas,' Ainslie retorted, standing rigid.

'You're very good at telling people how it should be,' Elijah said. 'Very good at telling people how to get there—the trouble is you give them the compass and take the map.'

'What?'

'I needed you at the funeral today.'

'You ignored me.'

'That didn't mean I wasn't glad you were there.'

'What you said after—'

'Was wrong,' Elijah finished for her. 'Unforgivable, it would seem. I was angry—angry that I had listened to you, that I had believed maybe things could be different—and then, when I was proved right, I was angry again when you contradicted me in front of the social worker...' Their disappointment in each other simmered in the long silence. 'If I lose you, I lose Guido too.' He gave a tired shrug. 'It would seem I already have.'

He left her then—left her with just the scent of him and a final glimpse of his fatigued face.

Slipping into the cool bed and staring at the ceiling, Ainslie knew that if it was about winning a fight then seemingly she just had.

And if it was about making a point then Ainslie had done very well for herself.

But as she lay in an empty bed on Christmas Eve, twitching with insomnia, over and over his face whirred into her vision. Seeing the grooves of exhaustion, close-up witness to the agony he endured, she relived the dark day, *felt* the deep chasm of his grief, and knew, *knew* that she hadn't won a thing.

That tonight Elijah lay alone with his thoughts.

And that surely she'd let him down when he had needed her most.

CHAPTER TEN

He knew!

Despite his tender age, despite the horrors of the previous days, somehow Guido knew today was special. For the first time he slept through the night. His eager squeals snapped Ainslie awake at six a.m., and as she headed to his room she collided with a very tousled Elijah, who stood in nothing more than a pair of black hipster trunks that left very little to the imagination. Ainslie flushed as she apologised to his naked chest. Actually, they left rather a *lot* to her imagination.

'*Buon Natale.*' His face bruised with lack of sleep, grumbling and surly, still Elijah set the tone and called a rapid truce, his mouth finding hers for a brief second, his hand pulling her in at the waist. 'Merry Christmas, Ainslie.'

The central heating must surely have been left on high overnight, Ainslie concluded, because this vast London house in the middle of an English winter was positively stifling. Her lips stung from his brief kiss, the taste of him lingering as Elijah scooped up Guido, who was holding the teddy she'd poked into his stocking, and carried him downstairs. Ainslie followed behind, smiling at the baby, but looking at his uncle's back. The keyboard of his ribcage had her jaw clenched. She wanted to reach out, to stroke the keys, wanted to play him like a piano. Wanted *not* to notice the luscious swell of his quads as he squatted down and chatted to Guido, wanted *not* to notice the heavenly flat planes of his abdomen as he stood up, or the swirl of hair around his mahogany nipples. But it was either that or look at his face—which was something she was having terrible trouble doing this morning.

'Everything okay?' Elijah frowned as she stared somewhere past his shoulder and nodded.

'Everything's fine,' Ainslie croaked, as Enid emerged from the kitchen, a pinny tied around her vast purple dressing gown and wearing a pair of reindeer ears and flashing Santa earrings. Ainslie could have kissed her for the effort she had gone to—so she did.

'Merry Christmas!' Enid beamed, not remotely fazed by Elijah's lack of attire as he came over and kissed her too.

'Buon Natale!' Elijah responded.

There was a smile fixed on Ainslie's face as Enid assumed the role of camera person, taking instructions from Elijah who had, in two seconds flat, worked out how his sister's digital camcorder operated. After a couple of goes Enid grasped it too, and she stood filming as Elijah headed over to the mountain of presents. Only somehow, as Elijah sat with his nephew, as he helped him open each gift in turn, Ainslie realised that her smile was there because it *was*. Watching Guido's delighted reaction, feeling the love and thought his mother had put into each and every loving gift, she was determined not to sit miserable—because this little slice of time Enid was capturing for Guido still had his parents' presence.

'Merry Christmas, Enid!' Elijah held out a parcel. 'You can stop filming now.'

'For me?'

Embarrassed, delighted, abashed, Enid opened her present—a vast box of luxury cosmetics, and on the top a silver envelope which she carefully opened.

'A spa retreat? My goodness!'

'A weekend away for you and a friend! To take at your leisure...' Elijah waved away her stammering thanks. '*We* thought you might need some time to unwind after putting up with us.' He shot Ainslie a look that emphasised the *we*.

'And just another little thing...' Ainslie said, retrieving Enid's gift and quickly tearing off the label that was signed from her alone, trying to remember that, for the housekeeper's benefit at least, they really were a couple.

Which meant she'd had to buy Elijah a gift, of course.

And somehow it had seemed important at the time that she didn't charge it to his credit card. It had been impossibly hard on her budget to buy for a billionaire who could have whatever his heart desired, and suddenly the stupid digital picture frame she'd bought for him seemed woefully inadequate as Elijah pulled it out of the gold wrapping paper. Biting on her bottom lip as he turned his present over, she saw an expression she couldn't read appear on his face for just a moment before he looked her in the eye.

'Thank you.'

And surely he was cross. Surely if she really was his fiancée, if she really *were* allowed to love him, she should have shown it better. This beautiful, expensive man should be pulling back meticulously giftwrapped scented paper, crowing in delight over Ferragamo wallets or Tiffany cuff-links, quirky little gifts that made him smile.

'There wasn't much time…' Inexplicably tears were pricking her eyes. 'What with Guido and everything…' Fleeing to the kitchen was easier than breaking down in front of them. Her lips clamped together as she tried to hold it in, sniffing back tears. She opened the fridge and stood, hoping the cool air would take the heat out of her face.

'Why did you rush off?'

'I'm just getting some milk for Guido.' She was still at the fridge, with her eyes screwed closed now, desperately trying to keep her voice sounding normal.

'Enid can get that!' Elijah pointed out. 'You didn't wait for your present.'

His hand was on her shoulder, turning her around to face him and her eyes blurred more as they came to rest on the box he was holding, the tears she'd been holding back spilling out when she opened it.

A ruby, surrounded by diamonds, dangled beautifully on a silver-coloured chain.

Silver-coloured because even to Ainslie's untrained eye this wasn't costume jewellery. No manufactured stone could ever be as deep and as blood-red and as mesmerising as this one, and only real diamonds could ever sparkle like these.

'It's too much…' She choked out the words, because it was too much. This was a gift befitting this man's *real* fiancée—not a quick fill-in. 'I should have spent more…' Her mind was darting, grabbing onto anything that flitted into it rather than facing the truth.

She *wanted* it to be real.

Wanted the hands that were now holding the pendant, the hands that were now going under her hair, the hands that had made love to her, to be hands she could hold…always.

'What are you talking about?'

'Your present…'

'I like it.' She wasn't sure if he was talking about her present or the jewel that, when he released the chain, slipped cool and heavy between her breasts. They both stared down, his hands still behind her hair, warm fingers on the back of her neck. Her nipples liked it too—popping out like two disloyal bookends each side of the ruby.

Disloyal because she didn't want him to know how much she wanted him.

But she did.

'It's too much,' Ainslie choked again. But Elijah was having none of it.

'You like nice things,' he teased. 'And we don't want you stealing.'

If it was a joke it wasn't funny. 'You know I didn't steal.'

'I did know—remember?'

He had known, and she did remember.

'Don't I get a kiss?'

'Why…?' Ainslie's voice was still laced with hurt. 'Isn't it just another perk of the job?'

Oh, God, why, instead of snapping back, did he have to smile at her anger? Why, instead of coming up with some crushing reply, did he kiss her angry face, kiss each salty tear and then her eyelashes?

'I say thoughtless things at times,' he whispered, absolutely echoing her thoughts. 'But then at other times…'

She didn't want to kiss him, but she did. As he traced her eyes, her cheeks, as his fingers traced her throat, she wanted him so badly on her mouth. Like eating hot porridge from the outside in, Ainslie thought faintly, as her mouth twitched with desire. Working through the warm bits when you really wanted the hot bit in the middle, with the thick golden honey on the top.

'No...' Her mouth said what her body couldn't.

'Why not?' He breathed the words into the shell of her ear, his tongue teasing the lobe. Both of his hands were behind her now, resting on the fridge, their lips their only contact, and for a crazy second she wanted to climb into the fridge behind her and cool her flaming body down. Either that or press it against him, grab his face in her hands and kiss him so hard he'd be sorry—sorry for teasing, sorry for playing, sorry for hurting her.

'We mustn't embarrass Enid!' It was an emergency response—albeit pathetic, Ainslie realized—but somehow appropriate as Enid herself came in, and Elijah broke contact with a lazy smile, his hands still pinning her.

'I don't get embarrassed!' Enid boomed.

But Ainslie did. Especially when Enid's eyes fell on the necklace and she put on her glasses to take a closer look. Elijah made a funny sucking noise as he chewed on his bottom lip, suppressing a smile as every eye in the room focussed on Ainslie's still rather flushed décolletage. Her wretched nipples were still standing to beastly attention as Enid took her time.

'Just lovely!' Enid announced. 'Certainly not fake!'

'Absolutely not,' Elijah agreed solemnly, then added, with a wink for Ainslie's benefit, 'You can always tell.'

Then there were the phone calls.

To her parents, her brothers, her sister. Ainslie felt awfully decadent, ringing Australia on the mobile phone he'd bought her—but, as Elijah had pointed out on several occasions, he'd rather she didn't use the home phone.

'You're all right, though, darling?' Ainslie could hear the knot of worry in her mother's voice.

'I'm fine,' Ainslie assured. 'I've got a really good job.'

'But you said that about the last one,' her mother pointed out. 'Look, if you need money, or things aren't working out, we'd want you to tell us.'

'And I would.' Ainslie lied. How could she not? They were in Australia, for goodness' sake—literally on the other side of the world. She was hardly going to ring them with every little drama. 'But there isn't anything to tell. Things just didn't work out with Angus and Gemma, and this other job came up at the perfect time.'

She gave a tiny grimace to Elijah, but he was on a call of his own, talking in Italian, his rich deep voice making it difficult for Ainslie to concentrate on what was being said. Just as she went to move to another room Elijah had the same idea, moving into the study and closing the door behind him.

'And they're nice?' her mother checked. 'This new couple you're working for?'

It was just so, so much easier not to correct her. Just so much easier to say yes.

Clearly Elijah had a fair amount of *Buon Natales* to get through, because he stayed in the study for ages. But somehow, *somehow*, it was still a magical Christmas—somehow a little miracle did occur. Because despite the grief and despair of before, everyone did their best to make it happy. Everyone in the house gave everything they could to make it a special Christmas for a very special little boy.

Elijah, when he finally emerged from his calls, was loose and funny for once, stubbornly refusing to get dressed till long after breakfast, which consisted of strong coffee and thick wedges of *panettone* that melted on Ainslie's tongue as she bit into the candied orange and lemon zest. Christmas carols sang out from the television as Enid set to preparing Christmas dinner, and Elijah played with his new toy, taking out the memory stick from his sister's camera and placing it into the digital frame. Guido was delighted as images of himself and his parents whirred again and again before his eyes.

'Homesick?' Elijah caught her in a pensive moment as she stared out over her wine glass.

Coming down from the bedroom, showered and scented with Enid's gift of bath oils, and dressed up for Christmas dinner, she had caught her breath as she'd seen the table Enid had laid. The huge dining room had shrunk somehow with love. Holly and crackers and candles and vast bowls of satsumas decorated and scented the table, and a turkey that would surely feed them till *next* Christmas proudly took centre stage. It had hit her then—hit her as she'd sat down and seen Elijah, all clean and shaved and dressed up for dinner too, in an immaculate fitted white shirt over dress trousers, not smiling a brave smile, but actually managing to have fun. And when Tony had joined them, and they'd pulled crackers, and this great brute of a man had sat with a party hat on as they had all laughed at silly jokes, and Guido's smiling face had been replaced with utter disgust as he'd spat out his Brussels sprouts. It had hit her that somehow they'd made it work. This hastily arranged patchwork job of a family had somehow got it right—had somehow managed to find Christmas.

'Yes.' She answered his question honestly—because she *was* homesick.

Not at this moment for Australia, though, and not at this moment for her family.

Instead she was homesick for the future—for the nostalgia that would surely hit her whenever she looked back and remembered this day.

'We'll be back about seven, then!' Enid buttoned up Guido's coat as Tony took the nappy bag and stroller to the car. 'In time for Guido's bedtime.'

'Thank you for this!' Elijah thanked her, then bent to kiss his nephew. 'Be good for Enid,' he warned.

'He won't be!' Ainslie giggled as the door closed.

'I didn't want her here,' Elijah admitted, 'but she's actually been wonderful.'

'She has,' Ainslie agreed, suddenly shy and awkward now that they were alone, and wondering what to say next. Only she didn't have to—it was Elijah who broke the rather awkward silence as they sat down by the fire.

'I'm sorry.' And it wasn't thinly veiled, or aimed in her general direction, it was absolutely directed at her, and he stared right into her eyes. For the first time since the funeral, since his horrible, horrible words, they were properly alone. 'I was bitter and sad, angry and...' He struggled for a moment to find the word. *'Confuso?'* he offered.

'Confused?' Ainslie suggested.

'It is not a word I normally use…' He pushed out a breath. 'Normally I know exactly what to do—what I am doing, what needs to be done. Confused is not me. I took it out on you—and for that I am sorry.'

'You'll work it out,' Ainslie said. 'You're doing so well with Guido and…'

'It is not just Guido I am confused about.'

Sapphire eyes held hers.

'Then what?'

'Us.' He said it so simply it was Ainslie who was confused now. 'This was not what I was expecting.'

Which made sense—it was the only thing in this crazy life they had created that did make sense. Except for his kiss.

A kiss that had been needed last night, a kiss that had been waiting in the wings the whole morning. When finally their lips met she sobbed with longing, trembled at the feel of his mouth as it came home to hers. A kiss that made sense because to deny it would be illogical. To not move her mouth with his, to not capture his tongue as it parted her lips would be denial to the nth degree.

White cashmere stroked her face as he slid her jumper over her head and the cool of late afternoon greeted her flesh—despite the heating, despite the fire. But she only felt it for a trice. Elijah, kneeling on the floor now, pulled her into the warm embrace of his arms as he kissed her again. His expert hands dealt with her bra and his expert lips moved where his eyes had been since before breakfast. His black hair stroked her chest as his mouth worked on, his hand fiddling with the zipper of her skirt, still suckling as he guided her bottom, making light work of her skirt and panties till she was naked except for her shoes.

'Elijah!' Embarrassed to be so very naked whilst he was still so very dressed, she moved to right the imbalance. Only he wasn't listening, was pushing her back on the sofa in one easy motion and pulling her bottom down in a seemingly practised manoeuvre.

'Relax,' Elijah growled—and she promptly didn't! Between intimate kisses he ripped off his jumper and set back to work. 'Relax,' he said again, diving eagerly between her legs.

'I can't...' she quivered, wondering if she should just fake it to get it over with. She was assailed with visions of Enid walking in, banging her gloves before releasing Guido from his stroller, but—oh, heavens above—it did feel nice.

'I put the chain on the door.' He countered her thoughts, countered her everything. With every wriggle of her discomfort his concentration deepened—as if he was actually enjoying himself.

'I *want* to do this...' He answered her thought and suddenly she didn't want to think, couldn't really think of anything other than this. Couldn't think of anything other than Elijah, with his soft, soft lips, coaxing her with little flicks of his masterful tongue, sucking her most tender centre as she swelled beneath him. A moan began building in her throat, her fingers knotting in his hair now, and he read each gasp, each guttural moan, just did it so right she was putty in his hands. She could see her knees trembling, could see her thighs convulsing, could feel his hot breath, the dart of his tongue. And then he stopped, for a beat of a second that had her weeping. 'It is *my* privilege.'

He captured her clandestine pulse with his lips till there was surely nothing else to give, nothing else to take. He depleted every reserve till she was utterly spent, and only then did he kneel up, looking into her reeling eyes as he pulled her down in front of the fire. She could see him rising over her, see the curved outline of his shoulder in the fading light, hear the last spits of the fire as it died, unattended, and glimpsed the potent length of his erection that replenished her. She felt the greedy relish of an inexhaustible supply as he stabbed inside, her name a mantra as he said it over and over, as he bucked inside, as he sent her into freefall.

'I feel guilty for feeling...' He didn't finish his sentence. He didn't have to. The fire had gone out, the light had long since gone. Just the fairy lights guided them.

'I know.'

'With all that has happened.' He was on his back, his chest rising with each breath, his stomach hollow as her fingers played with his dark mass of hair. 'You change my life.'

Her hand stilled as she heard the reverence in his words. The dewy glow of their lovemaking was too long gone for these utterances.

'You've changed mine too...'

His curse wasn't perhaps the expected response, but was entirely merited when the door was buckling under the weight of its chain—and a frantic thirty seconds ensued. They pulled on clothes and hid knickers, arriving breathless and drunk on guilt to open the door as Enid marched in, with Tony carrying a dozing Guido, and promptly stamped her feet and banged her gloves.

'You're sure about letting me use Tony to take me to my sister's?'

'Absolutely,' Elijah unusually enthused—just a hint of colour on his normally deadpan face. 'How was it?'

'Okay.' Enid shrugged, breathing white air in the hallway as winter followed her in, picking up a bag of presents for her family. 'What did you two do?'

'Oh…' A useless liar at the best of times, Ainslie turned puce. 'This and that. So, how were the Castellas?'

'Much the same.' Enid gazed sadly over to Guido 'They didn't go to much effort. Still, they bought him a lovely present…all little glove puppets of animals. They got it at the airport in Italy for him. It's here…' She started rummaging beneath the stroller, but Elijah halted her.

'You've done enough—go to your sister's now, and have time with your family.'

'It's no trouble for me to put the little one to bed.'

'No,' Elijah insisted. 'We can manage.'

'Well, if you're sure,' Enid said, turning for the door and then changing her mind. 'I can't say I was expecting to, but I've actually had a really lovely day—it's been a wonderful Christmas. Oh, and Mr Vanaldi, just so you know—' this time as she headed for the door she didn't turn around '—you've got your jumper on inside out.'

Ainslie adored that he blushed.

Even a few hours later, as they lay in bed, he simultaneously stroked her thigh and gnashed his teeth in a wince when Ainslie suddenly remembered how they'd been caught. His sallow cheeks actually darkened as over and over she tried another tack to dispute what Enid must have thought.

'Maybe we were trying on our new Christmas presents?'

'Ainslie...'

'Or we got too hot...' She let out a peal of nervous laughter, then a groan. 'She thinks I'm a nymphomaniac—I mean, she's always catching us. She even told me off for leaving my wet nightdress at the bottom of the shower.'

'She'll think we're acting like any normal engaged couple,' Elijah soothed, and changed the subject. 'Actually, my friend Roberto would dispute that—but then his fiancée isn't anywhere near as good-looking as you.'

'And we don't have the ghastly pressure of a wedding to put us off!' Ainslie attempted, but it was hopeless, and they both knew it—especially with what he offered next.

'Maybe we just found each other?'

And she wanted him to seal it with a kiss, wanted him to take her in his arms and kiss her again. But Elijah was suddenly pensive.

'They stopped to buy a present?' Elijah frowned. 'When I heard the news I took my passport, wallet and laptop. I had to buy a phone charger and adapter plug at the airport...it wouldn't have entered my head to buy Guido a present.'

'People react differently, I guess,' Ainslie said, and though she didn't want to spoil the moment, somehow she knew honesty must prevail. 'Dina said something to me at the funeral.' He didn't push, didn't say anything—just held her till she was ready to reveal. 'She didn't say it directly, but—well, she offered me money to leave you...' And she waited for the rip to drag her under, for the inevitable explosion, only it never came—two strong arms wrapped more tightly around her.

'Sleep now.' Elijah kissed her hair. 'It's okay.'

He could feel her relax in his arms—her problem shared,

perhaps, but not halved. He was tempted to rouse her from her slumber, to tell her his fears. But what purpose could that serve? And if he did tell her—why would she stay?

Staring down, he saw the cupid's bow of her mouth, her eyelids flickering in sleep that eluded him, and he *wanted* her to leave—wanted to wake her now and tell her to get out of the cesspit he was exposing her to.

Guido.

His brain tightened, his heart pounding in his chest as it struggled to keep rhythm with the sudden division of loyalties—wanting her to go, needing her to stay.

Needing *her*.

'Go to sleep.' He said it out loud again, only this time to Maria—to the soul he could feel hovering, guarding her baby, willing him to listen. 'I will take care of it—*Buon Natale*.'

CHAPTER ELEVEN

'HE SHOULD be with Enid.'

'Sorry?' Creeping back into bed at dawn, having settled Guido, Ainslie frowned into the darkness.

'Enid should be the one getting up to him at night. She is employed as a live-in housekeeper and nanny—it should not be you getting up to him.'

'I don't mind, though…' Ainslie yawned, hoping to get back to sleep, waiting for the warmth of his arms. But whatever they had found last night seemed to be fading with the dawn.

'It is not a question of minding—if you were my real fiancée you would not be waking to a baby all night—I will have his crib moved in the morning,' Elijah said, his mind made up, and rolled on his side, away from Ainslie.

But she was having none of it. She sat up in bed and talked to his broad shoulders, watching them stiffen as she defied his sudden decisions.

'If I were your real fiancée I certainly *would* be waking up to him—and if I were your *real* fiancée, then we'd be discussing this sort of thing, rather than you jackbooting about, giving out orders.'

'Then it's just as well that you're not.'

Watching Tony take down the crib and move it up to the top floor, Ainslie felt as if she herself were being dismantled—everything she sometimes glimpsed in Elijah, the man she so foolishly had thought she was getting to know, had been taken and moved and put back together again. Only no matter how she looked, how she tried to pretend it was okay, it didn't fit its new surrounds.

'I'm going out for the afternoon.' Elijah found her in the master bedroom, standing where Guido's crib had been, staring out of the window and glimpsing Guido's future.

'Is that how it's going to be for him?' Ainslie turned to face him. 'Left to be amused by the nanny while you go out? Sleeping out of earshot so he doesn't disturb your rest?'

'You blow things out of proportion.'

'No, Elijah, I don't. What the hell could be so important that you have to go out on Boxing Day? Ms Anderson's right—this should be time you're spending with him, forging some sort of bond, not distancing yourself…distancing him.'

'Guido doesn't seem to mind—he's downstairs with Enid, playing with his new things.'

'He's fifteen months old, for goodness' sake!'

'Exactly my point!' Elijah shrugged, but didn't leave it there. 'In fact, the only person who seems to have a problem with my going out is you, which leads me to question your motives, Ainslie. Don't use my nephew to try and trap me with a guilt trip, just to satisfy your own curiosity. I'm going out.'

And in that lull between Christmas and New Year, when

you never knew if the post office or the bank was open, when the decorations were still up and there was no need to go out because the fridge was full to bursting, it was almost as if the universe gave people a chance to find each other. Only Elijah didn't seem to want to take it.

Elijah paced the floors as if he were in some tiny enclosure. When he wasn't on the phone, or in the study on his computer, he ignored the services of his driver and took himself out at every opportunity, leaving Ainslie to amuse herself and giving herself plenty of time to think.

'I'll be a couple of hours.'

'You're going to work?' Enid blinked, voicing Ainslie's thoughts exactly. 'Why?'

'There are a couple of properties I want to look at.'

As Enid shrugged and headed out of the kitchen Elijah explained further. 'I have a lot of properties in London—a lot of contacts. There's no reason to stop working just because I'm stuck here.'

'*Stuck* here?'

'I didn't mean it like that.'

'But it's the holidays.'

'Which means bills are starting to come in—the perfect time to put in a low offer.'

'And make a fortune out of other people's misery?'

'It's my job.' Elijah shrugged. 'And one I do well. Buy yourself something for the New Year's party—it will be black tie, which means—'

'I know what black tie means!' Ainslie snapped.

'I was about to say that we'll have to ask Enid to babysit. Can you see to that?'

'I'll tell Tony too.'

'We're getting a lift with friends—I've given Tony the night off.'

Oh, it was a very nice life—if that was what you wanted.

A babysitter on hand and a driver to whisk her wherever she wanted to go. Trailing around the shops whilst Tony walked behind her, carrying the bags. Her mission was to choose a new wardrobe for little Guido more befitting his new status, and, on Elijah's instructions, a set of luggage for him too, in readiness for his upcoming jet set existence. Oh, and an outfit for herself for the New Year's Eve party Elijah had told her they were going to.

Told her.

A very nice life for some. Only it wasn't what Ainslie wanted—not for her and certainly not for Guido.

Especially when that night *again* Elijah missed Guido's bath and bedtime. When *again* his 'couple of hours' stretched to midnight, and dinner out was apparently required to close whatever deal was being made. When he climbed in bed beside her, even though he pulled her in close, Ainslie could sense his distraction, could feel the restless energy beside her. She knew he was working up to telling her something, staring at the curtains before finally he managed to say what was on his mind.

'I might have to go to Italy for a few days…'

'You can't take Guido out of the country.'

'I know…' Elijah gave a long sigh. 'We have to go to this party on New Year's Eve, but then I have to go. I'll fly out on New Year's Day.'

'But surely…' Ainslie bit her tongue. She didn't want to

nag, didn't want to question, but shivers of jealousy and doubt seemed to be climbing up her oesophagus. That he could even *think* of leaving now was an enigma to her. 'You've got an appointment with Ms Anderson on the second.'

'Which you're going to have to handle. Look, Ms Anderson has to realise that I have a life, a job—a job that I've put on hold since the accident. I have commitments, employees. I walked out on my life with two minutes' notice—surely, *surely*,' he hissed, 'she should be able to accept that I have things to do.'

How did he do it? Ainslie wondered. How did he make the unreasonable so reasonable? How did he always manage to twist things till the impossible made perfect sense?

Well, not this time.

'He's your *nephew*, Elijah.' She turned to face him. 'Your orphaned nephew who you're engaged in a bitter custody battle to keep. The Castellas are ringing every day—you know as well as I do that the second you leave the country they're going to demand he stay with them.'

'He will stay here!' Elijah retorted. 'In his home. And you are to be with him at all times—if the Castellas come to the door they are not to be let in. Look, if you're not up to dealing with the appointment I will ring Ms Anderson to reschedule, but the fact is I have things to attend to, and if that deems me an unsuitable surrogate father—then maybe I am.'

'You have no intention of changing, do you?'

'Why should I?' Elijah retaliated. 'Unlike you—I actually *liked* my old life. Off to the spare room again?' he drawled, as Ainslie sprang out of bed and pulled on her wrap. 'Are you going to run off every time you don't get your own way?'

'I was going to the loo, actually,' Ainslie bit back, heading down the hall and sitting on the edge of the bath, dragging in air and trying to calm down. But she couldn't.

Every word he'd said made seemingly perfect sense.

Only to Ainslie it didn't.

She could sense the shift that had occurred, could almost feel him slipping away...and not just from her, from little Guido too.

'You *should* go out.' Enid was utterly insistent.

Feeling guilty as all hell, Ainslie ducked her face from Guido's wet kisses so as not to spoil her professionally applied make-up. Wrapped in a bathrobe, so as not to blemish her rapid tan, and a silk scarf to keep her false curls from frizzing, Ainslie fed Guido his turkey and mash.

'It's New Year's Eve,' Enid pushed on. 'And if you are going to have Guido—well, he's going to have to get used to the fact you two go out.'

'But we won't as much.' Ainslie shivered, trying to say the right thing, but finding it harder with each and every word.

Elijah's mobile phone was constantly trilling, and his laptop was always on. Invitations thudded onto the mat as the world caught up to the fact that Elijah Vanaldi was in town. The thought of spreading her wings and fluttering into Elijah's real world had her dripping in cold sweat, but all that she could deal with—all that she could cope with blindfolded—if Elijah just met her halfway. If the man she had glimpsed, the uncle Guido so richly deserved, might somehow return.

Dragging her mind back to the conversation, Ainslie

knew she was trying to convince herself as much as Enid. 'We won't be going out as much. Not now we've got Guido to think of.'

'Of course you will,' Enid huffed in her no-nonsense way. 'I Googled him.'

'Googled him?'

'Mr Vanaldi—Elijah. So don't try and tell me that you two don't love the high life—your life isn't going to suddenly stop, so off you go and enjoy yourselves. After all you've been through you both deserve it.'

Maybe they did.

Maybe a night out *was* just what they needed. Perhaps she was starting to go stir-crazy, confined to the house and the park. Elijah was used to parties and glamour and running on adrenaline. Of course it couldn't just end because of Guido—he'd work out a compromise, and tonight so would she!

Staring in the full-length mirror, Ainslie almost had herself convinced! The pale pink raw silk, hand-beaded dress with matching coat had looked appalling on the hanger—like some rosé impersonation of the Christmas tree in the lounge. But once on—once set against a backdrop of spiralling blonde curls and a necklace to die for, with indecently high soft grey stilettos and lashings of silver eyeshadow—somehow, *somehow* it worked.

Unlike them.

Everything they'd found at Christmas seemed lost. The hands that had adored her hadn't been near her in days, the mouth that had kissed her derisive now, and she truly didn't get him—couldn't fathom that he would consider leaving for Italy so close to Social Services making its decision.

That he should simply walk away from something he insisted he wanted.

'You look lovely!' Enid beamed as Ainslie tripped down the stairs. 'Tony's in the kitchen—I'm just making him a cuppa.'

While we wait for Elijah.

She didn't say it, of course. It wasn't really the housekeeper's place to point out that Prince Charming was late for the ball.

Ainslie was so distracted she forgot Elijah's instructions not to answer the phone. She picked it up unthinking on the second ring, to find there in her hand and in her ear Elijah's real world: a throaty, sexy voice, talking in rapid Italian, purring like a kitten as Ainslie attempted to find her own voice.

'Elijah isn't here.'

'And you arrrre?'

She dragged her rrr's, Ainslie noted. The kitten showing its claws?

'Ainslie.'

'Oh—the stand-in!' A peal of laughter pierced her eardrum. 'Don't worry, Elijah told me about the old housekeeper, and that I must be careful.'

Something died a little inside Ainslie as Enid came out and placed a mug on the hall table.

'I can be discreet when I have to. Where is he? His mobile is off.'

'Who are you?' It was the bravest, yet possibly the most stupid of questions—one she'd already envisaged the answer to, even before it came.

'It's Portia!' came the confident reply—as if she should

already know, as if she really shouldn't have been so stupid as to think that a guy like Elijah came with his wings already clipped. 'His *real* girlfriend.'

After arriving home with about two minutes to spare, not even bothering to apologise, Elijah had washed and changed in a matter of moments, cursing as he did up his tie and combed back his hair. Dousing himself in cologne, he neither commented on her looks nor her mood.

But he noticed.

Could see her taut and pale in the mirror, more beautiful and fragile than he had ever seen her.

He didn't want to ask how she was, because it would kill him to hear.

Didn't want another row. Didn't want to justify going out when he didn't want to either.

He hated that he was going tomorrow.

Hated that he was making her stay.

Only he didn't want her to leave either.

'Come!' He offered his hand, knowing she wouldn't take it. 'Let's go.'

Elijah's *friends* were as awful as her mood. She hardly caught their names, and then they were chatting loudly and rudely in Italian as the driver whizzed them the couple of miles to their destination—a luxury residence with glittering views of the river, champagne flowing and a discreet procession of waiters bringing around the most delectable of finger food. But no amount of champagne could console her, and food, no matter how delectable, couldn't give her comfort tonight.

Elijah had introduced her to a small group, given her a

glass and then disappeared, as if dropping a dog off at the kennels, leaving her standing amongst his yapping social set, who were a different breed entirely. She tried to fit in, tried to blend and make small talk, but she was out of kilter—not just a step behind this glamorous, jet setting crowd, but lapped again and again. She listened without interest to talk of skiing holidays and nannies who had the nerve to want the night off on New Year's Eve!

And they all adored Elijah.

Ainslie had to grit her teeth as she attempted conversation, while out of the corner of her eye she watched as female after female came to offer him their condolences. Rather like the line-up Elijah had declined to take part in at the funeral. He consented now, accepting their kisses. Some were moved to tears—though not enough to mess up their make-up, Ainslie noted bitterly. But, hell, she *felt* bitter.

Bitter with him, bitter that these people, these awful, obnoxious people, could mean so much to him—that the man who measured up in so many departments failed so miserably in the one that mattered most.

'Come.' As the hands of the clock crept towards midnight he graced her with a dance, but it was way too little and way too late. He'd ignored her all night, too busy chatting up his rich banking friends to even *bother* chatting up her. She had tried not to be jealous, tried to remember she was here for Guido's sake. She'd tried to remember it wasn't his job to care about her. But after she'd seen him so relaxed and carefree in the expensive surroundings, seen the glitter of want in other women's eyes, her self-loathing was toxic—because, despite herself, despite everything, still she wanted him to.

Wanted him in way she had never wanted another.

Wanted not just a piece of him, but exclusive rights—something she was sure he was incapable of giving.

She knew that soon he'd tire of her—just as he had with Guido.

His hands were loose around her waist as they swayed, and it appalled her how much she wanted to rest in his arms, on his chest, to hold him, to smell him, to feel him just one more time. But she fought it, held back when she wanted to give in, ignored each pleading beat of her heart and resisted the call of her body.

'At least try to *pretend* you're enjoying yourself,' he hissed in her ear.

'Why?'

'Why?' His single word was shot with incredulity and frustration.

'These people are awful—I've tried talking to them—and you've ignored me all night...'

'Ainslie,' Elijah interrupted, 'you've got all the symptoms of postnatal depression without actually having given birth. And I've told you—I have to talk to these people.'

'To Portia too?'

His hand twisted on her elbow, guided her out to the freezing balcony, and his palpable anger was enough to have the remaining smoker take his last gasp before midnight then stub it out and run in.

'She rang tonight.'

'I have told you not to answer the phone.' Elijah shrugged. 'It's hardly my fault if you choose to ignore my instructions. Thank you for passing on the message.'

'I haven't yet.' Her voice twisted with bitterness. 'She

said she's your *real* girlfriend—that's what she told me. I guess it's your job to convince me otherwise.'

'Do you really think I didn't have a life before this happened?'

'Is she the reason you're going to Italy?'

'Portia?' He had the audacity to laugh. 'You think I am going for *Portia*?'

'Is that who you've been on the phone to all week?'

'You're jealous?'

'Yes!' Ainslie roared. 'And I'm sorry if I'm not worldly enough or sophisticated enough to say it doesn't matter that you're sleeping with her as well as me. But tell me this, Elijah, would your *real* girlfriend get up to your nephew at night? Would your *real* girlfriend love Guido the way I do? Would your *real* girlfriend—?' She stopped herself there—stopped because she didn't dare tell him she loved him, couldn't give him any more ammunition to fling at her when she was spent already.

'I never got round to finishing things with her.'

She winced at his disregard, knew that when her time came she'd be treated just as brutally.

'You are so ready to think the worst of me.' Elijah shook his head at her reaction. 'Between the hospital and the undertaker and the lawyers and the funeral I forgot to tell the woman I had been seeing for all of two weeks that there was no place in my life for her. Ainslie, believe me when I say I have not given Portia a thought. I rang her yesterday and told her what had happened. But I was giving her an excuse, not a reason—and I was also trying to find out some information. You are right—Portia could never come close to all you have given…'

She could feel his breath on her cheeks, see the anger, the passion in his eyes that matched hers.

'In this hell I never expected to be happy. I feel guilty that I can smile, that you make me laugh, that I can hold you and forget when my mind should be on Guido, on my sister. That with all that is happening every hour I want you!'

And then he kissed her—kissed her because he couldn't make her leave, kissed her because, no matter how much he wanted her gone, still he wanted her here. His mouth claimed hers, because it was his, but she fought it, tightened her lips. His tongue probed and, like a hot knife through butter, they parted. He tasted of champagne and he smelt of reckless danger. Hot, hard kisses didn't belong in this argument, this passion that blurred the lines over and over, this want that made her weak.

She could hear the chant of the crowd, counting down to the New Year, and all it did was terrify her. She wanted him one last time before she gave up the addiction that was Elijah. She didn't want twelve o'clock to strike, didn't want it to be tomorrow—because then she'd have to give him up.

His hands weren't loose on her waist, as they had been on the dance floor, they were pulling her right into him. His mouth was pressing on hers and she was kissing him, loving him and hating him all at the same time as every chime of Big Ben rang in the New Year. This celebration was nothing in Australia, but it was massive here. Everyone, from the party inside, to the people on the balconies below and in the street beneath, was breaking into 'Auld Lang Syne', and still he kissed her, his erection pressing into her as he pushed her into the wall behind. He could have taken her there, and the fact that she wanted him to take her, that with every twist of the kaleidoscope somehow she always wanted him, made her loathe him all the more.

'I hate how you make me.' She was crying the more he kissed her, but still she kissed him back.

'You love how I make you.' His mouth consumed hers, his tongue lashing hers, flailing her with every stroke.

He kissed the breath out of her all the way in the taxi back home, kissed her up the steps and through the front door, kissed her all the way into the hall and up the stairs.

She'd give up first thing, Ainslie promised herself as her fingers coiled in his hair, as she kissed him back with a frenzy that matched his, as they made it to the bedroom but not to the bed.

He was pushing up her dress as he sucked at her neck, unleashing his fierce erection and then tearing at her knickers. Rough fingers were parting her thighs, and even though she was in killer heels he had to lower himself to enter her. It was uncomfortable as he stabbed inside her, but somehow it was tender. This raw need that consumed them both would soon would be soothed with sweet release. His palms pressed into her hips, his fingers digging into her bottom, holding her, supporting her as he warmed her core. With each thrust he satisfied her yet had her wanting more—more of him. Her orgasm dragged him in deeper, and she was clinging on tighter with each intimate beat as he pulsed inside her, a heady rush consuming her as he groaned out her name.

When it was over—when later they were lying in bed, waiting for the morning that would take him away—he said the words she'd dreaded.

'Marry me…'

Under any other circumstances it wouldn't have hurt to hear him ask—only this wasn't about love, and it wasn't uttered in a moment's liberation post-orgasm. Ainslie knew that. This was about Elijah moving his pawns into place, Elijah thinking ahead, Elijah working the board to claim what he considered his. Two little words she had somehow known were coming from a man who knew how weak she was for him. She was terrified that she'd say yes, wondered how she could possibly find the strength to say no.

'Don't answer yet.' He hushed her troubled mind with his lips. 'We'll talk when I return.'

And, because she was at his bidding, Ainslie didn't know whether that gave her a few hours or maybe a few days to come up with her answer.

CHAPTER TWELVE

ELIJAH'S impeccable work ethic didn't quite translate to his home life. There was no call to check on Guido, and he certainly didn't ring to check on Ainslie. And wherever he'd left the message for Ms Anderson it hadn't been delivered!

'This really is most irregular.' Less than impressed, Ms Anderson had checked on a sleeping Guido and was now grilling Ainslie in the formal lounge.

'He has to work,' Ainslie defended. 'He has things that need to be sorted. He left everything when the accident happened, so he's taking a couple of days to clear things up so that he can come back and concentrate on Guido.'

'Which will be when?' Ms Anderson pushed. 'I want to see him with his nephew—see how they're interacting.'

'Elijah should be back in a couple of days,' Ainslie said firmly,

'Well, make sure that he is! The Castellas are going to be most upset, and frankly I don't blame them. If he can't be with his uncle, surely he should be with the rest of his family.'

'Guido's at home here...' Ainslie swallowed, trying desperately to remain assertive. 'To move him now, for a couple of days while Elijah is away, would just unsettle him.'

'I know that,' Ms Anderson snapped. 'I hope your fiancé realises that if it wasn't for you, if it wasn't for the fact you're his fiancée and are presumably going to have a large part in Guido's life, I'd have no hesitation in allowing Guido to spend some time with his other relatives—and I'll be telling the Castellas that. You can tell Mr Vanaldi too. His money doesn't impress me—I do not want this little boy raised by a string of hired help when there's a loving family who dearly want him.'

Keeping in her sigh of relief when Ms Anderson picked up her bag and made to leave, Ainslie saw her to the door. 'I'll have him ring you as soon as he returns.'

'See that he does!'

'Her bark's worse than her bite!' Teatowel in hand, Enid found Ainslie letting out her breath against the closed door.

'Is it?' Never had she been more grateful for Enid's solid presence. Bone-tired from it all, Ainslie let herself be taken to the kitchen. She sat in the womb-like refuge Enid offered and sipped on tea and dunked biscuits. Like fighter pilots scrambling, her brain tried to locate its target.

Only it kept moving.

'Maybe she's right,' Ainslie said finally, and Enid stopped unloading the dishwasher and came and sat down. 'I mean, if Elijah can miss such an important appointment because of work what else is he going to miss? The Christmas play? Parent-teacher interviews? Bathtime?'

'He's got things to sort out…' Enid soothed, but Ainslie shook her head.

She'd Googled him too—and any doubt she'd had that Portia might be the reason Elijah had gone to Italy had been quashed. Elijah, it would seem, didn't even stretch to dinner and a hand-hold to dump a girlfriend—from the bitter interviews she'd read, several women would have considered themselves lucky if they'd even got a text message. Which left work the only reason he was there. And that didn't fare any better with Ainslie, because if commitments *had* to come first, then where did that leave Guido?

And where did it leave her?

A convenient wife?

She could almost glimpse it, and it terrified her.

She was terrified that she'd accept his diamond crumbs, accept his lifestyle, accept his lovemaking, accept all he would offer, if it meant he would come home to her—while all the time knowing that if circumstances had been different he'd never have given her a second glance.

'I don't know what to do.' Helpless, Ainslie turned to Enid, sought guidance even though she couldn't reveal the whole truth. 'I don't know what is best for Guido—maybe he *would* be better with the Castellas. Just because Elijah loves him, it doesn't necessarily mean he's right.'

'Are you getting cold feet, pet?' Enid poured more tea. 'I can't say I blame you—with the life your fiancé leads it's going to be you raising him. And before you ask I'm not going to say anything to my sister. She's good enough at her job,' Enid said, not just loyally but with honesty. 'She really will do her best to work out what's best for Guido.'

'The perfect nuclear family, you mean?'

'No,' Enid said.

'Does she even *have* kids?' Ainslie's voice was rising now, but Enid stayed calm.

'Her girlfriend does...' Enid gave a small smile at Ainslie's raised eyebrows. 'So she more than most knows it isn't necessarily about a mum and a dad, nor a father who makes it home each night—it's about a loving household. Which this is.'

Oh, it was—for Ainslie at least. The fighter pilots had located their target now and were taking aim at her very core.

She loved him.

Which blurred everything.

Love, as Ainslie was fast realising, was a crazy thing, that made you rewrite your rules, that made a mockery of your own questions, that told you to just keep quiet when maybe you should speak up.

And speak up she would!

She would demand the truth before she made her decision—not just about where he had been, but about where they were going. To live without his love would be agony enough, but to live by his rules would be hell.

Her own rules were simple, Ainslie realised—honesty and respect were a small price for him to pay if she gave him her heart.

A touch calmer after her decision, if not entirely happy, for the first time since they'd met she let the world in. She decided she'd ring a couple of her old nanny friends this evening and see if they were interested in catching up some time. Picking up the paper for the first time in the longest time, she actually read—caught up with events instead of just reading her horoscope—and smiled at the sound of Guido waking over the intercom.

'I'll go,' Enid said.

'No, I will...' She went to stand, but froze midway, her eyes catching on the paper, reading the few small lines over and over.

Enid ignored her and fetched Guido from his crib. Ainslie's shocked face was the one that greeted the little boy when Enid brought him down.

'I need to go out!'

'Is everything okay?'

'Of course....' Her mind was going at a million miles an hour. Her first instinct had been to just grab her bag and run. Only Elijah's instructions that she keep Guido with her held her back, had her doing up his coat with trembling hands, putting on his hat, clipping him in his stroller and then bumping him down the stairs.

'It's really no trouble for me to watch him. Or I could call Tony for you—he's just on the phone...'

'It will be nice for him to get some air!' Ainslie forced a smile and, knowing Enid was watching from the window, forced herself not to run, chatting away to Guido as she headed for the underground, checking over her shoulder as she hit the high street, frowning as she swiped her Oyster card.

Surely not! Ainslie decided as she plunged into the underground—as if Enid would be following her!

Such flights of fancy flew from her mind the second she emerged at her destination, running now along the familiar street, tears filling her eyes at all he was going through.

And when she saw his tired smile as he opened the door it was entirely natural to fall into his arms and both give and receive a cuddle.

'Oh, Angus,' Ainslie sobbed, 'I just read it in the paper. I only just heard. I'm so sorry for all that you're going through.'

CHAPTER THIRTEEN

'WE'RE fine!' Just as nice, and just as assured as he always had been, for the hundredth time Angus reassured her.

Ainslie was sloshing in tea. His mother, who had flown down from Scotland to help, had made them a vast pot, then taken Guido to play with Jack and Clemmie and left them to get on with it.

'And despite what the papers say it really wasn't a shock. Our marriage has been over for ages.'

'Then why did you stay together?'

'The plan was to keep things going till both the children were at school. We got a nanny so that Gemma could keep her career and I would hopefully make enough money in the meantime, before I ended up a single dad—which isn't an easy thing to be when you're an A&E consultant.'

'And a celebrity doctor.'

'Pays well!' Angus gave a tired grin back. 'I don't want them brought up by nannies.

'I've had help from one of the nurses at the hospital, Imogen—she's Australian like you, and now mum's here—honestly, I've got it all under control.'

'So you really are okay?' Ainslie asked Angus.

'I really am,' Angus confirmed. 'What about you?'

'I'm doing okay.'

'You're welcome here, Ainslie...you know that.'

'That's good to know.' Ainslie smiled as he glanced at his watch and winced.

'Celebrity doctor calls!'

'I'd better go too.'

'Ainslie...' Angus frowned as he saw her to the door and she strapped in Guido. 'When Gemma accused you...'

And she'd never been more grateful for Guido's terrible manners—never been more grateful for a fifteen-month-old throwing a hissy fit as she clipped him in. She didn't really want to tell Angus what had happened that day.

Some things a deserted husband really didn't need to know, no matter how well he was doing, and at that moment Ainslie decided again that no one, not even Angus would ever hear that particular piece of truth from her.

'Elijah!'

He was the last person she'd been expecting to see when she arrived home. And not only was he there, but his smile was wide, his mood buoyant. When they walked in he scooped Guido into his arms, raining his face with kisses before landing a deep one on Ainslie's mouth.

'Where were you?'

'Just walking.' Ainslie shrugged, wondering how she could tell him, or not tell him, and deciding to work that one out later.

'Enid said you rushed off—that you seemed upset.'

'I just needed to think.'

'Me too!' And even though Guido was between them,

suddenly it was just they two. Ainslie a bit shy in the knowledge that she loved him, and Elijah somewhat hesitant too. 'We need to talk,' he said softly.

'I know.'

'Really talk,' he confirmed. 'Because this little guy deserves what's best for him—and we deserve what's best for us as well.'

'I know that too.'

'Not here, though.' Elijah smiled, an easy, natural smile she had never before witnessed, and there was an ease to him that was as confusing as it was welcome.

'Enid?' He turned to the housekeeper as she walked in. 'Would you be able to watch Guido tonight? I want to take Ainslie out for dinner.'

'Of course!' Enid beamed, taking the little guy and leaving them alone.

'I have to go out for an hour,' he said, pulling her grumbling into his arms. 'I know, I know.' He smiled into her hair. 'There's just a couple of things I need to clear up.'

'Like what?'

'I'll tell you over dinner.' He kissed her thoroughly, giving her just a taste of what was to come later, before reluctantly letting her go and opening the front door.

'What?' He registered her frown. 'Ainslie, I really will tell you everything later.'

'It's not that. I just...' She laughed at her own paranoia. 'I feel as if I'm being watched—you haven't got Enid spying on me, have you?'

'Enid?' Elijah grinned as Tony opened the car door. 'No, I haven't got Enid spying on you.'

'Maybe Ms Anderson has.'

'That really is paranoid.' He kissed her again on the lips. 'I'll tell you everything tonight.'

He would.

She just knew.

And so would she.

Would somehow summon the courage to tell him she loved him—loved him so much that she couldn't be a fill-in fiancée or a fill-in wife, could only be the real thing—and if that wasn't what he wanted then she needed to know.

So she readied herself for their first proper date.

She bathed herself in oils and scent, and put on her very favourite knickers—hoping, *hoping* to find out if they were his favourite too. Winced as she sprayed deodorant under newly shaved arms then set to work on hair that was so spectacularly cut now that it just fell into glossy shape.

Her trembling fingers even somehow managed eyeliner, and the thrill in the pit of the stomach grew as she pulled on stockings and shoes and a certain little black dress that had been chosen for her. Her cleavage was spectacularly enhanced by a certain ruby—so much so that she didn't even need earrings, didn't need a single thing except whatever it was Elijah had to say.

Hearing his key in the door, she felt her nerves catch up a touch, causing her to breathe in a few times before dabbing at her lipstick and then heading down the stairs, ready to face her future.

His back was to her, and when he turned around the shy smile on her face faded as she saw his expression.

The loathing, the hatred in his eyes, halted her.

'Judas!' He spat the word, and it hit her like a slap. 'You lying slut.'

And this from the man she'd been about to confess her love to.

'Here!' He mounted the stairs in two long strides. 'Before your brain comes up with an excuse—I'll show you there can *be* no excuse. Walking?' he shouted, thrusting photos into her shaking hands. 'Thinking? You lie so easily you probably don't even know you are doing it.'

And his irrefutable evidence was there for her to see.

The friendly cuddle between herself and Angus sordid and sullied now as she flicked through the photos.

'You *did* have me followed!'

'Of course I had you followed. Did you think I would trust you with my nephew otherwise?'

'Yes...' Ainslie whispered at his hot angry breath. 'Yes—because stupid me actually thought that you did.'

'Did what?' he roared, as Enid came out to see what all the noise was about. Tony followed behind—his services seemingly not now required for tonight.

'Trust me.' Ainslie shuddered the words out. 'Somehow, in all of this, I believed that somewhere deep down you trusted me, and somehow—despite my head telling me otherwise—somehow I trusted you too.' Handing back the photos, she didn't offer any defence—didn't need to make excuses for herself to him. 'Clearly I was wrong—on both counts.'

'And that's it?' Elijah demanded. 'That is all you have to say for yourself?'

'That's it.' Ainslie nodded, sniffing back her tears and somehow standing proud.

'Tony?' She called to his driver. She couldn't even face going up the stairs to get her things, couldn't stand to be in his presence a second longer. 'Can you take me to a hotel, please? Enid...' She forced a smile at her lovely friend. 'I shan't be needing the spare room tonight.'

'Ainslie...' Elijah grabbed her wrist as she headed for the door, but she shook him off.

'I'm running, Elijah, but I'm not hiding. Tony will tell you where I'm staying, and just as soon as you send my things on I'll check out. Oh, and I'd hurry if I were you,' she added. 'You know how much I like nice things!'

And that was almost all she had to say for herself—she swore that from this day on she'd never defend herself to him.

'*You're* the Judas.' Ainslie called out as her parting shot.

So the charade they'd started continued.

No draughty hostel or serviced apartment for Elijah Vanaldi's ex-fiancée.

The plushest of London hotels, a famous name in her guidebook, was suddenly home for now.

Nothing was too much trouble when she arrived in the vast lobby in her little black dress, with a tissue sodden with tears.

A luxury suite was arranged in a trice.

Strawberry daiquiris and white chocolate ice cream with hot raspberry sauce was sent up on her endless demand.

She'd never wanted his money—Ainslie knew that—but she'd damn well spend it. Would stoop to his gutter level because he expected nothing less.

But it didn't help.

Nothing helped.

Nothing dimmed her pain.

Not the ninety-minute massage or the pampering facial. Not the wardrobe that had materialised as if by magic, thanks to the personal shopper the concierge, without a turn of his hair, had discreetly arranged.

And she wished he'd stop her credit card—wished, *wished* he'd send her her things. Ainslie sobbed into her very soft pillow and wished, *wished* that this horrible bit was over, so that somehow she could move on. So that somehow she could pick up the pieces and salvage what was left of her heart.

Only it couldn't last—the frenzied spending, the venom, the hate. It just wasn't her—the gold-digging woman she'd played for a night and a day was so far removed from the red swollen face that looked back at her from the mirror it made her wince.

'Enough!' she told her reflection—because it was.

She didn't need to wait for the master to send her things—didn't need to explain herself to him.

And it would have been nice to keep it, but it would surely hurt for ever to look at so she took off her necklace and placed it in an envelope with her note.

Handed it in to Reception as she settled her bill.

'Could you make sure that Elijah Vanaldi gets this when he contacts the hotel?'

'Of course.'

'It should probably go in the safe,' Ainslie added, turning around. That funny old feeling was back now, and she was sure, quite sure, she was being watched.

She probably was, Ainslie decided, slipping the receipt into her purse.

Clearly Elijah liked to keep an eye on his *things*.

Well, she wasn't one of his things any more. So, to the receptionist's discreet cough, Ainslie turned around and stuck up two fingers for the camera, deciding to have afternoon tea while she was there!

Only this bill she would settle herself.

CHAPTER FOURTEEN

COULD he forgive her?

Elijah asked the unthinkable for the thousandth time.

The house was a morgue without her.

The Christmas tree had been taken down, the decorations packed away, and just this vast empty void remained in his soul where the grieving must now begin. For all *he* had lost, for all Guido had lost too.

'*Ijah!*' A delicious smile dragged him from the depths, a face full of dribbles and an endless supply of wet kisses stared up from his knees, banana-smeared hands reaching out for a cuddle. '*Ijah.*'

'So you learn my name?' Scooping him up, Elijah gazed at him, stared into eyes that were like mirrors, and the answers he'd sought so hard to find were there for him to see.

His search had brought up nothing, his hunch had proved unfounded. He had found nothing to pin the Castellas with Maria's and Rico's death. Now, with Ainslie gone, when Ms Anderson found out—as she surely would—that it had all been a ruse, Social Services' decision would be inevitable. Elijah had conceded his playboy, jet-setting lifestyle really wasn't fitting for a small child, so, yes, maybe Guido *would* be better off with two parents and cousins. Even if to Elijah they weren't ideal.

There was just one detail he hadn't factored in when he'd been searching his soul to make the best choices for his nephew's future. One slight hiccough in all his mental calculations that Elijah hadn't spotted.

'I love you.'

For the first time in his life Elijah said it, and it was like opening the lid on a shaken bottle. Bubbles fizzed in, and he felt the utter release that came with such a simple truth.

'I do.' He smiled at his nephew, smiled because Guido neither noticed nor cared how monumental this moment was. 'Which means I'm going to have to keep you.'

'Ijah!' Guido chanted, maybe not so oblivious after all.

'Which may not please some people...' Elijah gave a grim smile. But he was ready for the challenge now—there wasn't a fight he couldn't win if he didn't put his heart into it.

Except one.

'What do I do?'

Again he asked Guido, and again Guido didn't answer.

'Hey...' Elijah kissed his soggy face. 'At least I'll get the sympathy vote from the single mothers at the play placc you go to...'

'Playgroup...' Enid said, walking in unheard. 'My sister just called. I was hoping to meet her for coffee—I thought I might take Guido.' Enid's voice was polite and formal, just as it had been since Ainslie had left, but he could feel her holding back, knew there was plenty she'd like to say to him—that he was a fool, an idiot, that he'd let the best thing that had ever happened to him walk out of the door. But Enid didn't have to say it.

Elijah knew it already.

'I suppose you'll be discussing us?'

'No,' Enid replied coolly. 'As I said, I'm having coffee with my sister. But she did say that she wanted to come back here and speak with you after.'

'Fine,' Elijah snapped, then relented—after all, none of this was her fault. 'Tony can drive you,' he offered, though privately he was glad of the excuse to be alone—really alone—with his grief. 'Feel free to tell her I'm not giving up on Guido.'

'Glad to hear it.' Enid's face softened. 'But it would be easier with Ainslie.'

'It would…' Elijah conceded. 'And a whole lot nicer too—but we'll be okay…' He ruffled Guido's hair. 'The two of us will make it work.'

Enid took Guido off to get him ready, which left Elijah alone with his thoughts—and for the hundredth time he berated himself for his haste to accuse rather than to listen. Maybe she'd just gone to say goodbye to Angus? Elijah wondered hopelessly as he logged onto his computer. One final time together for old times' sake? Hell, he'd done that on many occasions himself—why shouldn't the same rules apply to her?

They just didn't.

And they didn't apply to him any more either.

Picking up the little black box by the computer, he opened it, stared at the mocking ring.

He'd being going to ask her.

Properly.

Ahead of the Social Services decision. Because that had seemed important somehow.

On his flight home Elijah had realised that though the decision was vital to him, to *them* it didn't actually matter. He needed her for so much more than Guido.

Needed that loyal, feisty, funny, beautiful woman in every aspect of his life.

A woman who could even make him smile now, when he tracked her manic spending.

In the hours she'd been gone she'd done pretty well, but his smile faded when he realised that she must have checked out.

Somewhere deep inside he'd known that she would.

He was scanning the entries now—for a sum so little it shouldn't matter. The fact it wasn't there actually mattered a lot, brought tears to dry eyes. He realised she'd paid for his Christmas present herself. But again, somewhere deep inside he'd already known that she had.

But men couldn't be seen crying.

Especially when Enid informed him that she was on her way out and that his nemesis was at the front door.

'Should I show Dr Maitlin in?'

'No—I'll see him at the door.'

'It's not doing much good there…' For the first time Enid interfered, glancing down to the ring he was holding. 'Sitting in a box when it should be on her finger.'

'I'll tell her that, shall I?' Elijah's sarcasm didn't faze Enid. 'When I see her next?'

'Happen you should!'

Clearing his throat, Elijah stood, unclenched his fists, and vowed to himself that he wouldn't hit him, would only open the door. It was a promise he wasn't sure he could keep.

'Is Ainslie in?'

It took a supreme effort to tell him where she was staying—but the barb on his tongue still needed an out.

'You'd better hurry, though—it would seem she just checked out—or checked in with the next rich fool to come along.'

'Sorry?' Angus frowned. 'I was asking after Ainslie. I just wanted to clear something up.'

'Well, she's gone.'

'Fine...' Angus turned to go, and then changed his mind. 'If she does get in touch, would you ask her to call me?'

Elijah's fists balled at his sides. New Year's resolutions were fading fast and he was sorely tempted to knock his lights out.

'Only I think I owe her an apology.'

'*Aspetta*! Wait!' Elijah instructed, watching Angus's shoulders stiffen. Clearly he was a man not used to being told! 'Look...' Elijah closed his eyes and struggled to keep his voice even, because even if he might not like what he was about to hear he badly needed to hear it. 'Would you mind coming inside? Would you mind explaining what is going on with you and Ainslie?'

'Let's just leave it.' Angus was walking away.

'I read your reference for her...' Elijah gave a tight smile. 'I was hoping to clarify a couple of points—perhaps I should ring your wife?'

'You'd have to find her first.' Reluctantly Angus came in and sat down in the study. 'My marriage has just broken up, so believe me—I'm not in the mood for small talk.'

'Me neither.' Elijah gave a tight smile. 'Ainslie told me when I hired her that she was fired because she had been accused of theft.' He knew it was a white lie, but he needed to find out exactly what was going on here.

'She told you about it?' Angus frowned. 'And you still employed her?'

'Ainslie wouldn't steal.' Without hesitation he said it. He believed in her then just as he had on that day—and with that came the appalling realisation that she wouldn't cheat either. That the suspicious, mistrusting world he had inhabited all his life had blinded him to simple beauty. 'Ainslie would not have stolen your wife's necklace. I know that.'

'I wish I had!' Angus let out a long sigh. 'Look—I have no desire to give you the details, but at the time it didn't sit right with me, and I told Ainslie that. She came to see me yesterday—when she read in the paper that my marriage had ended—and unfortunately it never entered my head to ask her till she was leaving... She was too busy checking that the kids and I were okay. And then it dawned on me—she didn't steal that necklace; that would have been my wife's excuse to get rid of her. I wondered if perhaps Ainslie had found out that my wife was having an affair.'

'Was she?'

'Oh, yes!' Angus gave a wry laugh. 'All I asked from my sham of a marriage was that we were faithful—something it would appear my ex-wife couldn't adhere to.'

'And you did?'

'Absolutely.'

And the strength, the unwavering conviction in his voice, suddenly had Elijah feeling very small—very small indeed.

'I am going to see Ainslie now—hoping to see her,' Elijah added. 'If I do, I will pass on what you have said.'

'Thank you.' Angus shook his hand. 'And I'm sorry about your family.'

'She told you about my sister?'

'Ainslie wouldn't discuss anything like that. I spoke to you on the phone. The day of the accident.'

'It was you?' Elijah's face paled, recalling again the awful call that had changed his life in so many ways.

'I was the receiving doctor when your sister was brought in. I'm very sorry for your loss.'

'Thank you.' It was all he could manage. All he could manage as he was plunged from hell to hell—remembering Angus's kindness that day, the voice on the phone that had gently delivered the hardest of news, remembering again, living again, what had happened to his family, the fear that had gripped him until Ainslie had come along.

Until she'd waltzed into his life and somehow made it bearable.

Because without her he truly didn't know how he'd have coped.

'One other thing….' Angus cleared his throat, paused for the longest time before speaking again.

Elijah could never have guessed the indecision behind the strong voice—could never have guessed that what was about to be delivered was absolutely against Angus's usually impeccable better judgement. Angus could almost see his medical licence flashing before a BMA review panel, but somehow it seemed imperative to go on.

'You'll no doubt hear soon anyway—though I'd prefer that you didn't mention you've heard it from me…'

'Hear what?' Elijah's hackles were raised, the intuition, the gut instinct that had led him from the streets to a penthouse, telling him that this was big.

'A detective contacted me this afternoon… It would appear your sister and brother-in-law's case is being reopened—it would seem it's not quite as open and shut as it first appeared.' He gave an uncomfortable shrug. 'Just so you know.'

He *had* known.

From the minute he'd seen his sister at some level he'd known. But at every turn he'd been thwarted, called irrational, tired, paranoid. Yet he'd known that it had been no accident—and now it would seem he was about to be proved right.

Without her!

The words buzzed in his ears—his throat was impossibly dry as he tried to speak. 'Who was the detective you spoke with?'

'I'd rather not say. Wait till they contact you.' Angus was heading down the steps now, walking out onto the street. He jumped a touch as Elijah grabbed his shoulder, spinning him around. As a trauma doctor Angus knew what he was seeing, witnessed naked fear in Elijah eyes.

'I need to know!' he shouted, and Angus knew it wasn't at him. 'I think Ainslie is in danger.'

The detective wasn't so easily convinced.

Elijah—wanting to shoot from the hip, wanting only to go to her—paced the lounge like a caged lion as the detective insisted on details.

'You hired private detectives,' he pointed out. 'That explains why she thought she was being followed.'

'It does...' Elijah said through gritted teeth. 'And I hired a bodyguard for Guido. Initially I was worried the Castellas might try to take him, and when I became suspicious I hired a private detective. Your colleagues,' he added, with more than a dash of resentment, 'didn't take my concerns seriously when I rang them after I spoke with the social worker.'

'Maybe they did,' the detective replied. 'Given that the case is being re-examined.'

'I always thought that Rico's family might be behind this—from the moment I realised they knew this house was in Maria's and Rico's names I was sure it had to be more than a coincidence. So I went to Italy to check up on them.'

'Hoping to find what?'

'Something—anything. I wanted to see if they'd paid a deposit for the apartment they're living in now—if they'd paid out any large sums.'

'You accessed their bank accounts?'

Elijah nodded without guilt—because he hadn't a shred—just as he hadn't had a shred of guilt when he'd called in a favour at the New Year's Eve party. 'I had to go there—they wouldn't give me any information over the phone.'

'And had they?'

'No.' The detective opened his mouth to speak, then thought better of it. But Elijah answered for him. 'Their financial situation is dire.'

'That's not a crime,' the detective said. 'And neither is stopping to purchase a gift at the airport. If you thought there was danger—why did you leave?'

'Because I had to find out what was going on. I had my nephew moved to the fourth floor. I had a bodyguard posing as my driver, watching Guido all the time, and I had a private detective parked outside the house to keep an eye on Ainslie.'

'Where is the private detective now?'

'I called him off—I thought they were safe,' Elijah roared. 'I thought for once I was wrong, that I was just being paranoid. But Ainslie thought she was being watched again yesterday.' Elijah stared the detective straight in the eye.

'And was she?'

'Not by my detective—I was on my way to meet him.'

'You believe she's in imminent danger?'

Elijah nodded, and it was Angus pacing now—Angus who greeted an utterly bemused Enid and Ms Anderson when they walked in.

'Find Ainslie!' Elijah called to Tony, before he was even through the door, his voice nearing desperation as he tried to spell out to the detective just how dire things really were. 'They think we are still engaged. They have no reason to think otherwise. Without Ainslie—' he gulped in air as he said it. 'Without Ainslie I would not be granted custody of my nephew.'

'You know that for sure?'

'I think I was about to find out.' Elijah glanced over to Ms Anderson, who nodded.

'But the Castellas wouldn't know that—' the detective pointed out.

'The Castella family know,' Ms Anderson interrupted. 'I just informed them of them of my decision. That in my opinion, for now at least, Guido should stay where he is— with Elijah and his fiancée.'

'Stay put.' The detective was pulling out his phone. 'I'll get a uniformed officer to stay with you. Don't go getting any big ideas…' He waited till the two men obediently sat before racing out through the door. But the second his car skidded off Elijah looked over to Angus.

Elijah was already standing. 'He *is* joking—he doesn't just expect us to sit here?'

He knew how the Castellas worked. Had grown up on rough streets himself. The instinct that had got him through his childhood and teenage years had taught him a thing or three, and not to use that now—to leave Ainslie to the Castellas—was incomprehensible.

And if they harmed her—if they hurt her—if because of his actions, the world carried on without her…

Elijah closed his eyes as Angus sped off.

It was unthinkable.

CHAPTER FIFTEEN

SHE felt better—well, how could she not?

She had feasted on the tiniest of sandwiches, each delectable crustless finger a taste sensation, and on the most divine raisin and apple scones, smeared with strawberry jam and clotted cream, and tiny little pastries served on a three-tiered silver server—all for her! And the surroundings were to die for! Her mind was soothed by the music that wafted in the air around her, and with a glass of champagne in her hand, endless aromatic tea waiting to be sipped, it was hard not to believe that life wouldn't again be good.

Afternoon tea, she'd found out, usually had to be booked weeks in advance, but given she'd been a paying guest—well, she'd been shown right through. Had sat and people-watched and realised, with a very brave smile, that she was lucky to be here.

Lucky to sample a taste of a life that was so far removed from hers.

Lucky to have had him—even if just for a little while.

And as Ainslie stepped out onto the street, walked out under the arches and felt the late-afternoon sun on her face, heading where she didn't quite know, but would soon work out, Ainslie also knew that, whatever he chose to believe, Elijah had been lucky to have her.

She could ring Angus, Ainslie mused. Or then again perhaps not. She wasn't really up to being around anyone, wanted to be alone a little while longer to lick her wounds...

'Sorry!' So deep was she in her thoughts, Ainslie actually thought she had bumped into someone. It took a second for her to realise that this was no accident. Her bag was being tugged from her shoulder.

Her first instinct was to cling on, to scream for help—only she was mute, stepping into survival mode and knowing she should just let it go. A bag wasn't worth fighting over—so she didn't. She just let the strap slip down her arm, her heart pumping, wanting the man gone. Only it didn't happen. She could see her bag being tossed on the ground, and Ainslie glimpsed real fear for the first time in her life as everything seemed to move in slow motion—the stench of body odour hit her, the wail of sirens was growing louder and louder, and she had the horrible, horrible realisation that he had a knife. This man who had taken her bag had a knife—and he was going to use it.

She'd never expected to wake up to him again.

Had said goodbye to that dream already.

But maybe she *was* dreaming—because it didn't actually look like Elijah. The Elijah she knew didn't cry, and this one had been.

'He stabbed me.' It was the second thought that came into her head, and her hands raced to her body, trying to locate her pain.

'No!' He moved to soothe her, but he couldn't. She

could feel the needle of the drip in her arm, could see her blood on his shirt, could remember the knife.

'Oh, God!' Panic was building. 'What will I tell my mum?'

'That you didn't get stabbed.' He lifted up his shirt, showed her a very white dressing against a very nice stomach, and on his tired grey face he managed a smile. 'That was me. You fainted when you saw that I had been stabbed, and hit your head on the pavement.'

'You?' It didn't make sense, but it was starting to, like trying to remember a dream. Little fragments of images pierced her mind—a wedge of muscle against her, the pungent scent of her assailant overridden by a beautiful, familiar, masculine smell, and then drenching her the sweet, heady relief that Elijah was here, that she would be safe, that he would make everything right. 'How did you know to be there...?' Her head thrashed on the pillow in confusion. 'Were you having me followed again?'

'No...but I wish to God I had been though. Ainslie, I had you followed while I was away because I feared for you—and feared for Guido too.'

'Feared for us?'

'It wasn't an accident that killed my sister and Rico—it was a hit. Marco and Dina arranged to have them killed.' He held her hands tighter as he admitted what he'd exposed her to, and she knew it wasn't paranoia or hate that was speaking, knew she was hearing the truth. 'And yours was not a random mugging—though that was how it was supposed to appear. A mugging that got out of hand...' He actually flinched as he said it. 'You were supposed to be killed too.'

'Me?'

'You,' Elijah confirmed. 'Because without you I would never have been granted custody of Guido.'

She felt sick, actually physically sick, at the thought someone would want her dead—that someone, anyone, could care so much for money and so little for life.

He needed a shave. Funny the things you thought about. Funny that something so irrelevant should come into her focus as everything changed. But he really *did* need a shave—the designer stubble he'd worn yesterday was far heavier now. He looked like a gypsy, Ainslie decided, as he took her hand, and tears filled her eyes for what Guido would one day have to hear.

'The police have arrested and charged them….' Closing his eyes, he brought a hand to his chin, index finger pressed against his lips, dragging air in and out for a minute as he tried to find the formula to an unknown poison. 'I had my suspicions—suddenly they'd found out Maria and Rico had money…to me it seemed too much of a coincidence—but then I told myself I was being ridiculous, that they would never want them dead. The police at the time seemed confident it was an accident. And Ms Anderson—everyone—seemed to think it reasonable that, despite the differences between the families, they would want to take care of their orphaned nephew…'

She looked at him with new eyes now. The man who had to her seemed so bitter and mistrusting had been—but for all the right reasons.

'Tony isn't my driver—he's a bodyguard. I hired him to keep an eye on Guido. At first I thought they might try to take him, but then the more I thought about it the more I was convinced they were to do with the accident.'

'That's why you had Guido moved to the top floor?' A frown creased her brow.

'Tony watched the house at night.'

A smile that was utterly out of place shone for a second as she saw things differently. 'That's why he never gave you a lift?'

'Unless I was with Guido.' Elijah nodded. 'The fact that they stopped to buy a present at the airport...'

That long-ago bedroom conversation came back to her mind, his sheer bewilderment at their actions, which had revealed the depths of the pain he must feel.

'I couldn't fathom that, Ainslie. I vomited at the airport—I had to face the same as them—I could not have thought to buy a gift. I didn't go to Italy to break up with Portia. I had already taken care of that. I went to Italy to check things out. I broke into their home, looked through their things—that New Year party we went to was about chatting up an old friend who had a contact that worked in their bank, I couldn't do it over the phone—I had to go there to view their accounts. And, yes, they were poor, but there was nothing to indicate they intended to travel—nothing in their home that confirmed my doubts—so I let it go. I told myself I was being stupid. I arrived back in London and I rang the private detective I had hired to watch over you and Guido—he had nothing on them either, so I called him off. I was about to call Tony off too—and that was when the private detective asked to meet with me—he said it was nothing to do with the Castellas, but he had some photos that I might want to see.'

'Angus and I?'

He nodded. 'Angus came to see me this afternoon—

amongst other things he told me that the police had contacted him. Forensics had come back on the car, and it appeared someone had tampered with the fuel tank. It looked like a professional job—someone who knew what they were doing. Given the ferocity of the fire, it was lucky it was picked up. They got rid of Maria and Rico and they tried to get rid of you.'

'Why?' The most pointless of questions, because there could never be a right answer. 'For money?'

'It wasn't just about money—though that would have been their first motive. It was about hatred, about revenge... All I know is that they couldn't even wait—they wiped their nephew's parents off the face of the earth just to get their hands on his money and just to get back at Maria for being a part of me.' He stared down at her bemused face as she struggled to comprehend such atrocities, struggled to accept the world in which he'd grown up—*this*—Elijah berated himself over and over—the woman he had refused to trust. 'That is what hate does to you.'

'And that's why you're going to have to somehow learn to forgive them...' She smiled at his incredulous face, but he closed his mouth when she spoke on. 'For Guido's sake—or he's going to grow up filled with hatred too. Elijah—why didn't you tell me?'

'How?' he asked. 'How could I tell you my suspicions and expect you to stay? All I could do was protect you—at first it was for Guido—and then...' Even now he couldn't fully tell her of the fear that had gripped him, of the paranoia that had convinced him everything he loved was in danger of being taken. 'I needed you to stay, but I wanted you to leave.'

'You should have told me.'

'I tried to.'

She closed her eyes in regret—because he had.

'We were fighting for the same thing from different corners,' Elijah said softly. 'You could only see good, whereas I…'

'It would have been nice to meet in the middle.'

'I am going to speak with Ms Anderson.' He swallowed hard. 'I have to do what is best for Guido and she is right—my lifestyle is not suited to a small child, not suited to any child…'

And she couldn't bear it—couldn't bear the thought of little Guido being a number in the system. Surely whatever love Elijah could offer was better than that? And then she halted. Because it wasn't—wasn't good enough for Guido the same way it wasn't good enough for her.

'You have to do what you think is right.' Her voice was strained. 'You will see him, though?' Ainslie checked. 'You will ring and keep in touch…?'

'I'll see him every day!' Elijah frowned. 'Are you feeling all right? Is your head hurting?' And then he got it. 'He's mine,' Elijah said simply. 'I don't have to prove that to Ms Anderson and I don't have to prove it to myself—now I know it in my heart. I am going to move here. I don't want to unsettle him again. He needs to have the people and the things he loves around him for a while. Enid is good for him, and Tony is looking to retire, so maybe he would work for me too—as a driver this time…'

'What about your work?' Ainslie asked. 'What about the travel and the parties and the women…?'

'Everything in moderation,' Elijah answered. 'Especially the women.' His eyes held hers. 'I'm hoping to scale them right back, actually—down to one!'

'It's not that straightforward.'

'I don't want to be without you,' Elijah interrupted. 'Never, ever again.'

'Because of Guido?'

'Because of *you*.'

Which was the right answer. But still she pulled her hands away—because even if it was extreme, the hate that had led them to this point was an extension of themselves. He was so mistrusting, so unsure. She remembered again the hell he'd put her through—remembered again every hurt.

'I never slept with Angus.'

'I know that.'

'But you *didn't* know that,' Ainslie countered. 'Which means that you don't know me.'

'I do now.'

'Which is too late.' It was the hardest thing to do, to turn her back on a future she so badly wanted—but as much as she loved him, she loved herself more. 'Now I've passed all the tests suddenly you decide that I'm good enough? Well, guess what? I always was.'

'What was I supposed to think?'

'You didn't think; you just assumed—saw a photo…'

'I'm not talking about the photos!' Irritated, annoyed, the old Elijah was back, his bedside manner fading as he stood up and paced the room. 'I walk out of that hospital and on to the underground, holding my nephew, and I pray to God, to the universe, to anyone listening, for help—for something to happen, to show me the way. And I open my eyes and there *you* are.' He jabbed a finger accusingly.

'Everything okay?' A nurse popped her head in and frowned.

'Everything's fine,' Elijah snapped, and Ainslie nodded.

But the second they were alone, she rounded on him, furious, *furious*, that he thought he could talk to her like that—furious that she was lying in a hospital bed and being told off. She told him so!

'I was nearly stabbed this afternoon!'

'I *was* stabbed this afternoon!' Elijah countered.

'I've been mugged, attacked…'

'Scoffing down afternoon tea?' Elijah hurled just in case she was expecting sympathy. 'Booking massages and personal shoppers?'

'You can't talk to me like that.'

'So I'm supposed to just walk out?' He glared. 'Let you turn your back on the best thing that will ever happen to you? Because I'm telling you now—' his voice rose as she opened her mouth to argue '—no one will ever love you as much as I do.'

And he meant it.

Because only Elijah could shout it the first time he said it.

'I loved you even when I thought the worst—hell, Ainslie, I spent this morning wondering if I was mad because I was ready to forgive you for sleeping with a married man. I told myself that despite everything I believe in, every standard I'd set for the woman who would be my wife, that if it really was just one last time it would be better to forgive you than to lose you.'

It had never entered her head that his love might be greater than hers—that Elijah might forgive something she never, ever could.

'It was so much easier to doubt you than to believe in you.'

'Why?' She just didn't get it—honestly couldn't fathom why he had chosen, at every turn, to think the worst.

Till he told her.

Walking over, he sat on the bed and word for word he said it again—only softly this time, holding her hands instead of jabbing a finger. 'I walk out of that hospital and on to the underground, holding my nephew, and I pray to God, to the universe, to anyone listening, for help—for something to happen, to show me the way. And I open my eyes and there you are. *You!*' he added. 'The only person who didn't walk on, the only person who stopped. Who came back with me to a house I was dreading entering, who took care of my nephew. And who fell in love with me.'

She nodded—not embarrassed, not blushing—just nodded at the simple truth. Tears streamed down her cheeks as he struggled to explain what had taken place in that beautiful head of his.

'It was easier to think of you as a mistress, a gold-digger…'

'Easier?' Ainslie frowned. 'How could that be easier?'

'Prayers don't just get answered. You don't give out your wishes and expect an instant response. You don't just open your eyes and the woman you've always wanted is there. Miracles don't just happen.'

'But they do,' Ainslie countered.

Love—the miracle that occurred over the globe, thousands upon thousands of times every day. Random people the world over were looking up to find their soul mate looking back at them—the person, whether they realised it or not, who was the very one they were meant to be with.

'Especially at Christmas!' Ainslie said, as if it were obvious. 'Everyone knows that.'

Lifting up her hand and capturing his proud cheek, she looked back with love at the man who had rescued her too that night, who had rescued her again today, and who would, she knew beyond a doubt, rescue her any time she needed it.

'And I guess someone decided that we both deserved a miracle.'

EPILOGUE

HE LOOKED divine.

If she lived to be a hundred then the next seventy-two years, Ainslie realised, clutching her flowers, were going to be spent catching her breath.

Catching her breath at a man who really did stand a head above the rest.

Resplendent in a suit, and somehow holding onto the hand of a very spoilt and thoroughly over-excited Guido, who insisted on being the centre of attention, Elijah was the centre of hers. Even when Guido pulled out his corsage and stamped on it as heads turned to the arriving bride. Even when Guido spat in frustration when the best uncle in the world took the arm of the bride and walked up the aisle.

Ainslie followed behind.

'Do you really think it appropriate that she's wearing white?' he whispered into her ear later, the giver-away of the bride dancing with the bridesmaid.

'Absolutely.' Ainslie nodded dreamily, lifting her head from the haven of his chest to see Enid smiling shyly at Tony.

'What was that?' In a room of couples dancing, he stopped.

'A kick.'

'He kicked!' His hand moved to her velvet-clad belly—held the swell of their baby in his hot palm. He grinned. 'He kicked again! He'll play for Italia!'

'So might *she*!' Ainslie said pointedly.

'Good.' Elijah shrugged. 'Ms Anderson can coach her.'

And even on a thimble of champagne to toast the bride, and a gallon of sparkling water and orange juice, he made her drunk with laughter. Reprobate, irrepressible, yet somehow incredibly tender—Elijah: the miracle that just kept giving.

'Guido is going to be so jealous when the baby comes…' Elijah sighed into her hair.

'He's already jealous.' Ainslie grinned, watching as he pummelled the floor with his fists as Ainslie's mother, who was over for Christmas, tried to soothe him. 'Fancy us two having the nerve to dance and forget to ask him!'

'He's getting better, though?' Elijah checked, and she nodded.

It had been hard, because despite his tender age Guido had missed his parents—still missed them, Ainslie was sure—but they were doing their best to fill that gap.

'He's getting there.'

And so were they.

Their decision to stay in London had been hard, but the right one. His home was the one constant they could offer Guido when everything else in his little world had shifted. All their worlds had shifted—as the adoption had gone through, as Elijah had scaled back his work, as new relatives had visited from Australia. As *Ijah* slowly became Dad and, one recent day, Ainslie for the first time became Mum.

Yet they helped him remember—the digital photo frame Ainslie had so lovingly purchased often a source of comfort for the little boy who did actually miss his parents. Slowly Guido's house had become their home—and never more so than now. The tree was back in the lounge, a wreath was on the door just as it had been last year, parcels were hidden in the wardrobe, and the house was filled with all the laughter and tears that came with any family at Christmas—especially when the mother-in-law comes to stay!

'I love you!' Ainslie said, just in case he needed reminding.

'How could you not?'

It was Elijah who couldn't accept the compliment—Elijah who made a brave joke and a stab at humour. Elijah who woke her at night sometimes just to check that she was there, that this woman who had dashed into his life wasn't going to disappear in a puff of smoke, just as everyone he had ever loved before her had. 'You know I love you…'

He stared into her heart and beyond it, took her with that look to places they would one day visit, to two lifetimes that were now one and would share together each day.

'I do know,' Ainslie answered, because she did. 'But tell me again why?'

'Because,' Elijah said, struggling for a moment before succinctly delivering her the perfect answer. 'Just because…'

Special Offers
Bestselling Stars Collection

A stunning collection of passion and glamour from your favourite bestselling authors of international romance

Lynne Graham — Passion
On sale 20th May

Sandra Marton — Pleasure
On sale 17th June

Miranda Lee — Seduction
On sale 15th July

Carole Mortimer — Fascination
On sale 19th August

Sharon Kendrick — Satisfaction
On sale 16th September

Carol Marinelli — Celebration
On sale 21st October

Save 20% on Special Releases Collections

Find out more at
www.millsandboon.co.uk/specialreleases

Visit us Online

0611/10/MB3